Tres BARE

LACEY THORN

ELLORA'S CAVE
ROMANTICA PUBLISHING

$\mathcal{W}$hat the critics are saying...

ം

5 Enchantments "BARE SEDUCTION is exactly what the title suggests. It is seduction in the most bare of forms. Combine one woman, two men and more heat than any fire could ever reach and you have this hot and erotic tale from Ms. Thorn. This author has not only a great imagination, but also the ability to draw the reader in from the first word and hold them firmly in her grasp until the last. Very hot and satisfying, Ms. Thorn. Very satisfying indeed." ~ *Enchanting Reviews*

A+ Rating "BARE SEDUCTION kept me enthralled and had me feeling completely seduced. This is definitely one of the most erotica ménage stories I have ever read. [...] BARE SEDUCTION is a very inspirational erotic romance that will leave readers breathless and anxious to get their groove on!" ~ *Dark Angel Reviews*

4 Angels "*Bare Devotion* is fourth book in the *Bare Love* series and can be read as a stand-alone story but I would recommend reading the previous stories first. [...] The sex scenes were hot and spicy and wouldn't be considered at all "vanilla" due to the m/f/m action. All in all, I'm giving *Bare Devotion* 4 angels and will be looking forward to more books from Ms. Thorn." ~ *Fallen Angels Reviews*

"A sexy short story and a thoroughly enjoyable one, BARE DEVOTION is a sure-fire hit, whether you've read the previous stories or not." ~ *Romance Reviews Today Erotic*

An Ellora's Cave Romantica Publication

www.ellorascave.com

Tres Bare

ISBN 9781419958182
ALL RIGHTS RESERVED.
Bare Seduction Copyright © 2007 Lacey Thorn
Bare Devotion Copyright © 2008 Lacey Thorn
Edited by Helen Woodall.
Photography and cover art by Les Byerley.

This book printed in the U.S.A. by Jasmine–Jade Enterprises, LLC.

Trade paperback Publication March 2009

TRES BARE

ଔ

BARE SEDUCTION

BARE DEVOTION

BARE SEDUCTION

ဆ

Dedication

❧

*As always this one goes out to my best girl Shell —
everyone should be blessed with a friend like you.
And to my mom who struggles daily with the
complications of her breast cancer.
Keep fighting!*

Trademarks Acknowledgement

❧

The author acknowledges the trademarked status and trademark owners of the following wordmarks mentioned in this work of fiction:

Cheese Lover's Pizza: Pizza Hut, Inc.

Chrysler Crossfire: Daimler Chrysler Corporation

Crime-stoppers: USI Alliance Corporation

Dodge Durango: Daimler Chrysler Corporation

Dumpster: Dempster Brothers Inc.

Duplex: Altec Lansing, A Division of Plantronics, Inc.

Jacuzzi: Jacuzzi, Inc.

Ka-bar Knife: Alcas Corporation

Loofah: Loofah S. A. Corporation

Nautilus: Nautilus Inc.

Photoshop: Adobe Systems Inc.

Pilates: World Pilates Federation, owner, Elena Onishenko

Playboy: Playboy Enterprises International, Inc.

Plexiglas: Rohm & Haas Company

Smith & Wesson: Smith & Wesson Corporation

Spandex: Hager & Werken GmbH & Co

Spin: Mad Dog Athletics Inc.

Chapter One

ဢ

It was two days before her best friend's wedding and Cass Sinclair was heading back to Legacy. She was supposed to co-host a bachelorette party tonight and she wanted to get there in plenty of time to be familiar with everything. Since she had spent the last four months helping her dad take care of her dying mother she had been dependent on the groom's mom and his sister to take care of local details for her. Cass hadn't even seen the dress she was to wear yet but Catherine, the groom's mom, whom she had met at her mother's funeral had assured her that it would fit fine. It was a beautiful red dress that was fitted to the waist and fell in waves from there to just below the knees. It sounded beautiful and even better it was red, Cass' favorite color.

Cass' best friend Moira Madigan had met Detective Gil Daniels when she and Cass had stumbled onto a murder in progress on their way home one night. Gil and his partner Ben Marcum had been the detectives assigned to the murders of local women in Legacy. When Moira ran into the path of the killer it brought them all together and for Moira and Gil there had been immediate chemistry. Now here they were, Moira and Gil about to be married.

Cass was happy for Moira—heaven only knew that if anyone deserved a little happiness it was Moira. But part of Cass was jealous as well. She wouldn't mind a little happiness as well or at least an opportunity for a little happiness. She gave a snorting laugh. Who was she kidding? She wanted a night of mind-blowing, all-consuming, hot and sweaty, down and dirty sex with a great looking guy who was well-hung and not shy about it. Even better would be two guys who were well-hung and…Whoa! Where had that thought come from? She definitely needed to have sex and soon.

She had thought there might be a chance for something between her and Detective Marcum before she was called home to help care for her mother. But he had hooked up with Gil's sister Katie and now they were married and expecting a baby. So obviously she had read more into that than ever existed. Moira said they were perfect together, Ben and Katie and Cass wished them well. She just wished for a love like that for herself as well. After what felt like hours on the road she saw the sign for Legacy. Finally she was home.

* * * * *

The girls were all gathered at Doug's and Damon's house for Moira's bachelorette party. The guys had staked out Ben's house so Catherine had commandeered her middle son's home for the bachelorette party. It was now one in the morning and things had quieted down a lot. The strippers Catherine had shocked them all with were long gone as were most of the guests. Gil had hired a limo for the night so that none of the women would drive under the influence. Of course Katie wasn't drinking but no one had wanted her carting everyone home in the middle of the night.

Now it was just Catherine, Katie, Moira and Cass who had just arrived back in Legacy this afternoon.

"I should have checked in to a hotel before I came out here," Cass groaned from her reclined position on the futon couch.

"I told you that you could stay in the apartment with us." Moira said from her sprawled spot on the floor.

"I am so not staying with you and Gil. I've heard what goes on in that apartment." Cass laughed as Moira groaned and buried her head in her hands.

Katie spoke up from the doorway. "You're more than welcome to stay with Ben and me."

Cass and Moira shared a look and both started laughing. "I don't think that's a good idea either," Cass said.

Katie wasn't so sure about that look. "Did you and Ben date or something?" she asked pointblank.

Cass smiled and shook her head. "I had only just met Ben and Gil before I left to go stay with my mother." Cass still remembered the veiled looks and words between her and Ben though and didn't feel comfortable enough to stay with him and his new wife, Katie, Moira's soon to be sister-in-law.

Catherine spoke up then. "Do you have a place to stay at all, Cass?"

"No, I hadn't thought about it actually. I'm so used to living with Moira that I just didn't think about how her getting married would change all that."

"I said…" Moira started to say but Cass cut her off.

"Thanks but no thanks. I really don't want to listen to you having sex when I'm not having any." She looked up with wide eyes when she realized she's said that in front of Gil's mom. Cass had drunk way too much.

But Catherine just looked at her and started laughing. Then Katie was giggling. Next thing they were all sprawled out over the enormous living room chatting.

"So what did you study in college, Cass?" Catherine asked.

"Health and physiology." Cass replied.

"Cass went to school on a full scholarship." Moira volunteered.

"Wow. That's impressive." Katie replied. "Was it athletic?" Cass worked at the gym with Moira as an instructor. She had an incredible body. Cass stood about five-foot-three in her bare feet but from what Moira said unless she was at the gym Cass was usually in three-inch heels. She had golden brown hair that fell in waves to her waist and big brown eyes with flecks of gold in them. She had a lush figure with full breasts and hips. She was every man's fantasy and every woman's wish for "what I want to look like when I grow up." Even better was that she was a genuinely nice person. She was sweet, sincere and had a great sense of humor. Katie liked her.

"It was a cheerleading scholarship." Moira said. "And she studied gymnastics as well."

Cass rolled her eyes.

"I took gymnastics while I was in school," Katie volunteered. "I stayed in all the way through high school."

"Cool." Cass replied.

"Why are you reserved about letting people know you went to school on a cheerleading scholarship?" asked Catherine.

Cass heaved a sigh. "I guess I just get tired of people looking at me like I'm an airhead when they find out I was a cheerleader all the way through school including college. Cheerleading is a tough sport. It's not easy being the top of a human pyramid or tossed through the air. It's a very competitive sport that requires a lot of training."

"I bet," Catherine answered.

They sat in silence for a moment before Katie asked, "So can you walk on your hands?"

Cass laughed. "Piece of cake."

Katie shook her head. "I never could do that. I could do all the flips and tumbles you wanted but I could not stay on my head."

Cass bounced up. "It's all about hand placement and body control. Wait, I'll show you." She stood up and looked down at the short red dress she was wearing. "Well, not in this." She pulled the dress over her head and threw it on the futon behind her. She was left wearing a gorgeous in a silk and lace red bra and panty set with red high heels. She moved to the roomy hall that led from the front door to the living room.

Cass bent over and braced her hands on the floor. When she found her balance she eased her body over and up until she was in a handstand position. Slowly she made her way down the hall toward the front door with Moira, Katie and Catherine crowded into the living room doorway behind her watching with avid eyes. Moira muttered, "Shit!" before she realized the front door had opened and closed. The next thing she knew two hands wrapped around each of her legs and when she looked up her now braced body she saw two men standing over her.

They were each holding one of her legs against their far shoulders forcing her legs into a wide "v" shape. Cass caught her breath as she felt a hard sexual pull deep in her belly when she looked up at them. From the way they were looking down at her, the way their fingers were caressing her calves, they were feeling something similar. She wanted them both and could see them all entwined on a big bed naked as the day they were born, flesh to flesh to flesh. It was the most erotic fantasy she had ever had and she might have just acted on it if Catherine Daniels hadn't stepped into the hall just then and shattered the sexual spell.

"Doug, Damon, perhaps you should let go now so Cass can get dressed before anyone else comes in and joins us."

The two men helped her flip back over and gain her feet, their hands running over her thighs and ass as they "helped". Cass tried to step away. The dark-haired one who looked a little like Gil and was his the middle brother Doug held her arm and kept her beside him.

"The others are right behind us," Doug told the woman, whom he refused to let go of. "I'll show you to another room you can use to catch your breath and get dressed. Damon will bring your clothes."

Moira threw Cass' dress at the blond that must be Damon and he caught it in one hand while Doug pulled her down the hallway, past the living room where the women all stood and watched until he opened another door. He pulled her inside with him and Damon stepped through after them and shut the door. Cass was immediately caught between the two men's bodies so tightly that she could feel their large erections against her. She tilted her head back on Damon's shoulder allowing Doug better access to her throat which he was nipping and sucking at.

Damon leaned down and took her mouth with a kiss so carnal Cass felt singed by it. She had often fantasized about two men at once and she would definitely like to be the filling in this sandwich. But there were people in the other room and no matter how drunk she was she didn't sleep with men she didn't know.

Finding strength she didn't know she had, she pushed away and walked farther into the room away from where they both stood watching her.

"I'm sorry. I can't do this."

"But you want to," Damon said. It was not a question as they all knew the answer to that.

Cass looked up and was snagged by the two sets of blue eyes that met hers. "Yes, I want to but I won't."

"Then what's stopping you?" Doug demanded.

"I don't know you." Cass whispered.

"Then when everyone leaves we'll remedy that," Damon said before picking up her dress from where he had dropped it on the floor and tossing it to her. "Go ahead and get dressed for now."

"We'll wait for you out in the living room," Doug told her reaching behind him and tugging the door open. "Don't take too long."

With that the two men left her alone and Cass took a breath to clear her head, clamping her dress tight against her chest while she struggled to breathe, much less think. What in the world had she got herself into? And more importantly how did she get herself out of it?

Doug and Damon walked past the empty living room and straight to the open front door of their home where Catherine waited on the porch.

"Everyone went on home," Catherine said. "Cass doesn't have any place to stay tonight. I hope that you'll make sure she finds a place and gets there safely. She's a very nice girl." She looked pointedly at her son and his best friend. "I'd hate to see her hurt."

"She'll be fine, Mom." Doug stated before leaning down to kiss his mother's cheek.

"We'll see to that." Damon added kissing her other cheek.

"All right then, I'm going to take the limo home and send the driver on his way. I'll see you both at the wedding," she said, looking down at her watch, which now said two a.m., "tomorrow."

They both stood on the porch and watched until the limo pulled away. Doug and Damon had been friends for years. They had met in college where they played football. Now Damon was co-owner of Doug's family's construction company. Doug had inherited it by default when his Dad died two years ago. Doug was already working there and no one else in the family was interested in taking it on. The members of the Daniels family were all more than happy to sign it over to Doug. Now Damon was buying into it as well and they were working on expanding into other areas. They had talked about changing the name but surprisingly it had been Damon who had vetoed the idea. Daniels Construction was a trusted name and Damon saw no reason to change it.

"I've never seen your mom tipsy before," Damon commented quietly.

"What makes you think that?" Doug asked.

"She said that she would see us tomorrow at the wedding and the rehearsal is tomorrow not the wedding. The wedding is still a couple days away." Damon grinned and shook his head wondering if the beauty in the house was as tipsy. God he hoped not. He didn't want anything to keep them from what he knew they all really wanted.

They both stepped back into the house and while Doug locked up Damon checked the living room to see if anything needed to be picked up or put away. What he found was a tote bag spilled over by the futon. Scattered around it was a wallet, a make-up bag and a paperback book with two men and a woman on the cover in a very telling ménage.

"Need any help?" Doug asked.

Damon turned to him with a big smile. "Well, well, well, look what I found." He held up the book so that Doug could get a good look at the cover.

Doug's eyebrows lifted as he flipped the cover and read the back. "Damn, this might just be our lucky night."

Damon grinned. Right now they were both thinking about placing the sultry brunette in Doug's bedroom in the same place as the woman on the cover of the book still in Doug's hands—on her hands and knees taking hard cock at both ends. Smiling with anticipation they both headed to the door just a little farther down the hall.

Cass was pacing in the bedroom too mortified to go out and face everyone. She had her dress back on but still... How was she ever going to face Catherine Daniels and Katie Marcum again? They had both seen the way Doug and Damon had openly caressed her in the pretense of helping her flip from a handstand back to her feet. Moira on the other hand was probably laughing her head off. Cass smiled at that thought. She would do the same if it were Moira. What else was a best friend to do? But it wasn't Moira and Cass had no idea what to do to get out of this. She had no doubts that if the two gorgeous men who had left her in what she now knew was a bedroom decided to turn up the heat, she would most definitely be putty in their hands. What Cass needed was just a few more precious moments alone to think and plan. What she got was a clear signal that time was up as footsteps stopped outside and the door was gently pushed open. Cass Sinclair was out of time and as her own eyes met and clashed with those of the men stepping into the room she realized with an undeniable certainty that she was theirs for the taking.

Chapter Two

೫

Doug stepped into the room followed closely by Damon. Doug crossed in front of Cass and sat down on the side of the bed. Damon closed the door and the loud snick of the lock being turned seemed to echo in the room, making Cass watch him closely as he turned and leaned against the door, folding his arms across his chest. Cass had been caught in the middle of the room and now she was firmly trapped between the two very large and obviously horny men.

"I'm Doug Daniels, Gil's brother, Moira's brother-in-law after tomorrow. I'm thirty years old and co-owner of Daniels Construction. I'm financially secure, own my own home," Doug said, waving his hands indicating the house in general, "and have a clean bill of health as of my last check-up, which was six weeks ago. I'm six foot three, two-ten and you'll have to let me know if there's anything else you need to know."

Cass stared at him and shook her head. What in the hell was he talking about? And why was he telling her all of this?

Damon spoke from his casual stance against the door. "I'm Damon Roberts, honorary member of the Daniels family since I met Doug in college our freshman year. I co-own the construction company with him now and we share this house which we both designed and built. I'm also thirty, six foot two and two-twenty." Damon moved away from the door and started stalking toward Cass across the room. "Is there anything else you need to know to make it okay for you?"

Cass backed away from him and hit the firm body of Doug who had somehow moved behind her when she was focused on Damon. "What are you talking about?" she whispered when he stopped in front of her. Doug had his hands on her hips holding her firmly in place. Damon reached out and stroked the fingers of one hand down the side of her face.

"You said that although you wanted to be with us you couldn't because you didn't know us. We're trying to help you get to know us." Damon smiled down at her, clear intent in his eyes. He wanted her, they wanted her and God help her she was dripping wet with need for them as well.

Cass couldn't help the laugh that bubbled out but it turned into a groan as Damon moved his hand down her throat and began stroking the side of her breast as Doug moved so that she could better feel his hard cock rubbing against her back. She dropped her head back against Doug's chest, exposing the smooth line of her neck and he quickly bent forward to lick and suck along the smooth column of flesh.

"We want you, Cass. Do you know enough to be comfortable with us? Will you be with us or will you deny yourself?" Doug murmured against her flesh.

She wanted to give in to them and they all knew it.

"Call it a seduction if you want," Damon told her, "just don't say no."

Cass let out her breath with a moan when Damon cupped her breasts and used his thumbs to rub back and forth across her nipples. She was too hungry, too needy, too weak and there was no way that she could walk away from the ultimate fantasy of these two men. "Yes," she moaned, "God, yes, I want you, I want this night."

The next thing Cass knew her dress was being lifted over her head and tossed to the floor; her bra was unsnapped and eased from her body at the same time that her panties were being pushed down her thighs and over her heels. Then she was before them gloriously naked and they were eating her with their eyes. She was lifted and placed gently on her back across the bed. Doug and Damon stood for only a moment stripping quickly out of their own clothes—so quickly that she didn't know where to look and ended up not seeing nearly enough. Too quickly they joined her, Doug moving up to her face and kissing her intensely, thrusting his tongue into her mouth and claiming her with such passion that she felt lost, sucked under, left gasping for breath. Damon was kissing and licking his way across her flat abdomen working toward the wet folds of her gleaming pussy.

Doug worked his way back down her neck and across her collar bone before moving to the aching tips of her swollen breasts. Damon was nipping and sucking at the tender flesh of her inner thighs stroking his tongue closer and closer to where she wanted it. Then as if they had planned it they moved exactly where she needed them. Doug took her nipple in his mouth sucking it hard with firm pulls while Damon used his fingers to spread the lips of her pussy and thrust his tongue inside, feeding on her sweet flesh. It was a perfect seduction of all of her senses and she was an eager participant. Cass screamed and bucked against them in mindless pleasure. They were everywhere, hands, lips, tongues, teeth. There wasn't a part of her that was left alone.

Damon was working two fingers in and out of her tight pussy, sucking and licking her clit, pushing her closer and closer toward an orgasm that scared her with its pending intensity. Her nipples were red and sensitive from the constant attention of Doug, his fingers, his tongue, his lips, his teeth. He spared nothing in his assault. He used them all to pleasure her breasts, torture her nipples. She was there, right there on the edge clinging to a thin wire that suddenly snapped flinging her over, sending her head first into such mindless oblivion that she seemed to float somewhere over her own body.

They were gone she thought vaguely and then they were back. Damon moved between her wet thighs and placed the sheathed crown of his erection against her tight pussy. With one hard thrust, his big cock was buried fully inside her pussy, so deep that Cass felt skewered, so big that her pussy felt stretched beyond its limits.

"Too much," she pushed ineffectually against Damon's chest while he began working in and out of her, "too big." She wanted him so badly, but it had been so long.

"You'll be fine, baby." Damon's voice was pleading with her to agree. Cass smiled up at him and nodded. "I'll be fine. You're just a little more than I've had before." His grin was pure male pride and Cass felt a smile tug at her own lips. "Plus it has been awhile."

"Relax. I promise that you can handle every inch of me." He hooked his elbows under her knees spreading her wider for his thrusts. "You feel so good," he moaned against her ear.

Cass groaned with each of his fierce thrusts into her pussy. His cock filled her completely, stretching and burning sensitive muscles that hadn't been used in the last three years. She was getting slicker with every thrust though and it was feeling better and better. Damon increased his pounding rhythm thrusting harder, faster, deeper with every stroke. Cass arched her back and screamed. Damon latched onto one of her cherry red nipples and sucked fiercely, biting and nipping it with his teeth sending Cass over the edge. She bucked and cried out her release her pussy squeezing around his cock as he continued to fuck her hard and fast. He lasted five, six, seven more strokes before he threw his own head back and roared with his orgasm. He was buried so completely in her throbbing pussy that it reignited the fading embers of Cass' orgasm sending her over again taking her higher and higher. He fell against her chest burying her tiny body under the bulk of his. He kissed her with an intensity that rocked her, taking her mouth the same way he had just taken her body with firm hard strokes of his tongue that showed her no mercy. Reluctantly Damon pulled back and looked into her glazed eyes swamped by feelings he shouldn't have, had sworn that he would never have, not for anyone. He quickly rolled off of Cass and moved away from the bed.

Cass blinked in surprise and then Doug was there sheathed and ready between her thighs. His cock was just as big as Damon's only thicker and she gasped as he thrust violently into her, powering in and out of her pussy too turned on by watching her with Damon to take things any slower at the moment. He pulled her knees up beside his hips and she wrapped her legs around him, locking her feet in the small of his back. He held his weight on one arm braced by her head and used the other to capture and manipulate her clit. Every stroke of his cock was hard, fast and oh so deep. He possessed her pussy forcing her to take every inch of him with every stroke holding nothing back. She shuddered and screamed as he rode her slamming his thick shaft in and out over and over again. Cass came and still he fucked her, manipulated her clit and pushed her higher, harder, faster.

"I'm not sure that I can take any more," Cass whispered when she could find her breath. "Please, Doug, take it easy with me."

Doug slipped his cock gently inside her again this time stopping to rub his pelvic bone against her mound. "You can take it, Cass." He groaned with pleasure in her ear. "I'll be as easy as I can. You make me lose control baby. I look at you, feel your snug heat surround me, and I'm lost."

He pulled out and drove hard into her again then again then pinched and pulled at her clit making Cass arch her back higher, scream louder. "When you're with me you belong to me. This incredible body is mine to do what I want with. I fuck your pussy the way that I want and you'll enjoy every minute of it." He rubbed his thumb over her bottom lip, "and I'm going to fuck this gorgeous mouth too, watching my dick stroke in and out of these plump lips. And when you're ready I'm going to fill your tight little ass with every inch of my big boy while Damon fucks your pussy." He leaned close and whispered in her ear, "And you're not only going to let me, you're going to beg me for it."

"Oh God," Cass screamed as his words led her straight into another sharp orgasm. "Oh God! Oh, yes! God yes! Yes! Yes! Yes!"

Doug followed her, slamming his cock as far into her contracting pussy as he could, biting down on her earlobe as he released his control and spilled into the tip of the condom, her pulsing pussy continuing to milk and squeeze around him. It was more than a moment before he could catch his breath enough to say, "You can just call me Doug."

Cass looked at him in confusion until she remembered that she had been hollering "Oh God" at the top of her lungs. She giggled as he smiled down at her then bent and kissed her softly but oh so thoroughly, stroking her tongue with his own. He rolled off her and rested beside her on the bed. Cass closed her eyes and took a shallow breath struggling to slow her frantic pulse down. But they flew open when she felt hands wrap around her legs and tug her down until her bottom rested on the edge of the mattress, her feet dangled over the side. Damon stood there his erection sheathed in a new condom his face wreathed with desire and need. Need for her, desire for her and Cass felt shaken to her core by that look.

Damon thrust gently inside her, his strokes slow and easy this time. Doug stood at the side of the bed watching as he pulled the used condom from his reawakening cock then he murmured something to Damon as he headed to the bathroom. Damon groaned and pulled out of her pussy, his sheathed cock glistening with her juice. He pushed her legs up and over to her side guiding her with his hands into the position that he now wanted her in.

"Hands and knees, sweetheart," he urged her forward so that he could get onto the bed behind her. "Bring that ass back here to me. That's right. Arch that back more and show me what I want. Umm...that's good, sweetheart. So good," and with that he entered her again sheathing his cock back in the tight wet glove of her pussy. His thrusts were slow and steady making her moan as he pulled against the already sensitive inner muscles of her pussy.

Then Doug was back standing before her on the other side of the bed his long thick shaft bobbing and bouncing against his stomach. He eased onto the bed only stopping when his cock was perfectly positioned in front of her mouth. He wrapped his hands in her long hair and nudged the leaking head of his erection against her mouth. "Open wide, darling."

Cass opened her mouth as wide as she could and still he barely fit. She licked and sucked at the bulbous head stroking the drops of pre-cum from the slit with her tongue. She worked her lips around him sucking as much of him as she could into her mouth using her tongue to stroke and rub against the sensitive underside of his penis. Doug groaned and forced more of his cock into her suckling heat. He held her head exactly where he wanted it and began working his pulsing erection in and out of her mouth with slow strokes forcing her to take more and more until she choked on the big head of his cock as he pushed it into the back of her throat.

Both Doug and Damon groaned as she clamped down on their cocks squeezing her muscles as she fought against her insistent gag reflex. Reluctantly Doug pulled back enough to ease her discomfort. "We'll work on this, darling. Soon, you'll be able to take every inch of me without choking," he moaned as he thrust slowly and easily into her throat again. He worked his cock in and out of the tight wet heat of her mouth going as deep as he could, choking her occasionally as he fucked between the plump folds of her lush lips.

Damon was stroking faster in and out of her wet pussy. She could feel one of his hands resting on the small of her back keeping her angled for his pleasure as well as hers. His other hand was playing with her clit his fingers growing slick with her juices. Then he moved his hand around to her ass and wiped the wetness against her anus. Back and forth he went working her own natural lubrication into her tight back entrance until it was slick enough for him to slip a finger in.

Cass moaned and cried out around the thrust of Doug's cock in and out of her mouth.

"God, she's tight. I'll bet she's never had a cock in here before," Damon told Doug as he worked his finger in and out of her ass. "She'll have to be well lubricated before either of us will fit in here."

Doug gingerly removed his erection from Cass' suctioning mouth. "Would you like that, baby? Would you like to have us both at the same time like that?"

"Oh God, yes," Cass moaned thinking of all the times she had fantasized about just that. "I've always wanted to try that."

"We'll fulfill that fantasy for you, baby." Doug smiled at her slowly feeding his big cock back into the tight wet heat of her mouth. "And we'll make sure that you enjoy every minute of it, baby," he added as his gaze locked with Damon's.

Doug groaned as he watched Damon's finger slide in and out of her ass. He looked down at Cass' face enjoying watching his cock tunnel in and out, stretching her reddened lips wide with his girth. She looked beautiful with her skin damp and flushed from the many orgasms she had received from both him and Damon. She looked beautiful on her hands and knees between them one cock buried up her tight pussy and one sliding in and out of her damp lips, almost an exact replica of the picture that he and Damon had seen on the cover of the book she had in her bag. "I'm going to enjoy fucking that tight little ass, Cass. I'm going to enjoy working my cock into where no man has ever been and I'm going to make sure that it is everything you wanted it to be."

Cass moaned with fear and desire, fear at the thought of taking either of the long thick cocks there and a strong desire to experience it with this man in particular. Doug must have seen that desire reflected in her eyes because his eyes immediately dropped to a half-mast look of intense lust. He thrust faster in and out of her mouth forcing his cock deeper almost choking her with his girth and depth. Damon was riding her hard and fast now, his cock powering in and out of her pussy while he added another finger to the one he was already working in and out of the small pink pucker of her anus stretching her and making the tiny nerves there scream at this new sensation. The sight of his fingers working in and out of her ass was enough to push Damon over the edge. He pushed his throbbing erection violently inside her sopping wet pussy reaching into her as far as he could, shoved his fingers completely into her ass and rubbed them against his cock through the thin membrane that separated the two parts of his body that were buried in the body of this incredible woman.

Cass cried out and convulsed around him squeezing and releasing Damon's cock with her orgasm, milking him for every drop of his own. Doug joined them with a cry of his own pulling his exploding shaft from Cass' mouth and watching as the hot jets of cum shot from his cock to land on her lips and cheeks dripping down her chin and splattering against the dangling globes of her breasts. He groaned as she licked a drop of cum from her lips and then leaned forward enough to lick up and over the still pulsing head of his cock.

Damon was leaning heavily against her back and Doug still had his hands clenched in her hair, his cum thick and white on her face. Cass brought a hand up and used her fingers to catch more of Doug's release and bring it to her mouth. He tasted so good. Her body felt more alive than it ever had. Their seduction was complete. She had lost herself in them, mind, body and soul. Her heart, the one that had felt such pain when she watched her mother laid to rest in the earth, beat with a steady rhythm reminding her that she was still here, still alive. And these two men, Doug Daniels and Damon Roberts, were reminding her of more things as well. Reminding her that she was a woman. Reminding her that she was alive. And just maybe reminding her of the many possible ways to fall in love.

Chapter Three

℈

Cass woke up sometime later that morning feeling deliciously well loved. She was lying on her side between her two lovers with one thigh pulled up over Damon's hip. She could feel Doug behind her working his lubricated fingers in and out of her ass. Her eyes flew wide open and she locked them onto Damon's baby blues not realizing that she had pulled her body away from Doug's probing fingers until she felt the sharp slap against the cheek of her lush ass.

"Don't pull away from me, darling. I told you before we went to sleep that I was going to take you here and I remember the look in your eyes when I did. You want this as much as I do, as much as Damon and I do." He rubbed his fingers gently over her stinging flesh and thrust his fingers back into her ass scissoring them and spreading her wide preparing her ass for what he intended. "Just hold onto Damon while I work my way in, baby, hold on tight."

Cass felt his fingers pull out but they were immediately replaced with the engorged head of his long, thick cock. It was too big, the pressure too intense and she felt like she would rip open before he would ever get inside. Her hands flew to Damon's shoulders and when she looked up at him again there was no way to hide the tears filling her big golden brown eyes. Damon bent and kissed her softly licking the tears from her face whispering words of comfort as Doug continued pushing against her forcing his way into her virgin flesh.

Cass' breathing was strained as Doug pressed harder against her until finally the thick head of his cock popped through that first tight ring of muscles at her back entrance and her hot, tight ass closed around him with a firm grip.

Doug groaned and Cass cried out then beat her fists against Damon's chest.

"It's too big. I don't know if I can take this," she cried out as she clutched at Damon.

Damon caught her close and held her tight to his chest with one arm while he used the other to grasp her thigh and pull her leg higher against his hip opening her wider for Doug. "Shh, sweetheart, the hard part is over. Doug's already inside and it's too late to go back now. We told you that we would want you this way, Cass. Try to relax for him so that he can work that cock all the way into your ass. Then when he's buried inside you I'm going to start working my cock into your sweet little pussy, sweetheart. Then we're going to make you feel so good that you'll beg us to keep going, never to stop." Each of his words were interspersed with kisses, nibbles, licks and sucks at her mouth, her jaw, her ears and all along her arched neck.

Cass hadn't realized how well he had distracted her, relaxed her, until she heard Doug murmur at her ear, "I'm in, darling, all the way in this tight, sweet ass of yours. You feel so good clamped around my cock," he pulled out and slowly, gently eased all the way in again before suddenly stopping and tensing behind her. "Shit! I forgot a condom. I'll have to get one before we continue, darling, but I promise to be as gentle as I can when I work my way back in here."

"No," Cass yelled clamping the muscles of her ass and trapping him inside her making them both groan. "You said that you have a clean bill of health as of six weeks ago. Have you been with anyone since then?"

"No," Doug whispered in her ear. "Neither of us has been with anyone in six long weeks, baby."

"Then I don't care if you wear a condom or not. I'm on the Pill and have been for quite a long time so I'm protected against pregnancy, as protected as I would be with a condom anyway. Plus, it has been three years for me so I can tell you that I am safe and clean as well." She looked into Damon's eyes then before adding, "Neither of you needs to wear a condom if you don't want to." Cass rubbed her nipples against the smooth planes of Damon's chest reveling in the contrast between his smoothness and the rough hairy texture of Doug's chest against her back. "I've never had an unsheathed cock inside me before."

"I've never had sex without a condom, sweetheart," Damon said.

"Me, either," Doug added before moving in and out of her snug ass again. "But I'm willing to enjoy the experience if you want to."

"I really want to," Cass turned her head so that he could match his mouth to hers kissing her with the same slow thoroughness as he was using to stroke in and out of her ass. She groaned in pleasure enjoying the touch of his tongue, the stroke of his cock. He was doing his best to bring the pleasure through the pain and his efforts were working. She felt Damon move in front of her and felt his lips latch onto her nipple and suck it into his mouth. He worked his fingers in and out of her pussy made all that much tighter by the girth of Doug's erection buried firmly in her ass. It was incredibly sensual, extremely sexual and more intense than she had ever known and that was before Damon began to slowly work his own swollen member into her pussy.

Doug held her close to his chest his cock fully impaled in her ass unmoving while Damon slowly worked his way into her hot little pussy. Finally both men were fully enclosed inside her body and she felt so full, stretched past her limit by these two big men. She couldn't breathe, couldn't move and couldn't focus on any one sensation as her body felt bombarded by an explosion of sexual intensity when both men began sliding in and out of her body—one filling her as the other withdrew. It was more erotic than anything she had ever experienced before.

Doug and Damon took turns kissing her as they made love to her using the slide of a hand or the nudge of mouths to position her exactly how they wanted her. Their breathing was hard and labored, all three of them gasping and moaning at the intensity of the feelings that were coursing through them. Doug was the first to cry out and increase his motions in and out of Cass' ass. He could feel the tingle along his spine and knew that he was close to orgasm. Damon picked up his rhythm immediately and Cass cried out as the men began fucking her harder and deeper with every stroke. Her orgasm was right there before she realized it, breaking over her in wave after wave. She felt shattered, broken, so overwhelmed by the force of her release that she was temporarily blind and deaf to all else around her. The only thing that she knew and felt was the pure pleasure washing over and through her body in never-ending waves. She knew that she was screaming but it was as if someone else were yelling, "Oh God, Yes! Yes! Yes!" at the top of their lungs. She could feel Doug and Damon exploding in her body, filling her with the hot pulsing jets of their release, marking her with their cum. Cass thought for sure that she must be dreaming that nothing could ever feel this good, this all consuming and this powerful.

Then Doug nipped playfully at her ear lobe and reminded her gently, "I told you that you could just call me Doug, darling."

Damon laughed and said smugly, "Perhaps she was referring to me. You're not the only god in this bedroom."

"Umm…" Doug nipped at her neck licking the sweat from her flesh, "maybe not the only one but certainly the best."

"In your dreams, Daniels," Damon scoffed while he nipped and sucked tenderly at Cass' bottom lip.

Cass laughed at them before finally catching her breath enough to say, "You both were incredible. I've never had an orgasm like that in my life."

"That's just the beginning," Damon said.

"Only the beginning," Doug added and Cass sighed happily as she let her body go boneless between them. The beginning, she thought. She had promised her mother that she would live life to the fullest, no regrets and no what-ifs. Cass had sworn that she would experience life in all its divine glory and with a saucy grin she realized that she couldn't imagine being any fuller than she just was.

* * * * *

Doug had made Cass promise to sit with him and Damon at the rehearsal dinner before he would agree to take her into town to Gil's old apartment where Moira had moved Cass' car. Moira and Gil wanted Cass to feel free to stay there since Cass didn't want to stay in her old apartment with them. Gil's lease was paid through the end of the year and Cass was more than willing to stay there for the time being. She knew that all she had to do was let Jack Madigan, Moira's father and a surrogate father to Cass as well when she was away from home, know and he would find something for her in one of the many buildings that he owned, rent free, of course.

Now she stood on the sidewalk dressed once again in the red dress from the bachelorette party the night before and waited for Doug to lift the two big suitcases from the trunk of her car. There was no persuading him to let her carry them up to the apartment herself so she didn't even bother. Instead she followed behind him into the building pushing the elevator button and riding up to the second floor with him then following him down the hall to his brother's apartment.

It seemed funny to her that she and Gil had switched residences in just five short months. Cass revisited that thought and corrected, five of the longest months of her life actually. The apartment still held Gil's furniture so she was okay for now. Eventually she would want her own bed from what was now Gil and Moira's apartment but this would do for now. She pointed Doug in the direction of one of the guest rooms because Moira had told her that Gil's other brother Griff was staying part time in the apartment as well. She hadn't shared that little bit of information with Doug and Damon, deciding it was in her best interests to get out of their house and into the apartment before they knew. She had only spent one night with them and it was the most incredible night of her life but it was still only in the realms of a one night stand right now.

She wasn't kidding herself though. Both men had made it more than clear to her that they planned on seeing her a lot from now on. She didn't know how long things would last between the three of them but she planned on fully enjoying herself while it lasted. They were already showing signs of being possessive of her.

Doug dropped the suitcases beside the bed and turned and pulled her into his arms flush against his chest. With her three-inch heels, the top of her head just reached his shoulders allowing her enough room to reach her arms up and encircle his neck without putting too much strain on either one of them. He possessed her mouth with his. There was no other word for how he took control of the kiss and her with it. She felt the hard pulse of his erection against her even with the layers of clothing separating them.

Cass groaned with lust but still managed to push him away although reluctantly. "As much as I would love to have sex with you again, Doug, I just can't right now. I will barely have time to shower and get ready as it is. The rehearsal starts in a little over two hours. I need to unpack, iron my dress, shower and find time to make a few calls as well."

Doug smiled down at her before asking quietly, "Feeling a little tender and sore aren't you, darling?"

Cass could feel the heat in her cheeks but couldn't look away from his deep blue eyes. "Yes, I'm a little tender. It's been a long time for me and I spent the better part of the day today, since early this morning, doing nothing but having sex with you and Damon. I'm not used to being this sexually active."

"Especially with two men," Doug added making Cass blush even redder.

"Never with two men," Cass stated.

"Damon and I are very sexual. We like to fuck," Doug said bluntly, "anyway we can, wherever we can. We've been celibate for six weeks but I won't lie to you, darling, we will always be demanding with you in the bedroom. Or wherever we may be when we spread those creamy thighs of yours, on the floor, the table, the wall or a bed. It won't matter to us. Wherever. Whenever. However. Just as long as our cocks are buried somewhere inside that lush body of yours."

"We've only just met, Doug, and it was only one day…" Cass started to say but Doug cut her off with a very angry sounding growl.

"We may have only just met but you should have taken us seriously when Damon and I told you that this was only the beginning. Things are far from over between us, Cass. We'll be spending a lot of time together, getting to know each other even better. Don't you want the same?" he asked holding her close and rubbing his erection against her belly.

"Yes," Cass managed to whisper before Doug took her under his spell again with a slow thorough kiss that somehow managed to bring both of their bodies into full play. The only thing she could think was that it felt so right. He knew how to kiss, how to use his mouth completely to bring her to the edge of orgasm without ever touching her in more intimate places. He was as reluctant as she was when they pulled apart but they both knew that they had other things to do.

He grabbed her hand and tugged her back down the hall and through the living room to the front door of the apartment. Doug bent and kissed her again just a quick brush of his lips this time before looking into her smoky brown eyes that were now more gold than brown with her desire.

"Lock up behind me and make sure you use the bolt. Katie had someone get into the apartment when she stayed here and she was hurt pretty badly before help got to her."

"Katie told me about that last night when Moira mentioned staying here. She said that she hasn't been back to the apartment since. I can't say that I blame her." Cass smiled up at him and brushed her fingers down his face. "You don't have to worry about me, Doug. I'll be fine here."

Doug caught her fingers and brought her palm up to his mouth for a kiss before saying, "Throw the bolt, darling. I'll see you at rehearsal in just a few hours." With that Doug headed out the door leaving Cass feeling weak in the knees just inside. She locked the door and flipped the deadbolt knowing that Gil's brother Griff would have a key to it if he needed in. Shaking her head she hurried back to the bedroom as she tried to plan the next few hours so that she would have plenty of time to do everything that she needed to. But when she headed to the shower half an hour later after unpacking and ironing the gold gown that she planned to wear to rehearsal it was thoughts of Doug and Damon that accompanied her.

* * * * *

They went through the ceremony twice before they were all able to head over to the restaurant Jack had booked for the rehearsal dinner. It didn't surprise Cass that she was linked up with Doug for the walk down the aisle as they were both attendants at the wedding. The only two other attendants were Ben and Katie Marcum, the groom's baby sister and her husband. Griff, the youngest in the Daniels family, was an usher along with Damon.

She and Doug were making their way down the aisle toward the doors to the vestibule for the last time when he leaned over and commented on her choice of attire for the evening. She had chosen the gold dress because of the way it brought out the golden highlights in both her hair and eyes. The dress was an ankle-length sheath in back but opened up around her legs in the front all the way up to her knees. It was strapless and looked good on her with the strappy three inch gold heels she wore with it. Doug thought so as well.

"I really like that dress you're almost wearing. I'll like it even better on my bedroom floor," he murmured in her ear. "Are you wearing any underwear under that thing?"

Cass' eyes twinkled with humor as she whispered back, "Some things a man should find out for himself." No way was she telling him that the only thing under her dress was her skin, soft and golden from her tinted lotion. The dress had a built-in shelf bra and was way too tight to allow for panties of any kind. Cass had a feeling though that if she told him she was naked under her dress he and Damon would never let her get to the dinner on time if ever at all.

Doug growled low in his throat and Cass suppressed a giggle as they walked out the doors that Damon and Griff were holding open. Ben and Katie were right behind them and of course the bride and groom, Moira and Gil, had preceded them down the aisle. There was no missing the fire in Damon's eyes when he looked at her on Doug's arm. She felt a shiver go down her spine as she thought of all the things the three of them had experienced earlier that day. She was still deliciously sore between her thighs and the cheeks of her ass as well. It still amazed her, the things that she had allowed them to do to her, with her and, hell she had wallowed in every moment of their love play.

Sensing more than seeing Damon heading toward them she quickly released Doug's arm and headed over to Moira and Gil. "Your wedding is going to be absolutely beautiful," Cass enthused as she hugged Moira to her. "I'm so glad that I could be here to see all of this."

Moira hugged her back as well. "I'm glad too." Moira couldn't imagine celebrating so important a day in her life without Cass with her. "If you don't mind I'd like to ride over to the dinner with you. We haven't really had a chance to talk or anything yet."

"I thought you were..." Gil started to say but Moira interrupted him before he could finish whatever he had meant to say.

"I want to talk to Cass and I'll let you know at the dinner what my plans are," Moira told him. "That is if you don't mind me hitching a ride with you, Cass."

"No, that's fine with me," Cass said and hoped no one could see the relief in her eyes that she felt at the temporary escape from Doug and Damon and their overwhelming presence. She was still unsure of where they went from this point on, no matter what they said to her. She knew that they wanted her but for how long and was it only to be a sexual relationship between the three of them or would they do other things together? These were questions that she had been struggling with since Doug had dropped her at the apartment earlier.

Moira looked over her shoulder and grasped Cass' hand and tugged Cass after her to the outside door. "Let's get going then," Moira said stopping only long enough to give Gil a quick peck on the lips and a mumbled, "Take care of that please."

This prompted Cass to glance behind her and see what Moira was talking about. Doug and Damon were headed right toward where she, Moira and Gil were standing and there was no misreading the looks on their faces. They were looking at her like she was the only edible thing in the room and they were dying of hunger. She headed toward the door and this time she was the one pulling Moira behind her.

By the time the two women made it out to the car Moira was laughing hard and teetering on the two-inch heels that she was wearing with her green dress that perfectly matched her eyes. Moira was a beautiful woman at five foot six with long blonde hair and green eyes slanted at the corners that gave them the look of cat's eyes. The green dress she wore was looser than Cass' own dress and had lovely sleeves that stopped at the edge of her shoulders with ruffles of lace. The dress fell to Moira's ankles all the way around making it appear demure except for the deep v neck that revealed a tantalizing display of her creamy thirty-six D cup breasts.

"You had better quit laughing so hard, Moira, or you're going to pop a boob out of that dress you're wearing," Cass said as she noticed her friend's breasts sway and move closer and closer to the revealing v as Moira laughed.

"I'm sorry," Moira gasped out as she tried to control her laughter. "It's just that you should have seen the looks on Doug's and Damon's faces when we hurried out the door. Not to mention Gil's when he realized what I had left him to deal with. It was just too funny to not laugh."

"Just get in the car," Cass muttered as she pressed the unlock button on the key ring to her red Chrysler Crossfire convertible. Her dad had given it to her before she left to head back to Legacy. It was something that her mother had always wanted and he had bought it for her but Cass' mom had never gotten the chance to ride in it. Her father hadn't wanted to keep it but he refused to sell it so he gave it to Cass stating that she needed a sportier car than her little Neon. He had paid the insurance on it for the entire year in September so it was easy to switch title, insurance and everything to her name. Now all she had to worry about was gas and maintenance between now and next September.

Moira stroked her hand over the leather interior of the little two-seater convertible. "I love this new car of yours. You have to make sure that you really enjoy it for your mother. Let's put the top down and go for a ride on the way to dinner."

"Umm…you are the bride, Moira. Do you really want to be late to your own rehearsal dinner?"

"I prefer to think of it as a grand entrance," Moira added in a regal sounding voice before she broke down and started laughing again as she fastened her seat belt. "Let's just take a drive, okay?"

"No problem," Cass said as she turned the key and listened to the rumble of the motor before buckling her seat belt and putting the car into gear. Cass wasn't taking the time to put the top down though as she saw the men leaving the church behind them. Instead she pulled away from the curb and drove down the street.

"So what is on your mind, Moira?" Cass asked as she drove around Legacy taking the long winding way to the restaurant.

"I was wondering if you wanted to stay the night with me tonight at the apartment. It would just be just the two of us again for one last night together. Gil will spend the night at his old apartment with Griff and Doug and Damon and even Ben will probably drop by at some point. He doesn't want to spend the night without me but he's willing to do it because it's what I want. So what do you say? One more night with just us two girls?"

Cass could feel tears in her eyes and tried her best to blink them away. It seemed like so much time had passed since she had left to go home and help take care of her mother. Now that she was back Moira was getting married and everything would be changing. They wouldn't be roommates anymore. No more late nights with the two of them laughing and falling asleep. Now Moira would be doing those things with her husband. "I would love to, Moira. I'm so excited that you asked me to. It will be so great with it being just the two of us again."

"Yeah, plus I get to grill you about what happened after we all left Doug's and Damon's house early this morning. I have to say that a person would have to be dead not to feel the heat between you three," Moira said with a wiggle of her eyebrows.

"You could say that," Cass said without adding anything else. She didn't know what exactly to share with Moira about them and everything that had happened in such a short time.

"Just answer a few things for me while you drive. You don't have to go into detail yet," Moira emphasized the last word letting Cass know that she wasn't completely of the hook just being given a slight reprieve. "Just a yes or no will do. Okay?" Moira asked Cass.

"Okay," Cass nodded but kept her eyes firmly on the road ahead of her.

"Did you sleep with them? Both of them?"

Cass was startled by that question. "How could you possibly know that, Moira?"

"Let's just say that the whole Daniels family knows that they share their women."

"Women?" Cass asked softly.

"Woman of the moment," Moira corrected. "So I take that to mean that you did sleep with both of them."

"Yes," Cass whispered.

"Wow, woman! I have to admit that Doug's overt sexuality kind of scares me. He seems so intense. More than even Gil and, trust me, Gil is plenty intense for me."

"Yes," Cass replied causing Moira to laugh again.

"So did you like it?"

Cass took her eyes off of the road long enough to give Moira a you've-got-to-be-kidding look before stating, "Yes."

"Did you sleep with them both at the same time?" Moira flushed when Cass just looked at her and raised an eyebrow. "You know what I mean. I'm just curious is all. I'm plenty happy with Gil and I couldn't handle more than him but I'm still a little curious."

"Yes," Cass answered, "and before you ask, it was the best sex of my life."

"That good huh?" Moira murmured. "So was it just a one night stand or what?"

Cass pulled into the parking lot of the restaurant and parked the car shutting off the motor but not getting out yet.

Instead she turned to look at Moira. "Doug and Damon both said that it was only the beginning. I had to promise to sit with them at the dinner before either of them would agree to take me to Gil's old apartment without one of them staying." She laughed and shook her head. They were like two little boys with a new toy. It was amusing having them in her life.

"Did you tell them that Griff is staying there for a while until his new place is painted?"

"Hell no!" Cass exclaimed. "As possessive as they are both already acting I decided that it was in my best interest to already be in the apartment before they found that out."

"You do realize that Griff has probably already said something to them about that by now, don't you?" Moira shook her head and grinned.

"Probably," Cass admitted, "but I don't have to admit that I knew anything in advance."

"Oh I'm sure that Doug immediately went to Gil and asked if he had told you about Griff or not. And I'm equally sure that my soon-to-be-husband sold you up river."

"Great, what am I going to do now?" Cass asked just a little desperately.

"Well for tonight you're staying with me so that gives you a little reprieve but, Cass, what do you want to do? Do you want to continue seeing them knowing that they are possessive?"

"Yes, I want to see them for as long as I can, until it's over. I'm just a little confused and scared right now is all," Cass added.

"Scared?" Moira questioned. "If one of them is putting pressure on you then I promise you that..."

It was Cass' turn to laugh this time. "No, no one is putting any pressure on me to do anything that I don't want to do."

"Then what are you confused and scared about?" Moira asked with some confusion.

"I'm afraid that I won't be able to walk away from them unscathed when the time comes. I'm afraid that I'm going to do something stupid like fall in love," Cass admitted.

"With Doug, Damon or both of them?" Moira asked.

"Both of them," Cass confessed then reached for the door handle. "Now let's head in before someone sends out a search party for the bride.

Moira stepped out of the car, shut the door and met Cass by the front of the sports car. "I'm here for you if you need anything."

Cass hugged her and took her hand as they crossed the parking lot to the sidewalk that led to the front door of the restaurant. Cass felt a strange tingle on the back of her neck and couldn't help but glance back over her shoulder. There was no one there but she couldn't shake the feeling as she and Moira continued to the door that someone was watching her.

Chapter Four

ဆာ

Doug watched Cass and Moira walk in the door and had to get a handle on his need to walk over and pull Cass roughly into his arms. The little minx had skipped out on him and Damon at the church leaving as they had headed toward her. He had seen her eyes and Doug knew that she had done it intentionally. He couldn't help but wonder why. Right now though he had a hard cock from looking at her in that dress and planned to get her out of the dinner and back into his bed as soon as he could.

Damon had just headed across from the other side of the room where he had been talking to Moira's father, Jack Madigan, when his gaze met Doug's. Doug nodded at the unasked question in his best friend's eyes and they both made a bee line for Cass just as she was lifted and twirled around by a big blond looking Viking. That was bad enough but when Cass squealed and wrapped her arms around the big guy's neck, Doug and Damon both saw red. No one touched their woman.

The big guy bent his head and whispered in Cass' ear, "Hey, gorgeous I just wanted to welcome you home and tell you how sorry I am about your mom. If she was anything like you then she must have been one hell of a woman."

Cass kissed Shep on the cheek and squeezed him tightly, oblivious to the two men converging on them. Shep had been around since her freshman year of college when she and Moira had hooked up. Shep, Roman and Chetan, all friends of Moira's dad, had always been around checking up on Moira for Jack since Moira refused to speak to her father back then. Chetan, Cass had learned from Shep, came from the Sioux word for hawk and was pronounced chay-than.

44

Roman was so much like Jack that they could have been brothers. Both stood six feet five inches and had sandy brown hair, but Roman's eyes were an intense shade of grey. He worked mostly with computers and security software. He was quiet for the most part but when he spoke people usually listened.

They were all like older brothers to Cass although she and Shep had gone out once. There was just no sexual chemistry between them though and they were much happier as good friends.

Cass felt the slight tension in Shep's shoulders and heard him whisper, "Well, well, well, what have we here. Seeing anyone interesting, Cass? Maybe two someones?"

Cass glanced back over her shoulder into the dining room behind them and took in the scowls on both Doug's and Damon's faces and couldn't help but mutter, "Oh shit."

Shep, always a troublemaker, just slowly slid her down his body and gave her a kiss on the mouth doing his best to make it look like what it wasn't. When Cass finally felt her heels hit the floor, she tried to turn but Shep patted her on the butt and pulled her to his side. "You don't know what you're doing, you fool. They're going to kill us both," Cass groaned as she faced the fact that Shep wasn't going to let her go.

"I'll protect you, my sweet little dove," Shep crooned to her just as Doug and Damon reached them making both men scowl even harder.

"Cass," Doug gritted out from between his clenched teeth. "Come here."

Cass tried to step away from Shep's side but Shep kept his arm firmly around her waist keeping her at his side. Cass tried to make the best of it by introducing everyone. "Doug, Damon, I'd like you to meet a friend of mine Donovan Shepard, Shep. Shep, this is Doug Daniels, Gil's brother and Damon Roberts."

Neither Doug nor Damon responded except to nod at Shep. Cass could see the muscle ticking in Doug's tightly clenched jaw and Damon wasn't much better. She wasn't surprised when Doug said her name roughly again and held his hand out to her.

When Shep still refused to release her, Cass did the only thing that she could think of. She stomped on Shep's foot with her three-inch ice-pick heels and prayed that she wouldn't break a toe. Shep cried out in surprise but he released her quickly enough and gave her a hurt look that she wasn't buying for a minute.

"All you had to do was ask," he muttered in a hurt tone before walking with an exaggerated limp into the room.

Doug and Damon immediately stepped up to her and led her down the hall to the first door they came to. It was a small room with shelves along the walls stocked with cleaning supplies and toilet paper and paper towels. Damon stepped into the room and Doug pushed Cass in and followed her closing and locking the door behind them.

"What was the meaning of that little display out there? Is he a boyfriend?" Doug demanded immediately gripping her upper arms and pulling her to her tip-toes against his chest.

"Shep works for Moira's dad. I've known him since I was eighteen, Doug. We're just friends." Cass definitely had no intention of telling him that she and Shep had gone out once. Crazy she was not.

"Why did you leave the church when you knew we were headed for you?" Damon interrupted to question. "Are you afraid of us? Afraid of what we want?"

Cass glanced to her side where Damon stood since Doug refused to let go of her. Doug had relaxed enough to let her feet rest on the floor though. "No, I'm not afraid of either of you or what you want from me. Moira wanted to ride in my car and talk for a few minutes. She is my best friend and we haven't seen each other in roughly five months."

Doug and Damon took that in and decided to let that one go before Doug jumped in again and said, "Why didn't you tell me that my brother Griff was going to be staying at the apartment with you?"

"And don't even try to tell us that you didn't know," Damon added. "We already talked to Gil and he told us that he had personally told you about Griff staying there."

Damn! Cass thought. Moira had warned her that Gil would tell on her. She blinked up at them as she tried to decide exactly what to say without making it worse for her. "I wasn't sure how you would take that little bit of news so I decided to wait and tell you later once we knew each other better."

"That was your first mistake, darling. You should have told us before we heard all about it from my little brother. He was full of how he was going to be sleeping in the same apartment with Moira's hot little friend."

Cass was starting to get good and pissed now. "So?" she demanded. "I'm not going to apologize for not saying anything to you, Doug. We slept together that doesn't mean that you own me."

Cass gasped as Doug slammed her against his chest and Damon moved until he was pressed against her back. "We more than slept together Cass. We fucked and we made love. You were told that it was only the beginning but maybe we didn't make other things so clear to you. While you are with us you are with only us. Damon and I can get very jealous and neither of us likes to see you in some other guy's arms."

"Don't earn a punishment, Cass," Damon whispered beside her ear as he gripped her hips and bent his knees to rub his erection along her buttocks. "Because you will be punished if you do anything like this again."

"Pun...Punished?" Cass stuttered out the question as Damon nibbled and licked along her neck and shoulder.

"Oh, yes, darling," Doug said. "I won't punish you when we get you home later because you weren't forewarned of the consequences yet but next time you will be. While you are with us you are with only us. We know where you are so we can get a hold of you when we need to. Anything comes up you let us know immediately, baby. We won't control what you do but we will know where you are and who you are with. That's what it means to belong to us," Doug told her, "and you do belong to us. Next time, Cass, Damon and I are going to strip you naked and bend you over my knees and take turns turning that lush ass of yours rosy red. Do you understand, darling?" Doug asked as he nipped and sucked at her lips.

"Yes," Cass whispered too lost in the sensations they were causing to focus completely on what he was saying.

"That's good, sweetheart," Damon said as he rubbed against her ass again before adding, "I can't wait to get you back home and into bed."

"Umm…I'm not going home with you," Cass murmured as they continued to caress her.

"What?" both men exclaimed as they pulled back from her neck and shoulders and looked down at her.

"I'm staying the night with Moira tonight," Cass explained. "Just the two of us. Gil's staying in the apartment with Griff for tonight so that Moira and I can have one last night together. We've lived together for six years," she added with a small smile.

"Then we better use this little bit of time wisely," Doug said and that was all the warning Cass got before she was lifted against him and braced against Damon's chest. Damon lifted her dress up out of the way and both men were made aware that Cass was not wearing panties underneath. They both groaned and Doug made quick work of his belt button and zipper while Damon supported her body with his arms and chest hooking his elbows behind her knees and spreading her wide.

Doug groaned as he finally released his engorged cock and slipped it between her wet folds. "I know you're sore, darling, but I can't wait," he whispered tautly and then surged inside the hot confines of her pussy stretching her sensitive inner muscles with his girth and length. He rode her hard pounding into her while Damon held her open for Doug's every thrust. She arched her neck back so that her head rested on Damon's shoulder and keened loudly while Doug fucked her with rapid strokes of his big cock. Doug reached out leaning back a little so he could rub his thumb over her straining clit and she came with a scream just as he did. She could feel the wash of his hot semen all along her pulsing channel and struggled to catch her breath, overwhelmed by sensations she had never known.

While she was lost in the emotions ripping through her Doug put his spent cock away and the two men managed to turn her so that she was in Doug's arms braced against his chest his elbows hooked beneath her knees and Cass was now facing Damon. She wasn't sure exactly how they managed to turn her but before she could comment Damon was pushing firmly inside her already ravaged pussy. He rode her just as roughly as Doug pushing his cock in and out with hard quick strokes that had her panting for breath. Damon took her swollen over-sensitized clit between his thumb and finger and pinched at it bringing her quickly to the edge of another orgasm.

Doug, sensing how close she was pushed his hands up to her breasts lifting her legs higher, spreading her thighs wider and she came with a violent orgasm when he pinched both of her nipples between his fingers and gave them a twist. She must have screamed and may have passed out because the next thing she knew Damon was spewing inside her muffling his cries as best he could in her neck. They stayed that way for a few moments all of them trying to slow their breathing and lower their heart rates. Damon slipped out of her and tucked himself away before turning and grabbing some paper towels from the shelf. He cleaned her up while Doug held her to him placing kisses along her neck and jaw. When Damon was done, Doug slowly released her down his body lowering one leg at a time while Damon helped balance her from the front.

Cass could feel the love bites on her neck and shoulders and reached back to take the clip from her hair letting it fall free in waves all around her. She pulled some over her shoulders hoping to not only hide the love bites but the vivid peaks of her nipples as well. They were just getting ready to leave the room when there was a discreet knock on the door and Shep's voice spoke from the other side.

"Everyone's waiting on you three to start dinner so if you're all through now perhaps you could join us." They listened as he walked away and Cass felt her face flame with color.

"You don't think that anyone heard us do you?" she asked uncertainty in her voice.

Neither Damon nor Doug answered as they escorted her out of the room, down the hall and into the dining room where everyone stared at them. Doug and Damon could tell by the smirks on Gil's, Griff's and Ben's faces that they knew exactly what Damon and Doug had been doing with Cass but it wasn't until they sat down and Griff leaned close to stage whisper in Doug's ear, "Some acoustics this place has, huh?" that all doubt was removed. It was more than apparent that at least some of the people around the table had heard Doug, Damon and Cass making love in the closet. Doug and Damon just shrugged and ignored the whispers and stares of the people around them.

Cass was mortified. She would have loved nothing more than to slide beneath the table and disappear. No such luck for her though as she sat through two and a half hours of dinner and celebration before she and Moira left to head over to Moira's apartment for the night. Cass still had some clothes there in the bedroom that had been hers so she didn't need to head back to Gil's apartment. As soon as they were in the car Cass groaned and tapped her head against the steering wheel.

"I can't believe that happened to me. I could just die," she moaned.

Moira laughed and managed to get out between peals, "That was nothing. Wait till we get back to the apartment and I'll tell you about how I met Doug and Catherine for the first time."

Cass groaned and said emphatically, "It couldn't have been worse than this."

"You have no idea," Moira told her as Cass started the car and pulled out heading to the apartment they had once shared. "Trust me, you have no idea."

Cass just shook her head thinking that there was no way Moira could have been through anything as embarrassing as this.

* * * * *

"Totally naked!" Cass shrieked from her seat on the couch a little while later. The girls had opened a bottle of wine and Cass had filled Moira in on all that had happened with her mom while Cass was home with her. Moira and Cass had spoken often on the phone but it wasn't the same and some things could only be shared in person. Now the wine bottle was empty and added to what they had both consumed at the rehearsal dinner they were now feeling very good and moving on to more interesting topics.

"I swear to God," Moira laughed. "I walked out of the bathroom still wet with my robe thrown on but wide open in the front and there in front of me were Griff, Doug, Katie and Catherine. I was mortified," Moira laughed even harder at the memory doing her best to cross her fingers over her heart. "I swear. Then Gil stepped out behind in nothing but a towel and yelled at me for meeting his family naked before making them all leave so that we could have sex."

"He didn't," Cass sounded shocked but she could tell from Moira's face that he had.

"Oh, it gets even better. You see I had already met Griff prior to that at the club. I had fallen asleep in the women's sauna and ran into Eric in there," Moira shuddered as she said the name of the man who had stalked her and raped and killed several other women in Legacy. "Anyway, I ran out of there stark naked screaming at the top of my lungs. Gil was there and Griff was with him. Needless to say he saw me completely naked, front and back. That was the very first time that I met Griff."

"Oh, my God," Cass laughed, "how in the world do you still face them all?"

Moira smiled widely. "Honestly that was rather tame compared to my crowning moment of glory. Gil and Ben came over after work and I was dancing around with Griff while Doug danced with their mom and Katie looked on laughing. When Gil walked in he just swept me off my feet and into the bedroom where we had some very kinky sex. At the top of our lungs. With everyone in the living room able to hear."

Cass went off into peals of laughter rolling off the couch to land on the floor where she continued to roll around holding her sides. "Oh that is a crowning moment, Moira."

"Especially when I was yelling for him to fuck my ass at the top of my lungs," Moira added dryly, sending Cass off into peals again.

"At least I was only screaming 'Oh God,' and 'yes'," Cass uttered as she tried to catch her breath.

"Yes but everyone could hear the grunts and groans of both of the men in there with you," Moira added with a devilish grin.

"Oh Lord," Cass moaned, "who all heard me?"

"Let's see," Moira started counting on her fingers, "Me and Gil, Katie and Ben, Catherine, Dad, Chetan, Shep and Roman, Kit and Kat and all the rest of the staff, so roughly about twenty people."

"I will never be able to show my face in public again," Cass said matter-of-factly. "Everyone knows that I'm having sex with two men at the same time."

"Everyone would have known sooner or later anyway, Cass," Moira informed her. "They didn't exactly leave any doubt the way they both rushed to you when we hit the door. Does it really bother you?"

"To have everyone know that I'm sleeping with them both?" Cass asked. "I'm not sure. Everything is so new right now. I'm not really sure about how I feel about anything."

"Even Doug and Damon?" Moira questioned.

Cass couldn't stop the smile that bloomed on her lips. "No I'm sure about them. I want them so much. I've never experienced the things that they make me feel. It's incredible every time."

"Then what do you have to hide?" Moira asked bluntly. "Don't you teach the women who come to your stripper-cize classes to embrace the woman they are and to not allow others' opinions to bother them?"

Cass smiled at Moira, "Yes, I do. Thanks for reminding me of that. I refuse to act ashamed of being with both Doug and Damon. As long as we're happy, then who cares."

"Plus, it's not like the people who know and love them aren't already aware that they share," Moira added.

Cass shook her head and laughed again. "If they didn't before the dinner, they sure do now."

"It seems to be a family thing, so don't worry so much about it."

"What do you mean a family thing?" Cass demanded. "You've heard them have sex before?"

"No, not them. So far it's just been me and Gil, Katie and Ben and now you, Doug and Damon."

"You heard Katie and Ben have sex as well?" Cass said with shock on her face.

Moira shook her head. "Yes, Katie had just been released from the hospital after Butch, he was Jessica's boyfriend at the time…" Moira added.

Cass interrupted to question, "Now who is Jessica again?"

"She's one of the girls in Women's Group that Katie leads at the gym," Moira answered, "you'll meet her when you head back to work on Monday."

"Okay," Cass said, "now go on."

"Anyway Ben took Katie back to his house from the hospital and they got sidetracked in the bedroom and Ben forgot to tell her that he had invited all of us over."

"Who is all of us?" Cass interrupted again.

"Me and Gil, Doug and Damon and Catherine," Moira answered before continuing. "Anyway the back door was open so we came on in when no one answered and were just in time to hear Katie screaming at Ben how much she loved him fucking her ass."

Cass laughed uproariously at that revelation. "How in the world did she survive that?"

"She had just found out she was pregnant at the time so any time someone started to say something around her she would just mention the baby. That worked every time."

"That is a good one but it won't work for me," Cass moaned. She was still lying on her back on the floor and Moira was now lying on her stomach on the couch above her. Cass held her head between her hands and moaned again. "I think I drank too much wine. I don't think I can move."

Moira snorted but didn't move either. "Who cares? It's just the two of us so we can sleep out here if we want to."

"Yeah, we can," Cass agreed and started laughing again. Moira joined her and they both laughed so hard that they didn't hear the key in the door or even realize that anyone was there until a throat cleared from the doorway.

Both Cass and Moira glanced at the doorway and stared at Griff who was grinning at them. "I just left your husband to be," he told Moira as he headed over to them, "and your boyfriends," he added to Cass, "passed out at the apartment. I thought maybe I better head over here and check on you girls." He sat on the end of the sofa folding Moira's legs up to make room. "I could hear you two laughing through the door and since you didn't answer my knock I thought that I would just let myself in. I must say that I always pictured girls dressed differently at slumber parties," Griff said as he shook his head in mock disgust. "You've really let me down, ladies."

Moira snorted as she got gingerly to her feet. "You've already seen me naked, Griff," she said, "twice as a matter of face. I'm not providing a peep show tonight." With that she stumbled down the hall toward her bedroom with Griff following after her. He helped her into the room and eased her onto the bed fully clothed. He wasn't stupid. He knew big brother was very possessive of this woman he was marrying.

"Go away, Griff," Moira murmured her eyes already drifting shut, "I'm sleepy…" and just like that she was sound asleep.

Griff grinned as he tugged her shoes off but left her dress on. He didn't have a death wish and Gil would definitely kill him if he undressed Moira, no matter what the reason. He pulled the quilt over her and left the room shutting the door quietly behind him before heading down the hall to the living room where Cass was on the floor. Only she wasn't there.

Griff checked the kitchen and glanced into the open door of the bathroom before opening the next door down. "Sweet mother of God," Griff croaked as he took in the naked woman passed out on the bed in front of him. Cass had managed to drop her dress and shoes before she crawled up on the bed and went to sleep. She lay on her back one knee bent giving him a sweet view and her full breasts were high and firm. Her golden brown hair lay all around her and she looked better than any *Playboy* centerfold he had ever seen.

Griff had to swallow twice before he managed to step forward to tug a quilt up over her. Doug would kill him if he ever found out about this. He couldn't stop himself from taking one more look before he dropped the quilt over her and stepped away. He was definitely not prepared for the man standing in the open bedroom door.

"What the hell do you think you're doing little brother?" Doug asked as he stepped all the way into the room.

Griff shook his head and thought, "Why me, Lord?", before answering. "I was just checking to make sure she made it in here okay. She and Moira were both three sheets to the wind when I got here. I didn't know that she was naked, Doug."

"You sure looked your fill though didn't you?" Doug said.

"Well, duh," Griff said with a grin. "Any man would, heterosexual, homosexual, old or young. The woman has an incredible body. And I am a young heterosexual male with twenty-twenty vision."

Doug shook his head but felt a smile tugging at his lips. Griff was one of a kind and few could stay upset with him. "Just haul your ass out of here."

"No problem," Griff promised as he passed Doug and stepped into the hall. "By the way I thought I left you guys passed out at the apartment. How did you get in here?"

"You did leave Gil and Damon passed out. I didn't drink that much but I must have dozed off. I found your note when I woke up just a little bit ago that said you were headed over here to check on the girls and thought that I would head over as well. I found Gil's spare key and let myself in. Good thing I did too," he added.

Griff just grinned wider. "Guess I'll take off then. You make sure the ladies are up in time to get ready for the wedding and I'll take care of Gil and Damon." Griff started down the hall with Doug right behind him. "Wait till I tell

Damon you snuck out and spent the night with Cass all by yourself," he laughed at Doug's scowl. "You're going to owe him one, big brother."

Doug shoved him out the door and locked it behind Griff before heading back down the hall to the bedroom that held the very naked sleeping woman he desired. He shut the door behind him and pulled off his clothes before slipping beneath the quilt with Cass. Cass automatically moved closer to his warmth and Doug pulled her even closer until her head was resting on his chest. She stroked the fingers of her hand through the thick black curls on his chest and nuzzled her face against him. Even in her sleep Cass recognized that chest and moaned Doug's name as she snuggled even closer. Doug's heart seemed to stop at the sound of his name in the silence of the bedroom then pounded in his chest like a freight train. Just the sound of his name on her lips set his blood on fire and had his cock growing long and thick with lust. He turned to his side and clasped her more firmly against him realizing that this was the one woman he had searched his entire life for and he was determined to never let her go.

Chapter Five

℘

Cass came wide awake at the startled shout of Moira in her bedroom doorway but it took a few moments to clear her mind and compute Moira's words.

"Jesus, Doug, warn a girl would you," Moira scowled at the bed where Cass was now sitting straight up and Doug was still reclining back. At some point in the night the quilt had been kicked to the bottom of the bed leaving them both exposed and Cass gasped as she realized Doug was sporting a pretty impressive morning hard-on and that Moira was getting an eyeful of it. Doug didn't seem the least bit bothered by being caught naked and made no move to grab the quilt and cover himself.

"Next time maybe you'll knock," he said from his sprawled position on the bed.

"If I had known that you were here then maybe I would have," Moira retorted sharply.

Cass leaned over pressing her breasts against Doug's thigh and using her face and hair to block the view of his cock making him hiss with surprise and clench a hand in her long locks. "Could we finish this conversation later please?" Cass insisted. "Moira, if you'll excuse us I'd like to find out how Doug got in here without me knowing it."

"Sure, Cass," Moira stated before glaring once more at Doug and tugging the door closed. "Just hurry up, would you. We have about three hours before the wedding and you were going to help me with my hair and stuff," Moira called through the door then walked down the hall toward the front of the apartment.

Cass lifted her head as far as Doug's hand allowed and hissed at him, "What are you doing here? It was just supposed to be me and Moira."

Doug nudged her head back down toward his straining erection and promised, "I'll tell you everything—just don't torture me, darling. It's been hell lying beside you all night and not taking advantage of you. Have mercy on me, Cass."

Cass felt a smile tugging at her lips. The man was truly incorrigible expecting her to give him a blowjob before they talked. Then again who did she really think she was kidding anyway? She licked her lips and felt the saliva pool in her mouth as she eyed that perfect cock just inches in front of her face. She could already taste him on her tongue and she knew she wanted him in her mouth just as badly as he wanted to be there.

Leaning forward she swirled her tongue all around the pulsing head of his thick morning wood licking off the drop of pre-cum that glistened there before kissing and licking her way down the shaft to his tightly drawn balls beneath. She spent some time licking and sucking them laving the taut skin just under them while she used a portion of her hair wrapped around her hand to slowly work up and down his long length. She could hear Doug groaning above her and took pleasure in his every sound.

Doug tugged her mouth back up to his weeping cock and ordered huskily, "Just suck it, darling, and quit teasing me. I need you to suck it nice and deep into the back of your throat for me."

Cass used both hands to brush her hair aside and stretched her lips around the large girth of the bobbing head of his cock. She sucked greedily at it carefully working more and more of him into her mouth until she could feel him at the back of her mouth. She worked him in and out licking and sucking his flesh, scraping her teeth gently against the long length of him.

"All the way, Cass," Doug moaned, "into the back of your throat, darling. You can do it for me."

Cass eased her mouth down his cock pressing him firmly into the back of her throat and felt her gag reflex kick in as her throat constricted around his rigid flesh. She fought against her reflex as Doug palmed her head and held her firmly on him tilting his hips up to fuck in and out of her mouth with short rapid strokes that had him breathing harder and harder. Cass clamped her lips and sucked harder while she used her finger to rub against the thin skin that lay just under his taut balls. Doug came with a loud groan filling her mouth with the hot wet jets of semen again and again until he was finally completely spent and empty.

He released his hold on her head and relaxed back against the mattress allowing Cass to pull gently off his slowly softening cock. She took a few moments to gently lick the head cleaning any tiny drops of his release that she had spilled before moving up to rest her head on his chest and play with the black curls there.

"So how did you get here? When? I remember Griff showing up after Moira and I polished off a bottle of wine and saying that he had left you, Damon and Gil passed out at the apartment," Cass murmured as Doug ran his fingers through her hair.

"I didn't pass out, only fell asleep. I woke up just after Griff left and found Gil's spare key and followed. It's a good thing I did too, darling," Doug added with disgust.

"Why's that?" Cass queried.

"When I walked in I found Griff in this bedroom looking at you, baby, naked and sprawled on top of the bed."

Cass groaned, "Please tell me that you're kidding."

Doug actually laughed, "No such luck. He was checking to make sure you made it to the bedroom all right and wasn't expecting to find you naked. He looked and covered you with a quilt."

"He told you that he looked at me?" Cass squeaked.

"I caught him gawking at you," Doug corrected. "And as he informed me, 'What young heterosexual male with eyes wouldn't check you out?'"

"This just gets better and better," Cass groaned against his chest. "I think your mom actually liked me to start with. I can't imagine what she thinks of me now."

"I'm sure she probably thinks that if you can survive the dinner then you must be a keeper. It seems to be a thing in my family."

Cass giggled as she remembered all that Moira had told her. "I heard about that. I guess Moira is even with you now."

"Even with me?" Doug asked confused.

"You saw her naked and now she's seen you naked," Cass grinned saucily up at him before adding, "naked and aroused."

"I'd say that puts her one up on me," Doug declared dryly.

"Oh, no," Cass insisted. "One aroused cock equals two fantastic boobs any day. Not to mention you saw her everywhere."

"Where the hell did you come up with that comparison?" Doug demanded before shaking his head and easing away from her and off the bed. "Never mind, I'm sure that I don't want to know," he said as he grabbed his pants and started dressing. "I'll just get out of your hair so you and Moira can start getting ready." He looked down at her uninhibited naked sprawl on the bed. "I hope you're not sore tonight, Cass, cause I want to fuck you really bad and I'm sure that Damon does too."

"Umm…I want it too, Doug," Cass said. "But I have work tomorrow so I'm not sure if I can see you guys tonight."

Doug frowned down at her before replying. "We'll fit in somewhere. You can either come spend the night at our house or we'll end up at the apartment with you. We all have to work tomorrow so what difference does that make?"

"I was just saying..." Cass started to say then thought better of it. "Never mind. The bed at the apartment doesn't look big enough for all three of us so how about I just grab a bag after the reception and meet you guys at your place?"

"That sounds better, baby," Doug sat down to pull his socks and shoes on leaning over to kiss her when he was done. "We've got something special here, Cass, just give it a chance okay?"

"I will, Doug, I promise," Cass answered then shook her head. "But I can't always stay the night with you and Damon and you both can't stay at the apartment with me. There will be nights when I don't get home from the gym until late and I won't feel like heading out to your place. You have to be okay with that too."

Doug frowned but didn't say anything for a moment. "We'll see how things go, Cass. One day at a time."

Cass smiled even though she realized he would do everything he could to make sure she did what he wanted. "One day at a time," she agreed and with a nod Doug kissed her again and was out the door and gone. She had a feeling that he would have her moved in with him and Damon as soon as he could manage. Cass wasn't sure how she felt about that but she would have to decide pretty soon she was sure.

* * * * *

The wedding was beautiful and Cass couldn't help but shed a few tears when Moira and Gil exchanged their vows. A person would have to be blind to miss the love that was reflected their eyes as they repeated the traditional vows to love and honor and cherish each other till death parted them. Of course everyone laughed when Gil did a very thorough job of kissing his bride and then swept her up into his arms and carried her back down the aisle to the sounds of their family and friends cheering. It was a perfect beginning to forever for Moira and Gil, and Cass was very happy for her best friend.

As they headed down the aisle after Moira and Gil Doug squeezed Cass' fingers and smiled gently down at her and the tears reflected in her eyes. He felt his heart constrict as he took in the breathtaking beauty of Cass and was stunned anew by his deep feelings for her. They had only just met really but somehow it was as if he had always been looking for her. Being with her just felt right on so many levels.

They led Ben and Katie and the rest of the guests outside where Gil and Moira were already getting in the limo to head to the reception across town. The minister had already been paid and Doug had already taken care of having the flowers delivered to the reception hall so all that was left was for them to follow. He grabbed Cass' hand and headed toward his truck.

"I don't think so, big guy. I've got my own car here and I'm not going to try and get in that truck of yours with this dress and heels on," Cass laughed as she tugged him back toward the direction where her own car was parked.

They met up with Catherine, Katie, Ben, Damon and Griff in the parking lot. Damon stepped right up to them and took Cass' other hand in his. "I rode with Doug so I'd be happy to ride over with you, sweetheart."

Cass laughed as Doug scowled at Damon. She knew that they would never really fight over her but it was fun to watch them try to one up each other. Doug had scored major points on Damon last night by spending the night alone with Cass and Doug knew it.

"Yeah, Dougie," Griff taunted with a grin. "You had her all to yourself last night anyway so let Damon ride her, I mean with her, to the reception."

Doug and Damon both reached out and smacked Griff on the back of the head for his deliberate mistake but Griff just ducked and hid behind his mother, which was an amusing sight to see with him standing six foot six and his mother a diminutive five foot one. "Mom, Doug and Damon are hitting me again."

Catherine just shook her head and Cass had to bite her lip to keep from laughing at the "Why me?" look on Catherine's face. "That will be enough, boys. Damon, you and Griff can ride with Doug while I ride with Cass to the reception. I've always wanted a little red sports car," Catherine added just to rile her sons.

"A sports car!" Griff exclaimed. "That can't possibly be safe, mom. Besides your car's only a few years old."

Catherine smiled at Griff and shook her head. "Sometimes a woman just needs to break free and live, baby," she murmured as she grabbed Cass' arm and guided her away from the three speechless men and to the car. Cass pressed the button to release the locks and she and Catherine settled into the car without delay. Cass firing the engine and pulling away from the curb before saying, "You sure shocked them, Mrs. Daniels."

"Just gave them a little food for thought," Catherine murmured, "and it's still Catherine, Cass, especially in light of the fact that you're sleeping with my son."

Cass choked on what she had been about to say and sputtered and coughed making Catherine laugh gaily.

"Perhaps I should warn you, dear, that there are very few secrets in this family. I find myself often thinking that we are entirely too close but honestly I wouldn't change a thing. Well except for the fact that I keep hearing my children having sex," Catherine added dryly. "That can be a little uncomfortable for a mother, let me tell you. Anyway, I'm still the woman who has come to know and love you, Cass, the woman who held you after your mother's funeral while you cried. I couldn't be more delighted that you and Doug are together."

Cass took a deep breath and asked before she lost her courage, "And Damon? How do you feel about him?"

Catherine smiled and patted Cass' hand on the gear shift. "I love Damon just like he was one of my own and really he has been since he and Doug met in college. Damon was alone for a long time before then and he was so hungry for family and love. But that's not the point I'm trying to make. My point is that I know all about Damon and Doug or at least as much as I feel that I need to, or even want to, know. I've never judged my children and I don't intend to start now. What is between you and Doug and Damon is just that, between you. However, I will ask you not to hurt them."

Cass seemed surprised by this request. "I would never hurt either one of them. In fact I'm a little afraid of them hurting me."

"You're afraid that you may fall in love with them," Catherine replied.

Cass wasn't even startled that Catherine knew that. "Yes well, that is, I think I'm already starting to fall in love with them. Honestly I'm not sure how I feel about that. Don't get me wrong. I've always wanted to fall in love, get married and have children one day. I'm just not sure how that will all work with two men."

Catherine smiled and answered, "You'll figure it out, dear, together. I know that I'm not your mom but I do want you to know that I'm here for you if you need to talk to someone, a maternal figure if you will."

Cass felt tears mist her eyes again. "Thank you, Catherine. I may just take you up on that."

Cass pulled into the lot and parked toward the back away from other cars. She wasn't surprised when Doug's truck pulled in next to her. Before she or Catherine could even release their seat belts, all three men were spilling out of the truck and heading toward the little car. Catherine grinned at Cass and whispered, "I'll take Griff and head on in so you can have a few minutes with Doug and Damon. Just remember not to take too long."

With that Catherine was out the door and, latching onto her youngest son's arm, herded him across the lot to the door of the reception hall. Doug pulled Cass' door open and Damon held out his hand to pull her out of the low-slung Crossfire and away from the door. "I see you made it here safely," he murmured as he pulled her into his arms for a slow rapacious kiss. Doug slammed the door closed and Damon pressed her back until she rested against it. "I missed you, sweetheart. I would have loved to have woken up beside you as well this morning," Damon whispered as he nibbled his way along her jaw to her earlobe.

"Umm…" Cass moaned, "You can wake up beside me tomorrow morning." She could feel the heat of Doug's body at her side and reached her hand out to caress his chest. "Both of you can."

Damon grinned down at her and said, "I think we should make him sleep on the couch or lock ourselves alone in my room since he spent last night with you."

Cass giggled as Doug tugged her to him and grunted, "Not going to happen, buddy, you snooze, you lose."

Her giggles turned to moans as the two men maneuvered her between them so that she rested against Doug's solid chest with Damon pressed to her back. Damon rubbed his cock against her lower back while Doug's rested against her belly and she wondered just how much sleep any of them would get tonight. Before they could do more than nibble and kiss her lips, jaw and neck Cass pushed back and slipped from between them.

"We should get inside, guys. Doug and I both have speeches to give and I don't want to miss the first dance between the bride and groom." She held her hands out to them and walked between them across the lot. "We have the whole night ahead of us."

Doug and Damon both grinned at Cass and she laughed up at them. She was startled to feel that uneasy sensation at the back of her neck again and glanced back over her shoulder.

She couldn't see anyone but still felt like someone was watching her.

"What's wrong?" Doug asked while Damon looked behind them as well trying to see what she was looking at.

Cass pushed away the odd feeling and shrugged her shoulders. "Just anticipating the evening," she said making both men groan with frustration at the long hours that lay between then and now.

Cass was anxious when she, Doug and Damon managed to follow behind the exiting bride and groom a few hours later, until she caught sight of her car across the lot. She was furious then. They were all hurrying across the lot toward the back were they had left Cass' car and Doug's truck when suddenly Cass let out a shriek and started running. Doug and Damon hurried after her having no idea what was wrong until they got closer to her car. Cass was already bending over checking out where someone had used paint, probably a spray can, to write obscenities across Cass' paintwork. Both men could tell she was getting madder and madder as she took in each new word boldly painted on her car. *WHORE* was on the hood, *SLUT* on the driver's side, *CUNT* was on the back and the passenger side was graced with the rather tame insult of *BITCH*.

Damon pulled Cass into his arms while Doug dragged his cell phone out to call Ben and see if one of the many cops still at the reception could come out or get someone on duty to come out. While he talked quietly into his phone Damon did his best to soothe their very pissed off lover.

"I'm sorry sweetheart," Damon murmured. He was feeling guilty for their very public displays of affection with Cass. He and Doug hadn't even tried to be discreet and Damon was pretty sure that they were somehow to blame for the damage to Cass' car.

"Why?" Cass demanded. "You didn't do this to my car."

"No but still..." Damon started to say but Cass interrupted him.

"I felt like someone was watching me earlier but I didn't see anyone so I ignored it," Cass muttered angrily. "That was the second time I felt that way in the past two days."

"What!" Damon said sharing a look with Doug before Doug headed across the lot to meet with Ben. "Why didn't you say something earlier? Doug or I could have checked it out."

"I don't know," Cass cried out. "I wanted to get into the reception and I did check but there was no one behind us. You looked too. Did you see anyone?"

"No," Damon admitted as Doug headed back to them with Ben and one of the other police detectives in Legacy, Charlie Tate. "But then, I didn't know exactly what I was looking for either."

By then Doug, Ben and Charlie were there and looking at the slow trickle of people following them across the parking lot Cass exploded. "Oh, great, let's just invite everyone out to take a good look at my car. Let's take a poll and see who agrees with it."

"That's enough, baby," Doug gritted out. "I know that you're upset but that's no excuse to take it out on people who care about you."

Cass took a deep breath and tried and failed to smile. "I'm sorry, everyone, Doug's right." Cass admitted to the crowd now gathered. Besides Doug and Damon and Ben and Charlie, there was Griff and Catherine, Katie, Jack, Roman, Shep and Chetan. "It's just that this was my mom's dream car and look at it," she managed to whisper trying like mad not to burst into tears in front of everyone.

"Oh, sweetheart," Damon pulled her to his chest and Cass let go and cried. She was oblivious to the looks that passed between the two men in her life over her head.

Doug passed his keys to Damon and helped him get Cass into the truck. "Go ahead and take her home. I'll take care of this and get a ride to the apartment and get a bag together for her. I'll meet you when I'm done. Keep an eye on her."

Damon nodded and let Doug lift Cass up into the cab of the truck. "I'll take care of this for you, baby," he whispered as he kissed some of her tears away but they were quickly replaced by more. "I promise, baby."

Cass nodded and didn't object when Damon pulled her across the seat and belted her in beside him. She laid her head against his shoulder and continued to cry quietly, breaking Damon's heart with every silent tear.

Doug watched them pull away and turned to those around him. "What needs to be done?"

Ben and Charlie were looking at the car and sighing. Finally Ben shook his head and said, "We could haul it in to the police lot and fingerprint it but there is no way to know if we'll get anything especially taking into account all the people who may have touched it in passing. The best bet would be to tow it to a shop and have it repainted. I'd have an alarm put on it as well so that nothing worse happens to it without someone being alerted."

"Shit, Ben, I was afraid you'd say that," Doug groaned.

"I'll put a Crime-stoppers blurb in the paper and on the radio," Charlie added. "This is a pretty public lot so maybe someone saw something."

"Cass said she felt like someone was watching her earlier when we were headed in," Doug told them. "She said that it was the second time she'd had that feeling in two days."

"That's not a good sign," Charlie looked at the car again and shook his head in disgust that someone could defile such a car. "Any ideas on who could have done this?"

Doug took a deep breath and grunted out, "Our house was broken into a while back. Nothing stolen that we could place but we thought it might have been a woman we had seen a few times."

"Think she could have done this?" Ben asked.

"Maybe," Doug said. "She didn't take it to well when we called it quits."

Charlie pulled a pad of paper and pen from the inside of his suit jacket, "What's her name and we'll check it out."

"Nikki Damato," Doug said.

Shep stepped up then and asked in a deadly calm voice, "Do you think Cass could be in any danger from your psycho ex?"

"I'll take care of Cass. I don't need your help," Doug informed him before looking back to Ben and asking, "Any ideas on where to take the car?"

"I can take care of the car," Shep snapped out. "I know where she goes for service and can take care of everything."

"I'll do it," Doug snarled. "I said I don't need your help."

"You don't have exclusive rights to caring about her," Shep snarled back. "Cass is like a little sister to me and I'm not going to walk away just because you're seeing her now."

Catherine stepped up with Roman right beside her and informed them both, "That's enough, boys. Cass doesn't need you two fighting over her this way. Ben, you and Katie take Doug and Griff back to the apartment to pack a bag for Cass. Katie, you'll know better what she'll need for work tomorrow. Then Griff can take Doug home. Roman, you'll help Shep take care of the car?" Catherine asked the tall man beside her.

"No problem, R...Catherine," Roman corrected his almost slip.

"Good," Catherine said turning to take Doug's arm and pulling him toward Ben's SUV. "What is more important right now, Doug, getting home to Cass or fighting over who takes care of her car?"

"You're right, Mom," Doug sighed.

"Can I get that in writing?" Catherine queried her son with a smile making everyone laugh as they reached the big Durango that Ben had bought when they found out Katie was pregnant. "I'll see you all later. Give Cass a kiss for me," Catherine said before giving Griff and Ben a hug and kiss. She stopped in front of Katie and hugged her only daughter tightly. "You're ready, baby," she whispered in Katie's ear. "It's time to face it and lay it aside. I know that this may be hard for you. You haven't been back there since you were attacked and almost raped. But it's time to face your demons and lay them aside once and for all. You can do this." With that Catherine waved to her children and walked to her own car trying to discreetly look at the man still standing in the lot by Cass' car, the man she feared she was in love with.

Chapter Six

&)

Ben held tight to Katie's hand as they rode up in the elevator to the second floor of the apartment building. "You don't have to do this if you don't want to," he whispered into his wife's ear. Katie had not been back to the apartment since her attack. Instead she had gone straight to Ben's house and never left.

"Yes, I do," Katie smiled up at her husband. "Mom's right. It's time to settle my demons."

"If you're sure," Ben said.

"I'm sure," Katie murmured but she could feel her heartbeat speeding up as the elevator doors slid open and they headed down the hall. It took every ounce of willpower she had to force herself to follow Griff and Doug over the threshold and into the apartment that had often haunted her dreams since that last afternoon she had spent there. She knew that it was Ben's solid presence behind her that helped her face it. She almost faltered when Doug headed down the hall to the very room that Katie had used when she stayed there, the very room where she had been hit and almost raped.

"Come on," Doug called, lost in thoughts of Cass.

"Damn it, Doug, give her a minute," Ben snarled at him holding his wife's hand in his while she gathered her courage.

Doug turned at that and one look at his sister's face was enough to remind him of what she had lived through here in this apartment, in the room he now stood in. "God, Katie, I'm sorry. I wasn't thinking. You don't have to do this. I'll take care of it."

"I'll do it," Katie snapped as she took a deep breath and stepped into the room. "I'm sure Cass would appreciate having the things that she needs in the morning instead of what you might pick out."

"Thanks," Doug told her as she pulled a gym bag from the closet and began to open drawers her racing pulse calming as she pulled out more clothes than Doug would have ever thought of. "Does she really need all that?"

"Yes," Katie laughed, "she does. She teaches spin, step aerobics, kick-boxing and tomorrow is stripper-cize as well. She'll change a few times during the day and each class requires a different shoe…"

Doug tuned his sister out after he heard the words "stripper-cize". "She teaches stripper-cize?" he mumbled making Ben grin.

"Gil watched Moira teach that class as I recall and he said it was quite stimulating," Ben declared roguishly while Katie laughed. "Perhaps you should check it out, Doug."

Doug just gritted his teeth and waited patiently for Katie to finish putting the bag together for Cass. "Thanks, Katie," he said as he took the bag from her and headed out of the bedroom to get Griff. "I'll see you guys later."

Ben took Katie in his arms and held her close to him, "All right, baby?" he asked.

"I'm okay," Katie told him as Griff hollered down the hall to them to lock up when they left. Katie had been given a new key to the apartment when the locks were changed like the rest of the family since this apartment had become a stopping place for them all so locking up wouldn't be a problem.

Ben eased out of the room and Katie sat down on the bed overcome with memories. Ben was back quickly and shut the bedroom door and flipped the lock when he came back in.

"What are you doing?" Katie asked her husband.

"I made sure the front door was locked and headed back to ravish my beautiful wife," he said as he began pulling his clothes off.

Katie giggled, "You can't wait until we get home?"

Ben smiled as he stopped beside where she sat on the bed and reached for his zipper. "Sometimes the easiest way to conquer old memories is to create new, better ones," he said as he released his swollen cock from his tux pants.

"Umm..." Katie purred and licked her lips with anticipation. "I'm all for that," and she leaned forward and sucked his stiff erection into the back of her throat making him as weak in the knees as he always made her.

* * * * *

Damon carried Cass from the truck through the garage and into the house. She had stopped crying and was silent in his arms. That worried him more than her tears had. "We're home, sweetheart," he whispered to her. He carried her through to the big bedroom and set her down on the closed toilet lid while he turned the water on in the big Jacuzzi tub. He turned and began helping her out of her heels and then her dress like she was a doll instead of a full-grown woman. When she was completely naked, he sat her back down and began stripping off his own clothes. By then the water was high enough and he turned off the faucets and turned on the jets before lifting Cass into his arms and stepping into the foaming water with her.

Damon eased them both into the water and settled her between his legs, pulling her back against his chest and stroking his hands down her arms. "I'm really sorry that happened to your car, sweetheart."

"It's not about the car, Damon," Cass murmured. "Not really anyway. I guess I just connected it to my mom and it felt like someone was doing that to her to the only piece of her I have left."

"Oh, sweetheart," Damon hugged her close. "Your mom will always be with you whether you can see her or not. Trust me," he took a deep breath. "My mom died when I was just a kid but I've always felt like she was with me, watching over me."

"How old were you?" Cass asked.

"I was twelve when she died." Damon ran his fingers up and down her arms absently as he spoke of his past. "She caught pneumonia and since we didn't have health insurance she didn't go to the doctor and ended up dying of complications."

"I'm so sorry Damon," Cass whispered. "Did you go to your dad?"

"No," the answer was short and sharp and she could feel the tension in him. "I went into foster care until I turned eighteen. I lucked into a really great family. Mark, my adoptive father, was a teacher and the high school football coach."

"Ahh...Catherine mentioned that you and Doug played football together in college," Cass commented.

"Yeah, Mark was the best thing that could have happened to me at that point in my life," Damon confided. "He taught me to love the game of football which gave me a diversion, something to focus my attention on. I owe him a lot."

"Was he a single parent or married?" Cass questioned thinking that most foster parents had to be married to be certified by the state.

"He was married and had a little girl, Sheila, but his wife didn't care much for me so..." he let his voice trail off and Cass got the feeling that he had already shared more than he had intended to. She was surprised when he added, "Sheila was great though, followed me around whenever she could. I think she fancied herself in love with me and Doug too when I went to college. She was so mad when I wouldn't let her tag along with Doug and me when we visited for a few days for her mom's funeral. She sure had the temper to go with her red hair back then." He shook his head and gave a strained laugh and Cass could tell he was uncomfortable for having shared so much.

"You don't see them any more?" she couldn't keep from asking.

"Not in years," he replied vaguely and she knew there was so much more that he wasn't saying but she wouldn't press him now.

She turned slowly in the tub moving her legs to the outside of his so that she faced him and took his face into her hands. "I'm glad that you were there for me today. I may not have shown it at the time but I really appreciate you and Doug taking care of me," Cass whispered as she brushed her hands over his smooth chest and shoulders.

"You're our woman, Cass," Damon said. "Of course we took care of you."

Cass smiled as she leaned forward to nip along his jaw. She could feel the long, hard length of his erection nudging her stomach and it felt so good. Too good to waste. "You know when I woke up with Doug this morning I gave him a blowjob," she murmured against his lips. "Maybe I should give you the same treatment?" she questioned as she rubbed her nipples along his chest.

"Umm…" Damon murmured, "I'd rather you slid that slippery little pussy over me and took me all the way to your core, sweetheart."

"I can do that," Cass moaned as she suited words to action and slipped a hand into the water to guide him to her opening. He was thick and hard and felt so good as she slid slowly down his length taking him all the way into her. They both moaned with pleasure when he was fully seated in her pussy and Damon leaned forward to take her mouth in a kiss that was both sensual and erotic, filled with slippery tongues meshing and mating. He helped her to glide up and down his swollen member in a slow and easy rhythm that was like savoring a slice of euphoria, moaning as each new layer was uncovered and explored. They reached orgasm together, her pussy tightening around him and greedily milking him of every drop of cum.

Damon looked her in the eye and said from his heart, "I'm falling in love with you Cass."

Cass smiled and kissed him tenderly on the lips before divulging, "I think that I know just how you feel, Damon."

They took their time washing off, each taking turns soaping the other with the large loofah sponge on the shelf. It was a slow sensual massage of flesh against flesh filled with an eroticism that had them both wanting, no needing more. By the time they were squeaky clean they were both panting for breath and Damon's cock was tall and proud begging for attention again. They barely made it to the bedroom before the towels were dropped to the floor.

Cass pushed Damon back to the bed until he sat down on the side and then she pushed him until he was reclined on his back. "I've been looking forward to wrapping my lips around your big cock all day, Damon. So why don't you just lie back and enjoy while I take care of you."

Damon groaned as she braced her palms on his thighs and leaned down nuzzling her face in his groin. "Have mercy, sweetheart, I'm already on fire here," he told her.

Cass took her time licking and sucking and nipping every inch of his luscious cock. "I love the taste of you," she whispered against the head "so salty and sweet at the same time." She ran her tongue all around and under the sensitive head of his shaft sucking it but never taking it all the way into her mouth. "I wish Doug was here with us sharing this moment."

"You're really okay with the three of us together?" Damon managed to get out between his teeth.

Cass laughed against his flesh bouncing it on her jaw making him clench his hands in the bedspread and gritted his teeth harder. "It's a little late to worry about that now," she told him. "I am with you both and I like it. No, that's wrong. I love it. I'm afraid that you two will spoil me for anything else."

She was startled by the sharp slap on her rear that Doug gave her. He had entered the room so quietly while they were involved that she hadn't even realized he was there. "There won't be anyone else, Cass. You belong to me and Damon now and neither of us intends to give you up." He held her hips firmly in his hands preventing her from moving from her position bent over Damon's legs with her face in his lap. She heard the rasp as Doug lowered his zipper and shoved his pants down his legs and off. His cock was thick and hot on her back as he palmed and squeezed her ass.

"Move up the bed, Damon, and give me some room, would you," he told his best friend and waited till Damon was all the way on the bed before helping Cass move to straddle Damon. He moved away and she could hear him opening a drawer while he told her what he wanted her to do. "I want you to slide your pussy onto Damon's cock and sit there with him inside you not moving."

Cass took Damon in her hand and rubbed him along her folds lubricating him before sliding her pussy down his long length. They both groaned and Damon grabbed her hips and held tight to help keep them both form moving while they waited on Doug. She felt Doug get onto the bed behind them and move up into position behind her straddling Damon's legs as she was. When Doug reached her he nipped and sucked at her neck before pressing her shoulders forward and having her lay her upper body down on Damon's.

"Now hold still, baby, while I get you ready for me," he told her and used his fingers and the tube of lubricant he must have taken from the drawer to prepare her for his hard cock. It was erotic torture to lie there unmoving with Damon's cock buried deep in her pussy and Doug working his well-lubed fingers in and out of her ass.

"Hurry, Doug," Cass implored. "I can't take much more."

Doug groaned and replaced his fingers with his cock pressing firmly against her until he gained entry and slid slowly into the hot, tight vice of her ass. She gripped him like a tight fist squeezing him with every breath she took. "That's so good, baby, so good. I love the way you grip my cock with your hot little ass sucking me in as far as I'll go."

Finally he was all the way in and they all managed to stay still for one long moment each enjoying their own extreme pleasure—Doug in her ass, Damon in her pussy and Cass filled full of long, hard cock. They all sighed with pleasure and Doug and Damon began moving in a gentle glide in and out of her filling her at the same time instead of taking turns. She was filled then empty repeatedly and it was slowly driving her crazy driving her past her breaking point. The erotic pinch of pain that Doug brought with every stroke set fire to her blood leaving her teetering on the sharp edge between pleasure and pain. It was too much, then not enough, and all she could do to hold on. Then she couldn't as she felt like she was flung over a cliff and free falling into nothing. Pleasure rolled through her in flames of fire making every nerve scream from sensory overload and her fingers clenched tightly around Damon's shoulders.

Doug and Damon were still gliding in and out of her moving faster and going deeper with every stroke keeping her there, just there, consumed by pleasure, tortured with pain, until she was screaming with each new, more intense wave of orgasm that crashed over her through her. Then they were with her, both men yelling their own release as her body was bombarded with thick, creamy jets of cum released in hot pulses into her ass and pussy burning her with new pleasure.

They all three collapsed on the bed in a tangled mess and Cass never knew when they moved her, cleaned her up and eased her under the sheets and between them in the big bed that still smelled of the erotic sex they had shared. She never heard another sound until the alarm went off the next morning.

The alarm was on Doug's side of the bed and Damon took advantage of that small fact when Doug leaned away to turn it off. Damon reached for her tugging Cass and moving between her thighs burying his morning erection in her pussy with one sharp thrust. He rode her hard catching her knees in his elbows and spreading her wide for his every thrust. Doug turned back and watched with passion-heavy eyes stroking his palm up and down his own hard-on while he watched her and Damon. He lifted his other hand to his mouth and wet his thumb with his tongue before moving it to her clit and rubbing her with slow circles. Cass came with a cry just as Damon pulsed and spilled his own release inside her.

Damon lowered her legs and kissed her softly on the lips before moving away and letting Doug take his place. Doug entered her violently pounding in and out of her juicy pussy. Cass lifted her legs and pressed her heels into his shoulders arching her back and taking every hard thrust he threw at her. Doug rose up to his knees and cupped her ass in his hands filling her with his hard cock with rough strokes that had them both on the edge of orgasm in a matter of minutes. It hit them both at the same time and Cass panted for air as she came and came and came.

Doug eased her legs down and bent down to kiss her while he was still buried inside her. "Morning, darling. Flexible little thing aren't you."

Cass grinned up at him as she replied coquettishly, "I'm a gymnast and was a cheerleader all through school including college."

"My fantasy comes to life," Doug murmured as he coaxed her mouth open and teased her tongue with his. "I like waking up to you in the mornings."

"I could get used to waking up this way myself," Cass agreed.

Doug eased out of her and rolled off the bed unabashedly naked and stretching. "Why don't you hit the shower in here while I start coffee and then I'll jump in after you? Damon's got to head in early so I'll give you a ride into work today and one of us will pick you up later. We can grab dinner in town and see where things go from there."

"I forgot about my car," Cass said amazed. "I can't believe that I forgot about my car."

"Shep had it taken to the place you always use and it won't be ready till the end of the week," Doug told her. "Damon and I will play chauffeur this week."

"You actually let Shep take care of my car?" Cass asked him not even trying to disguise the shock in her voice.

"I wanted to get home to you." He shrugged not telling her of the pissing match he and Shep had engaged in at the time.

Cass eased out of bed and walked up to him hugging him tight thoroughly enjoying the feel of his hairy chest against her still sensitive breasts. "Thank you, Doug. That means a lot to me." With that she headed to the shower in the adjoining bathroom leaving Doug to watch the sway of her lush ass before he shook his head clear and headed naked to the kitchen to start the coffee.

Chapter Seven

ຄາ

Cass was sore and tired and she still had four classes left before the day was over. It took a lot out of a woman to have two such vigorous lovers at the same time. She had aches on top of aches on top of aches with no relief in sight any time in the near future. She headed down the hall toward Moira's office and the little fridge they kept there to get a bottle of water. Cass kept her personal things in the fridge in Moira's office instead of the one in the employee lounge. Usually she and Moira spent their limited down time together anyway either going over club business or personal plans.

Moira was off for the entire week on her honeymoon with Gil. They were spending a week alone in a cabin in the mountains in Tennessee and Cass sincerely doubted if they would ever leave the cabin. Gil had originally planned to take Moira to a beach somewhere but Moira hadn't wanted to be around anyone else so Gil had booked a secluded cabin in the middle of nowhere for them. The cabin came fully stocked with a hot tub and sauna with plenty of trails nearby if they wanted to hike and explore. No television, no phone and no one around for miles and miles. It had sounded perfect to Moira. It sounded perfect to Cass as well.

"Hey, Cass," Kat called, snapping her out of her thoughts, "Can I get you to look at this for a minute?" Cass turned and Kat was holding a catalogue with new workout equipment in it.

"I'm not ordering anything while Moira is gone unless it's absolutely necessary, Kat," Cass informed her.

"We're going to need to order some more balance balls and medicine balls," Kat told her. "The classes are filling up so fast now that I've had to limit the number because of lack of equipment for everyone. Plus we need some more bands for Pilates."

"If you'll make me a list, I'll make it priority one," Cass told her falling easily back into her role as assistant manager after all her time away.

"I'll put it in this catalogue and leave it at the front desk for you," Kat said. "They have some pretty good deals in here if you buy in bulk quantities, which we probably should so that we have some spares on hand."

"I'll take a look this week, Kat." Cass nodded at her. "Thanks."

Cass headed back down the hall to the office and actually made it inside this time before someone else stopped her.

"Hey Cass," Kip followed her into the office. "Here's today's mail."

"Just toss it on the desk," she replied as she finally opened the fridge and took out the coveted bottle of water. She opened it and tilted it to her mouth and took a long cool refreshing drink.

"So," Kip said, "Two guys huh?"

And water spewed every where while Cass coughed and heaved trying to catch her breath. She tried to glare at him but he just grinned unrepentantly.

"Don't get me wrong," he said. "I'm cool with that. You should know that Kat and I don't care about that stuff." His face softened when he spoke about his wife and coworker at Knowledge Is Power. Kat had been attacked by the same killer, Eric, who had stalked Moira. Luckily she had been saved from whatever he had planned for her by the arrival of a stray dog that attacked Eric and protected her. Unfortunately that had put Eric into Kip's path and Eric had used Kip to gain access to Moira and then knocked Kip out. Kat and Kip had survived though and the experience had made them realize just how much they loved each other and the two of them had married shortly afterwards. Kat and Kip had even gone back and found the dog, adopting him and naming him Warrior for his bravery.

Kip's next words showed how great a guy he really was. "We just want you to be happy, Cass, that's all." Then he spoiled it by adding, "and if what we overheard at the dinner is accurate then I would have to say that you are one happy woman."

Cass couldn't help it. She laughed out loud as he bobbled his eyebrows up and down and grinned at her. "Yes, Kip, they keep me very happy," she turned to the desk but tossed over her shoulder, "and satisfied as well."

Kip laughed and headed down the hall back to the nautilus room where he was personal trainer to many of their members and just a helping hand to others, leaving Cass to sort the mail and open anything that couldn't wait. She was surprised when she saw an envelope addressed to her. Her mail was sent to a PO Box at the Post Office and she still needed to go stop the forward she had put on it. She glanced at the letter noting almost absently her typed name with the club's address. She pulled the contents out and felt her heart stop as she realized what it was.

The letter was a cut-and-paste job with words and sometimes letters cut from what appeared to be newspapers and magazines and pasted onto the sheet of paper. Whoever had sent it was quite clear about what they thought of her and what they wanted to happen to her. But what chilled her most were the pictures that had been sent with it. They were of her with Doug and Damon in the parking lot at the restaurant where the reception had been held and even a few of her and Doug outside the apartment building where she was now staying. Her face had been smeared with something red in all of the pictures. It was chilling to look at and terrifying to know that someone felt that way about her.

Cass picked the phone up and called the first person she thought of. "Hey, Roman this is Cass. Is Jack there? Can you get ahold of him? Yeah, I need him to come take a look at something for me. Someone sent me some hate mail at the club and I don't know what to do."

Cass thought about calling Doug and Damon but there wasn't really anything they could do about it and she didn't have their cell numbers or their business number anyway. She would see them soon and would just wait and let them know about it then.

* * * * *

The men arrived in force. Jack, Roman, Shep and Chetan arrived with Ben and Charlie. Ben wasted no time in telling her that Doug and Damon were on their way as well.

"You called them?" Cass asked incredulously.

"You'll learn this family soon," Ben replied as he and Charlie pulled on gloves to look at the letter.

It was vicious in its content and explicit as well. Her name was placed at the top, each letter cut out in capitals and bold red in print. Following this were words cut and pasted in a vast display of colors, fonts and capitalization from the tame like "bitch" and "jezebel" to the more harsh like "cunt", "slut" and "whore". Then the threats began. Threats that Cass would die by burning like the witch she was. Whoever had sent the note was clearly disturbed.

Charlie was the first to notice that there was no postmark on the envelope which could mean any number of things, including that the person had been in the building and slipped it into the pile of mail collected on the receptionist desk. So at some point that day between the time the postman delivered the mail and the time that it had been brought to Cass, the letter was added. This meant that whoever was sending the threat felt confident enough to come into Knowledge Is Power and not fear being noticed. That or it was someone who was already a member. Not comforting thoughts either way for Cass.

Shep had his arm around Cass' shoulders while Jack and Roman discussed safety precautions to take with Ben and Charlie. Security had been updated with the whole stalker incident with Moira but no one had thought about the mail as a threat. Now they were talking about bodyguards and posting a guard at the front desk.

"You can't post anyone at the front desk," Cass said. "This is a place of business first and foremost. According to Moira we had plenty of members who were scared after the shooting in the building who are just now feeling comfortable and secure enough to return. I won't have them scared again."

"We're talking about your safety here, Cass," Shep informed her. "I don't think that there is a single person in this room who will risk that for anything."

"Moira would put you first Cass and you know it," Jack reminded her.

"I know that," Cass said, "but there's no need to. There are enough cops who come here now to work out when they're off duty that they could keep a discreet eye open while they were working out. Most of them probably already do anyway. If one of you four wanted to stay during the day and shadow me, then that would be fine as well." She looked to Jack, Shep, Chetan and Roman. "I'm not going to hide though. I've got a job to do, a bigger one with Moira on her honeymoon and quite frankly I've missed it. I love what I do and I plan to continue doing it for a long time."

"Not if someone stops you," Shep said, "permanently."

"So far it's only threats, words painted on my car and now the letter," Cass returned. "How do we know that's not all they have in mind?"

"We don't," Charlie said, "but you should be prepared either way. One of you stay with her at work." He turned to look at Shep, Jack, Roman and Chetan. "And we'll put word out so that the cops who work out here will keep their eyes and ears open as well. We don't want to scare whoever this is off by going overboard. If this person does plan something it would be better if it occurred here instead of elsewhere. We can keep on top of things here a lot more easily."

"Thank you, Charlie," Cass said. "I knew I liked you."

Charlie cursed under his breath as he felt the deep flush heat his face and neck. Sometimes it sucked being so light skinned with his vivid red hair and pale blue eyes. At only six feet he was one of the shortest people in the room along with the one they called Chetan but Charlie didn't have Chetan's physique so that left him feeling odd man out. He had always been more of the brain type than the brawn which made Charlie both good and feeling challenged at his job. "No thanks needed," he mumbled, "Just doing my job."

Thankfully a commotion outside distracted everyone from him and Charlie was able to relax. He was no good in social situations.

Doug burst through the open door and scowled at the crowd of men around Cass who looked far too naked for his taste in her sports bra and tight leggings. He scowled even more darkly as he realized that this was probably how she dressed for her job every day. He didn't like it. Not one bit. It was probably a good thing that Damon was still at work. Only one of them could leave right now with things in full swing at the housing addition they were building and Doug was more dispensable right now since most of his stuff was on foundations and structural support while Damon was in charge of all the wiring and making sure everything inside was completed above code.

He walked around the desk and pulled Cass from Shep's side into his arms dropping a kiss on her head before looking at Ben and Charlie. "How bad is it?" he asked without preamble.

Ben held the letter up in his gloved hands so that Doug could get a look at it. Doug flushed redder with every word that seemed to jump off the page at him. He squeezed Cass closer to him and only loosened his grip when she pushed against his chest in protest. She was a lot shorter in her tennis shoes than her usual three-inch heels and the top of her head only reached the middle of his chest. Looking down he had a perfect view of her voluptuous breasts displayed in the sports bra she had on. "I'll take you home for the day," he told Cass.

She looked startled, "I'm not going anywhere. I have more classes today before I can leave. Actually the next one starts in half an hour so I really need to wrap this up, gentlemen," she said to the room at large.

"You can't stay after this," Doug said.

"I can and I will," Cass fired right back. "Ben and Charlie agree with me. Shep will stay the rest of today until I'm done." She looked over to Shep for confirmation.

"Sorry, no can do, love." Shep shook his head at her. "I left Griff alone on a job we're on and I should get back and check on him soon."

Before Doug could take issue with what his little brother was into, Roman spoke up. "I'll stick around for the rest of today and we'll work out a schedule among us for the rest of this week. Does that sound all right with everyone?" he looked pointedly at Doug, which irritated Cass.

"That sounds fine with me," Cass replied, "now if you'll all excuse me I need to get ready for my next class."

She didn't make one step before Doug pulled her up short and hauled her back up against him. "That sounds fine, Roman. If you guys wouldn't mind, I'd like a few minutes alone with Cass."

Cass was really pissed when she watched them all leave trailing out one after the other including Shep who closed the door behind him only taking the time to glance at Doug and say, "Take care of her," before exiting as well.

Doug sat in the chair behind Moira's desk and pulled Cass onto his lap. "Now, darling, before you take your punishment do you want to tell me why you chose not to call either Damon or me?"

"Punishment?" Cass gulped. He didn't look like he was joking in the least so she hurried to add, "I didn't have any numbers for you. You can't be angry with me for something that was out of my control."

"Not buying it, baby," Doug told her. "Katie is in the building and Moira has all of our numbers in this lovely little planner book that she keeps on her desk. So you had plenty of access to finding them if you really wanted to."

"I didn't even think to look in the planner and I honestly forgot about Katie being downstairs," Cass tried to explain.

"Then we'll just have to make sure that you don't forget again." He stood up and headed over to the door where he flipped the lock then turned back to face her. "Take off your clothes, Cass," he ordered her while he stood there with his legs braced apart his arms crossed over his chest.

"Wh-What?" Cass demanded.

"You heard me," he said and just stood there. "Take off your clothes, Cass. Now."

Cass took one look at his face and saw the hurt there. Hurt she had caused by not turning to him and Damon first no matter how much she hadn't meant to. She slowly pulled off her clothes and shoes until she stood naked in front of him.

"Turn around and bend over the desk. Brace yourself with your arms." He told her still just watching. Cass reluctantly did as he said. "Spread your legs," he said, "Wider." Cass complied and felt flushed not with fear as she would have expected but if she were honest, excitement and longing.

She could feel Doug move behind her, heard the pop of the button on his jeans and the slow rasp of the zipper as he lowered it. She felt his hand caress the silky smooth flesh of her ass and just when she started to relax he gave her a sharp smack that made her cry out and her pussy moisten. "From now on, the first call that you make will be to either me or

Damon," he gave her a sharp smack on the other cheek. "Do you understand?" he asked her softly.

Cass nodded vigorously, lost in pleasure but he smacked her again and demanded. "Answer me!"

"Yes," she cried out as quietly as she could as another smack landed across the burning cheeks of her ass. He had told her how he liked to be in control, to know what was going on with her and where she was. He was dominant and possessive but she knew that it was because he cared for her. There wasn't a mean bone in his body and although the smacks to her ass stung and left her cheeks reddened from his palm, she knew exactly what they were. Foreplay.

Doug held his hand over her red cheeks keeping the burn on her flesh. "You are with Damon and me now Cass. That means that you no longer turn to any other man to help you. Do you understand that?"

"Yes, yes," she hastened to answer him not wanting any more smacks on her ass. She could feel her juices spilling down her thighs from her pussy and was startled at how excited she was by this. No, she didn't want anymore smacks. She wanted him. Now. Taking her just as hard and fast as he could.

"I don't like seeing you so undressed in a room full of men, Cass. It makes me crazy with lust," he moved behind her and pulled her up on her tiptoes so he could line his cock up with her wet opening. "It makes me want to stake my claim in a very public way. Do you know how close I was to laying you out on this desk and fucking you while they watched? Don't push me that way ever again, Cass. Don't defy me or I'll do just that. I don't care who watches me fuck this pussy or this ass," he punctuated this last with another sharp smack to her buttocks. "You are mine." He rammed his cock into her dripping cunt and started a violent pounding that had her struggling to stay on her feet. "Mine," he grunted as he slammed in and out of her, his cock hitting deeper with every stroke. "Mine," he whispered again and Cass knew that he spoke with awe and not possession. The truth was she was his just as he and Damon were hers and she liked it that way.

She was keening and moaning her own pleasure struggling to keep from screaming, confused by how his dominance was arousing her to the point of orgasm so quickly. She loved him like this, loved his loss of control and his all-consuming need to claim her in so primitive a manner. She was so close to release she could feel the knot tightening in her womb as the slow burn filled her blood.

Doug smacked her ass just then, sending her over with a deep throaty moan, "You're mine," he grunted. "Say it! Say who you belong to," he demanded of her.

"You," Cass panted. "I belong to you, Doug. I belong to you and Damon." She glanced back at him over her shoulder and added, "And you belong to me. Only me. You and Damon. Mine. All mine."

Doug came inside her with a low groan that vibrated through his chest and collapsed against her back struggling to catch his breath while Cass did the same beneath him. He pulled out and turned her to him tilting her chin up so he could see into her golden brown eyes. "I love you, Cass. Don't ever forget that. I want to be the man you turn to. I need to be that man."

Cass was stunned by the sheer emotion on Doug's face. He was always so strong, so invincible that she hadn't realized just how much he had come to care for her so quickly. She and Damon had discussed it. She knew that Damon was falling for her and she had admitted that she was falling for them as well. But it was in this one unguarded moment that she realized that it was already too late for her. She had fallen head over heels in love and there could be no going back for any of them.

Cass cupped Doug's face in her hands and smiled with all her newfound feelings shining brightly for him to see. "I love you too, Doug. I love both you and Damon. I will never lose sight of that again."

"Was I too rough on you, baby?" Doug asked her softly reaching his hand around to rub her ass gently.

Cass grinned up at him and shook her head. "Never, big boy. You could never be too rough for me."

"I'm glad to hear that. I know that I can be aggressive during sex especially when I'm afraid," he added.

"You have nothing to be afraid of," Cass replied.

"Someone is sending you letters, damaging your property," Doug told her. "And I've never been more afraid in my life. I don't know what I'd do if anything happened to you. That's why I want to know where you are. I can't protect you if I don't know."

Cass smiled up at him realizing maybe for the first time just how much he did love her.

Doug pulled her close and bent to kiss her. It was the most beautiful kiss of her life magical, melting her, a perfect blending of two souls. In it lay the promise of forever. One eagerly given and wholeheartedly accepted.

Chapter Eight

ഇ

Cass walked into her bedroom at the apartment and pulled her suitcases from the closet. Roman had spent the rest of the day with her and then brought her home where he had searched the apartment before finally leaving her safely locked inside to wait for Doug and Damon to arrive. She knew they would demand that she go home with them. She figured that she would save everyone time by already being packed and ready to go.

Thanks to her afternoon delight with Doug she had been pressed for time to reach her next class which happened to be a spin class. She usually took it easy on Mondays especially since she was just getting back into the groove of things herself. Thanks to Doug though, her ass was sore and the seat felt uncomfortable prompting, her to initiate a lot of hovering over the bike seat and the ever unpopular popcorn jumps that had you sitting down on the bike only to hop back to a standing position. It was a hell of a workout though, a high intensity exercise that burned calories as well as making the muscles in your thighs and glutes scream for mercy.

All Cass had wanted was to spend half and hour in the sauna to de-stress and unwind but Roman had forbidden it since Moira was attacked and almost raped in the sauna. It was in the woman's center and Roman wouldn't be able to go with her and protect her. Cass had understood even if she did wish otherwise. So here she was hurrying through a shower so that she could repack clothes she had just unpacked instead of taking the long hot soak her body was begging her for.

When she was dried, dressed and had everything packed though, no one had arrived yet. It was already seven thirty and Cass who hadn't had dinner yet was getting hungry. She was ready to walk down to the corner to the pizza shop when she heard a key in the door and Griff walked in. His clothes were rumpled and stained and he smelled like week-old garbage.

"What in the world happened to you?" Cass asked as she tried to discreetly cover her nose.

Griff grimaced as he looked at her. "I know... I know... I stink. I had a little run-in on the job."

"No offense, Griff, but maybe you should think of doing something else then," Cass spoke through her hand which she was now holding completely over her nose and mouth, her need to not smell the stench outweighing her need not to hurt his feelings.

Griff just shook his head and grinned. "Nah, I really like it." At her raised eyebrow he clarified, "The job. I would have been fine but the damn stairs gave out when I tried climbing onto the balcony of an apartment building and I fell into the Dumpster ripe with garbage." He looked down at himself and grimaced with distaste.

"Maybe you should stay away from Station Street," Cass managed to get out. "Please, Griff, go take a shower and burn those clothes."

"How did you know I was on Station Street?" he asked.

"That's the only place I know of in Legacy where you would find a building with faulty balconies and Dumpsters filled with over-ripe garbage. God, Griff, take a scalding hot shower and literally burn those clothes. You have no idea what could have been in those Dumpsters. Count yourself lucky that you didn't get cut or jabbed with a dirty needle."

"I'm going, I'm going," he mumbled as he let her shoo him down the hall toward the bathroom. "I'm starved though. Can you order some dinner? Or are you heading out the door?"

"I was just thinking about heading down to the pizza place on the corner. Any favorites?"

"Umm...I'll take a large with every thing. If you're expecting Doug and Damon, you better get a few. Plus Shep is heading over too," Doug told her. "My wallet is in my back pocket," he nodded at his hip. "There should be a couple of twenties in there."

"Thanks, Griff, but I've got it this time," Cass told him as she grabbed her purse and headed for the front door. There was no way she was touching him right now. "Just have that smell gone before I get back or no one will have an appetite."

Cass hurried out of the apartment building and turned to walk the short distance down the sidewalk to the pizza parlor on the corner. Griff was in the apartment and she was only walking a few feet. It was broad daylight still. She was lost in thought and didn't see the car pull away from the curb behind her and begin slowly following her Cass was just planning to enter the busy pizza parlor when her cell phone rang. She moved farther out on the sidewalk to answer the phone not surprised to hear Doug's voice.

"Where are you?" he asked without preamble.

"Well, hello, Doug. I miss you too," Cass said. "The day has just dragged on without you."

Doug chuckled, "Okay, sorry. Hi, baby. I've missed you. Now where are you? Damon and I are at the apartment and no one's answering."

"Griff's in the shower. Please do not get him out too soon. He fell into a Dumpster of ripe garbage and he smells of it," Cass told him. "I'm right on the corner getting ready to order some pizza for dinner. Griff and I are both starving."

"We'll meet you down there in a few, babe."

"Okay," Cass sighed as Doug disconnected on her. She turned to enter the pizza parlor to place their order planning to come back out and wait on Doug and Damon. She ordered four large with everything and one small cheese lovers for her and was told that it would be about twenty to thirty minutes.

She had just stepped out onto the sidewalk when she heard the squeal of tires and looked up to see a car speeding down the road. *What an idiot*, she thought as the car barreled toward her. She just had time to make out a woman behind the wheel when the car swerved toward her without slowing down.

Cass jumped back on the sidewalk trying to seek shelter behind a parked car. The car careening toward her jumped the curb, sideswiped the car beside Cass and jerked back onto the road disappearing in a squeal of tires and brakes around the other corner. Cass was shaking so hard she thought she might literally shake apart when suddenly she felt arms grab her from behind and jerk her roughly back into a hard chest. She shrieked until the soothing sound of Damon's voice made it through to her.

"It's okay, sweetheart," Damon was saying. "We're here now. We're here."

Cass turned in his arms and burrowed against his chest. Damon held her closely soothing her with his hands and voice. "Doug's calling Ben on his cell. If we don't want a big public scene, we better calm you down before he gets over here," Damon whispered in Cass' ear as he placed kisses along her cheek.

Too late for that, Cass thought as she heard someone approaching. She felt Doug even before he wrapped his arms around her and pressed against her back. People were pouring out of the pizza parlor and other places of business and Cass knew they were the center of attention. It wasn't every day that a woman was caught in the arms of not one but two men on the streets of Legacy. Cass knew they were causing a sensation but realized that she just didn't care. She needed to feel their arms around her. If not for the car parked at the curb, she would have been hit and possibly killed by whoever was driving that car. She was almost positive that it had been a woman but it had happened so quickly that she couldn't be one hundred percent sure.

Doug and Damon held her close between them both running their hands over her body to assure themselves that she was unharmed, both placing kisses on her face and hair. Cass reveled in their touch, feeling safe and secure in the shelter of their arms. She didn't care that people watched, didn't care what anyone thought. She felt Damon start to pull away and grabbed his shirt with her hands holding him close.

"Don't leave me," she begged.

"I'm not, sweetheart," he tried to soothe her. "I just don't want to cause you any embarrassment. People are watching us, Cass."

"I don't care. Let them watch. I love you and Doug and I need you both to hold me for just a moment, please," Cass looked deeply into his eyes watching Damon's soften with emotion at her words of love. "Just for a few minutes I want you both to hold me."

Doug and Damon tightened their arms around her, glad to fulfill her request regardless of their curious audience. They were still together when Ben arrived followed by a blue and white Legacy police car with two uniformed officers inside. Ben came to them while the two officers immediately split up. One went to canvass the crowd to see if anyone had seen anything. The other tackled the irate man who was yelling about his car. Ben must have spoken to the officers over the police radio on the way to the scene filling them in on what had occurred.

Doug and Damon stayed close, standing on either side of her like quiet sentinels while Cass went over what she had seen. She explained to Ben that she was just hanging up from talking to Doug when the car came down the street and swerved toward her hitting the parked car instead. She thought it was a dark blue four door but wasn't sure what make or model since it had all happened so fast. Doug and Damon had seen the car speed down the street but hadn't realized what had happened and didn't pay close attention to it. They all agreed that it was a four-door sedan and all agreed it was a dark blue. The paint transferred to the parked car appeared dark blue and Cass noticed one of the officers scraping some off into a little baggie.

"We'll check the paint and see if we can't get a dealer match on it. Most car companies have their own particular shades of color so we might be lucky and find out what four doors were painted with that particular color. We'll get it to the lab and hope," Ben said as one of the officers approached them.

"What did you get, Simons?" Ben asked the young officer. Cass couldn't help but take notice of the young cop, how beautiful his ebony skin was and how he had the most startling green eyes she had ever seen. He was shorter than the other men, maybe five foot seven or eight but he was stunning. When he spoke it was in a deep baritone that sent shivers down her spine. No one that beautiful should have that incredible a voice as well. It just wasn't fair.

"Let's see," Officer Teddy Simons answered. "The car was blue, black, dark green and one lady swore it was dark brown. The driver was a black, white, Mexican man/woman with blondish brownish ebony hair." He shook his head in frustration. "Basically we got squat."

Ben shook his head and grinned when he noticed Cass staring so intently at Simons making Doug and Damon notice this as well. Doug nudged her and Ben laughed.

"Cass Sinclair, this is Officer Teddy Simons of the Legacy Police Department. Simons, this is Cass, Damon Roberts and Doug Daniels, Gil's brother." Ben introduced them.

"You can quit staring at any time, Cass," Doug said dryly making Teddy grin showing perfectly straight blinding white teeth.

"It should be a sin for a man to be so beautiful," Cass said, making Ben, Damon and Doug shake their heads and Teddy laugh.

"Why thank you," Teddy told her still grinning big. "I have to say that you're quite beautiful as well."

"And quite taken as well," Doug said with a fierce frown at the flirting policeman.

Teddy laughed. "I can tell you're Gil's brother. You're too much alike not to be, same fierce expression, same black hair, same blue eyes, same height, same possessiveness. Where do you Daniels hide these beauties?"

"Knowledge Is Power," Cass told him. "It's a gym here in town where a lot of cops have started coming to work out." She looked at his bulging muscles. "You look like you work out. You should come check us out."

"I'll be sure to do that." Teddy grinned at her shaking his head as Doug pulled her closer to him. "Possessive," he murmured.

Doug just grunted but Damon, Ben and Cass all laughed. Cass cuddled close and whispered to Doug. "I love your possessiveness," she told him making Doug smile softly down at her.

Ben sent Teddy back to the station with the paint chips and assured them that he would personally follow up on this incident. He urged Cass to be careful and not to go anywhere by herself again then headed back out. Damon went in to retrieve their pizza order and then they all three headed back to the apartment. Griff was thankfully cleaned up and smelling better when they got there and Shep was sitting on the couch flipping through the channels on the television. They all sat around the living room while Cass and Damon and Doug explained what had just happened to Griff and Shep.

"You okay, sugar?" Shep asked Cass.

"Yeah, I'm fine now," she assured him. "Thankfully Doug and Damon were there exactly when I needed them." She placed her hands on the thighs of the men who sat on either side of her on the smaller sofa in the room diagonal to both the television and the couch that Shep and Griff were seated on.

"Chetan will be with you tomorrow and Wednesday at the club. Griff and I have Thursday and Friday." Shep told them all. "Someone will be with you the whole day while you're at work. Your car won't be ready till the beginning of next week so Griff can take you to work in the morning and whoever is watching you will make sure you get back here after work."

"She'll be staying with us from now on so Damon or I will get her to work in the morning and then pick her up here or at the club before we head home," Doug said and Cass could feel the tension in him and knew that he was just waiting for her to argue with him.

"My bags are already repacked and waiting in the bedroom," she said instead, surprising him and Damon both. "I'm ready whenever you guys are."

Doug stood and pulled her to her feet. "I'm ready to head home for a shower," he said. "I'll get your bags and we'll go." He placed a quick kiss on her lips and went down the hall to gather her stuff.

Damon slipped his arm around her and hugged her close bending to place a kiss on her lips as well. "I'm glad you didn't argue, sweetheart," he whispered for her ears only.

"I've already been punished once today," Cass whispered back rubbing her bottom. "Once was enough."

Damon's eyes fired with lust letting Cass know how much it turned him on to think of Doug spanking her. Cass knew that she was in for another night of slippery erotic sex when they got her home. She was looking forward to it.

They barely made it in the door before Damon had her against the wall and was pulling her shirt over her head and unfastening her bra. He immediately latched onto her nipple and sucked it vigorously flicking it with his tongue, nipping it with his teeth. Cass felt Doug pulling her skirt and panties down her legs and stepped out of them at the prompt of his hand. He was on his knees in front of her and when he had her completely naked he placed one of her legs over his shoulder and tasted her pussy with a slow glide of his tongue. He licked and nibbled at her flesh savoring her like a much loved dessert. The contrast of Damon's harsh suckling and Doug's slow savoring was an aphrodisiac in itself.

Cass bucked and cried out but neither man was ready to release his hold on her. Damon moved from nipple to nipple until both were swollen red and throbbing before moving up her throat with soft nips and bites marking her with his need. Doug continued to slowly explore her quivering pussy with soft laps of his tongue and gentle nips at her wet folds and throbbing clit. He continued to bring her to the brink but would not allow her to go over. After three near orgasms that were so close Cass could almost touch them Doug finally relented sucking her clit while stroking two fingers in and out of her sweet pussy letting her crest over that edge into oblivion.

Cass cried out her pleasure sagging against the hands that held her as she grew weak from the intensity of her release. Damon swept her up into his arms as Doug stood and then followed her and Damon down the hall to Doug's big bedroom. Damon placed her gently on the bed and she watched with hooded, passion-glazed eyes as they disrobed and made to join her. Cass stopped them at the edge of the bed lying flat so that their long thick cocks bobbed in her face. She took them in her hands and stroked each with a slow glide of her palm down their length.

She leaned forward and took Damon deep into her mouth sucking and licking his willing flesh while she continued to stroke Doug with her hand. Damon palmed the back of her head and fucked slowly in and out of her suckling mouth moaning at the pleasure she was giving him. Doug placed his hand over the one she had wrapped around his erection and pumped both up and down his cock squeezing her fingers tighter around him. Both men were moaning and Cass was enjoying every touch, stroke of hand and tongue and taste she was given. Both men pulled away and Damon joined her on the bed while Doug opened the bedside drawer and removed a large tube of lubricant.

Damon reclined back on the bed and pulled Cass astride him lifting her until his cock was pushing against her slick pussy begging for entrance. Cass took him in her hand and guided the large head of his cock so that it was pushing into her forging the way for the long length of his staff to follow. He lifted and lowered her a few times before taking a deep breath and pulling her down to him leaving her ass up and ready for the lubricant Doug was squeezing onto his fingers.

Doug pushed two fingers into her ass making her cry out at the unexpected invasion. She knew that he was going to take her there but he usually took time preparing her, lubing her until she fairly dripped. This time he seemed beyond the slow buildup. Gone was the slow exquisite torture of before. He thrust his fingers fully inside her working the lube deep before removing his fingers and applying more. His fingers disappeared and she could hear him slathering more lubricant onto his cock before he placed the plum-shaped head against her ass and pushed his way inside.

It was torture for a woman to feel so full, so complete, so desired by two such well-endowed and talented lovers. Their cocks were fully seated inside her and she was already close to orgasm. They started a hard fast rhythm gliding in and out of her in synchronicity filling her and emptying her with every quick stroke. Damon popped a nipple still swollen and red from his earlier attention into his mouth and nipped softly at it while Doug reached a hand down between her and Damon's bodies as Damon leaned back a little and plucked her clit between his thumb and forefinger.

Cass broke with a sharp keening moan not knowing what to scream, whose name to cry out as her orgasm ripped hard contractions through her belly and the inner muscles of her pussy and ass bit down on the cocks sheathing in and out of her body. Doug and Damon both joined her crying with their own releases as they pumped hot jets of creamy cum into her body. Slowly Doug and Damon turned so that they all lay together side by side by side on the bed. They lay joined for a long time lying on their sides with Cass still speared on their softening cocks struggling to catch their breaths. It was several minutes later before anyone made it to the shower.

Chapter Nine

ᔰ

Cass received another letter in the mail the next day at the club. This one had been mailed locally and was just as descriptive. The words *WHORE* and *CUNT* jumped off the patched-together page at her but she had to laugh when she saw the phrases *SEXUAL DEVIANT* and *GANG BANGER*. Doug and Damon were pretty awesome in bed but they weren't actually a gang. Someone was really taking exception to her new — and in her opinion improved — sex life.

Cass sighed and waited in the office with Chetan for Ben and Charlie to arrive and take charge of the letter. Chetan had been careful not to touch it with his bare hands instead using a pair of gloves he pulled from the pocket of his low-slung jeans and a pen from the desk to open and lay the letter out for them to read. Cass enjoyed having Chetan with her. He was unobtrusive, just there always in his quiet way keeping constant watch over everything around him.

She had known Chetan as long as she had known Shep but really knew very little about him. He was of Native American descent but she didn't know any specifics. His skin was a warm toffee color, his hair a jet black ponytail hanging down his back but his eyes were a smoky gray, deeper and darker than Roman's. He was the shortest of the group of men he worked with at only six feet but he was toned and muscular and his eyes dared anyone to think they could take him. Shep had told her once of how good Chetan was with his hands in a fight and the man could wield a blade like no one else. According to Shep there was always a Ka-bar knife on Chetan somewhere.

Cass sat back in the chair behind Moira's desk and looked over Chetan from head to toe. He was wearing low-slung jeans that cupped his ass and molded to his hard, well-muscled thighs. He had on a gray pullover t-shirt that almost matched the color of his eyes and on his feet were sneakers. She had no idea where he could have hidden a knife on his body. Chetan just smiled at her which made Cass flush when she realized how intently she had been checking him out.

"It's a good thing your guys aren't here now," Chetan spoke softly, his natural voice low and sexy. "I don't think they would appreciate just how hard you're eyeing me, sweet stuff."

"I was just looking for your knife." Cass told him bluntly. "Shep says you never leave home without it."

"Shep talks too much," Chetan said and nothing more.

"What are Shep and Griff working on that they couldn't be here today?" Cass asked just to fill the silence.

"Don't know," Chetan said.

"Griff fell into a Dumpster yesterday," Cass laughed as she remembered. "He reeked so badly that I begged him to burn his clothes."

"That right," Chetan said.

Cass huffed out a breath and tried again. "So, Chetan, how long have you known Jack?"

"Long time," Chetan answered.

"Where are you from originally?" she asked and flushed again when Chetan raised an eyebrow at her. "I mean that you're not originally from Legacy."

"Nope," Chetan replied.

"So where are you from?" Cass was getting irritated.

"Here and there," Chetan told her with a smile that let her know that he knew exactly how he was aggravating her.

"Anyone ever tell you that you talk too much?" Cass fired at him.

"All the time, sweet stuff, all the time," he answered as Ben and Charlie finally arrived at the open office door.

"So you got another one," Ben said as he and Charlie pulled gloves on and looked over the letter and envelope.

"Same typing, same cut-and-paste job." Charlie spoke softly as he looked over everything. "Who opened it?"

"I did." Chetan reclined back in his chair and watched. "Used gloves."

"Good, good," Charlie muttered. The pure viciousness of the letter's contents upset him. "No prints found on the last one except Cass' which makes sense since it was stuck in the middle of the pile of mail. This time I'm afraid that there are going to be too many prints since it went through the mail. We'll take it in anyway and see what we get." He sounded frustrated.

"Thanks, Charlie," Cass spoke and touched him softly on the arm.

Charlie flushed bright red again and glared when Ben laughed at him. "You're welcome, Ms. Sinclair. I only wish that we could figure out who's sending these to you. I hear that you were almost involved in a hit and run last night."

"Yeah, thank God there was a car for me to jump behind or I would have been road kill at the rate the car was coming at me." Cass shuddered as she remembered the car speeding toward her.

Ben reached out and put his arm around her giving her a friendly hug. "You're safe now, Cass, and we're going to do all that we can to make sure that you stay that way."

"Thanks, Ben." Cass smiled at him and his attempt to reassure her.

"And here I thought you were my own personal white knight," Katie said from the door making Chetan grin, Cass laugh and Ben jump.

"Damn, woman, you scared me half to death," Ben grumbled as he headed to his wife who was just starting to get a little bump where their baby lay in her tummy. He immediately reached a hand out and rubbed her with a soft caress of his fingers. "How are you and baby feeling today?"

"Baby is fine," Katie told him. "I'm hungry."

Ben looked at Katie and saw the heat in her eyes realizing exactly what she was hungry for. "What luck," he told her in a low purr, "I was just getting ready to take a lunch break. Why don't I go feed you, sugar?"

Katie laughed and they left the room arm in arm oblivious to everyone else.

Charlie sighed as he watched them head down the hall, "There goes my ride back to the station."

"No sweat," Chetan told him. "Cass doesn't have class for another hour so we can give you a ride back and stop for something to eat on the way. Looks like this is your lunch break."

Cass looked at Chetan with awe prompting him to say, "What?"

"My God, Chetan, that was the most I've ever heard you say. I think it was close to two whole sentences, all at once."

"Careful, sweet stuff," Chetan told her as he clasped her arm above the elbow and led her out to his car with Charlie following behind them.

* * * * *

It had been another long day for Cass and she was dog tired. She followed behind Chetan down the hall to the apartment door standing back and waiting for him to unlock and take an initial scan inside. He held the 9mm Smith & Wesson handgun loosely at his side taking no chances after two letters and one attempted hit and run. He pulled her in behind him and placed her just inside the door as he searched the apartment for any hidden intruder. He seemed to spend a little extra time in the bedroom she was using and she saw why when he came back out and shut and locked the front door.

"Someone's been here," he told her. "They weren't too happy."

Cass followed him back down the hall and gasped as she took in the state of the bedroom. The few clothes that she had left behind here were older workout clothes and a few odds and ends so that she would be able to shower and change while she waited on Doug and Damon if she needed to. Everything was ripped and the pieces littered the floor. The bed looked as if it had been shredded with a knife. Lamps were shattered on the floor, broken pieces everywhere. Her purse-size perfume and deodorant, body lotion and other odds and ends that she had left were stomped into a mess on the floor. The red lipstick she had left had been used to leave a message on the mirror.

THE WHORE SHALL BURN was printed in bold red letters that no one could miss and the rest of the lipstick was smeared into the mirror and top of the dresser.

Cass was devastated as she took it all in. Someone had broken in and done all this damage because they hated her. She heard Chetan talking on his cell phone and knew that he was probably talking to Ben. This stuff wasn't even hers. This was Gil's stuff and she could only pray that none of it was family heirlooms that would be irreplaceable. The lamps had been pottery pieces that she thought were fairly new but the bed and dresser were older, more solid pieces than could be found today. She would replace everything that she could and pray that Gil would not be too upset with her.

She heard voices heading down the hall toward them and looked up to see Doug standing there. She had no idea how long she had been standing there looking at everything but it must have been a while, at least long enough for others to arrive anyway. Her gaze locked onto Doug's and she was across the mess and in his arms burrowing close, breathing in the reassuring fragrance that was uniquely him. Here was her comfort, her safety assured in the hard clasp of his arms around her body. She shuddered as she wondered for the first time if she could be placing him in danger. The thought of him or Damon being hurt because of her made her eyes widen with new fear.

"I need to find somewhere else to stay," she whispered.

"You already have," Doug told her. "You're with Damon and me now."

"No," Cass shook her head almost choking on the words she needed to say. "I can't stay with you any more. It's not safe."

Doug frowned down at her. "You'll be safe with us, Cass. No one will get you at our house."

"Look at this mess, Doug. Look what this person has already done. She's destroyed your brother's things all because of me." She yelled at him but Doug just shook his head at her.

"They're just things," he spoke quietly, calmly, in direct contrast to her increasing anxiety. "They can be replaced. You can't."

"Neither can you," Cass yelled at him suddenly revealing her real terror. "She followed me here. What's to prevent her from following me to your house?"

Doug gripped her arms and pulled her flush against his hard chest. "I am. Damon is. We'll protect you with our lives if we have to, darling."

Cass looked up at him tears filling her eyes and pouring down her cheeks. "Don't you realize that's what I'm afraid of? I can't lose you. Either of you. I won't risk you."

"You won't have to," he told her softly wiping her tears away with his fingers. "Don't you see that we would protect you anyway? You're everything to us. We would never be the same without you."

"Oh, Doug, I love you so much," she whispered cupping his face in her hands and pulling his lips down for a slow soft kiss.

"I love you too, baby," he murmured before taking her mouth again in a kiss that was erotic in its very simplicity. She let him hold her while they waited for the police and she was still in his arms when the officers left hours later. At some point Shep and Griff had arrived, informed by Chetan of what he had found. The bedroom Cass had been using was the only room that had been tampered with, but Griff looked through his stuff as well to be sure. Finally when the last of the police left Damon arrived looking stressed and angry.

"I saw all the police cars out front and nearly killed myself rushing up here," he said as he pulled Cass into his arms and squeezed her tight. "What the hell happened here and why didn't someone call me?" He glared at Doug.

"No one called me either," Doug informed Damon. "I found all this when I got here to pick Cass up. I did call you though and leave a voicemail message. Check your phone."

Damon picked his phone up and looked at it. "Damn thing's on silent mode still. I forgot to turn it back on after the meeting I had with the electricians." He cuddled Cass closer and nuzzled his face into her hair. "I'm sorry, sweetheart. It won't happen again."

"I'm fine, Damon," she assured him. "I wasn't here when whoever it was broke in."

"We all done here now?" Doug asked Ben and Charlie who were still there.

"Yeah, for now," Ben told him before turning to Cass. "That's two letters in two days, an attempted hit and run and now this. Be very careful, Cass. Don't go anywhere by yourself. Period."

"Another letter?" Doug asked looking hard down at Cass. "Never mind," he said before she could answer. "We'll talk about it at home." He turned to look at the four other men in the room—Shep and Griff and Ben and Charlie. "I want Cass to stay at the gym from now on until one of us comes to pick her up. No more coming here." He looked at Griff and added,

"Get the locks on the door changed and have Mom take care of getting someone to clean the mess up before Gil and Moira get back. We'll see you all later."

Doug and Damon herded Cass out of the apartment, down the hall and into the elevator. Cass could feel the anger pulsing off them in waves and knew that she was in big trouble for not calling them earlier when she had first received the second letter. She had thought about it but then she and Chetan had left to take Charlie back to the station and pick something up to eat. She had hurried to be at class on time when they got back to the gym and in the rush of the day had just forgotten to call them. Once Doug had her in his truck and Damon was following behind them in his Doug confirmed her thoughts.

"You're in big trouble, darling," Doug told her. "You know why?"

"I should have called you earlier when I saw the second letter in the mail," Cass replied.

"You're damn right you should have, baby. When we get home you're going to go straight to the bedroom and strip naked. You'll sit there and wait for Damon and me to come in and give you your punishment." He looked at her hard before asking her, "Understand?"

"But Doug," she tried to say but he interrupted her.

"Understand, baby?"

Cass shook her head and swallowed the fear choking her as she looked at his hard face. "You're so angry, Doug. Please don't hurt me."

Doug looked surprised at her words. "I would never hurt you, Cass, no matter how angry I am. You will be punished though because you disobeyed what I told you. But you have no need to fear me, baby."

Cass nodded and swallowed again feeling anticipation and fear as well as an erotic hunger for what she knew was coming. She knew his discipline would consist of a spanking, his hand or Damon's or perhaps both of them smacking her ass and turning it a soft shade of red. Cass could feel her pussy growing wet just from the thought of that punishment and shook her head in disgust at her own eagerness for the feel of a hard palm striking her ass. She was both terrified and amazed at the sexually submissive woman she became when she was with Doug and Damon. How had her life come to this?

Chapter Ten

❧

Cass sat on the edge of the bed stripped completely naked and listened anxiously for the sound of footsteps coming down the hall that would tell her that Doug and Damon were finally coming to her. How had her life come to the point where she was eagerly awaiting her lovers to come and discipline her, craving the sharp smack of their hands on the cheeks of her ass warming them and making them blush red? She had been sitting there for ten minutes but it felt like hours to her. She refused to budge knowing how much this moment meant to all of them. It was a way to deal with the fear and the helplessness that both of her lovers felt. It was a way to reassure everyone that she was alive and well. So she sat and waited her pussy dripping with anticipation and her ass tingling for the first sharp smack it would be given.

The turning of the door knob startled her. She hadn't heard them coming to her and yet now here they were. Damon stepped into the room first. He was dressed in loose stretch pants and one look at her sitting there naked and waiting and his cock was long and hard, tenting the material. He was barefooted and bare-chested, his wavy blond hair showing where he had been running his fingers through it.

Doug stepped in after him dressed in nothing but sweats as well. His cock was thick and hard pushing against the band just below his belly button seeking a way out of its confinement. His chest was covered with the thick mat of black hair that Cass had come to love spreading across his chest and trailing down his abdomen in a straight line that pointed the way to heaven. She licked her lips prepared for anything, for everything, or at least she hoped so.

"Stand up, baby," Doug ordered, stopping only to shut and lock the door behind him before crossing the room to stand beside Damon in front of the bed.

Cass rose hesitantly now that the moment was here unsure of her desire to submit and obey but all it took was one look into their eyes to remind her. Damon sat on the bed where she had been and Doug opened the drawer in the bedside table and removed a tube of lubricant and a very large plug which she had the uneasy feeling was for her ass. Doug's next words removed any doubt.

"I want you to bend over Damon's knees and brace your arms on the floor, baby," Doug told her as he opened the tube of lube and began using it on the plug in his hand.

"What...What are you going to do with that?" Cass couldn t keep the question in.

Doug didn't look at her as he worked the lube onto the plug making it glisten, "You're going to bend over like I told you to and brace your arms on the floor. Then Damon is going to spread those pretty cheeks and lube that tight little ass for me while I get this plug nice and slick." He finally looked at her when he spoke next and there was no missing the desire and dominance in his face. "This is part of your punishment, Cass. You should have called one of us like you were told to do. *Immediately.*" There was no disguising the fear in his voice, the look of helpless frustration in his eyes. "Now you're going to take this plug in your ass and then you're going to take your spanking. Now bend over and get in position."

Damon patted his knees and pulled her over to him. Cass took a deep breath and slowly lowered her body until she was in the position Doug wanted her to take, stomach balanced on Damon's knees and her hands braced on the floor. She could feel Damon spreading the cheeks of her ass and then the nozzle of the tube of lubricant was inserted and the cooling gel filled her ass. Damon slowly inserted one finger into her, working the gel deep inside her, preparing her for that plug. His finger was removed and replaced once more by the nozzle then two of his fingers plunged into her, stretching and shafting her ass with hard strokes. The fingers were removed and the nozzle filled her again forcing more of the cool lubricant into her ass. Then there was nothing, no nozzle, no fingers. Cass held her breath and waited, her nerves on edge, her body quivering for something she didn't know how to prepare for.

"Brace your body with your hands, baby, and press back into the plug when I push it against your ass," Doug told her and she felt Damon spreading her ass even wider as Doug bent over them and positioned the plug.

It was large and it burned as Doug worked it into her, the hard rubber unforgiving as it stretched and bit at the sensitive tissues of her ass. Cass cried out as it finally lodged fully inside her and both Doug and Damon removed their hands. She could feel their eyes on her ass looking closely at where she was speared on the rubber plug. Every movement made the plug shift inside her, rubbing against the nerves there and making her cry out in pleasure, in pain, in confusion. Her breathing became shallow as she tried to limit her body's movement and accept the hard plug in her body.

Just when she was starting to relax the first blow landed on her right cheek making her clench around the plug and tearing a scream from her throat at the sensations that caused. Another blow fell on the left cheek and she clenched and screamed again.

"You know why you're being punished, sweetheart," Damon told her. "You have to learn to keep us informed of what's happening with this. You could have been seriously injured," and another blow fell on her tingling ass.

Cass cried out as she clenched on the plug begging for release, from the spanking, from the plug, from the fiery need pulsing in her womb and coating her pussy with slick juice. The blows continued to fall like rain and a finger was pushed into her dripping cunt fucking her in rhythm with the spankings pushing her higher and higher toward an orgasm that felt like it would surely rip her apart with its intensity. Cass screamed and bucked as she finally splintered tightening on the fingers fucking her pussy and the plug filling her ass until she felt like she would crush them. Her body wouldn't come down, the large plug keeping her keening as her orgasm whipped through her until every tiny touch sent more small tremors through her.

She felt the plug pulled from her ass and she was turned until she was astride Damon and he was pulling them both back on the bed making room for Doug to join them. Damon shoved his sweats down out of the way and his hard pulsing cock slammed into her still convulsing pussy spearing her so deeply it felt like he was in her stomach. She was shoved forward so that her arms braced automatically on the bed above Damon's shoulders and he latched onto a rigid nipple violently sucking and biting it with his teeth. Doug rammed his cock into her ass and set in motion a fierce pounding that Damon readily joined in.

Cass didn't recognize herself. It was like she was an animal snarling and rutting with her mates as she gave as good as she got. She pulled her nipple from Damon's mouth and bit down hard on the spot where his neck met his shoulder making him buck beneath her shoving his cock so deep it was a painful pleasure. Doug leaned forward and bit her in the same spot and they all slammed into orgasm with harsh guttural groans.

It was a long time before anyone was able to move and even then it was only to fall to the side so that Cass was cradled between the two men their hands softly stroking her.

"Sweet Jesus," Doug moaned, "I've never had sex that intense before."

"Me neither," Damon replied softly kissing Cass on the lips before asking, "Are you okay, sweetheart? Did we hurt you?"

Cass gave a throaty purr that had both men growing hard again. "You hurt me so good," she leaned forward to give

Damon a hard possessive kiss stroking his tongue with hers before turning to give Doug the same treatment sucking his tongue into her mouth and rubbing it with hers. "Hurt me again, Doug. Fuck me like an animal," she begged him her eyes burning with the need to feel her men taking her again.

Doug jumped up from the bed and went quickly to the adjoining bathroom and Cass could tell from the running water that he was cleaning his rock-hard cock so that he could take her pussy this time. He was back instantly his cock shiny and still wet from the bath he had given it and Cass couldn't stop herself from leaning forward and nipping his shaft with her teeth before running her tongue around the bulbous head and sucking him deep into the back of her throat. Doug cried out filling his hands with her hair and fucking his cock into her mouth as she sucked him. Damon was palming and gently slapping her ass with one hand while he fucked her pussy with two fingers of the other hand.

Finally Doug pulled his pulsing cock from the tight wet heat of her mouth wanting to feel the slippery heat of her sweet little cunt around him instead. He shared a look with Damon and then Damon's hands were gone and he was lying on the bed. Cass started to turn and straddle Damon but Doug caught her shoulders and shook his head no. He helped her to place her knees on either side of Damon's hips but she was facing away from Damon looking at Doug instead. She felt Damon positioning his cock between the cheeks of her ass and then she was being filled with his hard length. Doug helped her to lie back against Damon's chest and Damon locked his legs inside hers and spread both of their legs wide.

Doug looked down at her and smiled a predatory look in his eyes. "I'm going to fuck your pussy, baby. I'm going to fuck it hard just like you asked me to and you're going to scream for me."

He rammed his pulsing hard-on violently into her pussy like the animal she wanted him to be. He shafted his large cock in and out of her the motion working her on Damon's rigid length buried so deeply inside her ass. Damon turned her head and took her mouth in a fierce kiss sucking and biting at her lips and tongue while Doug bent forward and bit sharply on her nipple before sucking it into his mouth. Damon left her mouth and bit her on her neck on the opposite side from that already bearing the mark of Doug's teeth. He sucked the flesh against his teeth and Cass screamed at the rough love bite. Doug lifted his head and turned his neck so that he could bite down on the other side of her tender neck. Cass arched and cried out wrapping her arms over Doug's shoulders and lifting up just far enough to bite down on the skin above his nipple.

Doug cried out and slammed hard inside her grinding his pelvis into hers while his cock pulsed and shot load after load of his hot seed inside her clenching pussy. Damon reared beneath her cramming his spurting cock deeper and deeper with each hot load of semen he spent inside her ass. And Cass reveled in every hot blast they gave her taking it all and wanting more. Her own orgasm wasn't as intense this time pulsing through her in soft waves but no less wonderful than the one before. Doug shifted to the side turning her and Damon with him so that they were all on their sides once more their harsh pants and gasps for breath filling the air.

Cass reached a hand back and clasped Damon's fingers and used her other hand to take Doug's hand. "I love you both so much. I'm so glad that I found you, that you wanted me as much as I wanted you."

"I love you too, sweetheart," Damon replied kissing her shoulders. "We'll never let you go now."

But it was Doug's response that took her breath away. "Marry us, baby. Marry us and never leave."

* * * * *

Cass was still reeling from those two words as she went through the motions of teaching her classes the next day at the gym. *Marry us* seemed to echo through her head, through her heart and she couldn't seem to focus on anything else. She could still see the way that Doug had shuttered his gaze when she had just lain there not knowing what to say. She had hurt him with her silence and Damon as well though he did his best not to show it.

The truth was that she wanted nothing more than to marry them and live happily ever after but life was never that simple especially when you were talking about one woman and two men. There were laws against that type of arrangement which meant that she would have to choose one of them to marry and leave the other to live with them and hope that he didn't feel left out or hurt by her choice of the other. How could she do that? How did you choose between two men who meant everything to you? It was like someone telling you that you had to choose which arm to keep knowing that the other would be cut off but still available to use when you needed it. She just couldn't choose and because of that she had hurt them both anyway.

Cass was despondent when the letter arrived again in the mail. She let Chetan call Ben and Charlie at the police department while she called Doug and Damon at their office.

"Daniels Construction," a cheery female voice answered, "How may I help you?"

"Hello, may I speak with Doug Daniels or Damon Roberts please?" Cass asked.

The voice wasn't so friendly this time, "May I ask who's calling?"

"This is Cass Sinclair," Cass answered "they'll know who I am."

"I'm sorry, Ms. Sinclair," the voice stated sounding anything but. "Mr. Daniels and Mr. Roberts are in a meeting right now and cannot be disturbed." Then the woman hung up on her. Cass stared at the phone in surprise. Then she got pissed.

She sat silently stewing while Ben and Charlie arrived and took the letter. Cass hadn't even bothered to open it this time recognizing it from the typing on the envelope. Charlie opened it with his gloved hands and flushed red as he looked at it. Ben and Chetan looked over his shoulder. Ben coughed and looked away and Chetan gave a low whistle before looking over at her.

"What," she demanded beyond pissed and steadily heading to full-blown anger as they continued to look at her.

"Perhaps it would be better if you didn't see this one," Charlie told her as he started to fold the letter up again.

"Oh no you don't," Cass said and grabbed the paper from him not caring that her hands were bare and would leave prints. She gasped when she turned it around and looked at it. Not a letter this time but a picture. The picture showed a very naked woman lying spread-eagle on her back on the floor of a room she didn't recognize, her body outlined in chalk. The head was Cass'.

"That's not my body," was the first thing Cass could think of to say. "How the hell could someone put something like this together?" she demanded.

"It's pretty easy if you know how to cut and paste on a computer. Most come with some version of Photoshop now," Charlie told her. "We already know that she has pictures of you from the first letter she sent."

"You said 'she'," Cass pounced on that admission. "Do you know that for sure or just a guess?"

Charlie looked at Ben for help and Ben shrugged and answered. "The woman made a mistake when she broke into the apartment. We were able to get a shoe impression from the carpet. Not enough to know who but enough to know that she was wearing a woman's athletic shoe size eight. Katie is a six and you are a seven so that leaves you two out. No other woman has been inside that apartment in quite a while so we're fairly certain that the person doing this to you is a woman."

"A woman," Cass said and her eyes took on a hard sheen. "Then I know just who to ask about this." She held the letter in her hand and looked at Chetan. "Get your keys and let's go."

"Umm," Charlie uttered stammering as he tried to get her attention and get the letter back from her. "Could I get the picture back from you?"

"Hell no," Cass told him. "You haven't made any headway with the first two so why bother with this one? This goes with Chetan and me."

Ben shook his head to cut Charlie off before he could even try to say anything else. "Cass," Ben tried, "this one could be the one with prints on it. Don't let your anger help her to win."

Cass glared at him and turned to eye the copier in the corner of Moira's office. "Can I at least make a copy then before you take it to the station and let everyone see what they'll think is my naked body?"

"Yes," Ben told her seeing no other way to get the original back from her. "Cass, I promise that only the people directly involved in this case will ever see this picture. That's me, Charlie and Officer Simons who's still interviewing people about the attempted hit and run and helping check with the Post Office about the letters. Charlie will run it for prints himself. That's it. No one else will see it." Charlie nodded his head in agreement with this.

Cass held the original back out and Charlie took it in his gloved hand and placed it in a plastic bag with the envelope. Cass pulled the copy from the tray on the printer and turned back to Chetan with fire in her eyes. "Ready to go?" she asked him.

He shook his keys and nodded.

"Maybe you should wait to see Doug and Damon, Cass," Ben tried to say but she cut him off with a hard look.

"What I do or don't do with Doug and Damon is nobody's business but mine. I am to call them and keep them informed when anything happens." She informed them all with a truly evil smile that had all three men stepping back. "Funny thing is though that when I tried, their secretary hung up on me. Imagine my surprise at that. So now I am going to go see them like a good little girl and tell them what I received in the mail today." She turned to Chetan and snapped out, "Let's go. Now."

Ben shook his head as he and Charlie followed Chetan as he followed Cass down the hall to the front desk where she informed the rest of the staff that she would be gone for the rest of the day and that they could reach her on her cell if they needed her. She spoke briefly to Kat making sure that Kat and Kit would take care of closing up for the night before she led the three men out of the building to the lot where their cars were all parked. Ben stood on the sidewalk and watched as Chetan helped her into his truck and shut the door.

"Don't let her kill the secretary," Ben hollered at Chetan watching as he made his way to the driver's door.

"Will do," Chetan told him, "but the boys are on their own."

Ben shook his head and glanced at Charlie. "I'm sure glad that I have Katie."

Cass was still steaming when they pulled up at the site where Daniels Construction was working. The trailer that housed the mobile office was off to the side of the houses they were building and Chetan drove his truck until he could park in the gravel right in front of it. Cass hadn't thought about what she was wearing until she slammed out of the truck and all work stopped as the men gawked at her. Only then did she remember the tight sports bra and tiny shorts she was still wearing from her last spin class. She was too pissed to care and paid little attention as the men hooted and whistled while she walked to the door of the trailer.

She slammed it open not caring who was inside or even if Chetan was following her. She zeroed in on the woman behind the desk but was sidetracked when a door opened and Damon stepped out with another man she didn't recognize. Damon looked surprised to see her and he should.

She walked right up to him and slammed the hand holding the picture against his chest. "I got this in the mail today. Just wanted to let you and Doug know so there wouldn't be any misunderstanding later." She scowled at him oblivious to the curious stare of the other man.

"Sweetheart," Damon tried to soothe her, "you could have just called."

"Funny thing about that," she smiled in a deadly way at him just as an irate Doug stormed in the door behind them. "I tried to."

"What the hell are you doing here dressed like that?" Doug demanded heading straight for her just as oblivious to the others in the room as she was. He grabbed her arm and turned her to him.

"If you don't want me showing up fresh from work dressed like this then make sure you take my calls when I do call," she yelled at him.

Damon stepped up behind her and she found herself trapped between the two men.

"Baby, you better explain yourself," Doug said in a low voice that she recognized as the one he used when he was getting pissed about something. *Well good for him*, she thought.

She shoved away from between them then turned and fisted her hands in their shirts tugging them both down to her. She kissed Damon first, a hard fast kiss that revved his motor and left him wanting more before she moved to Doug and gave him the same fierce treatment. "I don't need to explain myself. Not now. Look at the picture I gave Damon. I received it in the mail today. And don't even start, Doug," she told him when he opened his mouth, "I did try to call."

With that Cass pushed them away and stalked to the desk where she leaned down so that she was face to face with the wide-eyed woman who sat there, giving all three men behind her a glorious view of her lush ass hugged in Spandex. Their secretary was young, maybe twenty-four or -five with short brown hair and big green eyes made to look even bigger by the glasses she wore. Cass made sure she had the girl's complete attention before she spoke. "Next time I call," she glanced down at the name plate on the desk before continuing, "Ms. Sharp, I expect to be put through immediately. They," she indicated Doug and Damon who still stood behind her, "are mine. When I call it is important and I either want to speak to one of them or you damn well better take a message. Do I make myself clear?" she demanded of the cowering girl.

"Yessss," the girl stuttered out never taking her eyes off Cass.

"Good," Cass nodded before turning back to Doug and Damon. "Now give me the key to the house. Chetan's going to take me home and I'm going to relax and spend a nice quiet afternoon by myself. You will not follow me home. You will leave me alone because you love me and you know that I need to be alone right now," she told them as she waited with her palm out for the key she requested.

Damon's lips twitched with a smile but Doug's eyes shot erotic fire and promised payback when he got home. He pulled his keys from his pocket and held them out to her. "Take my truck home and I'll hitch a ride with Damon." He latched onto her wrist when she took the keys and used it to pull her to him. "You go straight home and nowhere else, baby. Not while this psycho is still out there." He pulled her roughly against him and kissed her until she moaned rubbing against his bulging erection like a cat. "You can have two hours, baby. Two hours alone before Damon and I head home."

"Okay," she agreed lost in his touch, his kiss until Damon turned her into his arms and took her mouth in a primal kiss that had her rubbing against him as well. With lust-glazed eyes and nipples so hard with need they were rigid points beneath her sports bra, she turned and left the trailer with Chetan shaking his head in amusement as he followed her.

When Cass left Tyler Andrews turned to Doug and Damon and saying, "That's one hell of a woman you have there." Tyler's cock was a hard bulge straining his pants after watching the display that had taken place in the office. Tyler knew two things at that moment—that discussion on the upcoming project he was working on with Daniels Construction was over for the day and that he was in dire need of a willing woman for a good long fuck. Perhaps he'd look up his old buddy Shep from his Ranger days and see what Legacy had to offer.

Doug and Damon nodded their agreement with his comment and agreed to meet with Tyler again early tomorrow morning for breakfast to continue with plans for the office complex they would all be working on next.

Tessa Sharp couldn't take her eyes off Tyler's lush brown locks and his perfect ass in the tight jeans he wore. She remembered the twinkle in his big brown eyes when he had actually stopped and chatted with her earlier. Perhaps he would be more receptive to her than others had been. Then again, she thought with a frown, he had kept his eyes glued to the busty brunette as well when she had been in the office. Tessa's frown turned into a fierce scowl. Was it too much to hope for a man to look at her like that, with lust in his eyes?

She had worked for Daniels Construction since she was eighteen taking over her mother's job when her mom retired early. Tessa had been a late surprise for her parents who had been in their forties when Tessa was born. Eight years she had been with the Daniels and not once had Doug or Damon looked at her that way. Eight years of being a convenience more like office furniture than a person. She glared at Doug and Damon who were watching out the window still looking at the busty brunette she was sure. Some day they would realize all that she did for them and regret not paying more attention to her.

Chapter Eleven

℘

Cass reclined back in the big Jacuzzi tub moaning with pleasure as the pulsing jets of water hit along different points of her body soothing and relaxing away all her aches and pains. Now if she could just cleanse her mind as well. There was too much there, too much for her to think about, to deal with. It was driving her mad.

Chetan had followed her home not leaving until she was safely inside Doug and Damon's secure house with the alarm armed once again. She had explored the house not leaving any door closed to her curious eyes. She had happily discovered the door that led down to the basement which had been turned into a state-of-the-art home gym. There was a treadmill, a stationary bike, a rowing machine and a cardio glide. There were free weights and benches, three different size medicine balls and even a dry heat sauna. But what caught and held Cass' attention were the punching bags and kickboxing dummy in one corner of the room.

She had shed her socks and shoes, taped up her hands and feet and went to work shedding her aggression and anger with hard punches and sharp kicks that had the dummy rocking. She spent forty-five minutes de-stressing and was dripping sweat by the time she stopped. After cleaning up the matted floor after her workout and hitting the lights, she climbed back up the stairs and realized she was down to only half an hour before Doug and Damon arrived.

She headed straight to the big bathroom in Doug's room and topped up the tub with water as hot as she could stand before stripping and taking her clothes back out to the hamper in Doug's bedroom. The water was high enough when she returned that she could start the jets and sink deep into the bubbling water. It was pure heaven after everything that had transpired since her return to Legacy to grab a few minutes of alone time and try and corral her thoughts.

She still hadn't come to any decisions when Doug and Damon entered the bathroom. She watched through half-closed eyes as they both shed their clothes and joined her in the big tub. Doug slipped behind her and settled her against his chest while Damon lounged in front of them running his toes up and down her legs as he looked at her.

"I've had a hard-on for two hours, sweetheart," Damon told her. She could feel Doug's impressive length against her back and wiggled closer to it.

"I'm happy for you," she told Damon and at Doug's dry chuckle added, "both of you."

"You know that you're going to have to pay for that little scene at the office, baby," Doug informed her as he bent to trail kisses along her slim neck exposed to him with her hair piled loosely on top of her head with a clip.

"Oh, no," she told him, "if anyone should be punished for that, it's you two." Cass turned and glared at him over her shoulder. "I was only making sure I kept you up to date on what was happening. Following the rules you two gave me."

Damon winced, "Sorry about that, sweetheart, neither of us thought to make sure that Tessa knew to put your calls straight through to us. She thought you were someone else and was trying to protect us."

"Protect you often, does she?" Cass asked with a bite to her voice.

"Careful, kitten," Doug nipped at her skin then laved it with his tongue, "your claws are showing."

"You believe in discipline right, Doug?" she asked him with a purr in her voice that had both men warily looking for a trap.

"Yes," Doug hedged, unsure of where she was going with this.

"I took my punishment like a good little girl, didn't I?" she asked him. "I didn't fight you or deny you."

"No, baby, you didn't," Doug answered her carefully.

"Why was I punished again?"

"You know why, baby," Doug told her. "You didn't do what you were supposed to. You made us worry when all you had to do was call and fill us in."

"Umm…" Cass murmured sliding her foot up and down the length of Damon's erection, "sort of like I tried to do today. Whose fault is it today, Doug? I tried to reach you and I couldn't," she pouted.

Damon groaned as she continued to stroke his cock with her foot and thrust it against her while he answered, "That was our fault, sweetheart. It won't happen again."

Cass leaned her head back and licked and sucked at Doug's neck while she slid one hand back between their bodies and stroked his cock with slow, teasing pulls making him groan and lean his head back against the edge of the tub. When she had him where she wanted him she moaned out, "You're going to take your punishment like a good little boy, aren't you, baby?"

"Yes, oh yes," Doug groaned oblivious to her words focused only on the hard slide of her hand along his cock.

Cass moved her feet so that Damon's cock was caught between them and whispered to him, "And you, Damon, going to take it like a man?"

"Fuck yeah, sweetheart, like a man," he groaned.

Cass moved her hand and feet away from her lovers' bodies and stood up letting the water sluice off her body back into the tub. "Good," she said stepping out and grabbing a towel off the heated shelf. "I'll be waiting for you in the bedroom." Her smile was so big that they both knew they were in trouble.

"What did we just agree to?" Damon asked Doug as they both stood and grabbed a towel.

"I have no idea," Doug answered him, "but I think we're in big trouble here, buddy."

Damon grinned and laughed.

"What the hell are you laughing at?" Doug demanded as he finished drying and wrapped the towel around his waist.

"Just wondering how Cass is going to punish you," Damon replied tongue in cheek. "I don't think you'll fit over her knees but I sure would like to see her spank your ass."

"You sick perv," Doug told him before adding as they headed to the bedroom where Cass was waiting, "Don't forget you'll get yours too."

"Shit," Damon said as they entered the bedroom and saw the ties Cass had laid out on the bed.

"Come on over here, big boys," Cass purred at them. "I'm ready to play."

Damon headed over first followed by a silently cursing Doug. Both men stopped in front of her and were startled when their submissive lover gave them a hard look and commanded, "Drop the towels." When they didn't immediately comply, she slapped a tie between her hands and told them, "Now!"

"Yes, ma'am," they replied and the towels hit the floor. Damon's eyes were twinkling merrily showing how much he was enjoying her little show but Doug's burned with a deeper darker lust letting her know that he would remember and repay her for everything. She was looking forward to it.

She turned to Damon first and made him walk around to the other side of the bed and lie down with his head down by the baseboard. She tied his hands together with one of the ties and used the loose end to bind his hands to the bottom bedpost on the far side stopping to bend down and reward him for his cooperation with a penetrating kiss stroking and sucking his tongue with hers.

When she turned back to Doug, he just looked at her and said, "You know that you're going to pay for this don't you, baby?"

She surprised him by pulling his head down and nipping at his full bottom lip whispering for his ears alone, " I'm counting on it, big boy."

Doug's eyes flared fire and he willingly let her position him at the top of the bed with his arms tied together and then bound to the bedpost at the headboard so that he lay next to Damon on the bed each facing in opposite directions. With a deep sigh of anticipation she walked back around the bed and crawled on top of Damon facing away from him rubbing her pussy on his hard belly. She leaned forward pressing her hips back until she bumped his chin with her dripping folds and took his cock into the lush heat of her mouth.

Damon groaned and bent his head up to lap and suck at her folds trying desperately to drive his tongue inside her tight pussy or to reach her engorged clit. The vixen who had taken over Cass' body wouldn't let him though pulling away from his mouth and saying "No, no, no," over her shoulder. She worked her pussy back down over his abdomen leaving a trail of juice behind stopping only when she felt the head of his cock lodge against her. She placed him between the folds of her sex and ground down against him making them both cry out with pleasure.

She reached forward and palmed Doug's huge erection in her hands swiping her thumb over the leaking tip and bringing it to her mouth sucking it clean while he watched her with hooded eyes. She leaned forward and took him in her mouth sucking and licking him but never giving him what she knew he wanted while she continued to rub on Damon's cock with her pussy.

"Fuck me, Cass," Damon told her, "put that sweet pussy on my cock and fuck me."

"Not yet," she moaned around the swollen head of Doug's cock. "You have to take your punishment first." With that she switched positions maneuvering her body so that she could grind along Doug's length while she fondled and sucked at Damon's pussy-coated cock. She reached a hand down and held the head of Doug's cock against her pulsing clit pleasuring herself, tormenting him. She licked and sucked the juice she had left behind on Damon keeping her eyes locked on his so he could see how much she was enjoying herself.

"When I get my hands untied, sweetheart, and believe me I will," Damon told her showing her the darker more dominant side that he usually kept under control letting Doug fulfill that role instead, "I'm going to shove my cock in your sweet little cunt and make you scream for it. And you're going to scream, sweetheart. You're going to beg for it."

His expression, his very words coupled with Doug's deep groan behind her sent her tumbling over the edge into orgasm. She could feel her juices spilling out of her pussy soaking Doug's cock and balls. She forced herself to pull away from them and leave the bed where she stood looking at them spreading her legs wide so they could see her gleaming slit. She took her breasts in her hands, kneading and pinching them tweaking the nipples to impossibly tight points before lifting one up and bending her head to suck the tight bud into her mouth making both men cry out and strain against their bonds.

Cass smiled at them and released the nipple with a loud pop before sucking the other one into her mouth. When both nipples were swollen and wet from her mouth she released her breasts and moved her hands slowly down her body until she reached the lips of her pussy. Using one hand she spread them wide opening herself so they could see as she used the other hand to rub across her puffed up clit pinching and rubbing the bud gritting her teeth at the pure pleasure that filled her. She moved the other hand down the slick lips of her pussy and dipped two fingers inside thrusting in tandem with the strokes against her clit bringing herself closer and closer toward orgasm.

Cass threw her head back forgetting her avidly watching audience and living in the moment each thrust of her fingers working her closer to peak until finally with a deep moan she pushed her way over the edge grabbing her orgasm and riding it with all she had. She never knew how they released their hands so quickly but before she could come down they were there turning her and guiding her until she was on her back on the bed and Damon was above her. He smiled down at her wickedly and then impaled her on his cock slamming into her like he had promised her. He rode her hard plunging his engorged rod violently in and out of her forcing her to take every inch he gave her.

Doug held her arms high above her head not allowing her to touch either of them or herself torturing her as she had tortured them. He bent his head forward and latched onto one of her nipples as Damon latched onto the other one. They both sucked greedily at her flesh punishing her with lips, teeth and tongue. Damon forced a hand between their bodies and pinched the tight bud of her clit pressing it hard between his thumb and forefinger sending her catapulting into another orgasm as he continued pounding into her. One, two, three more hard strokes and he cried out his own release spilling his seed in hot pulsing waves deep into her quivering womb. He leaned down and kissed her just as savagely as he had fucked her raping her mouth with his tongue leaving no part of her unclaimed by him before slowly moving off of her and collapsing beside her on the bed.

Doug moved between her still wide-spread thighs and eased his long thick cock into her still pulsing pussy. He made love to her with slow sweet strokes that soothed and pleasured her all at once. He kissed her gently licking at her lips until she opened for him rubbing his tongue along hers. The role reversal wasn't lost on Cass as the men let her see the other side to them. Damon, always the more calm and loving of the two, let her see that he could only be pushed so far before his dominance took over. And Doug always the dominant one was showing her that he could be soft and loving as well sharing with her a tenderness that made her weep.

"Don't cry, baby," Doug told her bending to lick the tears from her cheeks.

"I'm just so happy, Doug," Cass told him as Damon turned to his side and came up on his elbow beside them. "I just love you both so much. Don't ever leave me. Promise me that no matter what comes at us we'll work through it together."

"Always, baby," Doug assured her as he continued his slow easy strokes in and out of her pussy.

"Forever," Damon agreed as he leaned down to kiss her deeply.

Cass lifted her legs up and draped them over Doug's shoulders lifting her pelvis into his thrusts. "Fuck me, Doug. Fuck me," Cass begged him.

Doug was more than happy to do what she asked, immediately speeding up his thrusts pushing harder inside her tight pussy. Damon moved back placing one hand on her breast and tweaking her nipples and using his other to stroke his fully aroused cock while Doug rode her to orgasm. When they came it was together their cries filling the air as Doug spurted in her pussy and Damon rose to his knees and coated her breasts and face with his thick streams of seed.

Cass smiled up at her lovers covered and filled with their semen the scent of sex heavy in the air. "Whoever said three's a crowd definitely didn't have the right three," she told them with a purr making them both laugh and grin with pleasure.

Chapter Twelve

ᔕ

Thursday was Cass' day off normally but with Moira still on her honeymoon Cass was in the office at Knowledge Is Power doing paperwork and printing out the paychecks for the gym employees. It apparently being her lucky day she was cooped up in the office trying to concentrate with Shep and Griff in the room keeping watch over her.

"Would you two knock it off for a while please? I'm trying to concentrate here. If I mess payroll up I'm going to be really pissed," Cass told them growing frustrated at the way they seemed to pick at one another. She was almost ready to call them Felix and Oscar or maybe more appropriately Bert and Ernie. Cass grinned at that thought and gave a small snort or amusement.

"What's so funny?" Griff asked her from his sprawled position in the chair across the desk.

"Nothing." Cass smiled at him and batted her eyelashes. "Just something funny I thought of."

"Want to share?" Griff asked her.

"I don't like to share," Cass told him.

"So the possessive type huh?" Griff kept the conversation going.

Cass thought about that for a moment before answering. "Yes, I guess I am with Doug and Damon," she finally said.

"So you like two guys at once," Griff asked her, "feels pretty good what with women having multiple orgasms and all that?"

Shep choked on laughter while Cass just raised a brow at Griff. "Thinking of trying two men at once, big boy? I'm sure you'll like it."

Griff turned purple and jumped to his feet. "Christ no! I was just wondering if women really enjoyed having sex with two men at the same time, that's all."

"Come on, sugar," Shep cooed, "don't be shy now. You can tell us."

"What is it with the new women in this family trying to turn one of the Daniels boys gay?" Griff muttered.

"Who else tried to say you were gay?" Cass questioned him, eyes wide with curiosity.

"Not me!" Griff defended with a huff. "Moira thought that Doug and Damon were gay."

Cass went off into peals of laughter at the thought of those two having sex with each other. She couldn't see either man agreeing to be on the receiving end. Literally. That made her laugh even harder. Shep and Griff were chuckling as well though more from watching her than from any thoughts of Doug and Damon.

"So," Shep finally said bringing up something that had been on his mind. "I hear you ran into an old buddy of mine from the Rangers yesterday."

Cass looked at Shep and shook her head. "I didn't meet anyone yesterday. I went straight home after seeing Doug and Damon and talking to their secretary."

"Yeah, my buddy was in a meeting with Damon when you walked in, about a project he's working on with them. He's a landscape designer and just moved here. His name is Tyler Andrews." At her questioning look he went on, "About six foot two, brown wavy hair and brown eyes, the one standing right next to Damon."

"Oh, God, I remember him vaguely but I was pretty angry at the time so I honestly wasn't paying much attention to anyone else at the time," Cass admitted with a groan. "What did he say about me?"

Shep grinned making Cass cringe instinctively. "He said you were one hot woman and incredibly sexy with the temper in your eyes. Called me last night and asked where he could find one just like you."

"Oh my God," Cass exclaimed, "he did not."

"I invited him to come take a look at the gym today knowing that you would feel the need to personally show him around and apologize for yesterday," Shep told her with mischief written all over his face.

"You are such a shit, Shep," Cass told him making Griff laugh and causing Shep's eyes to twinkle.

"Just looking out for you, babe," Shep assured her, "We wouldn't want anyone to think rudely of you or anything. I mean you didn't even acknowledge the man's existence."

Cass groaned and lowered her head to lie on her arms on top of the desk. "One day, Shep, some woman's going to put you through the wringer and I'm going to enjoy every moment of it."

"Never going to happen," Shep told her.

Cass looked up and smiled at him, "Oh, will you be a delight to see fall."

Just then there was a knock at the door and Katie opened the door and stuck her head in glancing around before her eyes landed on Cass. "Got a minute?" she asked her.

"Sure," Cass said, "come on in. I'm just finishing up payroll," she said as she glanced back at the computer screen before hitting print. "What's on your mind?"

"Moira and Gil will be back tomorrow and I was hoping maybe you would be willing to go over to their apartment with me and fix it up a little bit. Just a little cleaning to get rid of any dust and I have a couple of other things in mind," Katie told her.

"Oh, wow," Cass shook her head. "I should have thought of that. I would love to go over and get things ready for them with you. What time do you want to head out?"

"I'll be done here at three for the day," Katie filled her in. "Do you still have a key or should I call Jack?"

"I have a key and Howie is still at the security desk in the lobby of the apartment complex so we shouldn't have any problems." She looked over to Shep, "Is Jack there today or out and about?"

"Don't know," Shep told her. "Jack is Jack and goes where he wants without informing the little people. I know he was supposed to have lunch with some woman named Michelle today. She's been calling trying to catch him."

Katie gasped and everyone turned to look at her.

"Do you know something I don't?" Shep asked her.

"Lots I'm sure," she replied dryly making Griff and Cass laugh and Shep grin. She turned to walk out of the office and threw over her shoulder to Cass, "I'll meet you here at three and we can head over then if that's all right."

"That's great, Katie," Cass said. "Bert and Ernie here will be with me," Cass nodded at Shep and Griff.

Katie grinned and turned back around to look at her brother, "Wow, Griff, and to think that I never even suspected."

"Suspected what?" Griff asked but Shep just laughed and shook his head.

"That you were gay," Katie tossed before turning and leaving the room shutting the door behind her. They could hear her laughing as she went down the hall.

"Christ," he glared at Cass, "For the last time, woman, I'm not gay."

"Bert and Ernie are best friends on a kids' show, Griff. What's wrong with you? Why would you even think something like that? It's a kids' show!" She shook her head at

138

him and murmured just loud enough for everyone to hear, "Dirty minds."

"I didn't...I wouldn't...oh hell," Griff stammered. "Obviously I should try to be more sexually aggressive like my brothers."

"Yes," Cass replied her voice sugary sweet, "I mean no one thinks they're gay or anything."

They all started laughing again at that. She couldn't wait to talk to Moira again. She hadn't realized how much she had missed her best friend until Katie had reminded her that Moira and Gil would be back from their honeymoon tomorrow. Moira would help her make sense of the chaos in her head. If there was one thing that she knew she could count on it was that Moira would always tell her exactly what she thought.

Three o'clock was there before Cass realized it and she and Katie headed out with Shep and Griff for the party store by the mall to pick up a few things to take back to Moira and Gil's. Katie wanted to decorate with a few things and figured the party store was her best bet. Then they were going to stop at a few places in the mall. They had kept things pretty tame at the reception and were planning to make up for it now.

Cass and Katie rode in the back of Griff's car while Shep rode shotgun. They chatted about everyday things on the trip over. When they got there Katie latched onto Cass' arm and pulled her away from the men to look at the opposite side of the store. They stood looking at different colored streamers and balloons and Cass waited for whatever Katie had on her mind.

"So, you and Doug," Katie finally said.

"And Damon," Cass added not ashamed of her love for the two men.

"And Damon," Katie agreed. "How...are...well..."

Cass grinned at her, "Are you asking me what it's like to be with two men at the same time, Katie?"

Katie blushed red and hurriedly grabbed a couple of rolls of red and white streamers. "I guess," she mumbled.

"It's incredible," Cass told her. "The best part of all is knowing that they both love me and want to be with only me. But I'd be lying if I said that the sex didn't matter. Sex with them is..." she stopped, struggling to think of a word to describe what she felt with them but couldn't. "It's hard to describe. It's like nothing I've ever known before. It's like a delicious chocolate-covered caramel," Cass said her eyes shut an expression of pure ecstasy on her face, "rich, creamy, decadent and impossible to think of without blending the two flavors together." Cass licked her lips and sighed slowly opening her eyes to see Katie gaping at her. "What?"

Katie finally snapped out of it and giggled. "I'll never look at chocolate-covered caramels the same way again."

Cass grinned and laughed. "Come to think of it neither will I."

"You said that they love you," Katie said as they went through the store adding red and white balloons and a big Welcome Home banner to their pile. "How do you feel about them?"

"I love them," Cass confessed then looked at Katie. "If I tell you something, can you promise to not tell anyone else?"

Katie thought of all the secrets she knew and almost laughed. "Yeah," she assured Cass, "I can keep a secret."

"Doug asked me to marry them," Cass told her.

"Oh, my God," Katie beamed at her. "I knew it. I just knew it. So when?"

"I haven't answered him yet," Cass said.

"What? But you all love each other," Katie said as if love was the answer to everything. Unfortunately for Cass it was a little more complicated than that.

"I'd have to choose between them, Katie," Cass pleaded with Katie to understand something that she was struggling to deal with. "Legally I would only be allowed to marry one of them and take his name. I can't do that. No, I refuse to do that. I won't choose one over the other. I love them both."

"Lord," Katie told her shaking her head. "I hadn't thought of it that way and I bet neither have they. Did you tell them how you feel?"

"No," Cass said. "I've just been kind of ignoring the entire subject."

"Just talk to them," Katie urged her. "Maybe you can all come up with something together."

"You're right." Cass smiled at her. "I should have done that to begin with.

"Good," Katie said turning back to the front of the store. "Let's take care of this and head out."

"Did you see the adult toy store next door?" Cass asked her and Katie nodded. "Let's go in there for a minute. I have a few ideas of party supplies of my own."

Cass and Katie grinned at each other and standing arm in arm went to buy more supplies.

* * * * *

The apartment was clean and beautifully decorated. The front room was tastefully done with the red and white streamers and balloons and the Welcome Home banner. The bedroom was another story. Cass had bought a round Plexiglas mirror to mount on the ceiling above the bed and Shep and Griff had happily put it up for her. She and Katie had purchased red satin sheets and comforter that they had cleaned and put on the bed. Cass had purchased a red peek-a-boo bra and crotchless panty combo with attached garter belt and red stockings for Moira and one for herself as well in dark blue. They had bought Gil a matching pair of red silk boxers after Shep and Griff had laughed so hard at the men's thong they had picked out.

On the bedside table was a jar of chocolate body butter and on the dresser was a supply of body paints and brushes, flavored body oils and a pair of fur-lined handcuffs that Katie had insisted they get. Cass would have to ask Moira about that one because Katie wasn't talking.

Cass had made a few other purchases for herself and her men as well. She had bought both Doug and Damon a pair of silk boxers, Doug in dark blue and Damon in light blue. Then she had bought two pairs of fur-lined handcuffs and two blindfolds. Shep had quirked an eyebrow at that but thankfully not commented on it. Katie had laughed uproariously when Cass added a tub of chocolate caramel body butter to her purchases then winked and picked one up to add to her own overflowing basket of personal purchases as well making Cass laugh.

Now Cass and Katie sat on the sofa in the living room waiting for Shep and Griff to come back up. Both men had left earlier after Shep got a call on his cell, leaving both women safely locked inside the apartment. Cass had taken advantage and gone to the restroom to take a quick shower and change putting on her new dark blue underwear set and a blue sundress she still had in the closet in her old room. The dress had short cap sleeves but she had a white cardigan sweater in the coat closet so she was set having found a pair of white heels on the shelf in her closet as well.

Cass had poured them each a diet soda from the fridge and they had sat and chatted some more before turning on the television and watching a late afternoon talk show. The show was just starting to get interesting when there was a knock on the door and Cass jumped up to answer it.

Ben stood there. "I hear my wife is here causing trouble," he said entering the apartment and going straight to Katie who jumped up and threw herself into his arms.

Their kiss was carnal and sensual and Cass wondered if that was what people thought when they saw her and Doug or Damon kissing. Cass discreetly cleared her throat, "I'm going to head on into the kitchen and get a fresh drink if anyone's interested."

Ben pulled slowly back from his wife's lush lips nibbling down her throat as she arched against him with a low moan. "So I guess you missed me today," he whispered to her.

"I always miss you," Katie told him enjoying the feel of his teeth and tongue on her neck and earlobe.

"So Griff said you bought some interesting things at the naughty store," Ben told her. "And he blushed." He wiggled his brows at her and Katie laughed. "So what did you get, sugar?"

"Surprises," Katie told him but gave in with a laugh when he pouted his lip out at her and batted his eyelashes. "I thought maybe we could play cop again," she told him with a sly slant of her eyes.

"Umm…" Ben groaned. She was reminding him of the time they had stopped at a rest stop and done just that. "I make a great cop."

Katie pouted up at him and said, "That's too bad. I bought this little cop outfit at the store so that I could be cop this time. It came with a hat and cuffs too."

Ben's eyes glazed over with lust. He looked around to make sure that they were still alone before demanding, "Show it to me."

Katie slipped out of his arms and retrieved her bag from beside the sofa sorting through it for what she wanted. Finally she held up a skimpy light blue top that would barely cover her breasts with a badge on the left pocket. The bottoms were even better, a tiny navy blue skirt that might cover the cheeks of her ass. She pulled the hat out and set it on her head a very good likeness to the old dress hats. Finally she dangled the cuffs from her fingers and grinned at him. "What do you say? Want to play with me?"

"Oh, yeah," Ben told her gesturing her attention down to the very prominent erection straining against his zipper. "I definitely want to play."

Katie giggled and put her things back in her bag. "Let's go then."

Ben swept his wife close for another hard kiss before hollering at Cass, "We're heading out, Cass. You okay by yourself?"

Cass poked her head out of the kitchen cautiously before entering the room. "Let's see. Griff and Shep are here. Howie is still at the desk. And Jack is downstairs as well," she said before shaking her head sadly and telling them, "No, maybe you both better stay and keep me company."

Katie giggled again and Cass grinned at her. "Go ahead. You two have fun," she added making Katie giggle again and Ben flush red.

Cass locked the door after them and sat back down on the couch waiting for...just waiting. She flipped through the channels searching aimlessly for something to watch but truth to tell she had never been much for television anyway. She had just walked over to the bookshelf to look for something to read when the phone rang. It was Kat from the gym.

"Hey, I'm glad I caught you," Kat told her. "We just got a call from some woman who sounded frantic to reach you. She said that she was from Daniels Construction and that there had been some kind of accident there with Doug and Damon and..." Kat continued on but Cass didn't hear the rest. Dropping the phone she opened the kitchen drawer where Moira had always kept a spare set of keys to her car and thankfully some things hadn't changed. Cass flew out of the apartment, , cell phone glued to her ear, barely taking time to yell to Howie where she was going before she was out the door and gone. She prayed that one of her lovers would answer the phone and reassure her that they were both all right. What would she do without them?

Howie cursed under his breath and paged Shep to the desk hoping that he wouldn't take to long to answer, hoping that Jack didn't kill him.

* * * * *

Tessa finished up at her desk still in the office long after Doug and Damon had both left for the day. She was tired of the pats on the head like she was an obedient pet instead of a full-grown woman. She was tired of blending in and being way too convenient. She was tired of a lot of things. Tessa was ready to make a statement, a big one. She was going to shake things up but good once and for all. She picked up the phone and placed the most important call of her life.

* * * * *

Cass threw gravel as she slammed to a stop in front of the trailer at the housing Duplex that Doug and Damon were working at. Tessa's car was still in the lot and she hurried toward the trailer to find out what Tess could tell her about where Doug and Damon were, who was hurt, and how serious it was. She opened the door her heart in her throat as she thought of something happening to Doug or Damon. She never saw who hit her before she crumpled to the carpeted floor knocked out cold.

Chapter Thirteen

ഇ

"What do you mean she just left?" Shep snapped at Howie. "Did she say where she was headed? How the hell did she get a car?" Shep was furious, at Howie, at himself.

"She probably found the keys to Moira's car. Moira keeps it parked in the lot across the street." Howie tried to defend himself. "She said something about Daniels Construction and an accident."

"Accident," Griff jerked his cell phone out to call Doug. "Shit..." he mumbled as the phone rang and rang, "Answer the damn phone."

His call went to voicemail and he left his brother a terse message, "You better not be dead, bro, or I'm going to kill you. If you get this message call me. Cass is on her way to the construction site. Someone told her there was an accident." He flipped the phone shut and headed to the door. "I know where she's heading," he tossed to Shep. "Let's go."

They hurried out to Griff's car hoping for the best but they both had a bad feeling.

* * * * *

Doug felt his phone vibrate but when he saw his younger brother's name he decided to let it go to voicemail. He and Damon were in the middle of a meeting with the powers that be for their next project. It seemed that the gentlemen had a very specific idea of what they wanted in design and layout and wanted to make sure that Daniels Construction could handle it. Doug groaned as he listened to Damon try to tell them that there would have to be a few changes or they would have trouble with overloading the electrical circuits in a few of

146

the rooms. They wanted too much equipment available in one little room and Damon was doing his best to tell them the room would either have to be bigger or they were going to have to spread the materials out to at least two different rooms.

It looked to be a long night.

* * * * *

When Cass woke up, she found herself tied to a chair her arms bound so tightly behind her that her hands were numb and her shoulders were screaming in agony. She had no idea how long she had been there or even where she was. She blinked her eyes several times trying to focus on what was around her. The room she was tied up in was not finished, the walls open so that she could see the wiring. So she was in one of the houses being built in the addition by Daniels Construction unless whoever had her had taken her somewhere else.

As her eyes began to clear she noticed two things. One was that her head was pounding, probably from where she had been hit. The other was that there was someone lying on the floor a few feet away and if she wasn't mistaken it looked a lot like Doug and Damon's secretary Tessa Sharp.

"Tessa," Cass whispered hoping to wake the girl on the floor. "Tessa wake up."

'Tessa won't be waking up any time soon," a voice said from the shadowed corner of the room sending chills of fear down Cass' spine. "Tessa won't be waking up at all," the voice said and laughed.

Cass looked back at Tessa and for the first time noticed the odd angle of the girl's neck. It was broken. Sweet Lord, Cass thought, who could have killed Tessa and why?

"Why Tessa?" she asked hoping to make the voice step farther into the room so that she could see exactly what she was dealing with. "What did she do to you?"

"She figured out who I was," said a woman as she finally stepped out where Cass could see her. Her hair was a wild tangled mass of red curls that fell to her shoulders. She was maybe five foot nine and with the gun she was holding in her hand terrifying.

"Who are you?" Cass asked her trying to come up with some way to get herself out of this mess. Surely Shep and Griff would follow her when Howie told them she was gone as she knew Howie would. Depending on where the woman had taken her surely help would come if she could just keep her talking long enough. "Why are you so upset with me? It is you, isn't it? The letters, my car, the attempted hit and run? It was you, wasn't it?"

"Yes," the woman screamed at her, her face flushing dark red with rage as she stomped toward Cass. "You whore. Nothing but a whore. Just like all the others. But he's mine." She screamed this in Cass' face spraying her with spittle as she raged at her. "Mine! And I'm done sharing him with anyone."

"Are you Nikki?" Cass asked remembering the name of the woman Katie had told her about, the woman they thought had broken in to Doug and Damon's house.

"Ahh…Nikki Damato," the woman said. "She was so easy. So naïve." The look in her eyes let Cass know in no uncertain terms that this was a person with one too many screws loose. Cass was in big trouble and it looked like she was on her own. The woman looked at Cass her eyes glazed with insanity. "I killed her, you know. They'll never find her body." Her laugh was a high-pitched girlish giggle and all the more chilling for that fact. "No one even suspects it's me," she continued seemingly lost in her own world, which was just fine with Cass. "He came home for the funeral but everything was different then. He wasn't mine anymore. But that was okay, I would have shared. They like to share," she whispered to Cass.

"Sheila," Cass whispered recalling Damon telling her about the little girl in his foster family who had fancied herself

148

in love with him. It didn't look like Shelia had ever grown out of that notion.

The woman snapped back into the present and glared at Cass, "How do you know who I am? You're not supposed to know," she told her sounding like a petulant child who had just had her big surprise spoiled.

Cass thought she heard a noise and prayed hard that help was finally here while she scrambled for something to say. "Damon told me all about you," she told Sheila.

"He did?" Sheila asked her face softening in a real smile for the first time since Cass had seen her. It made her look so young and innocent, so child-like, except for the shiny metal of the gun she held in her hand.

"Yes," Cass said shaking her head, "he is so proud of you. He couldn't say enough about you."

Now Sheila looked doubtful and demanded of Cass, "What did he say?"

"That you were a great girl and that he missed you and hoped to see you again soon," Cass said praying Sheila would buy it.

Sheila screamed and pulled at her own hair. "You lying whore! Nothing but lies! He doesn't want anything to do with me. He quit writing to me and calling me when Daddy told him I was going insane. Like my mother, Daddy said. Crazy! It was the last thing he ever said." She turned wild eyes to Cass waving the gun in her hand, "Do I look crazy to you?"

There was no way that Cass could truthfully answer that because Sheila looked crazy as hell and Cass didn't want to get shot any time soon. She had seen Shep slipping in out of the corner of her eye when Sheila was in full rant and knew that Griff was somewhere nearby. All she had to do was keep Sheila's attention focused on her and give them a little more time.

"No, of course not," Cass told the crazy bitch. "What do men know anyway? Why would your dad say something so awful about you and your mom?"

Sheila giggled again leaning close and whispering to Cass, "Oh she was crazy my mother was. Heard voices in her head all the time," she told her in a singsong voice. "She killed herself. The voices must have been mad at her," she said and giggled again.

"But not you," Cass told her praying the guys made their move soon.

"No my voices don't want me dead," Sheila said turning and pointing the gun at Cass' chest. "They want you dead."

Griff jumped into the room and hollered causing Sheila to jerk the gun up and fire just as Shep tackled her from behind.

Cass screamed expecting to feel the bullet lodge somewhere in her body but felt hands behind her instead untying her bound hands and releasing them. She moaned as fire shot through her fingers as nerves sprang to life and her shoulders protested with a sharp pain when she moved her hands in front of her to clap and shake the feeling back in faster.

Shep was having trouble with the hellcat redhead and finally hit her on the jaw with his fist knocking her out. He bent down and whispered in her ear, "Sorry, sweetheart, the voices told me to." He quickly stood up and went over to Cass.

"You okay?" he asked her, his hands automatically running over her and checking for breaks or bullet holes.

Cass fell into his arms taking them both to the floor. "Thank you! Thank you! Thank you for getting here in time." She shuddered at what might have happened if they hadn't made it, if she had been on her own. She looked around for a minute searching for Griff and finally saw him on the floor behind the chair. "Griff, you all right?" she asked as she crawled over to him still too shaky to even try to stand up.

Griff moaned. Cass knelt beside him and cried out when she saw the blood soaking through his shirt. "The crazy bitch shot me," he mumbled. "I really liked this shirt."

Cass searched frantically and finally ripped her dress to get something to hold against his wound to try and stop the blood. She leaned over Griff her breasts flush against his face as she pushed down on his shoulder. Griff turned his head and she almost thought he was nuzzling against her breasts but when she glanced at him he moaned in pain and whimpered, "It hurts."

Shep grinned as he watched Griff milking the situation while Shep called 9-1-1 for an ambulance. Griff rubbed his mouth back and forth against Cass' chest, opening wide and leaning up to moan convincingly around one of her nipples. When Cass found out what he was doing she was going to kill him.

Shep frowned as he noticed the amount of blood Griff was losing. He walked over and handed his phone to Cass where the 9-1-1 operator was still on the line waiting with them for help to arrive. He squatted down by Griff and gingerly moved the makeshift bandage aside to get a better look at where the bullet had hit. Griff groaned as Shep moved him around. The bullet had hit high on his shoulder and was a through and through so the only thing Shep could come up with was that a blood vessel or vein had been nicked or Griff was just a bleeder. Either way after Shep's years in the Rangers and playing medic for Jack's crew on some of their jobs he knew Griff would live.

Cass saw the grin twitching his lips and demanded, "What is it? Is he all right? Please, Shep, tell me that he's going to be all right!"

Griff nuzzled her nipple and mumbled around it. "I'm dying, beautiful. Kiss me?" he asked.

Cass looked down at Griff where he was way too close to her nipple and then glanced up to see the huge grin on Shep's face. "What?" she demanded.

Shep laughed and said, "He'll be fine, Cass."

Cass glared down at Griff ready to yell at him for scaring her but Griff's eyes were closed and his lips were actually still. "Oh, my God! Shep, what's wrong with him?"

Shep leaned over and looked to make sure Griff wasn't just playing possum to get away from Cass and shook his head. "He's passed out."

"I thought you said he'd be fine," Cass reminded him.

"He will be," Shep grunted. "Trust me, I've seen worse." Shep shook his head with disgust and grinned, "Stupid wuss passed out from a little shoulder wound. I can't wait to razz him about this."

"That's not very nice, Shep. He took that bullet for me," she told him, her voice echoing with her guilt.

"And you paid him for it, darling, believe me," Shep said.

"What do you mean?" Cass asked him.

"Hell you held him and let him nuzzle all over your nipples, didn't you?" Shep laughed at her expression.

"He wasn't… I didn't…" Cass tried to stutter out before glaring down at the unconscious Griff. "Why you little rat!" she said but Shep could hear the relief in her voice.

They could hear the sirens getting closer when Griff's cell phone suddenly starting ringing. Cass grabbed it, opened it and pushed the talk button when she saw Doug's name on the caller ID. "Doug," she sobbed everything getting to her.

"Cass," Doug asked. "Where are you? Where's Griff? I missed his call earlier and wanted to see what he wanted. What's the matter, baby?"

But Cass was finally falling apart so Shep eased his arm around her and took the phone just in time to have Doug yell in his ear. "Calm down, buddy. Everything's fine now. Didn't you get Griff's voicemail?"

"No, I just called him back first," Doug snapped out. "Now what the hell is going on? Where are you guys?"

"We're in the last house on Cliff Road," Shep told him.

"Cliff Road," Doug repeated. "That's where we're working. What the hell are you doing there?"

"It's a long story," Shep sighed as Cass' tears started to wind down. "Just get here. I'll explain it all then. The ambulance is here so I need to go."

"What ambulance? Who?" Doug demanded answers but Shep had already hung up.

"I don't know," Doug said. "Shep said the ambulance was there but he didn't tell me who was hurt."

"Toss me your phone," Damon said and Doug flipped it to him with a questioning look. "I'll check voicemail and see if that tells us anything more. You just drive and get us there as fast as you can."

They arrived just in time to see the ambulance pull away lights flashing and siren screaming. Shep was standing there with his arm around Cass. As they got closer they could see the blood on her. Doug let out a roar and ran to her with Damon mere inches behind. They pulled her into their arms and ran their hands over her checking for where the blood was coming from. Police were coming in and out of the house and Damon gasped when he saw Sheila led out in handcuffs.

"What the hell?" he breathed out.

"She tried to kill me," Cass whispered grabbing his hands and pulling him firmly against her somehow knowing that he would need to hold her when she told him what all had happened. "She was the one. The car, the letters, everything was her."

"Sweet Lord," Doug muttered. "We knew she wasn't all there but I thought you said Mark put her in a facility?" Doug asked the last to a shell-shocked Damon.

"He did," Damon murmured clasping Cass to his body needing to know that she was all right.

"I think she killed him," Cass said. "She killed Tessa Sharp too."

153

"Tessa," both men exclaimed.

"Why Tessa?" Damon asked.

"She said that Tessa figured out it was her and that she was going to tell. I don't know whether that's true or not," Cass confided to them in a shaky voice. "She's not all there. She killed Nikki too. She said that you both belonged to her and she wasn't sharing anymore." There was no way that she would ever tell Damon that Sheila had meant him and not both of them. She could already see the guilt on his face and she would not add to it no matter what.

"All of this," Damon whispered, "because of me."

"No," Cass shook her head vehemently in protest. "You didn't know. She wasn't all there, Damon. There was no way that you could have known."

"She's right," Doug agreed from his position flush against Cass' back. "As far as we knew, Sheila was in a mental hospital."

Damon closed his eyes and gritted his teeth. He had almost lost the one woman he would ever love because of the girl he had once seen as a sister. He looked down at Cass and ran his fingers down her tear-streaked cheeks. "Where did she hurt you, baby? What did she do?"

"I'm fine," Cass assured him leaning back to include Doug as well. "I have a little bump on my head and some chafing and bruising on my wrists where she tied me up but other than that I'm okay."

Both men lifted her hands each pulling one to his mouth and placing kisses on her abused wrists. "The blood," Doug asked, "where is all the blood from?"

"It's not mine," she whispered turning to Doug. "The ambulance. She shot Griff, Doug. She shot Griff."

"Flesh wound," Shep said before Doug and Damon got too excited. "He'll be fine. You might want to have people head to the hospital though. I'm sure he'll expect everyone to be there." Shep's lips twitched again as he remembered the way that Griff had worked Cass for sympathy before he passed out.

"I'll call Ben," Damon said. "He and Katie can swing by and pick up your mom on their way to the hospital. Find a cop and see if we can leave with Cass." Neither man would leave without her.

Doug turned and waved to one of the officers. He wasn't surprised to see Officer Teddy Simons come over.

"You okay?" Teddy asked Cass his voice soothing like deep, dark hot chocolate.

"Fine." Cass looked up at Doug and over to where Damon stood on the phone. "Now."

"We need to go to the hospital," Doug told him. "My brother Griff was shot. I'd like to get there and see what's going on with him."

"No problem," Teddy told him glancing at Shep. "You going to stay?" he asked and Shep shook his head knowing that someone had to. "Go on to the hospital then," Teddy told Doug. "I'll let Detective Tate know that's where you are when he gets here. He can talk to you there just as easily."

"Thanks," Doug told the police officer knowing that he owed his brother Gil for this favor he'd been granted. Cops tended to take care of their own and Doug didn't doubt for a moment that they wouldn't have been allowed to leave if Gil wasn't a cop. Gil! What a mess his brother was going to come home from his honeymoon to find. Of course knowing Gil he would be sorry that he'd missed all the excitement. Then again he had just spent a week in total seclusion with his hot wife so he wouldn't be too disappointed.

Doug took Cass into the office so that she could use the bathroom to clean up a little bit. The blood on her dress would just have to stay for now but at least she was able to clean it off her hands and arms. Even covered with his brother's blood she was the most beautiful woman in the world to him and the thought that he could have lost her terrified him. She met his eyes in the mirror and smiled at him, her love for him showing on her face. Tonight he would ask her again to marry him and Damon and this time he would make her answer them.

"Hey, Doug," Damon called walking to the open door of the bathroom, "take a look at this." He held up a typed sheet of paper for Doug to see.

Doug took it from him and skimmed it, shook his head and read it through more closely.

"What is it?" Cass asked them.

"Tessa's resignation," Damon told her. "She wanted to find some fun and adventure while she still could."

"I wish she had left sooner," Doug murmured.

"Me too," Doug agreed.

By the time they arrived at the hospital Ben was already there with Katie and Catherine. Jack, Chetan and Roman were there as well and Doug figured Shep must have called them. Doug immediately went to his mother wrapping her in his arms and holding her close. Cass felt Damon grab her hand and looked up at him drowning under the weight of her own guilt as she looked at Catherine knowing that she, Cass, was the one responsible for Griff being shot.

"She won't blame you," Damon whispered to her pulling her close and giving her a soft kiss on the lips. "No one blames you for this."

"No one blames you either," Cass told him. "If you promise not to feel guilty then neither will I," she assured him.

"It's a deal," Damon told her giving her another soft kiss on the lips but they both knew that their respective guilt would take longer to go.

Cass felt a hand on her shoulder and turned to find herself wrapped in Catherine's arms. "I'm so glad that you're okay," Catherine told her giving her a squeeze.

"I'm so sorry," Cass said to her.

"For what?" Catherine asked.

"Griff took a bullet that was meant for me," Cass told her. "If not for me he wouldn't have been shot."

Catherine smiled and patted her cheek. "Sounds more to me like if not for Griff you might not be here at all which would have killed Doug and Damon as well. Besides, like I told Doug, the doctor has already been in to assure us that Griff will be fine. They'll patch him up and keep him overnight but thank God the bullet went straight through his shoulder."

"But all that blood?" Cass asked.

"According to the doctor it was normal," Catherine assured Cass. "Griff is young and healthy and he'll be fine. If I know my son he'll milk this for all it's worth though so prepare yourself."

Cass laughed and said without thinking, "Oh, he's already played me."

"What did he do?" Doug asked as he pulled Cass from his mother into his arms.

Cass flushed red as she noticed everyone looking at her and scrambled for something she could say. Shep made her want to fall through the floor when he responded from behind her.

"He nuzzled up real close and personal while she leaned over him trying to stop the bleeding. That boy's good," he told them as he walked over to join Jack. "She didn't even have a clue what he was doing. Christ," he laughed, "he had her convinced he was dying before he passed out."

"He passed out?" Roman asked.

"Wuss," Chetan said with a tiny grin.

Cass could feel herself growing redder as all the men looked at her. She felt like they all knew exactly where Griff had been nuzzling. Doug and Damon held her between them letting her burrow into them obviously happy that it didn't bother her that everyone knew that the three of them were together. She knew they would hold her for as long as she needed as closely as she needed. They would never let her go.

Chapter Fourteen

❧

Cass was never so glad to be home and she had most definitely come to realize that this was home here in the house that Doug and Damon had designed and built. Doug carried her into the house and headed straight to the bedroom setting her tenderly on the side of the bed while Damon watched with hooded eyes from the doorway. She knew what they needed—what she needed—a way to reaffirm that everyone was fine. And she knew just how to initiate it.

Cass stood and turned her back to Doug. "Can you unzip this for me?" she asked him lifting her hair out of the way to help him. "I'll be happy to throw this dress in the trash and never see it again."

She heard them both catch their breaths as the dress slid down her body and pooled around her feet on the floor. She kicked it away lifting her hands to drop the ties that held the cups up on the peek-a-boo bra and exposing her erect nipples before turning to give them the full view of the dark blue underwear she had bought at the naughty store.

When she turned Damon was already beside Doug and both men reached out to stroke a finger across one of her nipples while they eyed her from head to toe.

"What's this you're almost wearing, sweetheart?" Damon asked her his voice husky with desire.

"A little something I picked up earlier just for you two," she whispered, her own voice a husky purr. "I was hoping that you would like it."

"Oh we like it," Doug answered for both of them reaching down to lower his zipper and release his bulging cock from his now too tight jeans. "You look beautiful, baby."

"It gets better," she told them with a wicked grin before she turned around and bent over the bed giving them an eyeful of pussy revealed in all its pink glory in the crotchless underwear.

"Oh, baby," she heard Doug groan as Damon whispered an awed, "Beautiful."

Hands touched her, fingers stroking her wet folds before slipping inside the hot velvet of her tight pussy. Another finger joined the first two and she knew that both men were pushing into her flesh sharing her pussy. A finger brushed across the swollen nub of her clit and Cass arched her back and cried out. She looked over her shoulder and caught her breath as she watched both men sliding their hands up and down their cocks while they played with her pussy.

"Love me," she asked them, her heart in her eyes, "Love me."

The hands moved away working buttons and snaps and zippers as they stripped for her and joined her on the bed. They pushed her back on the bed and took up positions on either side of her. Damon bent and tasted her lips first, kissing her with a slow soft tenderness that expressed better than words how much she meant to him, how much he loved her. When he finally lifted his head Doug was there plunging his tongue violently in her mouth filling her with his passion relaying his fear and need for her all at once. Gradually he settled into the kiss, slowing, calming his strokes of tongue and teeth, gentling as she met him need for need.

Damon moved to her nipple sucking and laving it with his tongue, nipping it with his teeth before sucking her fully into his mouth. Cass cried out and Doug moved down to her other nipple bathing it with the same treatment. Cass placed a hand on the back of each of their heads holding them tightly to her breasts wanting them to stay there forever.

Fingers slipped down her belly two hands making their way to the promised land. One stopped and plied her clit between thumb and finger while the other moved lower sending two fingers straight into her pulsing channel fucking her and driving her wild. It was too much for Cass to take. She slammed into orgasm drunk with love and lust gasping for breath as the fingers continued torturing her pushing her higher and higher.

Before she came down Doug was between her spread thighs pressing his cock home inside the wet heat of her pussy. He fucked her with a desperation that made her want to cry his eyes bright with a need to have her, to become a part of her, to never leave her. Cass lifted her legs and bending her knees wrapped them high around his back lifting her pelvis higher into his driving thrusts. "Harder," she moaned as she felt Doug hammering into her. "Faster," she cried though she knew he couldn't. She held him when he came, his orgasm filling her with him; his cum, his sweat, his very soul. She held him till the shaking stopped for both of them and he finally kissed her softly and moved away to lie on his side next to her refusing to release her completely from his touch. He smiled and ran his fingers softly over the curve of her shoulder and along her throat.

Damon slid between her thighs and entered her with a solid thrust home. He wasn't as hard with her, as demanding with his body but his need was just as strong, his fear just as easy to see. She rose into him meeting him stroke for stroke showing her love in the sweet giving of her body the warmth in her eyes that for the moment was only for him. He slammed inside her forcing his cock as deep as it would go and held it there letting her body milk him of his seed as she reached her own orgasm. He collapsed beside her on her opposite side. They held her between them stroking her body with gentle caresses soothing her after the turbulent love they had shared.

"I love you," Doug told her, "with my body, my heart, my very soul. I can't breathe without you anymore, baby. I can't live. Not without you."

"I love you too," Damon whispered at her other side. "You have all of me, everything I am. I died a thousand deaths when I thought you might be hurt or injured. I couldn't get to you fast enough. I need you like water."

"You have to marry us, Cass," Doug told her and Damon nodded his agreement.

"There is no us without you, sweetheart," Damon added his own words to Doug's. "You have to marry us."

"I can't," Cass told them not wanting to hurt them but seeing it on both of their faces before she could continue. "Don't you see? Legally I would only be able to marry one of you not both of you," she looked back and forth between them begging them to understand how she felt. "I could never choose between you. I refuse to."

"That's easy then," Damon told her. "You marry Doug."

"Wait a minute," Doug said to his best friend. "Why me? Don't get me wrong. I want that more than anything but I'd be okay if she married you instead."

"I know that, buddy, and I appreciate it but hear me out for a minute," he said before either of them could interrupt him. "Doug has family; his name can bring you a security that mine can't, an extended family that I don't have to give to you."

"Now wait just a minute," Doug said. "You know that my family has always accepted you and they always will. And they'll accept Cass as part of the Daniels family whether she has my last name or yours."

Damon shook his head in frustration. "I know that. I'm not explaining myself well enough here." He took a deep breath and tried again. "I know that I'm a part of the family, a Daniels whether I have that name or not. I will always have that. It has meant more to me than I could ever tell you. Your family took me in when I felt like I had no one. Mark had drawn away from me out of necessity to take care of Sheila." He looked so sad when he said this that both Cass and Doug reached out to touch him to reassure him. "Your parents didn't care where I came from. They accepted me and loved me because you did. You were then and have always been the brother I never had and you accepted me as a brother even though you already had two. I want that for Cass too. I want her to be a part of that officially. I want her to be a Daniels."

"Oh, Damon," Cass hugged him close understanding exactly how he felt. "I'll do it as long as you're there with us. I'll marry Doug, take him as my legal husband and then we'll have our own private ceremony where I'll marry you. Just the three of us," she told them. "Will you both wear a ring?"

"Most definitely," Doug told her. He was awed by the generosity of the two people with him. Cass the woman of his soul who had agreed to marry him and Damon the brother of his heart who had given him the best gift in the world when he had urged Cass to marry Doug, to take the name of Daniels. "You take it too," Doug blurted out.

"What?" Damon and Cass asked him.

Doug grinned and laughed with joy. "Hell, you said it yourself. You're already a member of the family, a Daniels. So why not change your name to Daniels?"

"Can you do that?" Cass asked Damon.

"I think so," Damon told her and they both looked at Doug.

"Sure you can," Doug assured them. "You fill out some paperwork at the courthouse, pay a fee and have your name legally changed."

"Is it really that easy?" Cass asked amazed.

"Well, I'm sure there's probably a little more involved with it but I've known people who have changed their names before so it can't be too hard. We'll check into it when we apply for a marriage license. What do you say, Damon? Want to officially become a Daniels brother?"

"What will your mom say? Gil, Griff and Katie?" Damon said his mind reeling at the thought of becoming Damon Daniels.

"You know they love you and would be all for it but we can bring it up at Gil and Moira's welcome home Saturday night if you like." Doug told him while Cass looked at Damon with pleading in her eyes.

"Yeah, let's do that," Damon agreed relaxing and smiling with them. "If everyone agrees then I'll see what I need to do to become Damon Daniels."

"Ohh I like the sound of that," Cass told him.

"How do you like the sound of Mrs. Daniels?" Doug asked her.

"I love it," Cass told him. "They're the most beautiful words I've ever heard."

Cass, Damon and Doug went to the jewelry store the next day to look at rings. Cass wanted a simple wedding band to go with the engagement ring that both men insisted on buying for her. The jeweler was more than eager to help them anticipating a big sale after the engagement ring he had already set aside for them.

"What about these?" he asked them, pulling out a tray with bands with diamonds and other precious stones in them.

Cass was looking at another set though on the tray still behind glass. "That's the one," she breathed. "Those right there."

The rings she was pointing to were simple white and yellow gold bands that were made to look like the colors were braided together two of yellow and one of white. Looking at them made her think of the three of them joining their lives together and all becoming one.

Doug looked where she was pointing and smiled, "They're perfect, baby."

"I love them, sweetheart," Damon said from her other side.

The jeweler pulled the tray out and let them take a closer look.

"Yes, these are the ones we want," Cass told the little man behind the counter. "Two men's bands and one for a woman."

"Two," the little man started to say and then thought better of it and cleared his throat. "If I could just size your fingers?" he asked holding up a set of sizers on a ring like keys. He took Cass' ring finger first and measured it before looking up at the man and asking, "And which of you is the groom?"

"I am," Doug and Damon said in unison.

The little man batted his eyes and looked at Cass not saying a word.

"They both are," she told him smiling at the two men she loved with all her heart.

"Well," the man coughed, "what a lucky woman."

"The luckiest," Cass agreed, "the luckiest."

* * * * *

Damon was nervous on the way to Gil and Moira's apartment the next night and Cass and Doug did their best to assure him that everyone would be happy for them. It was his chance to have the family he had always wanted and never really had.

Moira answered the door on the first knock and pulled Cass close for a hug. "Oh my God, Shep told me about what's been going on with you since I've been gone," Moira squeezed her softly and Cass squeezed right back. "Are you really okay?"

"Yes," Cass told her, a huge smile on her face as she reached back and took Doug's hand and then Damon's in hers pulling them inside and next to her. "I've never been happier in my life."

Moira grinned back, "I see that."

The only one missing was Griff who was still in the hospital and wouldn't be released until Monday morning. Gil's family was there, Katie and Ben, Doug and Damon and Catherine. Moira had Jack, Roman, Chetan and Shep who were all gathered together talking to an Asian woman.

"Who's that?" Cass asked Moira.

"My aunt apparently," Moira answered. "I guess she and dad share the same father. Dad just found out so he brought her to introduce her to everyone."

"I take it Jack's okay with it?" Cass asked.

"He's delighted, to look at him," Moira said and catching his eye smiled fondly toward him. "I'm happy for him."

It appeared that it was a night for family to celebrate and Doug wanted to add to that joy.

"I have a question to ask the Daniels family, a request of sorts," Doug said gathering everyone's attention as Cass and Damon came to stand beside him. "Damon has been a part of our family since I met him in college. You've all accepted him and never left him out."

"Well of course," Catherine said unsure of where this was going. "Damon is family. That is all there is."

Doug smiled at his mother and tossed an I-told-you-so look at Damon. "Damon, Cass and I would like to ask all of you, the Daniels that is," he looked pointedly at Shep who just grinned at him, "how you would feel if Damon legally changed his last name to Daniels."

"Oh that would be wonderful," Katie cried.

"Can you do that?" Moira asked.

"Yeah," Ben said, sharing a look with Katie, "you can."

Catherine stood up and walked over to them hugging Doug before turning and tugging Damon's face down to her. "You have been my son since you followed Doug home that very first Thanksgiving and laid claim to a piece of my heart and their father's as well. You may not have come from my body but you have always been my son. I was only waiting for you. I couldn't think of anything more perfect than to have you legally become a Daniels."

Damon hugged Catherine to him burying his face in her hair to hide his tears while he tried to get control of his emotions. She was more than he had hoped for, her words a balm to his heart which had cried out for a mother since he was a twelve-year-old boy and lost his.

Cass cried openly beside him her tears dripping down her cheeks while Doug held her. Moira and Katie shed tears of joy as well while the men blinked their eyes to hide how Catherine's words of love had moved them as well.

Doug cleared his throat when he could and told everyone, "On that happy note I have another announcement to make. Cass has agreed to marry us. Well me legally but both of us in her heart."

There were smiles and hugs from this unique family who saw no wrong in one woman living the rest of her life as the wife of two men, not as long as the three of them were happy. They were supportive and understanding in a way that few families enjoyed.

Catherine smiled. She was happy with her life. Her oldest son was happily married to a great woman. Her daughter was happily married and expecting her first child. Her middle son, no sons, were getting married to a great woman and her baby boy was finally back home where he belonged. She had a magnificent lover who made her feel young and carefree instead of like the fifty-seven year old widow she was. For the first time in two years she could think of her husband of thirty-four years with a smile and not tears. She was a lucky woman.

Catherine slipped into the kitchen carrying some of the empty containers from the dining room table with her to refill. She wasn't surprised when Jack slipped in behind her. She knew this day was coming, that eventually he would say something to her. She had been hopeful that it would be a while, a long while.

"You can't keep hiding things from your kids, Rin," Jack told her calling her by the nickname her lover had given her. "It's not fair. Not to you, not to him," he nodded to the door behind him, "Not to any of them. If you don't do something soon, you're going to lose him. We're all going to lose him." And with those words Jack Madigan stepped back into the chaos in the other room showing no sign of the agony he felt for his best friend. Roman deserved the same love and acceptance that Catherine had given to Damon that she gave to all of her children. She feared that they only saw her as a mother and wouldn't be able to handle her having a relationship as a woman. He feared she might be right but he prayed they were all wrong. Because Roman wouldn't hide much longer no matter how much Rin begged him to. Instead he would walk away from her, from Legacy leaving the only family he had behind for the woman he loved.

BARE DEVOTION

Dedication

❧

This book is dedicated to all the men and women who fight the flames, giving all that they can to serve and protect. You selflessly give of yourself, risking everything to ensure the safety of others. It can never be said enough – from the bottom of my heart… Thank you.

Trademarks Acknowledgement

❧

The author acknowledges the trademarked status and trademark owners of the following wordmarks mentioned in this work of fiction:

Jeep: Daimler Chrysler Corporation

KY Jelly: McNeil-PPC, Inc

L'Oreal: L'Oreal Corporation.

Nautilus: Nautilus, Inc.

Plexiglass: Rohm & Haas Company

Trans-Am: Sports Car Club of America

Wild Turkey: Austin, Nichols & Company, Inc.

Ziploc: S C Johnson Corporation

Prologue

∾

He struck the long match and held it in his hand, enjoying the sweet smell of sulfur that filled the air and the first bright flame. The scent of gasoline was thick and he couldn't resist the urge to breathe deeply, filling his lungs with the smell of his handiwork. He glanced into the room one last time taking in the two sinners entwined on the bed that he had prepared so thoroughly for this funeral pyre. Everything was as it should be.

It amazed him still how foolish people could be, how accommodating to him. They never checked under the bed, never saw what he had placed there. They never noticed the minor changes he made to their rooms, changes that enabled the flames to attain their goal, his goal. They never paid attention to the sweet smell that seeped from their pillows, pulling them into a deeper sleep, granting him the time he needed to prepare their cleansing.

He closed the door with a sharp click and finally ran the lit match along the wall, igniting the gasoline. He watched with glazed eyes as the blue flames fed hungrily from the fuel and the walls surrounding the bedroom began to burn. The snap and crackle filled the air and he held his gloved hands out to it as if to warm them in the fire. This was his favorite moment. The hiss of fire, the pungent smell filling his lungs and the beauty of the flames as they leaped and grew around him.

Fire—such a wondrous gift to man, a means of purification. Didn't the Lord speak to him through the flames as He did to Moses? And now it was his turn to bring God's message to the world. It was his destiny to purge the world of sinners with the fires of damnation and hell. *For the days of reckoning were upon us and the time to repent was long past.* He was The Messenger and his message was clear.

With his hands still in the air he delivered his message, "Temptation comes from the lure of our own evil desires. These evil desires lead to evil actions and evil actions lead to death. James 1: 14-15." He nodded his head and smiled at the congregation of lost souls in his head as he watched the flames a moment longer.

Then he turned and walked away, opening the front door and closing it softly behind him. He carelessly dropped the used match on the porch where it would be easily seen. It was his way to show that The Messenger had been there. In a quiet voice he spoke again, "For the wages of sin is death. Romans 6:23."

With that he nodded his head once more and walked away smiling and whistling "Onward Christian Soldiers". For tonight, his work was done.

Chapter One

ဆာ

He used the key she had given him to open the apartment door, entering quietly and shutting and relocking the door behind him. He knew exactly where to find her at this time of the morning. She would be in the kitchen sipping her first cup of coffee, preparing to start her day. If it were up to him they would be sharing that routine every morning for the rest of their lives. She had children though, fully grown children with lives of their own, who she refused to upset. She hid her relationship with him, seeing him in private, refusing to acknowledge in public what they had come to mean to one another.

He had gone into this relationship with his eyes open. She had only been a widow for two short years and it had taken him a month of smooth talking to even get her into his bed, despite the sparks that ignited between them. She had been up front with him, just sex, discreet sex, and no one was to find out. She was a woman, yes, but a mother first. That had been fine with him until he got his first look at her naked.

She was a breathtaking woman at the age of fifty-seven. She still had the sleek shape of her youth, her thighs still lean and her skin smooth. Her breasts might not have been as high and firm as they once were but they were beautiful to him. He especially loved the little pudge of loose flesh at her waist, a subtle reminder of the four children that she had carried inside her body. Then he had bent to taste her. Just a gentle glide of his tongue between her glistening folds and he was hooked, couldn't get enough of her.

He was no spring chicken himself at forty-six, but with her it was like he was a randy teenager again. He just had to breathe her unique scent, hear her voice or, better yet, see her and his cock jerked up to attention, eager with anticipation. He knew what it was like to be inside her, to feel the harsh contractions of her pussy around his cock and tongue. He knew the way her brown eyes would darken to chocolate when she came, the little noises that she couldn't hold in.

He also knew of the unconditional love that she had for her children. So unconditional that she would rather deny her own happiness than risk upsetting them. But he was through letting her, through walking away and pretending that he wasn't in love with her. He was through sneaking around and hiding in the bedroom when someone showed up unexpectedly. It was decision time. Once and for all, she would have to decide if he was worth it, if they were worth it. But first he would remind her just what she would be giving up if she chose to walk away.

He entered the kitchen and there she was. Her brown hair lay softly around her shoulders still tumbled from sleep, her eyes still soft with her dreams. She was wearing a soft chenille robe and he knew from experience that she would be naked underneath it. She looked up with a startled expression when he walked in, her eyes widening, her breath catching before panting out in small breaths.

"Roman," she said, "I...I wasn't expecting you today." She grasped her robe with one hand seeming unsure of what to do or say.

"Rin," Roman called to her holding out his hand as he sat down in a chair at the table. "Come here, darling."

"What...What are you doing here so early in the morning?" Catherine asked as she crossed to him.

"Aren't you glad to see me?" he asked and the look in his eyes was sharp, as if he was searching for some answer from her. An answer to a question he hadn't asked and she was so afraid of.

"Of course I'm glad to see you. Don't be silly, Roman." But he never just showed up unannounced, especially not using his own key. What if one of her children had been with her?

"But they're not here, are they, Rin?" She startled as he answered her unspoken question. How had this man come to know her so well?

"I'm sorry," she whispered. "You deserve so much better than me, than this. Maybe you should…"

"Don't piss me off, Rin. There is no one any better than you. Not for me. Now come show me how much you've missed me." His eyes were silver flames of desire and a thrill of excitement worked through her as she thought of how lucky she was.

She still couldn't believe that he was with her. Oh, she wasn't that bad, but still. At fifty-seven she had seen over ten more years than he had. Her hair was still brown, with the help of L'Oreal, and she was still slim and trim, mostly because she stayed active. She stood only five foot one and her frame wouldn't allow for extra weight. When she had married her husband at the age of twenty-one she had barely weighed ninety pounds. Now thirty-six years later she fluctuated between one hundred and one hundred five pounds. Her skin was still good from years of lotion and staying out of the sun. But it still stunned her that such a sexual man would choose to be with her.

Roman was tall, standing six foot five inches, two inches taller than her husband had been and two of her sons were and one inch shorter than her youngest son. He had sandy brown hair and light grey eyes that changed to almost silver when he was turned on. He still had the rugged muscular physique of the Marine that he had been and she knew that he still continued with a daily regimen of push-ups and sit-ups and a run whenever he could. He was perfection in her eyes and perhaps the smartest man that she had ever known. He was incredible, wonderful, and she was falling in love with him more and more every day, something that truly terrified her.

Her late husband Mick Daniels had only been gone for two years, although some days it felt like longer and some days it felt like just yesterday. He had been the love of her life and the only man she had ever slept with before Roman. Mick had been almost eighteen years older than her but they had loved each other instantly and married as soon as she convinced him that there would never be another man for her. She had loved him from the first moment she met him when she was eighteen. He had been the one to encourage her to go to college and see a little more of the world before they settled down. It hadn't made any difference to her though. She had only had eyes for him. As soon as she graduated with her degree in business administration they had married and she had happily stayed home. Their children and their home had become her priorities, second only to him.

Then one day Mick fell from the scaffolding at a building site that his company, Daniels Construction, had been working on. He was in his early seventies at the time but still fit. Although their son Doug worked for the construction company, sometimes Mick still went up on the sites. She had wished a million times that he hadn't that day. His neck had been broken in the fall and he had died instantly. A part of Catherine had died that day as well, a part that would always belong to Mick. But Catherine had moved forward, knowing that she had to for her four children. She had pushed her pain aside and comforted her children, made them the only priority in her life. Unfortunately, she had never stopped. Now when she had this second chance at happiness she found herself shying away, afraid of how her children could be hurt by her choice. To them she was a mother and their father had been and would remain the only man in her life. She didn't know how to open their eyes to the fact that she was still a woman. She had been dropping hints since she had sold the family home and moved to Legacy when her oldest son, Gil, had become engaged. In fact, Gil had recently married Moira

Madigan and they had celebrated with a private welcome home just a week ago when the happy couple had returned from their week-long honeymoon in the mountains of Tennessee.

It was through Moira that Catherine had met Roman. Moira's father, Jack Madigan, was the best of friends with Roman. The two men had been in the Marines together and she still wasn't sure what all they had done after leaving the service before Jack had opened Midnight, Inc., a securities company that did a little bit of everything. Midnight was the name that Jack had been called in the Marines. Roman's name was actually Caesar Davis, but few people knew that and no one called him anything but Roman or Mr. Davis.

Jack had spoken with Catherine briefly at Moira and Gil's welcome-home celebration, warning her that if she didn't quit hiding her relationship with Roman and forcing Roman to hide it as well, she might lose Roman. Jack thought that Roman might pack up and move away from them, leaving Legacy behind for good if she didn't quit hiding behind her children. She needed to act like the woman she was and be honest with her children about her relationship with Roman. Catherine prayed with all her heart that wasn't the reason Roman was here so early in the morning. She still didn't know what she should do. She didn't want to hurt her children, but the more time she and Roman spent together the more she knew that she loved him.

"I'm waiting Rin," Roman spoke again, pulling her out of her thoughts and back into the here and now.

"What…" she started to ask as she stepped close to him but she cut herself off with a loud squeak when he lifted her off her feet and sat her on the table in front of him.

"I've come for breakfast," he murmured, reaching for the belt to her robe and removing it. He opened her robe slowly, reverently, like unwrapping a present, and his grey eyes went silver when he took in the beauty of her naked flesh beneath. "Do you know what I want to eat, Rin?"

"What?" her voice came out husky with need. She moaned at the feel of his fingers on her thighs spreading her legs wide so that he could scoot his chair up between them. She leaned back on the table bracing her weight on her arms and Roman lowered his face, breathing deeply of the scent of her passion.

"Smells sweet and delicious," he told her, running the fingers of one big hand between her glistening folds. "Perhaps I should sample a little first." He bent further forward and ran his tongue along the plump lips of her sex, gently tasting the dew that lay there. "I was right," he whispered, "delicious." His fingers spread her lips wide and he dove into her with his tongue, pumping into her channel with shallow strokes before swiping upwards and caressing her swollen clit.

She cried out her pleasure as he sucked and ate at her pussy. He was ravenous for her taste and let her know it. Catherine gasped for breath as he pushed her toward orgasm with nothing but his mouth—the soft stroke of his tongue, the sharp nibbles of his teeth, the greedy suction of his lips. Finally he latched onto her clit, sucking it harshly into his mouth, and thrust two thick fingers into her pulsing channel. With two quick strokes she reached orgasm, drowning him in her release. She relaxed back onto her elbows as he slowed his caresses but never ceased his torment.

"I need you, Rin," Roman looked up at her and she knew that she could never deny him anything, never again.

"I'm yours," she told him, talking of things greater than the moment. "I'm all yours."

Roman surged to his feet between her sprawled thighs and the chair skittered back and crashed to the floor. He made quick work of the button and zipper of his jeans and pulled his long thick cock out into his hand. It was lush and full, already seeping with desire. She licked her lips, remembering well the taste of him. He hastily grabbed the condom from his front pocket and ripped it open with his teeth, wanting to don it as quickly as he could. But Rin stopped him with the gentle glide of her fingers over his arm until she reached his fingers and took it from him. God, he loved this woman. She was fire and ice and everything he had spent his entire life searching for.

"Let me," she whispered and put action to her words. Using one hand she started at the base of his cock and softly let her grasp run along its turgid length till she was holding the crown in her hand. "So soft and yet so hard," she sighed as she used her other hand to place the condom over his tip and then used both hands to glide it down his swollen shaft. When she looked up at him her eyes were the deep chocolate that he had come to treasure. "Take me, Roman. Take me to paradise."

He moved forward lining his cock up with her slick entrance before grasping her hips and thrusting deep. They both shuddered at the feel of that first powerful stroke that joined them as one.

Roman held still, filling her with every inch of his pulsing erection and reveling in the tight clasp of her channel. She felt so good to him, like the other half of his soul, and he was devoted to pleasing her, sexually and emotionally. He wanted her completely—body and heart, mind and soul.

Rin gasped for breath as he began a slow, easy rhythm that had her on the cusp of orgasm almost immediately. He made her feel so young and beautiful. There were times he made her feel like a naïve virgin. The things he did to her, that she did to him, were far different from the vanilla sex that she and her first husband had shared. Oh, she hadn't known at the time that it was vanilla, but Roman had opened her to new things, new positions that should be impossible for her. He made her laugh, really laugh, for the first time in a long time.

Roman's pace increased until his balls were smacking against her ass with every harsh thrust. He moved one big hand over and opened her so that her clit was exposed to his thrusts as well and she came, tightening like a vise around his pumping shaft. Their cries mingled together filling the kitchen and apartment with the sounds of pleasure as he exploded into the condom with hot jets of his creamy cum.

She lay flat on her back on the table gasping for breath and Roman leaned down and gave her a slow passionate kiss, his tongue a soothing balm against her own. "I love you, Rin," he murmured softly before kissing her again. "Remember that."

"Remember that?" she asked with panic filtering into her eyes and soul as she recalled Jack's warning that Roman would leave if she didn't stop him. "Why? Are you going somewhere, Roman?"

"I have to go out of town for about a week." He noticed the panic in her eyes and, easing her up into a sitting position, wrapped her in his arms and held her tightly to his chest. "I'm not leaving you, Rin. It's a business trip for work. But I do want you to think about us while I'm gone." He tilted her face up so that she was forced to look into his eyes. "We can't go on this way anymore. You have to make a decision, Rin. I'm either a part of your life or I'm not."

"You know that I want to be with you Roman," Rin tried to explain again, "but the kids. Especially my boys. I just don't—"

Roman cut her off placing his fingers on her lips and giving a gentle shake of his head. Sadness filled his grey eyes when he replied, "No more excuses. I'm too old to be sneaking around, hiding how I feel about you. I love you, Rin. You either love me or you don't."

Temper flared and she gave him a little shove away from her, though it did nothing to move him. "It's not that simple, Roman, and you know it."

"It could be," he answered, moving his hand down to dispose of the used condom and put his cock away, zipping and buttoning his jeans. "If you want it enough then it could be."

"Damn it, Roman," she began again but he silenced her once more with a kiss.

"I don't want to argue with you anymore, Rin." He looked down at the watch on his wrist. "I'm running late. I should have left over an hour ago but I wanted to see you first. Just promise me that you will think about it while I'm gone." He leaned close and stopped when his lips hovered mere inches above hers. "Promise me ?"

Catherine was lost in him pulled under by the love that reflected in his eyes. "I'll think about it, Roman, but..."

He kissed her softly, not wanting to hear again how much a relationship with him would hurt her kids. "That's enough for me, Rin. That's all I intend to ask of you right now."

He deepened the kiss, wanting to leave her with a reminder of how great they were together, how devoted he was to her. Gradually, he eased away from her stepping back and taking in the sprawl of her body on the table. She was gorgeous with her robe open and revealing the beauty of her naked body, her opened legs giving him a glimpse of so much more. Her hair was still tousled from his loving and her lips were red and swollen from his kisses. Her cheeks glowed with the bloom of youth, or at least youthful passion, and it was all he could do not to step forward and have her again.

Instead he ran his fingers gently over her cheek and smiled. "I'll call you," he promised, then turned and left the kitchen and the woman he loved more than anything else behind. It was the hardest thing he had ever done, and as a Marine turned mercenary, he had made some rough choices. He opened the front door and let himself out of the apartment using his key to lock it behind him. He stood there for a moment wondering how he would live if she didn't fight for him, for them. It would kill him to be without her.

Catherine sat on the table and gave free reign to the tears that seeped from her eyes and fell like rain down her cheeks.

How could she let him go? Yet how could she put him before her kids? How could she ever decide what to do in just a week?

Chapter Two

ഌ

Halloween was only a week away and Katie was looking forward to the costume party that Cass was throwing at the home she shared with Katie's brother Doug and soon-to-be brother Damon. It didn't seem that long ago that Cass had met Doug and Damon and the three of them had fallen in love. Doug and Damon were known to share women and it was no surprise to Katie that when they had fallen in love it had been with the same woman. And since Cass' best friend Moira was already married to the oldest Daniels son, Gil, Cass was already like part of the family.

And now Damon would be officially family soon as well Damon Roberts would be known as Damon Daniels as soon as the paper work went through and then there would be a wedding to plan. Although, legally Cass was marrying Doug and taking the last name of Daniels, the three of them had decided that Damon would officially take the name of Daniels as well. After all, the Daniels family had always been there for Damon and he had always wanted to belong with them. He already did belong, but if taking the name meant that much to him, then the family was all for it. And after the official wedding another smaller more private ceremony would take place with the there of them uniting. Katie couldn't be happier for them. Maybe this was exactly what her mother Catherine needed to snap her out of the funk she was in.

Catherine had always been the rock of the family, the one constant in their lives. Now she was changing before their eyes. Doug and Gil didn't really see it, each wrapped in the intricacies of their own lives and loves. And Griff refused to see it, refused to see their mother as anything other than just that, their mother. But Katie saw more, the hunger that flashed in her mom's eyes when Catherine thought no one was looking. Katie saw it and, as a woman understood, what it meant.

Katie had even caught her mom with a man not too long ago. She didn't get a good look at the guy her mother was with, just the back of his head, but she still had an idea of who it was. For some reason her mother wasn't ready to share that part of her life with Katie. So Katie was giving her plenty of time. Her mother deserved to be happy and Katie was bound and determined to make her brothers aware of that.

"Hey there, sugar," Ben came up behind his wife and wrapped his arms around her to cradle her stomach, rubbing the spot where their baby rested. She wasn't due until the middle of May and her stomach was still flat, but Ben still couldn't stop touching her abdomen or placing kisses there every night before bed.

Katie turned in her husband's embrace and went up on tiptoe to kiss him. The kiss took on a life of its own and they both were lost in the passion of their embrace for long moments before reality intruded with the sharp ring of the phone

"You better get that," Katie murmured as he eased away. That was the way it was when you were married to a detective. He could be pulled away at a moment's notice on cases that she didn't even want to know about.

"Marcum," Ben snapped when he picked up the receiver. "Yeah. When? I'll head out now and meet you there," Ben glanced down at his watch before replying again. "Give me about ten minutes. Yeah. See you in a few."

"Gil?" Katie queried, already knowing the answer as she watched Ben put his shoulder holster back on and check his weapon before sheathing it.

"Yeah," Ben stated. "Call came in before he left the station." He looked over at his wife and smiled wearily. "We gotta take this one, sugar. I don't know when I'll be back. Don't wait up for me."

"I love you," Katie said and accepted the chaste kiss he placed on her mouth.

"Love you too, sugar," Ben said and, grabbing his jacket, headed out the door.

Katie wanted to yell at him to be careful, to stay safe. But Ben already knew that and she knew in her head that he would never do anything to endanger himself or his partner, Gil, Katie's brother. But the case he was on now worried her, in more ways than one. Legacy had another madman on the streets and this time he was stalking right into the very homes of its residents. No one knew how, when, or why. But death had come again to terrorize them and this time it brought with it fire.

* * * * *

Detectives Ben Marcum and Gil Daniels took in the blackened structure before them. It had once been a beautiful home owned by a young couple just starting out their lives together. Now it was their tomb. The one the department was desperate to catch had struck again and although Ben and Gil hadn't been cleared by the fire marshal to enter the house yet, they were certain of what they would find. And it wouldn't be pretty.

This would be yet another fire attributed to the phantom who was attacking the residents of Legacy. He somehow managed to gain entrance to a home. Whether invited in or not they didn't know, as thus far no one had been left alive to question. But the final scenes were always the same when Ben and Gil finally were allowed in, which was only after the fire marshal did his job determining the cause of the fire. Then the structure had to be considered safe enough for them to view the scene of death before the coroner removed the bodies.

The bodies were always found lying on the bed entwined in a lovers' embrace. The autopsies would show that the victims were drugged prior to the house being set on fire, but the cause of death was always directly related to the fires, asphyxiation from smoke inhalation. The coroner was always quick to tell them that it was better that the victims were drugged before he burned them. It would be far worse to know what was coming and be powerless to stop it.

"Hey Gil, Ben," Blake Summers called as he exited the house and headed toward them. Blake was the fire marshal in Legacy and had been for the last three years. He was in his early forties, with sandy brown hair and piercing brown eyes. He had moved to Legacy after a bitter divorce and taken over as the town fire marshal when the job came open. "It's all clear," he said taking in the protective gear they were both already wearing. "You can come in now. Just be careful not to touch anything. I'll lead you to the bedroom."

"Unfortunately, we know the ropes by now Blake," Ben grumbled. "Start the same way?"

"Yeah," Blake's sigh was full of disgust. "The door and outer walls of the bedroom were soaked in accelerant—gasoline seems to be his choice—and then with a flick of a match he lit it up."

"You get the match?" Gil questioned, eyes taking in every little detail as they worked their way back to the main bedroom.

Blake held up a clear baggie with the match in it. Just that. A match that could have come from any box of long matches that most people used to light their fire places with. Hell, the only reason they ever found the match was because he always left it on the doorstep or porch, depending on what the house offered. Like a macabre calling card.

The stench in the bedroom was overwhelming and it took all Ben had not to gag at the ripe smell of burned human flesh and hair. He glanced at Gil and knew that his partner felt the same way. But even worse than the smell was the sight of the devastation that a fire could wreak on a person.

The bodies were burned beyond recognition and dental records would have to be used to identify both victims. Gil prayed that the coroner was right and that they didn't wake up during the fire. It turned his stomach to see what this guy did to these people. And for what? The sick thrill of playing God? Of holding the power of life and death in his hands? Or for some other, more personal, reason? He prayed they found their answers soon and put an end to this guy's reign of terror.

"Anything new with this one?" Gil asked gruffly turning his head from the bed and heading out the door. The only evidence in this room was long gone, consumed by the flames. And what little might remain Blake and his crew would uncover once the bodies were removed. It was way past time to stop this fire-crazed madman.

* * * * *

Ally could feel it in her blood. She was getting closer to him. This time, she prayed that she would be in time to find him, to stop him. She squeezed her hands tightly around the steering wheel as she drove. This time she would find him and stop him for good. At the very least she would make sure that he paid for the lives he took so carelessly, for the lives that had meant everything to her.

She glanced at the sign and laughed softly as she read, "Legacy thirteen miles". Legacy, she thought, what an appropriate place for things to end. For as he felt it was his Legacy to kill, she felt that it was hers to stop him.

* * * * *

Catherine paced her apartment like a caged tiger searching for a way out. Roman had only been gone for one day and yet it felt like an eternity. She was desperate to hear from him. Some part of her was still afraid that he wasn't planning to come back to Legacy, back to her and what they shared. And technically he wasn't. At least not like things had been in the past. Now he was forcing her to make a decision, forcing her to admit to the world that she had taken a lover, replaced her deceased husband with someone younger.

If she were honest, then she could admit that it wasn't the world that she was worried about, just the small part of it where her children lived. She had no idea of how Gil, Doug, Griff and Katie would react to her and Roman being together. Catherine hadn't even dated that they were aware of in the two years their father had been gone. But Mick was gone and all of them had moved on with their lives.

Gil was now married to Moira. Katie was married to Ben and expecting their first child. That made Catherine smile as she thought of how much Mick would have loved to be around for his grandchildren. He would have made a great grandpa, the best any little boy or girl could hope for. But she would do everything to make up for Katie's child not having Mick. And how would Roman be around children? He didn't have a child that she knew of. And it dawned on her how little she really knew about him.

They had shared some amazing conversations but most of them had been about her family, losing Mick and how her kids were doing. Roman often spoke of Jack and Jack's daughter Moira and she supposed maybe that was the closest to family he had. It stunned Catherine to realize how much she hadn't discussed with him. She didn't know much about his life before now or what events in his life had shaped him into the man he was.

She had known everything there was to know about Mick, as he did about her. This was all so frustrating to be thinking of starting over at the age of fifty-seven. And that was exactly what Roman was asking of her, to start over, with him. God help her, she wanted to, wanted it with every breath. This brought her full circle back to the reason why she wasn't. Her children.

Doug was busy now with Damon and Cass. Damon's papers should come through any time and then his name would officially be Damon Daniels. Catherine was planning a surprise birthday party for him to celebrate his official "birth" into the Daniels family. And then there was the wedding of Cass to Doug in the official ceremony, and to both men in a family one. Catherine shook her head and laughed. She should be shocked by that but she wasn't. She had known Doug's and Damon's sexual practices since they first starting sharing women back in college. That wasn't something you could keep secret and people were all too willing to tell tales, especially to the mother and family members.

Catherine just wanted her children to be happy and if Doug, Damon and Cass could be happy together, then let them. Gil and Moira were obviously happy and Catherine was looking forward to the day when they decided to have children of their own. Gil would be a great father and Moira would be the perfect role model as a mother—strong, fierce and independent. And Catherine's baby girl, her Katie, was having a baby. Ben and Katie would be great parents. Ben was protective and loving and Katie was just the same. All of her children were happy and healthy in relationships of their own. Surely they wouldn't deny her the same thing.

Griff. He was the one who would be the most vocal about her and Roman. Griff would not be happy about it. Catherine had been dropping little hints and clues for months now and Griff, the only one of her children not in a relationship, always made comments about her being a mom and not thinking like that. Mick had spoiled him. With Gil gone in the service and Doug off at college, Griff had been the son left at home and Mick had often had long talks with him. Catherine wasn't sure what all the conversations had been about and didn't really feel a need to know, since they were between father and son and should be private. But she knew that Mick had told Griff that it was important to watch out for and protect his mother and sister, a task Griff took all too literally.

Catherine had some major decisions to make, but right now she just wanted a long soak in a hot tub and a glass of wine.

Chapter Three

ဆ

Ally stood as close to the home where the latest fire had taken place as she could. No one seemed to be around, but she had learned that often it was the things that you couldn't see that you should fear the most. All she needed was a chance to take a look at the scene to see what he had done this time, to find out if he was still using the same method of destruction. If it was then he would have left some part of himself behind and she would pick up on it. Then she would know for sure if this was the same person she had been hunting and not a copycat. She prayed it was him.

She was a profiler of sorts who often worked with local police departments when she was able to connect with a case, but she was currently on personal leave due to this particular madman. The Messenger. She had known two of his victims personally, her mother Roni and her mother's life partner Tory, who Ally had always referred to as Aunt Tory. Her mother had been her whole world and Aunt Tory had been a very important part of that world. Ally never knew her father, though her mom and Tory spoke of him with love. He had died just before Ally was born, killed by a drunk driver. She didn't know the full dynamics of the relationship they had all shared but she had gathered the gist of it as she grew older. Basically they had both been his wives and when he was gone they had turned to one another. And that is what had got them killed.

It also explained why she was here following him and hoping to finally stop him. This was the first time he had set fires again since killing her family. It had taken her a while to pinpoint exactly where he was but as soon as she did she'd headed out. One way or another, The Messenger must be stopped. She would see him die as violently as he had killed others. She would see him burn. Now if she could just get inside the home without getting caught.

He watched the shadow ease closer to the side of the house, edging around to the back door, he assumed. Blake didn't know what had made him come back by the house tonight but was glad that he had. He may have just caught the man they were looking for. He eased his cell phone out and called the cell number he had for Detective Gil Daniels.

"Gil, it's Blake," he said as soon as he heard the voice on the other end of the line. "I'm here at the last house and there's someone trying to sneak in."

"So our guy came back," Gil exclaimed. "I'll call Ben on the way. Don't do anything stupid, Blake. This guy has killed six people so far. Don't take any chances."

Blake ignored Gil's warning as he hung the phone up with a snap. There was something wrong here. The shadow was too small, too petite to be a man. And if what he was thinking was correct, then what the hell was a woman doing here at this time of night? What did she have to do with this investigation?

"Shit," Blake muttered and headed at a slow run to the side of the house where the shadow was already disappearing around the corner. He had to stop her from getting into the house. He was hoping to take a fresh look at the scene in the morning and didn't want to lose any trace evidence he might find.

Blake took a running leap planning to tackle the small figure in the soft grass just off the back porch.

Ally heard a noise and turned around to peer behind her. She had time for a startled squeal and a feeble attempt to backpedal before the large figure took her tumbling to the ground, finally landing with him on top of her, his big body sprawled between her spread legs. Ally gave a soft gasp at the sparks that flowed through her at his touch.

He was big, but then most people were when compared to her five-foot height. People constantly referred to her as a fairy with her diminutive height, long black hair and green eyes.

Blake leaned his full weight on the woman beneath him. And he could tell that she was all woman. He could easily feel the shape of her full and obviously unconfined breasts, the heat of her sex against his growing erection. Shit, he thought, trying to adjust his position between her thighs. He had obviously been way too long without a woman. He needed to get laid and soon.

"Get off me," the woman gasped, doing her own wiggling that only brought her flush against his full-blown erection. They both stilled at the delicious sensations that coursed through their bodies. It felt good. It felt right.

"Not yet, sweetheart," Blake told her, giving up all pretenses and relaxing his body down over hers. "What the hell are you doing here?"

He could see the wheels spinning behind her eyes and wanted to laugh when she replied with a shrug. "I'm looking for my aunt's house. Obviously I've got the wrong address."

"Am I interrupting something?" Gil asked from behind them, causing two sets of startled eyes to glance his way.

"Just getting to know the lady better," Blake said as he lumbered to his feet. "How did you get here so fast?"

"I was just around the corner when you called," Gil murmured, a smile tugging at his lips.

Ally's eyes widened as she took in the sheer size of the men in front of her, looking even bigger from her position on the ground. The one who had interrupted them was long and lean, but she could easily see that he would be a force to be reckoned with. But it was the other man, the one who had held her so intimately on the ground, that her gaze kept returning to as she slowly came to her feet before them.

The moon was finally out of hiding and she could get a good look at him. He was gorgeous. He had to be well over six feet, at least an inch taller than the lean guy, with wide shoulders bulging with muscles. Thick, wavy, brown hair settled around his shoulders and it was all she could do not to moan her pleasure at finally seeing him. He was sex personified. Rough, dirty, raunchy sex. And the bulge straining against his zipper was impressive.

"Uh...umm," Blake cleared his throat as he caught her eyeing the straining length of his erection. Yeah, his cock was hungry for her and the blush that stained her cheeks assured him that she knew it. "You want to try again to tell us what the hell you're doing here?"

"I told you," she said quietly sticking with her earlier story. "I thought this was the address of my aunt's house. Obviously I was mistaken. I'm sorry to have bothered you both," she managed as she tried to nonchalantly ease away. "I'll just be on my way."

Blake snaked a hand out and snagged her by the wrist, his fingers easily wrapping around her small bones with room to spare. Fuck she was delicate. She'd never be able to handle the rough ride he would love to give her. Blake shook his head, clearing that thought from his mind. "I think maybe you better stick around until you decide to tell us the truth," he stated firmly.

She was exquisite, dressed all in black with her ebony hair braided down her back. Her eyes were big green orbs with a slight tilt at the corners that gave them a feline appearance. Actually they reminded him of Moira's, Gil's wife. The woman whose wrist he held was dainty, standing maybe five feet even, but her curves were all in place and very pleasing to his eyes. Blake had always considered himself a leg man, but taking in the straining mounds of her lush chest complete with pebbled nipples had him salivating. He wanted to strip that little catsuit off her, throw her down on the ground and fuck her till neither of them could move. His cock pulsed in his jeans and he could feel the pre-cum that was seeping from its tip and prayed it wouldn't leave a wet spot on his jeans. Oh yeah, he definitely wanted to fuck her.

"I'm not sure what I could tell you, gentlemen," Ally tried unsuccessfully to pull out of the hold on her wrist. "Maybe I should call the cops. I don't even know who you are."

Gil eased his hand inside his leather coat and pulled out his detective's shield. "Detective Gil Daniels, ma'am," he told her. "And the gentleman holding onto you is our fire marshal, Blake Summers."

"Pleasure," Blake told her and neither of them was sure exactly what he was referring to.

"Ally St. John," she told them, easily using her mother's maiden name in case they decided to run a check on her. "It's been a pleasure, but I'd really like to leave now," she added, tugging uselessly on her arm. She had to get away. No one had mentioned anything yet about her catsuit or the fact that she was wearing black leather gloves, and she'd like to keep it that way. The last thing she needed was to be hauled into the local police station. If they checked on her they would find her real name attached to several cases where she had assisted the police.

"Can anyone join this party?" a new voice spoke up as a tall man came around the corner.

Ally blinked unsure of what...who she was seeing. It couldn't be. And yet it was. She hadn't seen him in years, not since they were both in their teens, not since he had left his family behind so many years ago. It was a fate they both shared when it came to Preston St. John, the patriarch of the St. John family, Ally's uncle and Tommy's father. Lord knew that Preston had disowned his sister as quickly as he could. There would be no foolishness in his family and being openly bisexual could definitely be considered a blight on the St. John name. Ally strained to get a better look at the man who kept coming closer. It was him and she had never been happier to see anyone in her life.

"Tommy? Please tell me you're not a figment of my imagination," she begged, tugging at her wrist again and almost falling when she found it released.

"No, that's my partner Detective Ben Marcum," Gil answered.

"Ally? No way!" Ben exclaimed as he headed toward her. Ally ran and flew into his arms, laughing. Ben spun her around and squeezed her tightly against him. "What the hell are you doing here, Ally Cat?"

Blake clenched his hands at his sides startled by the jolt of jealousy that coursed through him at the sight of Ally in Ben's arms. Hell, it wasn't like him to be possessive with women anyway especially one he didn't even really know. Besides, chances were good that if she ended up in his bed they wouldn't be alone in it for very long, since Blake had a good friend in Legacy whom he shared his women with. And with just that thought his cock swelled larger. Blake gritted his teeth trying to clear the erotic vision from his head, the vision of Ally on her hands and knees taking him and another man at the same time. Luckily his thoughts were interrupted.

"Tommy?" Gil questioned. "What the hell is she talking about? What is she doing here? And how do you know her?"

Ben opened his mouth to reply when Ally cut him off with a strangled sob that tore at his heart. The Ally he remembered never cried.

"She's gone, Tommy," Ally cried softly against his chest. "They're gone."

"Who's gone?" he questioned already fearing her answer.

"Mama," she cried out, giving way to the tears that she had held back for so long. "Tory and Mama are both gone."

Ben ran his hand affectionately down the back of her head, letting her cry in the comfort of his arms. "Tory and Roni both," he spoke softly.

"Who are Tory and Roni?" Blake asked.

"Roni is — was — her mother," Ben informed them quietly. "Tory was her...aunt." He looked his partner cum brother-in-law Gil in the eye before adding softly, "Her mother was my aunt."

Gil and Blake glanced over at Ben with startled expressions as it dawned on them what he was saying.

"Are you saying—" Gil started to ask when Ben interrupted them.

"Yeah, Ally is my cousin," Ben stated and began gently leading her to his SUV. "And I'm taking her home where she can get comfortable and tell me just what's going on."

"I'm coming with you," Blake stated bluntly not knowing why he was insisting just sure that he couldn't let her out of his sight just yet.

"Fine," Ben said nodding his head. "I'll see you there."

Gil nodded and headed to his Trans-Am already opening his cell to call Moira. There was no way that he was missing out on this. Something was going on and he planned to find out exactly what it was.

Ally cried quietly in the passenger seat on the way to her cousin's house. There was so much going through her mind and she could only be grateful that she had found Tommy again. But why did they call him Ben?

"Why did that other detective call you Ben?" she asked her cousin softly. The cousin she had always known as Thomas Austin St. John — Tommy.

Ben let out a long sigh before answering. "I changed my name, Ally. When I left the family behind, I legally changed my name to Ben Thomas Marcum."

"You changed to your mother's maiden name," Ally nodded in understanding. "You always loved spending time with your Grandpa Tom."

"Yeah," he agreed.

"So is life better for you now," Ally inquired. "As Ben Marcum I mean."

There was no doubting the huge smile that lit his face. "My life is perfect," Ben assured her. "When we get to my house you'll meet my wife Katie."

"Wife?" Ally was startled at this revelation.

"We're expecting our first child in May next year," Ben told her. "You'll love Katie. Hell, you'll love the entire Daniels family. They're good people."

"That detective back there introduced himself as a Daniels," Ally replied, refusing to comment on the rest of what he said. In her life, good people were only nice to her when they needed something from her. Otherwise she was referred to as the daughter of the lesbians.

"Gil," Ben nodded as he pulled into a big house and parked by a fenced-in backyard. "He's Katie's brother and my partner. And my best friend as well."

He jumped out of the SUV and walked around to help her out, shutting the door and beeping it locked before tugging her hand and leading her through the gate and to the back door of his home.

A woman stood there silhouetted in the light from the room behind her. It was remarkable to Ally the physical similarities that they shared. Katie—she was sure this woman had to be his wife—was petite as well, with short black hair and a slim build. She wasn't overly chesty like Ally, instead appearing more in proportion with her small frame. Her eyes were a magnificent blue that reminded Ally of the detective named Gil. In fact the closer she walked toward the woman the more obvious it was that the two were related. She couldn't help wondering if there were any more of them and if they were all so beautiful.

Katie opened the door and Ben swept her up in his arms making her shriek with joy. Ally felt like a voyeur when her cousin wrapped his wife in his arms and kissed her passionately cupping her ass in his big hands and squeezing the cheeks. She went to step discreetly back out of the doorway and backed right into a very warm, very aroused male body.

Hands gripped her waist and she knew exactly who was touching her before he leaned low and whispered in her ear.

"This family is very openly affectionate," Blake spoke into Ally's ear, breathing in the sweet scent of her shampoo. "You'll get used to it if you stay for very long."

Ally just nodded, unable to breathe, much less speak, with him so close to her. His erection felt huge against her back and she wanted desperately to feel it pounding inside her wet pussy. Something about him called to her and she knew that before this night ended she would be in his bed. She glanced over her shoulder and the look in his eyes said that he knew it too.

"Go on in, guys," Gil spoke as he came up behind them. "Ben, put her down and let's all sit down and talk. Some of us have wives to go home to."

His comment startled Ally and her eyes locked once more with Blake's, asking without words if he was married, if there was someone else. He shook his head and breathed in her ear, "Not me. There's no one," before patting her on the ass and nudging her into the kitchen where Ben and Katie were finally coming up for air.

Ally went to slip around the table and take a seat but Ben grabbed her and pulled her close to his side. "Katie, I want you to meet my cousin, Ally Samms. Ally, this is my wife Katie."

Katie smiled and reached to give Ally a hug, but before she could get more than, "It's a pleasure…" out of her mouth both other men in the room exploded.

"Samms," Blake snarled unsure why it upset him so much that she had lied about who she was.

"I thought you said your name was Ally St. John?" Gil questioned at the same time.

Ally took a deep breath and closed her eyes.

Ben muttered under his breath while giving Ally a pointed look and Katie just shook her head before grasping Ally's hand firmly in hers and pulling her toward the open door that led further into the house.

"If you gentleman will excuse us," Katie began, although all three men knew she wasn't really giving them the option. "I'm going to show Ally where she can wash her face and freshen up just a little bit before you all start in on whatever you have planned." She turned to face Ally then and smiled. "You have some dirt streaked on your cheek and some leaves and things in your hair. Follow me and I'll help you out."

"Thanks," Ally managed. It had been too long since she had anyone who really cared about her. It seemed like all of her time recently was spent pursuing the man responsible for taking that away from her.

She followed Katie up the stairs and was startled when instead of a bathroom Katie led her into what had to be the master bedroom. Katie showed her to the bathroom and encouraged her to jump in the shower really quickly while Katie found something for Ally to wear. The shower sounded like heaven and Ally wanted to give in.

"But they're waiting for me," Ally said.

"Then let them wait," Katie replied, looking so closely at Ally that she hoped her cousin's wife wasn't noticing the dark circles under her eyes. She crossed her fingers that Katie wouldn't comment on the fatigue and worry that she was sure showed on her face.

"Relax," Katie told her softly. "Whatever problems there are will still be there when you're done. Only you might feel better equipped to handle them." Katie gave her another hug before moving back once more. "I hope that you will consider me a new friend, Ally. I'd like to get to know you better.

Besides, you are family," Katie grinned at the look of confusion on Ally's face. Hell, at this rate Ally would have the other woman convinced that she never had another soul in the world as a friend. "That makes you an honorary Daniels, Ally. I can't wait for everyone to meet you. How old are you, anyway?" Katie asked and Ally could almost see the wheels already spinning in her head.

"I'm twenty-six," Ally replied slowly, wondering where this might lead.

"You look so much younger," was all Katie said as she left the room pulling the door closed after her.

Ally stood there for a moment taking it all in. She could hear Katie moving around in the other room and knew she was laying out clothes for Ally to wear. For the first time in what felt like forever Ally felt hope. With a weary sigh she turned to the shower, starting the water and quickly stripping and unbraiding her hair. No matter what Katie said, Ally knew that the men were waiting for her and she had no plans to make them wait any longer than she absolutely had to.

* * * * *

Ally could hear the voices in the kitchen as she was coming down the stairs, her hands gliding over the banister. It sounded like there were more people there than before. Ally felt self-conscious in the clothes that Katie had left out for her. The jeans were fine, if a little snug, but the top was another matter entirely. The t-shirt that probably looked great on Katie was tight on Ally and as Ally hadn't been wearing a bra under the form-fitting catsuit, her breasts were blatantly displayed beneath the tight material. At least they were still high and firm but Ally would give anything for one of her comfy sweatshirts to hide beneath.

As she edged closer she could make out the discussion that was taking place in the kitchen.

"She knows something," Blake reiterated for the third time. "Why else would she show up at the latest crime scene?"

"He's right Ben," Gil admitted. "And who did she say died? How did they die?"

"I know as much as you do at this time," Ben said. "We didn't talk much on the way over because Ally was too upset. And let me tell you, that is not like the girl I knew at all."

"What do you mean?" Blake asked.

"Ally has always been strong," Ben looked sad for a minute. "She's had to be. Ally's mom and my dad are—were— siblings. But my dad shut himself off from the rest of his family because they didn't fit the social image he wanted. Ally's dad died before she was born and all she's had in her life have been her mother and Tory. I can't imagine how alone she must feel with them gone."

"Doesn't she make friends?" Shep, who had stopped by to speak with Ben, asked from his spot next to Blake. He and Blake had been fast friends from the moment they met, and had many things in common. Since then they had shared a lot with each other. They had met for the first time through Blake's cousin, Tyler Andrews, who was also Shep's old Ranger buddy. The men enjoyed each other's company and spent a lot of time together.

"No," Ben interjected quickly and shook his head, not knowing exactly how to describe Ally without making her sound weird. "Ally is a loner, mostly because she's had to be."

"Had to be why?" Blake asked.

"She just is," Ben said sharply and there was no missing the anger in his voice. Katie stepped in front of her husband and leaned her back against his chest knowing that he would automatically wrap his arms around her. Ben took a deep breath and held his wife close to him. "Ally is very sensitive. She always has been. Her mother and Tory protected her as best they could but there was no way to hide the things that Ally could see."

"Are you talking some voodoo shit?" Gil cut in sharply.

"Look, Ally just knows things some times," Ben admitted with a look on his face that dared anyone to comment.

"Wow," Katie's voice broke through the tension. "So can she speak with ghosts and stuff like that little boy in the movie? Or is she more like that John Edwards on television?"

Shep grinned, Gil shook his head and Blake and Ben laughed, eliminating the rest of the tension in the room. But the woman standing in the doorway just heard people laughing at her again. She didn't know what she had expected from her cousin, from the other man who called to her soul, but laughter was not it. She stepped softly into the room and Katie gasped when she caught a brief glance of the sorrow on Ally's face before it was quickly gone, leaving only a blank expression in its place.

"I'm glad that I've provided you with a night's entertainment," Ally said softly—too softly. "Thanks for the shower and clothes," she told Katie. "I'll make sure to get them back to you when I get back to my car and check in at the hotel."

"You're more than welcome to stay here, Ally," Katie said.

"Of course she'll stay here," Ben said.

"No," Ally said. "Who would want to have someone around with all their voodoo shit?" Gil flushed. "If I can just get a ride back to my car then I'll get out of your hair."

Blake and Shep had both been looking at Ally's change in clothes. Shep took in the long thick black hair, the petite frame, the big green eyes and the delicious mounds of flesh so vividly on display in the borrowed t-shirt. Then he took in the way Blake was already viewing her so possessively. Shep grinned. His cock was as hard as steel under his zipper and knowing Blake the way he did, Shep knew it wouldn't be long till Blake was fucking her too. Blake would claim her first, but then it would be time to share and the erotic images skating through

Shep's mind already had him hard and ready, eager for his part.

Blake stood up from the table glad that he had untucked his shirt earlier to cover the full-blown erection he still sported when he arrived. Now his cock was long and thick again and there would be no way to miss it in his tight jeans. "I'll take you to get your car," he said then held up his hand to cut everyone off before they could speak. "It's been a long night. Let's get together tomorrow to discuss everything." With that he took Ally by the elbow and went to skirt around the table.

Ben released Katie and stepped in front of them, his eyes going automatically to Ally. "Are you sure you don't want to stay here?"

"I'm sure," Ally stated quietly.

"I can take you to get your car, we can talk," Ben told her just as softly, regret ripe in his eyes for the pain he had never meant to cause her.

Ally shook her head no. She knew what was coming with Blake and she needed it. "No, we'll talk tomorrow." She reached up and touched her hand to his face before turning to go with Blake once more.

Shep was already at the door. "You need any help?" he asked Blake with a devilish grin that threw Ally for a loop. This man was big, as tall as Blake. But this one was a blond Viking in modern clothes. She could easily imagine him plundering and conquering her in every way imaginable. She must have made some small sound because his feral gaze hooked on her and there was no mistaking the lust in his eyes. His glaze flicked down to her breasts and she could feel her nipples hardening further and poking out of the material. He grinned in triumph and Blake glanced down at her turgid nipples then. Ally refused to acknowledge her body's response and just stood there letting them look.

Blake pushed her gently out the door in front of him. As she brushed past the Viking she swore she felt him brush a finger across her nipple.

"Not yet," she heard Blake tell the other man. "Tonight's mine, Shep."

So that was his name. Shep. But what did Blake mean not yet? And did he mean what she thought he meant? She felt the moisture in her pussy and hoped she didn't soak the jeans, as panties were something else she wasn't wearing. She just didn't feel comfortable borrowing such intimate apparel from a stranger. And cousin's wife or not, Katie was still a stranger.

Ally snapped out of her thoughts when Blake grabbed her hand and led her to his truck, opening the passenger door and boosting her up inside. She watched as he shut the door and moved around to the driver's side and hopped, in firing the truck up as he slammed his door and belted in.

Ally remained quiet as he drove back the way they had come. This time she took in the scenery around her, looking at the town called Legacy as they drove through it. It took her a minute to realize that they were headed on another road out of town and not toward the fire charred home where her car was parked around the corner. She glanced over at Blake.

"Where are you taking me?" she asked though she felt sure she already knew.

"To my place," Blake stated, glancing casually over at her. "Any objections?"

Ally shook her head slowly back and forth. No, she had no objections to what was coming.

"You know that I'm going to fuck you," Blake said plainly so there were no surprises when he got her to his house. "We may not make it past the front door the first time. I want you that badly, Ally."

Her eyes were wide, not with fear but with a raging lust of her own. "I want you too," she admitted in a husky whisper.

"Have you ever been with a man before, Ally?" Blake asked. "'Cause I don't know that I can be gentle with you right now. The need is too strong."

Ally thought of the two men she had slept with in her life. They both seemed like boys when compared to the man sitting across the truck cab from her. "I'm not a virgin," she told him. No need to tell him that it had been at least five years since she had engaged in sex with a man.

"Good," Blake replied as he pulled into a driveway and hit the remote for his garage.

Ally briefly glimpsed the brick one-story home before he enclosed them in the garage. The truck turned off and he turned to her, releasing first his seatbelt and then hers. His eyes were hot and dark with need and she could tell that the lust was riding him hard.

"You have ten seconds to get out of the truck and head into the house, Ally," he told her, his voice rough. He nodded toward the door that must lead into the house. "That's about as long as I'll make it. Ten seconds, Ally. Then I'm going to fuck your sweet pussy till you scream."

Ally gulped, reached for the door handle, and flung it open, then gave it a shove to close it and bolted for the house door.

Chapter Four

෨

Blake sat for a few seconds watching Ally hurry away from him to the door leading into the house. Had he misread the signals? Was she scared and not really interested? Then she stopped as she opened the door that led into the house through the utility room and smiled at him over her shoulder before continuing on inside. She was playing with him, taunting him to catch her and take her. And he would not disappoint her.

Blake slipped from the truck and quietly shut the door. He kicked his shoes off inside the door Ally had left open and shut it gently. He grinned when he saw her shoes kicked off there as well. His belt slipped free and he tossed it aside, then undid the top button on his jeans and pulling his shirt over his head. When he found her, it would be a rough first mating. Blake shook his head. Mating? Where the hell had that thought come from? It would be a quick fuck the first time and, looking at her diminutive size, he might not last as long as he hoped once he plunged his cock into her pussy.

On his sock-covered feet he crept into the kitchen and almost groaned when he saw the t-shirt Ally had been wearing tossed on top of the table. He continued through the house and shuddered when he came across her jeans lying in a puddle in the middle of the hall. Was she naked now? Was she already in his bed spread and ready for him? He rubbed his hand along his hard denim-covered length and gave it a squeeze. Fuck he wanted her badly. He took a deep breath and continued down the hall and pushed open the slightly ajar door to his bedroom. The sight that greeted him nearly brought him to his knees.

Ally knelt on his bed knees spread wide with one hand playing in the lush, wet folds of her sex. Her scent of arousal filled the air and made Blake groan again. Her other hand was pulling and teasing her plump nipples, which crowned the most amazing breasts he had ever seen. Her hair hung around her like a curtain and he couldn't wait to get his hands in it. But it was her eyes that grasped him and wouldn't let go. There was so much there, so much more than just the lust that was riding them both right now, a promise of something better than Blake had ever known.

Blake reached down to unzip his pants as he just barely managed to walk the rest of the way across the room to her. When he stopped in front of her, his cock was wrapped in the fingers of his hand as he used the other to shove his pants and boxer briefs down out of the way.

Ally moaned and dropped down to all fours before he could focus. Her lips wrapped around the large head of his cock and she sucked him into her hot little mouth until she meet his fingers. Blake groaned at the feel of her mouth as well as the sight of her round ass high in the air behind her. If things worked the way he hoped, she would be in just this position again soon with one man in her mouth and another stroking in and out of her sweet little cunt. Oh yeah, she looked just perfect in this position.

Ally's firm suction brought him back to the present and he gently wrapped his fingers in her hair and pulled her mouth away from him. She let go with a loud pop and gave another swipe of her tongue over the weeping slit of his crown before looking up at him. She licked her lips like she was savoring the taste of him and Blake almost came right then and there.

"You taste amazing," Ally informed him.

"I'm glad you think so," Blake replied as he knelt on the bed in front of her and used his hands to ease her back up the bed so that he could lie her down and cover her like he wanted. "I promise to let you eat your fill of me later, Ally."

"I'll hold you to that," she smiled and arched her body up into his rubbing her hard nipples all over his hair covered chest. "I love your chest, Blake. I love the feel of it against my skin, against my nipples."

Blake moaned and leaned down, pinning her chest to the bed with his, crushing her nipples into him. He took her mouth with his and plundered her the way he had wanted to the last time he had her under him when they were both still dressed and lying on the ground. This was so much better. She tasted better than he imagined and he only let her mouth go when they were both gasping for air. He could feel her fingers digging into his shoulders and he loved it. Her thighs were already grasping his hips and Blake could feel the moisture from her pussy on his stomach.

He reached down between their bodies and slid his finger in the wetness rimming her opening before going back up to torment the engorged bud of her clit. Ally moaned and thrashed beneath him and finally, on the third pass, Blake buried his finger in her cunt. It was heaven—tight, wet and hotter than hell around his digit. Yeah, he'd last maybe two seconds. Only one thing for a man to do and that was to ensure her pleasure before he ever took his own.

He bent his head and took one of her nipples firmly between his teeth, sucking and nipping her flesh while he plunged his finger in and out of her. She was so tight. He wondered how long it had been since she had last had sex. He slipped a second finger inside and Ally cried out, pumping her hips up to greet his plundering hand, pressing her clit against his palm. Ally came with a harsh cry and a rough clawing of his shoulders. She wasn't as delicate as she looked, Blake thought taking in the wildcat who was convulsing beneath him in what had to be a powerful orgasm. She was clenching his fingers with her sheath and her juices where soaking them both. God, she was the most gorgeous picture he had ever seen.

He pulled his fingers from her and pushed her thighs wider, lining his cock up with her still-pulsing center. He couldn't hold back any longer. He entered her fully with one hard thrust and almost died at the pure pleasure that wrapped around his shaft and worked its way up and back down his spine. His balls were already high and tight with his seed. And that thought stopped him cold. He wasn't wearing a condom. Fuck!

Ally must have sensed his intent to pull out of her snug heat, for she slipped her hands down to dig grooves into his buttocks and urged him to continue. "Don't stop," she gasped. "Please don't stop."

"Just a minute," he groaned as he lunged for the bedside table drawer and the box of condoms inside.

He watched Ally's eyes as he ripped one open and hastily rolled it on. He was back between her thighs in mere seconds, sheathing himself once more in her lush sex.

"Yes," Ally screamed. "Fuck me. Fuck me so good."

That was all Blake needed to hear to start up a pounding rhythm that had them both too breathless for words. He could feel his orgasm building and knew that there would be no holding back the flood. Then he felt Ally clench around him and watched with amazement as she reached another orgasm. She was exquisite. Two more hard strokes and he was grinding his cock as deep inside her pulsing channel as he could get before flooding the condom with several harsh blasts of his thick semen.

He collapsed on top of Ally, only managing to push his upper body to the side, not wanting to pull completely out of her just yet and from the tight grip of Ally's hips on his, it seemed as if she felt the same way. Finally, long moments later, they both relaxed, Ally's legs slipping from his to rest on the mattress. Blake heard a shuddery sigh and when he glanced over, Ally was asleep. He tried to ease his body away as softly as he could, not wanting to awaken her. He removed the filled condom and, tying it off, wrapped it in a tissue before tossing into the trash can by the bed. When he was back beside her, he gently pulled her into the cradle of his arms and pulled the folded afghan from the foot of the bed over them, not wanting to risk waking her by pulling the covers down beneath them.

Blake looked at the sleeping woman in his arms and knew beyond the shadow of a doubt that he would never be able to let her go.

* * * * *

It was the ringing of the phone that brought Catherine awake, abruptly shattering the sweet dream she was enjoying. She fumbled for the bedside lamp and, turning it on, blinked at the clock, noting that it was twelve-thirty in the morning as she reached for the phone.

"Hello," Catherine murmured sleepily, praying that there wasn't another emergency in her family. It seemed that they had experienced more than their share lately.

"Rin, did I wake you?" Roman's voice soothed her from across the line. "What time is it there?"

"It's about twelve-thirty," Catherine replied.

"Shit. I'm sorry, honey. I didn't realize," his voice sounded weary, like he was ending a really rough day. "I didn't mean to wake you up. Go back to bed and I'll try to call earlier tomorrow."

"No," Catherine cried out. "I'm awake now and I don't mind. I was hoping to hear from you."

"Miss me, honey?" Roman questioned and she could hear the need in his voice.

"Miss me?" she asked instead, unwilling to admit just how lonely she was without him.

"Every moment, honey," he whispered to her, "with every breath I take."

"I miss you too," she admitted quietly, an easy thing to do in the privacy of her bedroom.

"Are you naked in that big bed, Rin? All alone and naked?" His voice was deep and seductive sending shivers of desire coursing into the very heart of Catherine.

"You know I am," she whispered, as if afraid someone would overhear her.

"Don't be embarrassed, honey," Roman told her. "I can't touch you but I can tell you what I want you to do to yourself."

"Phone sex?" Catherine gasped, shocked and interested at the same time. Perhaps more shocked because she was interested.

Roman's chuckle came over the line, rich and full. "I'll let you return the favor, Rin. You can tell me exactly what you would like to be doing to me. I'd love to hear your voice saying all those naughty things."

"I'm not sure," Rin whispered softly, "that I can do this, Roman."

"Close your eyes, honey, and lay back in the bed," he encouraged her and Catherine found herself obeying instantly. "Now slip one hand under the cover and rub your nipples with it."

Catherine followed his order and felt the hard stab of her aroused nipples against her palm and fingertips. Her hand felt good and it wasn't like she had never touched herself before. What woman who had reached her age hadn't? But she had never done it while talking to a man, be he a husband or lover, on the phone. It was exciting and scary all at the same time. Her mouth opened in a moan as she thought of Roman's hands and the way he liked to pinch and roll her nipples between his fingers before taking them between his teeth and flicking his tongue against her willing flesh. She moaned again as she pinched one and then the other going back and forth. She could feel the slow glide of liquid coating her sex and seeping out onto her thighs.

"Oh, God, honey," Roman's voice was even huskier. "My cock is pulsing and begging for relief. You don't know what it does to me to hear you like that, aroused and needy. I want to pop one of those cherry red nipples in my mouth and suck it hard."

She cried out again and, without thought, started sliding her hand down over her stomach toward the center of her need.

"Are you touching your sweet pussy now, Rin? Are you dipping you fingers into that sweet cream?"

She definitely heard the pop of a button and the rasp of a zipper coming over the phone. "Are you taking it out?" she asked too lost in the moment to be embarrassed but still cognizant enough to control her words.

"Oh yeah, honey," he groaned and she could picture him kicked back on the bed, one big hand wrapped around the pulsing erection rising toward his belly button. She'd watched him do that before, watched him while he watched her undress for him.

"How wet is that pussy, honey?" he asked her, stroking soft and slow along his cock. "How many fingers are you putting in that sweet cunt?"

She blushed just like she always did when he used the "c" word. There was just something about it that was dirty.

"Talk to me, honey," he begged softly. "Tell me what you're doing, what you're touching."

"I'm... I'm touching myself," Catherine managed in a husky voice.

"Where at, honey?" Roman encouraged her to answer.

"My...my...between my legs," she managed to say.

Roman's chuckle flowed over the line again. "Close your eyes, honey, and talk to me. It's just you and me, Rin. Tell me where you're touching. Where are your fingers?"

Catherine groaned and closed her eyes again. She was startled when she realized just how comfortable it made her. "I'm running my fingers through the wet lips of my sex, circling my clitoris and coating my fingers."

"Ahhh…" Roman groaned loud. "There is just something so dirty and erotic about the way you say clitoris, honey."

He was always pushing her to talk dirty to him when they had sex, loving the sound of the words on her lips. She wasn't a prude, but a woman had to have a certain amount of modesty. Or at least the ones of her generation did. Still, she felt her temper flare just like it always did when he made comments like that, just like he knew it would. And he knew it would get him just what he wanted from her.

"Do you want to hear me talk about how wet my pussy is? How much I want to feel your cock inside me right this minute?" she asked him, her voice rough with anger and excitement.

"God, yes," Roman moaned. "Tell me how tight you clasp around your fingers. Tell me how good it feels, Rin. Let me tell you how good it feels to me."

Catherine pushed two fingers deep inside her channel and pumped them slowly in and out. She braced the phone between her shoulder and the pillow and moved her other hand down to trace tight circles around the bud of her clitoris. "I'm using two fingers. It feels so good, so good. But I can't hit the spot that I need to. I want you inside me, Roman. I want every long hard inch of you pumping in and out."

"How do you want it, honey?" he asked. "You want it slow and easy or fast and hard?"

"I want to start slow and easy. I want to keep it that way until we just can't take it anymore. Then I want you to take me as hard and as fast as you can. That's what I need," she told him.

"You're killing me, Rin," he groaned. "My cock is ready to explode. Just the thought of how your cunt would clasp me makes me swell bigger. I want to fuck you, Rin. I want to fuck you until you scream my name."

"Yes," Catherine cried out, her fingers stroking faster, searching for that spot that Roman always knew how to find, the spot that would give her the release she needed. "I want that to. I want you."

"Say the word, Rin," he encouraged her moving his hand faster along his shaft. He could feel the tingle along his spine, the swelling of his balls, and knew that if she would just say the word they would both find the release they needed. "Say the word, honey. Say it!" he demanded.

"Fuck!" she screamed, her orgasm washing through her and turning her mind to mush. "I want you to fuck me, Roman. Fuck me."

"Rin," he groaned as he shot his cum all over his rock-hard stomach. "I knew you could say it, honey. I knew that you would enjoy this. You did enjoy it, didn't you, honey?"

"Yes," she sighed softly, tired after such an intense orgasm. "I did enjoy it, Roman."

"I miss you, honey," he whispered softly. "I'll be back soon and we'll sit down and talk. Okay?"

"Yes, we'll talk," she murmured drowsily already falling asleep. "I can't lose you, Roman," she admitted quietly, all her shields down, lingering on the verge of sleep. "I love you."

"You..." Roman heard the soft click of the phone and knew that she had hung up before falling completely asleep. She had said that she loved him that she couldn't lose him and it was like a jolt of energy shot through his system.

Roman jumped out of bed and whistled on his way to the shower. Life was great. He hadn't even told her that he would be coming back before the end of the week. She loved him, he thought, and his grin widened. She loved him and somehow that gave him all the hope he needed.

* * * * *

He watched the woman in the bar closely while he nursed the wine that was in front of him on the table. It was okay for him to drink wine since even God's son Jesus had turned water into wine. But it wasn't okay for her to drink the way that she was, to dress the way that she was. She was just like all the rest, a whore who flaunted herself in an attempt to lead men astray. She was one of the devil's weapons and as God's messenger it was his responsibility to silence her. More importantly, it was his job to cleanse her of the sins that coursed through her feminine form and do his best to save her mortal soul. Oh yes, he had plans for the jezebel, but for now he sat and watched, waiting to see which man showed himself to be weak of the flesh and in need of cleansing as well.

Chapter Five

ഇ

Ally awoke the next morning to an empty bed and since Blake's side wasn't even warm, she knew that he had been gone for some time. She glanced at his bedside alarm and was startled when she saw that it was already ten in the morning. She never slept this late, which made her realize just how long she must have been running on fumes. And sex with Blake last night had obviously relaxed her more than she had thought. She had wanted more than just the one time, but sleep had pulled her under and refused to release her. Now he was already gone and who knew when she might see him again.

Ally snorted as she swung her legs over the side of the bed and stood up, grimacing slightly at the pull of muscles that hadn't been used in quite a while before last night. As far as she knew Blake might not even want a repeat of last night. All of this was probably just another one-night stand for him. She'd just take a quick shower and see about catching a ride out of here before he came back up.

She padded across the carpet and smiled when she noticed her clothes folded on top of his dresser. Well, technically they were Katie's clothes, but still. She pushed the door open and glanced across the hall where another door stood open, revealing a bathroom. Thank heavens, because she didn't really feel comfortable padding naked through his house searching for a shower.

She tiptoed across the hall and almost laughed out loud at how ludicrous she must look. Who in the hell was she trying to be quiet for? It appeared that she was all alone, either that or someone was extremely quiet. She shut the door with a snap and flipped the lock just in case Blake came home or had a roommate or something. She opened the cabinet and drawers

217

until she found a rubber band that someone must have left at his house. She used it to put her hair up in a loose bun so that it wouldn't get so wet.

The shower was fantastic. Just what she needed to sooth her sore muscles. Well, it would suffice until she could get access to a hot tub and a full-body massage. Now that sounded like heaven. She shut the water off and pulled the curtain back to reach for the towel and let out a shriek when she noticed the golden god from last night sitting on top of the closed lid of the toilet. His eyes took in her naked body, flushed red and dripping wet from her hot shower. His name was Shep, she remembered as she snatched the towel and held it in front of her.

"What the hell are you doing in here?" Ally demanded, doing her best to wrap the towel around her without giving him any more of a show then she already had. "How did you get in here? I thought that I had locked the door."

"You did," Shep smiled and it was like watching a little boy try to sweeten his way out of trouble.

"Then how did you get in here?"

"Locks are one of my specialties," he murmured, finally standing and holding his hand out to help her out of the shower. Ally took his hand and stood dripping onto the throw rug in front of the shower. "Need some help drying off?"

"No, I don't," Ally stated firmly, but it was all she could do not to burst out laughing at the gorgeous man in front of her. He reached out and pulled the band from her hair.

"I'll have to tell Chetan that you took his hairband," Shep declared pocketing the band and reaching back to twine his fingers in her long locks.

"Che—what?" she asked, unsure what he had said.

"Chay-than," Shep enunciated slowly. "It comes from the Sioux word for hawk. A gift from his mother so he wouldn't forget where he is from."

218

"Interesting," she said, pushing his hand away from her hair and trying to slip past him and out the door. "Now if you'll excuse me."

He let her slip past him but followed her into the bedroom, where the clothes were on the dresser. She turned to shut the door and felt overwhelmed for a moment at how close Shep was standing behind her. He was as tall as Blake, maybe six foot four, and it startled her to realize that she barely came up to his diaphragm in her bare feet. She had been wearing her black boots last night with her catsuit and put them on with Katie's jeans as well. With their chunky block heels she had been closer to the middle of Blake's chest and then she had been on her back and it hadn't mattered.

Shep reached a hand out and brushed his finger across her hardened nipple, which was pressing against the towel. "Cold?" he asked softly.

"Let me guess. Warming me up would be another one of your specialties," Ally commented as she swatted his hand away and took two steps back from him.

Shep's grin stretched wide across his handsome face. "Absolutely," he agreed. "Anytime that you need heating up, you just let me know, sweetheart."

"I'll keep that in mind," Ally shook her head. "Now if you'll excuse me I'd like to get dressed and find a way back to my car."

Shep nodded toward the bed and Ally glanced over at it. Someone had straightened the afghan out while she showered and she recognized the single bag sitting on top of it as the one from her car—her locked car. She walked over and opened it. Sure enough, that was her stuff in there. "How did you get my bag?" she asked, then shook her head and answered before he had a chance. "Locks are your specialty, right?"

"Yep," Shep agreed, then tugged a familiar set of keys out of his jeans pocket and tossed them onto the bed beside her bag. "But keys work just as well."

"How in the world did you get my keys?" she wondered out loud.

"Found them in your pants when I came in last night," Shep said with a smile. "Of course I'd already picked up that tight shirt. When I folded them I felt the keys and thought how appreciative you might be if I showed up this morning with your bag and your car." He grinned and batted his big baby blues at her.

Ally couldn't help it. She burst out laughing. "Tell me, does that usually work for you?" At his look she continued, "You just bat those blue eyes of yours and give that grin and what? Women just fall onto their backs for you?"

"Every time, sweetheart," Shep said as he backed into the hall and grabbed the door handle. "I can already see you falling under my spell. Before too much longer you'll be wondering what it would feel like to kiss me, to make love to me. And let me assure you," he winked, "it will be better than you can even imagine. I'll let you get dressed while I start a pot of coffee. Just come to the kitchen when you're ready." With that he pulled the door shut and she could hear him whistling as he walked away.

Ally shivered and shook her head. The weird thing was that he was exactly right. Hell, she was already at the point where she was wondering what he would be like in bed. She had a feeling that his charming boy next door smile and good humor hid a lot more than she could handle.

Ally followed her nose down the hall to the heavenly scent of morning nectar, otherwise known as coffee. She felt more comfortable in jeans of her own and a sweatshirt, plus she had the extra security of a bra and panties underneath. On her feet were her sneakers that had a two inch rubber sole, something that was important when you were only five foot even.

Shep was at the table playing what appeared to be a game of solitaire while another man reclined with the newspaper open in front of him. Both men looked up when she entered and gave her the once over. She felt like a piece of meat being dangled. She shook her head and turned to the coffee pot on the counter.

"What happened to the t-shirt?" Shep asked from his seat at the table. "I'm sure Katie wouldn't mind if you wore it again."

Ally turned around and burst out laughing at the scowl on his face as he took in her loose sweatshirt. "I'm sure she wouldn't, Shep, but I'm more comfortable in my own clothes."

The man with the paper folded it and stood from the table. Lord, he was a tall one, taller than anyone she had ever seen. He was long and lean with jet black hair and gorgeous blue eyes. He reminded her a lot of Katie and her detective brother in looks and she was pretty sure that he must be another member of the Daniels' family. And she was right. They were all extremely good looking.

"Let me guess," Ally said as he rounded the table, heading to where she was leaning against the counter. "You must be another of Katie's brothers."

"The only one that matters to you," he told her with an engaging grin. "I'm Griff," he reached for her hand and then startled her by bending and bringing it to his lips. He turned it up and placed a kiss on her palm and for a moment she found herself lost in the pure romance of it. "It is a real pleasure to meet you, Ally. I've heard a lot about you."

And that was all it took to shake her free. She tugged her hand from his and wrapped both hers around the warmth of the coffee mug. "Oh really," was all she said but she wondered just how much they knew about her already.

"Katie didn't do you justice when she described you to me," Griff said and turned to hold out a chair for her at the table. "She is hoping that you might be free to join us for dinner tonight."

"Not sure that Blake's going to go for that," Shep put in with a look at Griff. Ally shook her head. It was obvious that Shep was trying to tell Griff that she and Blake had slept together, but hell, she would think that was pretty clear. Why else would she still be in Blake's house when he was long gone? Blake was pretty good in bed. Okay, she could at least admit to herself that the man was the best lover she had ever been with. But bottom line was that sex, even great sex, didn't make a relationship. And that meant that it didn't matter what Blake thought.

"I'd love to," she said, which made Griff grin even wider and even had Shep fighting a smile. "I'll just need directions to the house, and the time, of course."

"I'll pick you up and we can ride together," Griff said and waved his hand at the chair he was still holding out. "Just tell me where you'll be."

"No thanks," Ally said indicating the chair. "I'm just going to finish this cup and head out. I need to find a hotel and get some stuff taken care of this morning." She turned to Shep and smiled. "Thanks for getting my car and bringing my bag in. Now if you two will just point me in the right direction I'll head back to Legacy and get settled."

"Do you already have a room somewhere?" Griff asked pleasantly.

"No," Ally admitted. "But it didn't look like excitement burg, at least not what I saw last night. Are you telling me that I might have trouble finding a room?"

"No," Griff laughed. "I was just asking. My family still has an apartment that no one is staying in at the moment. It was my brother Gil's till he hooked up with his wife Moira. Then Katie lived there before she married Ben. I lived there till I moved out. Come to think of it, even Cass stayed there."

"Cass?" Ally asked wondering if this was another member of the Daniels clan.

"You'll meet her eventually," Griff informed her. "She is marrying my brother Doug soon and then Damon."

"She's marrying two men?" Ally asked with disbelief. "Exactly where are we that such a thing is even legal?"

Griff and Shep both laughed. "She's only marrying Doug in the legal sense, but Doug and Damon sort of come as a package deal."

"They're conjoined?" Ally asked, horrified in spite of her unwillingness to offend anyone.

Griff doubled over laughing and she thought she heard Shep say something about them liking that comment better than the question of whether they were gay or not. Gay? What kind of family had her cousin married into?

"I'm sorry Ally," Griff said trying to catch his breath. "You'll understand when you meet them all." He reached out and took her hand in his giving it a reassuring squeeze. "And that will be tonight at dinner. It should be a smaller group, though, if both Chetan and Roman are still out of town."

"How many people are in your family?" she asked, allowing him to lead her toward the door. She noticed Shep pick her bag up from the hall and turn the coffee pot off before following them out the door and into the garage hitting the button on the wall as he followed them out into the drive.

"Well, see the thing about the Daniels is that we welcome everyone as family," Griff said and led her to where her car was parked at the curb. "We have a pretty big extended family, though not everyone is related," he glanced down at her and waited for her to click the locks open before holding open the passenger door for her.

"You plan to drive my car?" she looked up at him with arched eyebrows.

"Just thought it would give you a chance to sit back and acquaint yourself with the roads and town," he assured her and Ally shook her head and let him help her into the car. "I'll take you to the apartment first so you can check it out and see if you want to stay there for now. Then Shep and I will show you around town and stuff."

"And stuff?"

"Well, since I'm not sure what you're doing here," Griff said with a smile. "I'll have to play it by ear until you tell me what you plan."

Ally shook her head. Oh, he was good. She hadn't even realized that he was fishing for information on what she knew about the fires and The Messenger. "I'm not sure myself," she told him with a smile. Two could play this game. "I'll let you show me everything."

Griff nodded and shut the door. He and Shep stood by the hood of the car talking for a few minutes before Griff headed to the driver's door and Shep headed to a battered Jeep parked in the driveway. After his comments about coming in and finding her clothes, she wondered if he and Blake were roommates.

"Everything all right?" she questioned with a big grin as Griff sat down and belted in.

"Just fine," Griff assured her. "Shep's going to meet us at my sister-in-law's gym in about an hour. "That will give you plenty of time to see the apartment and the neighborhood."

"Great," Ally enthused and almost laughed when she caught the look on Griff's face. What was it about these guys that they were used to a woman falling under their spell and doing what they wanted? What were the women in Legacy like? And was everyone as good-looking as the ones she had met so far? And just what the hell did they feed these guys to make them grow so tall? It would be fun to stay and play awhile but first things first. She had to find The Messenger and end his reign of fire.

The apartment was completely furnished with two bedrooms. She liked it on sight and tossed her bag onto the bed in the bigger of the two rooms. She had seen the look Griff had thrown at the other bedroom and couldn't help but wonder what had happened in there to cause it. She might take a closer peek later and see if she could pick any vibes up.

Griff had walked her around showing her the pizza parlor on the corner and a few other businesses close by that she might have use for while she was in Legacy. Then they headed back to the apartment and he gave her a set of keys and shown her how to work the numerous locks installed on the door. When she had asked him about them, Griff had just shrugged and said that you could never be too safe. There was a story there somewhere she was sure.

Now they were headed for the sister-in-law's club. Moira, she thought her name was. She was the one married to the detective Ally had met last night, Gil Daniels. Moira owned a health club called Knowledge Is Power. Ally was actually looking forward to seeing it. If she was lucky maybe they would offer kickboxing, which was Ally's sport of choice.

The front entrance was a gorgeous design of Plexiglass that allowed anyone passing by to peek in at the lobby of the gym. The front desk was off to the left-hand side as you entered and there was a pretty girl sitting there who fixed her eyes immediately on Griff. Until she caught sight of Ally walking beside him, his arm thrown casually around her shoulders. Ally glanced up at the big guy and almost laughed when she realized that he had no clue the young girl was eating him with her eyes and getting madder by the second.

"So I'm too young to go out with, but she's okay?" the girl pounced on them as soon as Griff had walked them close enough for the girl to hiss it out.

"Now, Crystal," Griff said and flashed that roguish smile at the girl. "You know that your brother would have my head for messing with his baby sister." He reached a hand out and traced a finger down her cheek. "You know that, don't you, sugar?"

Ally almost gagged at the way he was playing the girl. Hell, even she knew that he was just being nice and wasn't the least bit interested in Crystal. But Crystal bought it hook, line and sinker, nodding her head in agreement.

"I know, Griff," Crystal sighed with all the angst of unrequited love.

"How old are you?" Ally asked her curiosity getting the better of her.

"Twenty," Griff replied while Crystal glared at her and muttered under her breath something about being the same age as Ally.

"Actually," Ally smiled at her, "I'm twenty-six. I just look a lot younger because of my height."

"Moira in her office?" Griff asked before Crystal could make any more comments to Ally.

Crystal glanced down at something on the desk. "She's in class for a few more minutes but she should be up soon."

"Katie downstairs?" he asked next.

"She should be in her office," Crystal said after checking the schedule again. "She doesn't have anything else until two p.m."

"Tell Moira I'm down there, will ya, sugar?" Griff smiled that winning smile and Crystal just looked at him and nodded.

Ally made it a few more steps before she burst out laughing. Griff just grinned at her and caught her hand up in his. Before Ally could make any comment a white-haired Mrs. Claus-looking woman approached them.

"Why, Mrs. Addison, look at the roses in those cheeks," Griff said as he bent to kiss her on the cheek. "When are you going to leave that husband and run away with me?"

"Oh, you rascal, you," Mrs. Addison said. "One of these days I'm going to take you up on your offer and send you running for the hills."

"Never," Griff assured her. "You'd make me the luckiest man alive."

Mrs. Addison actually giggled and patted his arm as she walked away.

Ally burst out laughing again. "You just can't help it can you?" she asked him. He gave her that "what" look with the arched eyebrow. "It doesn't matter how old or young a woman is, you just have to turn on the charm."

Griff looked down at her and shook his head sadly. "What kind of men have you been around that you think that? Every woman is a beautiful gift from God and she should be cherished and adored."

"You really believe that?" Ally asked quietly.

"Of course," Griff assured her and his face didn't seem to be hiding any mirth. "Women are the givers of life. They are the nurturers and healers. A man may have the ability to be stronger, faster and bigger. But when it comes down to it, the smallest female can easily bring the largest male to his knees with just a look. There is power in that and it should be respected."

"Philosophy," Ally remarked. "And who is Griff Daniels?"

"Anything you want him to be," Griff assured her, that killer smile back in place. But Ally couldn't help but see more in his eyes, an underlying sadness that made her wonder what woman had ever hurt this man.

"So where to now?" she asked instead, letting his secrets lie for the moment.

"Down to the lower level to Katie's office. She leads a woman's therapy group here and has even started individual counseling. I thought maybe we'd chat with her 'til Moira's done. Then I'll have Moira give you the grand tour and maybe talk you into sticking around long enough to enjoy the amenities of this place."

Ally smiled at the oh-so-readable ploy for information from her. "Maybe," she murmured. But she was laughing on the inside.

* * * * *

He held the match up to his face, breathing deeply of the sulfur scent while gazing avidly at the tiny burst of flame. Tonight would be the night that he would save another soul from the flames of hell by cleansing them with the flames of truth and justice. It was the path that God had chosen for him and he would not fail to see it done. He could feel the heat of the fire, hear the roar, the hiss and crackle as the flames consumed everything around them.

He knew the woman he was going to save. She was a jezebel, a harlot who fornicated with every male of the species. He had watched her in the bar, watched as she had paraded and enticed the weaker sex. He had watched until she had made her choice and left with a man. No one was in any doubt of what those two were planning. Not the way that they pawed at each other before they were ever even out the door. They were going to explore the pleasures of the flesh without the sanctity of marriage—a sin against the laws of God. Now it would be up to him to ensure that they repented and earned their way into the kingdom of heaven. They must pass through the flames of salvation. He would see it done as the Lord had commanded him to.

Chapter Six
ဆ

Ally was more nervous than she cared to admit. The only real comfort to her was that she had already met some of the people who were going to be at the dinner tonight. Ben and Katie would be there, Griff and Shep and the other detective Gil Daniels would be as well, since it was his apartment. Tonight she would once again see Moira, Gil's wife, Cass, Doug and Damon—the threesome in the family—Catherine, the matriarch, Jack, Moira's dad, and Roman and Chetan. That seemed like an awful lot of people to her and she wondered just how the hell they would all fit into an apartment. Why weren't they getting together somewhere else? Like Ben and Katie's house, for instance? It had seemed big enough to hold at least fifty people.

She paced the bedroom of the apartment that Griff had talked her into staying in and tried to figure out what to wear. Her few clothes were tossed on the bed where she could easily choose or discard from them. Finally she gave a nervous sigh and sat on the edge of the big bed, tugging a pair of jeans toward her. The nicest things she had at the moment were her lacy bras and panties, but somehow she didn't think those would be appropriate, although Griff would probably enjoy them.

That made her grin. Then she scowled as she remembered for the hundredth time that she hadn't heard from one fire marshal all day. She was a big girl. She'd been around the block a few times, but it still hurt. She had felt something with him, something she couldn't quite put her finger on. He had felt like a lot more than a one-night stand. She wanted him to be different and that more than anything had her feeling shaky. In all her twenty-six years, Ally had never wanted everything from a man, never wanted forever.

She stepped into her jeans and rose from the bed pulling them up and over her hips where they settled, leaving the toned flesh of her abdomen uncovered. She tugged on a simple black t-shirt that had the phrase "Pony Up" in glittering faux rhinestones across the chest. The top was snug and hugged her breasts, stopping at the top of her belly button. She reached into the box she used for jewelry and pulled out a belly ring with a rhinestone drop and replaced the sedate ring that was in at the moment. She wore that one when she didn't want it noticed and this one when she did. Not to mention that this one looked as sexy as hell.

She sat back down to tug her black boots on, giving her another three inches of height. Her make-up and hair were already done and she felt like she looked as good as she could. That was her mother's number one advice when Ally was feeling extremely nervous about something. Make yourself look as sexy and enticing as you possibly can and it will boost your confidence and calm your nerves. Her mother had been right.

As Ally went to answer the knock at the door, she felt a jolt along her spine making her part her lips and gasp for breath. The Messenger was preparing something. She wasn't as locked into him as she had been and she needed to repair that tonight. She would have to tell Ben that she needed something from the fires, preferably one of the matches that she knew The Messenger left behind. She needed to merge with him again, get back inside his mind, and she needed to do it soon. Hopefully before anyone else died.

* * * * *

"I think that you should see this," Gil said as he sat across from Ben.

"What is it?" Ben asked as he automatically took the thick folder from Gil.

"You're not going to like it, Ben, and I'm sorry about that. But I had to check," Gil stated firmly making Ben raise his eyebrows. "It's all about Ally St. John, aka Ally Samms. She's been quite active with the police department, Ben. Helping out with missing persons and it even looks like she's done some profiling for certain cases."

"I told you what Ally was, who she was," Ben glared. "You didn't need to check this out behind my back."

"Look at the first two cases in the file, Ben," Gil told him as he stood and grabbed his jacket. "I placed them in the front of the file even though they're the last two she helped on. One of them involved a little boy who your cousin helped find almost five years ago. Ally isn't as innocent as you want to believe, Ben."

"What the hell are you talking about?" Ben demanded, standing and slamming the file down on his desk with a loud thump.

"Ally killed a man."

"What?" Ben shook his head in denial.

"That's all it says," Gil stated as matter-of-factly as he could. "She shot and killed a man. Someone scribbled in self defense and it states that the DA decided not to prosecute at the time."

"Did you call and speak with the detective in charge?" Ben asked as his head spun.

"No, I thought that you might want to make that call yourself," Gil told him with a knowing look. "Either way, I'm here for you. I checked for you, Ben." Gil looked frustrated. "You know that someone else would have when they realized that we found her at the scene of the latest fire. I wanted to give you a heads up."

"Thanks," Ben murmured looking at the file like it was a bomb ready to explode and destroy his life. Maybe he was half right, he thought with a heavy sigh.

"You're family," Gil stated with a shrug. "That makes Ally family as well."

Ben watched Gil walk away and shook his head. That was Daniels' family logic for you. Nobody messed with family.

* * * * *

Griff couldn't take his eyes off Ally. The girl was absolutely gorgeous in her low-rise, belly-baring jeans and tight black top, the perfect outfit to show off her pierced navel. Her hair was a mass of black curls that hung over her shoulders, stopping in the middle of her back. But it was her eyes that got him, such a deep, dark green with flecks of gold in them. With the exotic tilt at the corners, she looked amazingly like Moira. The faces were similar. Of course they both had an awesome chest as well. But where Ally was short with dark hair, Moira was a tall blonde. Still, there was something there.

"You're awfully quiet, Ally," Griff stated, glancing over at her as he pulled into the open space in front of the apartment building. "Anything on your mind?"

Ally gave a vague smile. "Too much on my mind to even begin getting into."

"I've been told that I'm pretty easy to talk to," Griff assured her. "So anytime that you need someone just let me know."

Griff turned the engine off and Ally glanced over at the entrance to the apartment building. Waiting in front of it were Shep, a darker skinned man with a ponytail who she figured must be Chetan, and none other than Blake. She glared back at Griff and hissed. "You didn't tell me that Blake would be here."

Griff grinned. "Didn't know for sure. We invite him all the time since he and Shep became such good friends, but Blake can be a loner at times. He doesn't always come to our get-togethers. Then again," his eyes twinkled as he reached for his door handle, "we can often be a little hard to take when we're all together."

"Shit," Ally muttered and then was startled as her door was pulled open. She glanced up and fell into the smoldering gaze of the man she had spent last night with. He looked good — too good. And with her sitting in the car and him standing in the open door, that bulge behind his zipper was in the perfect place for her to lean forward and nip him with her teeth. It took every ounce of willpower that she had not to.

Ally released her seatbelt and vaguely heard Griff shutting the driver's side door. Blake's hand appeared and she took it as she stepped out of the car. Expecting him to step back out of the way, Ally instead found herself flush against Blake's rock-hard body. She glanced up at him and gasped when he lowered his head down and took her lips in a hungry kiss. His tongue slipped inside her mouth and rubbed along her own until she moaned. Somehow the door was shut and she was trapped between it and Blake. And God help her, she didn't want to move.

Finally, the sound of a throat clearing gained their attention and Blake pulled back from the kiss, allowing them both a much-needed breath of fresh air.

"Damn, honey," Blake whispered quietly for her ears alone. "You look fucking hotter than hell in that outfit. I wish we were already back at my place for the night. I know just what I want to do with you."

Before Ally could reply Shep was beside them. "Now that you've got that out of the way, you two ready to head up?" His grin was wicked, but Ally could clearly see the glitter of lust in his gaze.

"Yeah," Blake answered for them and took her hand in his firm grasp, turning to lead them to where Griff and the other man stood waiting just outside the entrance.

Holy Hannah! What had she got herself into? Blake made her body burn. Yet Shep caused a similar reaction. Maybe not quite as intense but definitely there. She remembered Blake telling Shep when they first met that the first time was his and she wondered again just what he had meant by that. And if it meant what she thought and these two planned on making an Ally sandwich what would she do? She'd never been with two men at the same time before and wasn't sure how that would work. She looked from Blake to Shep and back again and had to admit, at least to herself, that she was more than willing to give it a try.

Ally had met so many people that she didn't know if she could keep all the names straight. Griff had introduced her to his mother Catherine first, and Ally found that she really liked the matriarch of the Daniels family. Catherine was just about the same height as Ally with wavy brown hair that fell to her shoulders in a classic bob and big brown eyes. She must be in her late fifties but the woman looked so much younger. Ally could only hope that she would age half as well.

Katie and Ben were there but for some reason Ben wouldn't meet her gaze and she wondered if he knew about the night she had spent in Blake's bed. She was twenty-six and deserved a sex life just as much as everyone else did. If that was what was bothering her cousin, than he could just get over it. Besides, he lost the right to say anything to her when he walked away and didn't look back. She could understand him leaving his father and that ice bitch of a mother behind. Hell she could even see him leaving his older brother Pres behind, though she wondered if he was aware of the reasons Pres did what he did. But she couldn't understand why he hadn't contacted her or her mother. They had always been on his side and they hadn't deserved to be abandoned.

The ponytail guy had indeed been Chetan and although he was mostly quiet, when he did speak his rather a dry sense of humor made Ally smile. There was something about him that touched her and when they had clasped hands she knew he felt it as well. He had the power of vision just as much as she did, but for some reason he chose not to use it. She was intrigued by him and hoped to learn more.

Next she had been introduced to Moira, Gil's wife, and her father Jack. Moira was the owner of the gym Ally had been shown earlier in the day, Knowledge Is Power. Although she should have met the other woman there, work had kept Moira busy and Ally hadn't had the chance. Moira had the toned body one would associate with a gym owner and a bubbly personality that would make people feel comfortable around her. She instantly put Ally at ease and had her laughing at stories of little incidents that had occurred at the gym that day.

Jack was something else entirely. He studied her like she was a puzzle he was determined to solve. He was tall with sandy-brown hair and green eyes the same shade as his daughter's. Something about him tugged at her memory but she couldn't place it. She was happy when he excused himself and stepped over to speak with another man who Moira told her was Roman. Roman glanced over at them and nodded at something Jack said.

Katie joined them and the three women chatted and laughed. Ally felt like she belonged, as if she could actually be friends with these women, which was a new feeling for her. But then again, none of them had seen her in action yet and that sight usually changed everything.

"So, how long have your mom and Roman been together?" Ally asked Katie.

"What?" Moira asked startled.

Katie just nodded her head and smiled. So Roman was the mystery man in her mother's life. Now that Ally had mentioned it, she could see the looks they sent each other's way when they thought no one else was looking. How had she not seen it before? "For a few months now," Katie murmured and laughed when Moira squeaked and glared at her.

"How long have you known and why didn't you tell me?" Moira demanded of her sister-in-law.

"I've known for a while that she was seeing someone," Katie confessed quietly. "But I didn't realize who until Ally said something."

"Oh, Lord," Ally murmured. "I'm so sorry. I just thought...well...I should have just kept my big mouth shut."

"No, I'm glad that you noticed," Katie assured her. "All this time I've been wondering if it was Jack."

"My dad?" Moira laughed at that. "I can't see your mom with my dad. Roman...yeah, I can see that."

"He's a good guy?" Katie asked although she already figured what the answer would be.

"Roman is an amazing man," Moira assured her. "Your mom is a very lucky woman."

"Yep, she is," Griff agreed, walking up and joining them just in time to hear Moira's comment. "She married the love of her life and spent thirty-four years with him. She has four great kids who will watch over and protect her. And now she has her first grandchild on the way." Griff grinned at them all. "What more could a mother ask for?"

Oh, hell, Ally thought as Moira and Katie exchanged looks. Griff had no idea that his mom was seeing someone. Hell, it seemed as if he expected her to live the rest of her life as a widow and a mother. Ally didn't think he would take too well to the idea that his mother was seeing another man, no matter how long his father had been gone. Griff, the man who loved all women, had forgotten that his mother was still a woman as well. And when he did find out, the shit would definitely hit the fan.

"Hey, Ally," Ben walked over and joined them. "Care to take a walk with me and talk for a few minutes?" He pulled Katie up so that her back rested against his chest and placed a kiss on the top of her head.

Ally looked in his eyes and knew that he had found something out. Either about her mother's death, Ally's work with the police, or maybe even worse. She prayed he hadn't found out the worst thing. Before she could gather her thoughts enough to answer, the door to the apartment opened and two gorgeous men walked in with a beautiful woman.

Ally knew that this must bet the threesome Griff had told her about. She could see the love that they all shared and they definitely weren't shy about giving and receiving small touches in front of others.

"It's finally official," the brunette informed everyone. "The paperwork came in today. Damon is officially a Daniels now."

Congratulations rang through the room as the group was surrounded. Hugs and pats on the back were exchanged. It made Ally really sad to watch the open affection and love these people had for each other. The only people she had ever shared that with were now dead. She tried to fade into the background as those she had been talking to merged on the trio as well. Ben was laughing and joking and seemed to have forgotten about wanting to talk to her. She took another step back and collided with a hard body. A hard body that she recognized easily and instantly.

Blake pulled her tightly to his body loving the feel of her against him. Damn, he wanted to leave and take her back to his house. He wanted to fuck her 'til they were both screaming from pleasure. And he would soon, he promised himself. "They're an affectionate family, Ally. I told you that at Ben's house."

"Yes, you did," Ally agreed, but truth was she wasn't paying attention to anyone else in the room at the moment. It was too delicious to be in Blake's arms again, to feel him against her even if it was with their clothes on. "I didn't know that you were coming."

"I usually don't," Blake stated. "I'm not much of a people person. Never have been. But every once in a while it's good to get out and see what I'm missing."

He sounded a little sad and Ally couldn't help but wonder what secrets lay in his past that still haunted him. "And what is it that you are missing?" she asked softly. She heard him sigh behind her before he answered just as softly, his voice so close to her ear that she could feel his breath against her.

"Life. Family. And all that those bring to a person," Blake said. "Do you believe in second chances, Ally?"

Ally didn't know where this was leading, but she felt compelled to answer anyway. "I don't know. I do believe in fate and destiny."

"And what about love, Ally? Do you believe in love? Love at first sight?" His voice has gone husky and she almost jumped when he nipped her earlobe with his teeth.

"I...I don't know if I do or not," Ally admitted and was surprised that she could force the words out without letting loose the moan she was trying desperately to hold in. His teeth felt so good and she was desperate to feel them on other more sensitive places on her body. Her nipples peaked beneath her tight t-shirt and she prayed that no one would look their way.

"Come home with me again tonight?" Blake whispered in her ear before slipping his tongue in for a gentle exploration. "I need you in my bed, Ally."

Ally closed her eyes and took a shallow breath. When she opened them Shep was looking at her and Blake, and Ally could clearly see the lust in his eyes. "Just the two of us," Ally said without thinking and then could have bitten her tongue off at Blake's husky chuckle.

"That's up to you Ally," he gave a soft tug on her ear again with his teeth. "The two of us or the three of us. It doesn't matter so long as I'm with you."

"Do you and Shep share women often?" she asked.

Blake sighed and turned her in his arms so that they could see each other's faces. "I'm not going to lie to you, Ally. Shep and I are the best of friends. He has a key to my house and sometimes he comes over and spends the night. Sometimes he brings women with him and, if they're willing, then we share. I hear that it can be the most intense sexual experience that a woman has." He pulled her even closer so that her belly was flush against his thick erection. "Imagine the two of us worshipping your body with our mouths and hands and cocks. Two men, Ally, with you as their sole focus."

"Yes," Ally whispered, though she could feel the blush on her cheeks.

"You'll come home with me?" Ally nodded her head, but her gaze wouldn't meet his. Blake brushed his fingers down her cheek to her chin and urged her face up to look into his. "Just me, or both of us?" He wouldn't let her escape his gaze as he waited for her decision.

"Both of you," she whispered and felt his cock jerk between them. She couldn't believe that a man could be so turned on about sharing a woman with another man. She had always assumed that most men were possessive. But by the feel of Blake and his husky moan, he was anticipating their evening even more than she was. And she was definitely anticipating. But she was also nervous and just a tad bit worried if she would measure up to the women Blake and Shep had shared in the past. Could she handle two men at the same time? She looked up at Blake and remembered her earlier encounter with Shep. Maybe she could. Maybe she couldn't. But she sure as hell planned to enjoy every moment with the two of them that she could.

"Time to eat," Catherine called from the table where she and some of the others must have set out the food while everyone else had been talking.

Blake dropped a quick kiss on Ally's lips and caught her hand in his, tugging her along with him as he moved toward the table of food. That big hand felt so right in hers and Ally caught her breath with a jolt of surprise at the emotions bombarding her. She had assumed that the destiny that Legacy held for her was to stop The Messenger and end his reign of fire and terror. Now she found herself wondering if Blake was part of her destiny as well.

Chapter Seven

℅

Ally slipped into the kitchen, hoping that no one would notice that she was gone. She had counted fifteen people, not including herself, and discovered that the reason they all fit so well into the apartment was that none of them had any sense of personal space. Well, except for Blake, that was. Ally had found herself laughing at his attempts to keep some personal space between him and this extended family.

She wasn't surprised when she heard someone slip into the kitchen behind her. She was when she turned and saw Ben instead of Blake or Shep. She had noticed Blake and Shep speaking earlier and from the look of lust in Shep's eyes, she was fairly certain that the two had discussed what was to happen later in the evening.

"I'd like to talk to you about a few things," Ben said bringing Ally back to the present with a jolt.

"Like what?" Ally asked warily.

"I have your file, Ally, a file filled with all the cases that you've worked on in the past with law enforcement." Ben fought the need to hug her to him. Now wasn't the time for that. Now was the time to figure out a few things. "How were you able to help with the cases?"

"If you have the file then I'm sure you've already read about my skills Ben," Ally spoke with a calm tone, but her rigid posture showed how unwilling she was to have this conversation. "But let me fill you in anyway. I just seem to connect with some cases. Not all, but some. Usually I know once I've seen and touched an object in relation to the case. Sometimes I relate to the victim and sometimes I connect with the killer, or kidnapper, or rapist. It is not a pleasant experience. Once I connect I can see things through their perception. Sometimes scenes from the crime or leading up to it, sometimes I see where they are at the moment. I've been able to help the police many times, but usually only as a last resort."

"That's what I thought," Ben replied. There was no way he would tell her about all the derogatory remarks in her file. He could tell that she already had an idea of how cops felt when working with someone possessed of her particular talents. Most would treat her with skepticism, but some would be harsher in both their judgment and their treatment. He had read some of that in the file Gil had gathered as well. "Why didn't you tell me that Tory and Roni were killed in a fire?"

"It's not like we've had a chance to speak, Ben. I would have told you," Ally assured him.

"You had the entire day today to stop in at the station and see me," Ben argued. "Or you could have stayed at my house last night and talked."

"If you've read my file than surely you can understand why I didn't stop in at the station." Ally gave him a hard look before adding, "And last night I had other plans."

"I don't want to think about that," Ben muttered, knowing that she had left with Blake and fairly certain that she had ended up in the man's bed.

"I'm twenty-six years old, Ben. I make my own decisions and have for a long time. Besides, you didn't walk back into my life and probably never would have. I walked into yours."

"That's not fair Ally," Ben tried to argue.

"You walked away, Ben. Not just from your ass of a father and bitch of a mother but from all of us. The only person you saw as worthy was your grandfather. I'm sure he appreciated that." There was no disguising her anger as she spoke.

"I'm sorry, Ally." And he was. He and Ally had once been close when they were kids. Hell, there was many a time when he had been the one to step in and take Ally's side. "I would have found you eventually."

"You keep telling yourself that, Ben," Ally shook her head and walked to the fridge taking out a bottle of water. "Bottom line is that it doesn't matter at this point."

Ben heaved a harsh sigh. "When you showed up here you had no idea that I was in this town, did you?"

"No, I wasn't looking for you either," Ally said matter-of-factly.

"You showed up at a crime scene, dressed like a cat burglar. That wasn't an accident, was it, Ally?" Ben looked her in the eyes believing that she wouldn't lie to him. "He killed Tory and Roni, didn't he?"

There was fire in her eyes when she finally answered him. "Yes, he did."

"What do you know about this case?" Ben asked her.

"I'd like to know that as well," Blake said as he stepped into the kitchen with Gil and Shep. He wanted to go to Ally and take her in his arms but the vibes she was sending off were definitely saying don't touch me.

"Not now. Not here. I'll tell you but this is not the time." Ally turned away from them all and faced the sink wrapping her arms around her waist as if she felt the need to hold herself together.

"When everyone else leaves then," Gil stated firmly. "You don't leave 'til we get some answers."

"Fine," Ally snapped out, still facing away from them.

"There's one more thing that you're going to have to tell us as well, Ally," Ben murmured and something in his voice caused her to turn around. "I have to know if you killed that man."

Blake and Shep looked startled, but it was obvious that Gil knew exactly what Ben was referring to leading her to believe that both detectives had looked at her file. They wanted the truth. A simple yes or no to answer a question about something that was more complicated than they could ever know. Fine. She would give them just that.

"Yes, I killed him." Ally took the time to look all four men in the eyes before adding one more bombshell. "And my only regret is that I can't do it all over again."

Cass, Doug and Damon left first and Ally was sure that everyone in the room was certain of just how the threesome would be finishing the celebration that night. The love that radiated from them was obvious and Ally couldn't help but wonder how on earth Cass handled two such virile and dominant men. Then Ally glanced over to where Blake and Shep were talking with Griff and Chetan. She hoped that when this night finally ended she would find out that answer for herself.

Catherine left next with another woman who Ally now knew was Michelle, Jack Madigan's sister. They didn't look anything alike, really, and according to Katie, Jack and Moira hadn't even known that Michelle existed until the Asian woman had shown up in group therapy at gym Moira's gym. Katie said that Michelle was a very nice woman and from what Ally had seen so far she would have to agree. Ally smiled to herself as she caught both Catherine and Roman throwing looks at each other. She didn't understand exactly why they were hiding their relationship but from what she had heard Griff say earlier she had a pretty good idea.

Once the door closed behind the two women, Gil immediately turned to Ally. "You ready to talk now?"

Ally looked around at all who were still in the room. Blake, Shep, Griff and Chetan were over by the table, now cleared of food. Roman and Jack were sitting on the sectioned couch. Moira and Katie were still in the kitchen but the divider was now opened between the two rooms making Ally aware that probably everyone had heard the earlier conversation. Gil was just inside the closed door to the apartment and Ben was sitting in a soft easy chair.

"Are you sure you don't want to call the other five back so that they don't miss any of the good stuff?" Ally asked with sarcasm dripping from her voice. She was positive that the others would learn of what she said anyway and it pissed her off. But what could she expect. They weren't her family. She didn't have any family anymore. She shot a harsh glance to Ben. "Which shall I go into first? The pyro who killed my mother and is now doing his dirty work in Legacy? Or how about the man I shot and killed in cold blood? Which juicy story would you like me to share first?"

"Ally…" Ben started but she cut him off with a look of such disgust that it literally froze him in place.

"Don't try to play the protective, sincere family card with me, Tommy. Oh, excuse me, it's Ben now isn't it? We both know that you crossed that bridge long ago."

"That doesn't mean that I don't care about you anymore, Ally, that I don't love you." Ben looked at her and maybe for the first time really thought of all the ties that he had cut when he had walked away from his family. He had left everyone behind, family and friends. He regretted it after seeing Ally again. The only people he had meant to hurt were the ones who probably never cared—his mother, father and big brother.

"Maybe it means that I don't," Ally stated and complete silence filled the room.

"Ally…" Ben tried again.

"Don't," Ally turned away from him and walked as far away from everyone as she could get and still be in the room, which wasn't far. "Just don't." She took a deep breath and closed her eyes. "Which story do you want first?" her voice was calm and collected now but there was no disguising the hint of pain.

"Tell us about the murder, Ally." It was Gil who spoke and when Ally opened her eyes she was shocked to see compassion on the faces of the men in the room. It made her wonder just how many of them had the same skeletons in their closets.

"I was working on a case with local police." She began quietly, closing her eyes again and seeing it all play out in her head. "A local boy was reported kidnapped and his parents were desperate to find him. The mom brought in a teddy bear for me to see if I could connect with it, with her little boy." Ally took a deep breath before continuing. It was hard to remember this. It was this very case that had her walking away and refusing to try to help again, no matter what the circumstances. It was a time she would never forget. "His name was Justin. He was six years old at the time. When I touched the bear I connected with him instantly. I could feel his terror. The fear was clawing at him and I felt suffocated by it." Ally's pulse pounded as she continued, reliving the moments in her mind. "I could make out a room. He was in a room and someone was with him. Justin was sitting on a bed his knees drawn to his chest with his arms wrapped around them. He was just rocking and all I could feel was his terror. It consumed him and me as well. I was eventually able to make out some of the things in the room and one of the detectives recognized it as a tiny motel on the outskirts of town."

Ally's eyes were still closed tight as she continued. "I went with them. I'm not sure what made me insist but I did. Even then I felt something was off. But Justin's terror was just so… Well, when we got there it was all just as I described. I remember watching the police enter the room with guns drawn. I remember watching Justin's dad charge in shoving people out of his way. I watched as he drew a gun from under his shirt and shot the other man in the room twice. That was when I realized something that I should have picked up on before. Justin wasn't terrified of the man who took him." Her eyes opened and immediately locked with Blake's. "He was terrified of the man who had been molesting him. His father."

Ally heard a gasp from the kitchen but she couldn't look away from Blake. "When his dad turned to him Justin began screaming. I was the only one who knew why. I was filled with this little boy's terror. The closer I was to him the more intensely his emotions become mine. I must have grabbed a gun from one of the cops beside me. I heard the gun shots but it wasn't until much later that I realized that I was the one who had shot and killed a man."

"The mother never knew what Justin's dad had done to him until a few years later when Justin confessed it all to her. The man who took Justin turned out to be a local college boy who baby sat for the family occasionally. He was trying to save Justin and instead he was shot and killed."

"Oh, Ally," Ben started to her but stopped when she spoke again.

"Don't," she stated firmly. "I'm too raw right now. Don't touch me." She took a deep breath and continued. "I'm not sorry for killing him and if given the chance under the same circumstances I would do it all over again. The only thing that saved me was the fact that Justin's dad was pointing his gun at me at the time I shot, or so I was told. The DA decided against prosecution and I walked away."

"You didn't walk away, Ally," Blake said as he came up to her and, even though she held her hands out as if to ward him off, he pulled her snugly into his arms and against his chest. "Limped or crawled, maybe. But you didn't just walk away from it."

Ally's body shook with the silent sobs she refused to release but everyone in the room was aware of the toll it must have taken for her to relive those moments.

"I'm taking Ally home now," Blake said to the room at large. "She's had enough questions for the night. You can all meet at my house in the morning to discuss the fire. But for right now, she's had enough."

Ally was quiet on the ride to Blake's house and Blake didn't push conversation. She was aware that Shep would be following them shortly but couldn't drum up the same level of excitement that she had felt earlier. She was still raw from reliving the shooting and Justin's terror. She felt broken inside. There were things that she hadn't shared with everyone, things she never would. Like the way that she had seen the harsh memories of the countless nights of abuse that Justin had suffered at the hands of a man who should have protected him. Like the fact that she had been dating one of the cops, who had broken things off after that day telling her that he couldn't see her any more because dating the town freak would ruin his career.

"We're here," Blake said snapping Ally out of her morbid thoughts and bringing her back to the present.

She shook her head when she realized that they were already shut in his garage and the truck was off. "Sorry, Blake," Ally said with a sad smile. "Maybe I'm not good company tonight. Maybe I should just head back to the apartment that Griff showed me."

"You could," Blake nodded, then caught her off guard with a wicked grin. "But all your stuff will be here." She gave him a confused look and he continued releasing both of their seatbelts while he spoke. "Shep is stopping by there and getting your bag on his way here." He pulled her across the seat to him and held her close. "You shouldn't be alone tonight, honey. We don't have to do anything but hold each other. But you shouldn't be alone."

Ally could feel the tears burning the backs of her eyes. It felt like forever since she had really had anyone care about her though in actuality it was not quite a full year since her mom and Tory had been killed. Blake felt so right, so perfect holding her close but part of her was still uncertain, still afraid. How long before he pushed her away to save his career? How long until she was forced to move on and try to start over again?

"Come on," Blake said as he opened his door and pulled Ally out after him. "How about a nice soak in the hot tub? That might make you feel better." He tugged her into the house and headed through the living room to a patio door that she hadn't noticed earlier. He left her standing there in the shadows while he opened the door and flipped a switch that turned on a low wattage outdoor light.

His patio was beautiful. There was a huge grill against the back rail of the deck as well as a patio table with four chairs. There was something that looked like a couch with a low coffee table in front of it with two other chairs that matched the ones at the table. Then there were two long loungers and in the back corner to the left of the door was a huge Jacuzzi hot tub that looked like it could easily seat twelve people. Blake had removed the cover and hit a switch and Ally watched as the water began to churn and bubble. There was steam rising into the air around it and at that moment she wanted nothing more than to feel it on her skin. Her gaze landed on the box of condoms lying on the deck and she inhaled a sharp breath. A trickle of excitement worked down her spine and chills erupted on her arms.

"I can find something here for you to wear if you want," Blake stated as he walked back into the room.

"You keep women's bathing suits here?" Ally asked and almost laughed when Blake flushed.

"No," he said. "But I can find you a dark colored t-shirt to wear with your panties if you want."

Ally smiled and did laugh, then. He was just too sweet. "You've already seen me naked, Blake."

She could see the fire in his eyes that he was trying so hard to keep banked. "Shep will be here soon, Ally. If you don't want anything to happen then maybe we should all keep our clothes on for now."

He was trying to be good, putting her first and not pressuring her about her earlier decision to come back here and have sex with both men. But the truth was that reliving the moments earlier made her want tonight with Blake and Shep even more. She needed to feel alive, to feel free. She needed every wicked, carnal deed that the two men could dream up.

She smiled and bent to remove her boots, placing them to the side of the door. Her t-shirt followed and then she shrugged out of her jeans, taking her socks with them. She looked up at Blake and reached back to unfasten her bra and add it to the pile. She heard his indrawn breath when her breasts were uncovered and slid her hands over her nipples, stimulating them to harder points as she moved down to her panties. She eased them down over her hips and when they puddled at her feet, she used her foot to toss them onto the top of her other clothes.

She smiled at him, enjoying the fire in his eyes as much as the sight of the bulge straining against his zipper. "I'll be in the hot tub. Come and join me whenever you want to." With that she stepped out into the cool October air and hurried to the rising steam.

Blake watched from the door, enjoying the view of all her jiggling parts as much as the effect that the cool air had on them. Her gorgeous breasts were bouncing high on her chest and her nipples were hard tight points that made his mouth water with the need to suck them. The jewel resting snugly in her navel begged for his attention. Her ass was firm and perfectly rounded and he couldn't wait to take her from behind, to feel it against his stomach as he pounded into the welcoming heat of her pussy.

He groaned and reached for the hem of his shirt. He couldn't get out of his clothes fast enough and almost landed on his ass when he tried to jerk his shoes off without unlacing them first. Finally he was just as naked as she was and he hurried out the door to join her.

Her eyes followed him as he walked closer to the hot tub.

Blake was perfection striding toward her with his huge cock bobbing in front of him. She moved toward the steps and knelt there waiting for him. When Blake stopped at the tub, his cock was just where she wanted it and Ally leaned in and took him in her mouth.

"Ummm..." she moaned. "You taste so good." She licked around the crown, paying special attention to the notch just under the sensitive head. She used her lips to nibble along a particularly thick vein that ran underneath and followed it all the way to the base. She took the time to lick and suckle at his balls, enjoying the smoothness of the taut globes in her mouth.

"You shave," she commented, loving the fact that he didn't have a huge bush of hair covering his sex.

"I like to be clean and neat," Blake stated in a tight voice, reveling in the feel of her hot little mouth moving over him. "Just like you."

"I have some hair," Ally commented while she licked him like an ice cream cone, stopping every once in a while to suck at the head.

"I like that you do," Blake said. "You're trimmed and neat, just like a woman should be. I've never been one for hairless pussy. It just isn't right. Makes me feel like I'm with a little girl and that's just wrong."

"Ummm..." Ally said again as she took his long length as deeply into the back of her throat as she could and held it there for a moment. She heard Blake's harsh curse and knew he was holding tight to his control to keep from trying to ram it deeper. Finally she pulled back and licked at the head, again hungry for the drops of cum that were already easing from him. "I never thought of it that way before. But I'll admit that you have a point."

"Ally," Blake groaned when she took him into her throat again. "If you keep doing that, then I'm going to come and I really want to be inside you when that happens."

251

"You will be inside me," she grinned up at him and took just the head in her mouth and sucked it.

"Fuck, Ally," Blake grunted and pulled away from her, his cock releasing with a loud pop. "I want to be buried so far in your hot little pussy that you still taste me in the back of your throat when I come." He nudged her back from the steps and entered the hot tub. "Step up on the step there," he urged her and when she did, he knelt in front of her, lining his mouth up with her pussy. "Let's see if you taste as good as you look."

With that, Blake used his fingers to part her folds and licked her slit from top to bottom and back up again, stopping to suckle her clit. Ally gripped his shoulders with her hands to maintain her balance as he used his mouth and fingers to plunder and explore. He would work her to the edge of orgasm with his fingers and then back off and use his tongue to sooth and caress. Finally Ally couldn't take it anymore.

"Please, Blake," she begged him. "Please make me come."

Blake gave a harsh groan and buried two fingers in her core, thrusting and retreating with them as he used his whole mouth to stimulate her clit. The scrape of his teeth followed by the harsh suction of his mouth and then the gentle touch of his tongue was enough to send her crashing into orgasm. She knew that her screams were filling the air but was helpless to stop them. She felt Blake remove his fingers and replace them with his tongue and it was enough to trigger another round of small pulses through her.

"Enough," she finally managed, feeling as if she were going to collapse. "I can't take any more."

Blake pulled back and smiled up at her. "Too bad. This is only the beginning." He turned so that he could sit on the bench beside where she was standing and reached for the box of condoms. He dumped plenty out on the deck and grabbed one, opening it and standing to place it on his erection. He eased back into the water and pulled her onto his lap with her facing away from him. His hands disappeared under the water and then she felt the nudge of his cock at her opening. With one sharp thrust he was buried and Ally cried out at the bombardment of sensations.

"Put your arms up around my neck," Blake said and guided her so that she laced her fingers behind his neck. His hands came back to her nipples and he tugged and pulled at them while he gave small thrusts inside her.

"No, fair," Ally murmured to him. "I wanted to suck your cock."

"I'll let you suck this one," Shep said from the doorway and stepped out of the shadows to join them. He was deliciously naked and Ally caught her breath at the sheer beauty of him. He was as tall as Blake, only with shaggy blonde hair that fell around his shoulders. She could barely make out a scar high on his shoulder that looked like a knife wound and she could see the marks of what must have been bullet wounds. She'd once dated a cop and had seen the guys playing sports with no shirts on. She knew what a healed bullet wound looked like and Shep had many of them. He literally looked like a warrior and she could easily understand why women felt drawn to him.

Her eyes traveled downward as he walked toward them and she licked her lips at the view of his erection. It was everything a woman dreamed of and a few inches more. Shep was using his hand to stroke it from balls to tip as he walked. She couldn't wait to get her mouth on him.

"I saw you sucking Blake's cock, Ally. Watched him eat that pretty little cunt 'til you screamed. I watched those gorgeous tits bouncing with every breath and the way that your nipples flushed and hardened even more with your orgasm." He stepped into the hot tub until he was standing right in front of where she was sitting on Blake's lap. With them sitting on the top shelf and Shep standing on the bottom, the water was at the top of his thighs and his cock was right there in front of her.

"You want to suck my cock, Ally?" Shep asked again and stopped his hand at the base and held it out to her.

Ally unwrapped her arms from Blake's neck and leaned forward, crying out with pleasure at the way it changed the angle of Blake's cock and pushed it deeper into her pussy. She rested her hands on Shep's thighs and ran her tongue over the engorged tip of his cock, catching a drop of his semen when it slipped out. They both moaned in pleasure. Shep wrapped his hands in her hair and held it back out of her face so that he could watch her lick and suck at his flesh.

She felt Blake moving behind her and with his hands he guided her until she was standing on the shelf between where he sat and Shep stood. He used his hands to press her back into the arch that he wanted and surged high inside her again. She cried out around Shep's cock and panted for air. Blake was fucking her now, working his cock in and out of her, and each hard thrust jarred Shep's cock deeper into her mouth.

"Just suck on it," Shep told her when he went impossibly deep into the back of her throat and she gagged a little. "You just suck it and I'll work it in and out."

She did as he said and it was pure heaven. His cock was so long and thick that she couldn't get more than three-quarters of it in her mouth at a time, but she sucked greedily on every inch he fed her. Blake was pounding into her now and she was so close to coming again. He felt so good, his cock rubbing against her inner walls and the slight pull of tissue with every outward movement.

She was so focused on Blake's motion that she didn't realize how close Shep was until his voice caught her attention.

"I'm going to come," his mouth was a harsh line as he tried to hold it back. "If you don't want it then you need to let go."

Ally just sucked harder, anxious for the wash of his seed over her tongue and down her throat. Shep gave a cry and filled her mouth with his cock, holding it there as the first burst of seed left his cock. She swallowed it down and kept sucking while he gave small thrusts until he had emptied his cock. He immediately dropped to his knees in the water, moving her hands to his shoulders so that her breasts were in perfect position for him. He latched on to one nipple and sucked fiercely on it while he treated the other one to little pinches and tugs.

Blake moved one of his hands around to rub across her clit while he used the other to hold onto her hip. "Hurry, honey," he urged in a husky tone. "I'm going to come any minute."

Shep bit down on her nipple while Blake pinched her clit and Ally came with a scream. "Yes! Yes! Oh God, yes!" she moaned as she bucked against them. She felt Blake thrust into her two more times before he cried out his own release and emptied into her pulsing channel, filling the condom with his rich cream.

"Never this good," Blake gasped behind her, his hips flush against her ass as they both continued to pulse with their combined release. "It's never been this good before."

"Ummm…" was all that Ally could manage as she fought to fill her lungs with much-needed oxygen. He was right though. She had never had an orgasm so intense before, not even the first time with him. Shep stood up in front of them and she was amazed that his cock was fully aroused again after she had just sucked him off.

"Going to share that sweet pussy with me?" Shep questioned and Ally wasn't sure if he was asking her or Blake. She felt Blake tense behind her for a moment and then he must have nodded his consent because Shep focused on her. His fingers caressed her check and traced over her lips. "What do you say ? You want to go inside with me?"

She knew that this was what they had planned and God help her, she really did want to feel him inside her. She gave a slow nod of her head and gasped when Shep lifted her up into his arms and maneuvered them both out of the hot tub. "We'll see you inside," he tossed over his shoulder to Blake as he entered the house and carried Ally to where she knew Blake's bedroom was.

Blake sat up on the ledge of the hot tub, removing the spent condom and tying it off. He was in serious trouble here. What the hell was the matter with him? He and Shep shared women all the time. What made Ally any different? What was it that made him want to hoard her for himself and not share? He couldn't believe the jealousy that had seized him for a brief moment when Shep had asked if he could fuck her. Blake had fought against the sharp need to grab Ally close to his chest and holler "mine". Which just didn't make sense. He wasn't a possessive or even a jealous guy, which was part of the reason his first marriage didn't work. So what made Ally so different? He surged out of the water and hit the deck, moving quickly to join Shep and her in the house. He didn't know exactly what it was, but he knew that he had to be with her, sharing every moment.

Chapter Eight

∽

He watched her weave up the walkway to the little house on the edge of town, the home that he had followed her and the man to last night. He was displeased to see that she was obviously drunk again, but at least the jezebel seemed to be alone this time. Of course, the alcohol would help prevent her from smelling the chloroform on the special pillowcase that he had placed on her pillow. He knew just where to watch, knew just where her bedroom was. He'd give her ten minutes, then he would begin.

He was God's messenger and it was his calling to save the souls of the wicked, to cleanse the sins from their spirits with the fires of justice. After all he was an ordained minister, thanks to the ease of the internet, and now he bore the official seal of one sent by God to tend to the flock. For only through the flames of salvation would he save their souls and cleanse them so that they could walk in the halls of heaven with the Lord and Savior. Yes, he would save all the little children from their earthly prison.

The light switched off and The Messenger looked down at his watch. Four minutes and the baptism of fire would be set in motion.

* * * * *

Shep placed Ally gently on the bed and opened the bedside table to remove a handful of condoms before settling his big body between her splayed thighs. His mouth possessed hers, his tongue sinking in and exploring every inch of her mouth. His hands were busy manipulating her flesh from breasts to thighs, working her into another frenzy of need that she hadn't expected after her recent orgasm. Shep moved down to her breasts and worshipped them with his teeth and tongue while his fingers played in the pool of desire that lay between her legs. He knew just where to touch and the exact amount of pressure to use to send her keening toward another orgasm.

She heard a noise and looked up to see Blake standing in the doorway watching them. He was stroking one hand up and down his thick erection while he used the other to play with his balls. He looked so good to her, so powerful and god-like. She felt like his devoted servant who was willing to go to any length to ensure that he was satisfied. And she would. She watched as he walked to the bed and stood watching Shep pleasure her.

"Do you want a true ménage, Ally?" he asked in that husky voice that betrayed the need burning in him. "Or just like we did in the hot tub?"

"A true ménage? I thought that's what we already had." Ally looked from Shep's grin to Blake's taut features. "What's the difference?"

"What we had out there was pussy and mouth," Shep informed her, thrusting two fingers in and out of her core. "What he's asking is if you want to try pussy and ass." He slipped his coated fingers out of her vagina and pushed one into her anus to the first knuckle, letting her feel the pinch of tension as he passed the first ring of muscle. Ally cried out at the sensation and bucked against him.

"You like that?" Shep questioned as he worked the finger a little deeper using his other hand to draw her natural lubrication back. Ally moaned. It felt different, not over-the-top good but not bad either. She had heard other women talk about anal sex and was interested but also cautious.

"You want to try it, Ally? Two men thrusting inside you with nothing separating them but a thin membrane of your flesh? It'll feel so good," he promised in that velvet voice of his. "We'll make it feel so good."

"What do you want, Ally?" Blake brought her attention back to him. "It's up to you, honey. If you don't want to then it's okay. We'll do whatever you're comfortable with."

He blew Ally away with his knack for reading her and his willingness to cater to her wishes. She honestly knew that if she said no he'd be fine with it. He wouldn't pressure her to get what he wanted or make her feel bad. And damn it, he was making her fall in love with him a little more every moment. "I want to try," she replied and both men groaned. "On one condition," she added quickly and both men focused on her. "I want Blake to be the one, you know…"

Blake smiled and nodded. He wanted nothing more than to be the man to initiate her into anal sex. When done right, the woman's orgasm could reach new heights, especially when her pussy was receiving equal stimulation. "I'd love to."

Ally nodded and Shep moved so that he lay in the middle of the bed on his back. He reached for a condom and tossed it aside, grabbing another. He waggled his eyebrows at her and showed it to her. It was ribbed for her pleasure and Ally almost laughed. She didn't think that she would need that extra touch, not this time. He slowly rolled the condom on and then reached for her. He lifted Ally up out of the way and placed her on top of him, balancing her while she positioned her legs so that she was straddling his stomach. Her pussy was hot and wet against him and he couldn't restrain the urge to grasp her hips and grind her into him. She felt ready and the look in her eyes confirmed it.

"Lift up a little bit," Shep told her and reached a hand down to grab his sheathed cock and help her center her pussy above it. "That's it," he encouraged her as she lowered herself onto his thick stalk, easing down slowly, taking one inch at a time. It was killing him, but he let her do it the way that she wanted to, the way that made her most comfortable.

Blake stood at the side of the bed, watching, using his hand and a tube of KY Jelly to lube the condom covering his cock. He wanted more than anything to make this an incredible sexual experience for her and that meant taking the time to make sure that she was as prepared as he could possibly make her. When she was firmly seated on Shep's cock, Blake nodded and Shep eased her down so that she lay flush against him, her ass up in the air calling to Blake.

He climbed onto the bed behind them, carrying the tube of jelly with him. He took his lube-coated hand and eased his finger into her ass, then slowly moved it out again. He did this a few times before adding more lube and another finger. Finally he had three fingers moving in and out of her, stretching her wide for the thick head of his cock. He knew that was what would hurt the most, but once the head was in the rest would be smoother. He squirted a little more lube along the tip of his erection and removed his fingers from her ass.

"About damn time," Shep muttered as Blake pressed between Ally's back cheeks, seeking permission to enter.

"Easy honey," Blake soothed when he felt her tighten up on him. "I'm almost in…just a little more…" He popped past the first ring of tight muscle and slid the rest of the way easily with the amount of lube he'd used to coat them both. "Just hold still for a minute and let your body adjust to us."

Ally took a deep breath and then another. It was sheer torture to stay still between these two men while both of their cocks were buried inside her. Her ass burned, but not in a "stop" kind of way. It was more like an "it hurts so good" kind of way. Most of all she knew that she wanted them to move, wanted to feel the slide of their flesh in hers and know that they were enjoying it as much as she was.

"Fuck me," she moaned. "Sweet merciful heaven, just fuck me."

Shep's eyes flared and Blake's fingers tightened on her hips but they both responded by thrusting further inside her. She cried out at the sharp pleasure-pain that seized her and knew that she wanted more, so much more. Blake pulled out first until only the flared head of his cock was still tucked inside her snug back hole. When he powered back in, it was Shep who pulled out. Back and forth they went with one thrusting while the other retreated until they had the perfect rhythm down. Ally was crying out with the need to counter their thrusts, but two sets of hands held her exactly where they wanted her.

She had never felt these sensations before and just when she thought she couldn't take any more, the men changed the rhythm so that they were both thrusting at the same time and then retreating as one. She was full and then she was empty and it was an agonizing emptiness that she never wanted to feel again. She came in a kaleidoscope of colors and she could swear that she really did see stars. It gripped her and wouldn't allow her to come down, instead taking her to higher planes of pleasure that she had never reached before. The only thought that filled her head as she heard Blake and Shep cry out and felt the heat as their semen filled the condoms was that Blake was absolutely right. Having two men at the same time provided a woman with the best orgasm that she would ever have.

* * * * *

Catherine lay in bed wondering where Roman was and if he was planning to stop by and see her before the night was over. She had been surprised to see him tonight as she thought he was out of town for the week. He must have gotten back earlier than he planned and she hadn't been home today so if he called she wouldn't have known. She was one of the few people who didn't have caller ID and Roman wouldn't leave a message out of concern for her should someone else be there and find it.

The truth was that she didn't know which she feared more. Him not stopping in or him showing up and wanting his answer. She still didn't know what to do. She was afraid of what people would say about her dating a man ten years younger than she was. But she was learning she was afraid of him doing just what he had said, walking away and not looking back.

She loved Roman and it was a hard struggle to deal with those emotions. She had thought that her life had ended as a woman when Mick died. She had gone into full mom mode and that was it. Then Gil had come to Legacy. Katie and Griff had followed and Doug and Damon had headed this way as well. So Catherine had sold the home where she and Mick had lived, loved and raised their children and moved to a comfy apartment building in Legacy.

Then she met Roman. There was something about him from the very beginning. It was his deep grey eyes that seemed to say so much when he was so silent. The sparks had flown every time they had accidentally touched, or maybe not so accidentally. His eyes said he wanted her but God help her she didn't know how to deal with it. She was a fifty-seven year old widow who had only been with one man in her entire life, only loved one man. And she had spent thirty-four years with him, the prime of her life in love with him.

Roman had shown up at her apartment a few times to talk and once he had used the excuse that he wanted to check her security and make sure she was safe. Then they had met for coffee. Then he had shown up one rainy night with water dripping off him and Catherine had hurried to get him some towels. When she stepped back into the room he had already stripped off his boots and socks by the door and his shirt was off and hanging on the coat rack to dry. Catherine had caught her breath and just looked at him.

Roman was gorgeous, all hard muscle. He still kept his sandy-brown hair military short and she loved it. It sounded so corny when people said it but their eyes had connected across the room and sparks had filled the small living room. Before she knew it they were together and doing their best to remove the clothes from themselves and each other. He had swept her into his arms and carried her into the bedroom.

Roman had tasted and teased her body from head to feet before finally spreading her thighs and thrusting inside.

Roman had shown that he was a wonderful passionate lover. He was big on foreplay which, since she was in her late fifties, was important to her. And she had done things with Roman that made her blush and feel like a young girl again. Sex with Mick had been wonderful, but it hadn't been creative. Vanilla sex was what they called it nowadays and that was what she had with Mick. But with Roman it was new and exciting. The positions, the foreplay, the games and the toys. My God, she had even had phone sex with the man. And the things he talked her into saying. She liked it. No, she loved it and damn the man, she loved him too. But if she had to choose she wasn't sure that she had the strength to pick him over her children.

* * * * *

The sound of the phone ringing woke them up. When Blake rolled away to answer it Ally automatically turned to Shep and cuddled close to his warmth. Shep threw an arm over her and pulled her closer, still loving the feel of her naked body against his. When Blake began cussing they both opened their eyes and sat up. Shep pulled her onto his lap and held her while they listened to one side of the conversation taking place.

"What's the address?" Blake flipped the bedside lamp on and began looking for the small pad of paper that was always there. "How long ago did it start? Fuck."

"Another fire," Ally murmured softly and shivered at the thought of The Messenger getting someone else.

Shep glanced down at her pale features and pulled the thick comforter up and over them.

Blake was now looking for clothes to throw on. "I'll be there in ten minutes. Nobody goes in until I get there. Get it put out and wait for me. Yeah, yeah, yeah, I know. Just do it."

He turned off the phone and slammed it on top of the dresser where he ripped open a drawer searching for fresh jeans. "Fuck," he muttered again.

"It was The Messenger," Ally whispered and Blake turned to look at her.

"The Messenger?" he questioned.

"That's what he calls himself. He thinks that he is God's messenger." Her face was pale and her green eyes looked huge. "I want to go with you. Please Blake, if I'm going to reconnect with him then I need to be there."

"I can't take you with me, Ally. It's not safe."

But Blake would go in and that's when it first dawned on Ally just what his job meant. He might not fight the fires but he was the one who went in to determine what caused them and sometimes that meant going into unstable places. It was a risk every time he entered a burned building or home and searched for clues to why and where.

"I need to be there, Blake." He shook his head and Ally cried out. "The match. He always leaves the match he used on the front steps of the house."

"How do you know that?" Blake demanded. They had purposely withheld that bit of information hoping to weed out any copycats and, of course, those people who called in and confessed to everything.

"I've connected with him before, Blake." Ally pushed away from Shep and stood beside the bed. "I've been inside his mind. He's an ordained minister, but he didn't go to school, he received it over the internet. He thinks that what he is doing is the right thing in order to cleanse the people from sin." She walked over to Blake and looked up into his eyes. "I need to see something, to touch something that still holds his touch. It will connect me with him again and I might be able to help find him."

Blake didn't want to hurt Ally, but what the hell was he supposed to say? Sure come on down and use your super woo-woo powers while the cops and firemen all gather round and watch the show? Fuck! He didn't know what to do. He looked over her head at Shep and Shep looked just as surprised by what Ally had just told them.

"You don't believe me," Ally said and went to turn away. Blake grabbed her and pulled her naked body against his.

"That's not it at all," he assured her. "It's just that I can't let anyone on the scene right now. Even Gil and Ben, who are the detectives assigned to this case, won't be allowed to enter yet. I have to do my job first. It's not about you. It's about the job and making sure that there are no mistakes." He tilted her head up to look at him and placed a kiss on her brow. "In my job mistakes can get you killed. Trust me?"

Ally nodded but inside she didn't know what to think. Was it really about his job or was it about her being a freak? She felt Shep move up behind her while Blake hurried to dress. Blake pulled her close and kissed her until she melted against him before setting her aside.

"I'll be gone for a while, so why don't you try to get a few more hours of sleep." They both glanced at the clock that was showing two-thirty in the morning. "I'll be back later and Gil and Ben will probably be with me. We'll talk then and I'll see what I can get for you." He glanced down at her and hugged her against his long length one more time. "It's going to be okay. We're going to get this guy." With that he turned and hurried out of the bedroom.

Shep pulled her back against him and leaned down to nuzzle her neck. "Feel like sleeping?" he queried.

"No," Ally whisperd. She was too keyed up right now to fall back to sleep.

"Good," Shep said. "I know exactly what you need to help you relax." His grin was wicked and Ally caught her breath at all the possibilities that presented themselves in her head.

Two hours later, Ally was dripping sweat and every muscle in her body was screaming for a break. Shep had been right—this was exactly what she needed.

"Don't stop now," Shep told her. "You're just getting your rhythm down."

Ally laughed and sat on the mat anyway. Blake's basement was a fully stocked home gym. He had Nautilus equipment, free weights, treadmills, a rowing machine, medicine balls and even an exercise ball. But what she really loved was the corner that was filled with boxing equipment. That was where Shep had brought her. He had suited her up with tape and gloves and put her to work with a kickboxing dummy. She had no idea how he knew that was what she enjoyed the most, but he did. And it was the best workout she'd managed in a while. Now she was deliciously boneless and content to just lie on the floor.

Shep dropped down beside her. "Feeling better now?"

"God, yes," Ally moaned. "How did you know just what I needed?"

"I didn't," he laughed. Hell, all he had wanted was to toss her back into the bed and fuck her into exhaustion. But he knew that she wouldn't be as interested without Blake there to participate as well. He liked Ally and he'd enjoy her body as long as she and Blake were willing to share it with him, but he knew that she wasn't the one for him. She was meant for Blake and it made Shep happy to know that his friend would finally find some happiness. If anyone deserved it, Blake was that man. And from what Shep had learned about Ally recently it seemed like she could use a little happiness in her life as well.

"You want a hot shower now?" he asked. When Ally looked up at him with her big green eyes full of questions he couldn't help but grin. "By yourself. I won't join you unless you really beg and plead and maybe if you throw your naked body at me."

Ally giggled and then smiled softly at him. "You're a great friend, Shep. Blake's lucky to have you."

Shep sighed, thinking how much it sucked at times to be such a great friend. "I'd like to be your friend as well, Ally. If you'll let me."

"I'd like that too," Ally replied.

"Good." Shep rose to his feet and pulled a groaning Ally up beside him. "Then let's get you showered and dressed and we'll make some coffee. Then we can talk." He looked into her eyes so that Ally would see just how much he meant what he said. "I believe you, Ally, and I want you to tell me everything that you know about this Messenger."

Ally nodded and let Shep guide her back up the stairs to the bedroom. Maybe she had finally found someone who would not only believe her but help her as well.

Chapter Nine

℘

Blake was tired, hot and sweaty, wondering where the hell the day had gone. It was already six o'clock in the evening. Gil and Ben had arrived at the scene shortly after he had and they had all spent most of the day working with the task force assigned to these fires. By the looks of them they felt the same way. Now the count was up to four. Four fires with the same accelerant used, the same burn pattern, the same macabre outcome for the victims. They had to find this guy soon and stop him before he killed again.

The heavy scent of burned flesh and hair clung to him, or maybe it was just that he couldn't forget that smell. It was so much stronger than the smoke. The again, maybe it was just that the scent of smoke was a given in his job and the smell of burnt flesh was something a fireman never wanted to smell. Also one he would never forget.

"It's exactly the same as the last scene, right down to the material under the bed and the match on the porch." Blake stopped in front of Gil and Ben and shook his head. "One victim this time."

"Yeah," was all Gil said but they all knew that it was still one more than should have happened. "You heading back to your house now?"

It was an easy question, except for the little fact that they knew that Ally was there waiting for him. Blake gave a weary sigh. It was time to find out what she knew about the pyromaniac who was killing people in Legacy. No matter how much he didn't want her involved in this, she was. No matter how much he wanted to ignore the things she had done to help the police in the past, he couldn't. But more importantly, no matter how much he wanted to pretend otherwise, he was in love with her and that changed everything.

It had finally dawned on him when he had first seen the curled body of the woman on the bed, or what there still was to see, that she could be anyone. The woman from the diner, someone he saw in the gym or passed at the grocery store. They had seen a picture in the front room of her and she had been young and beautiful. For some reason it had made Blake think of Ally and what he would do if something like this happened to her. It would devastate him, cripple him and leave him an empty shell. He had sworn after his ex-wife had destroyed his life and walked away that he would never give another woman that kind of power over him. But the heart was a foolish organ, forgiving and accepting.

"Yeah, I'm heading back. You guys want to follow me there?" It was a silly question since they all had the same thing on their minds. Talking to Ally and maybe getting some answers that would point them in the right direction. Maybe she would provide the break they were looking for.

"We'll be right behind you," Gil stated with a glance at Ben, who nodded and turned away without a word. Blake thought maybe Ben was feeling just as protective of Ally. It was the least she deserved from him. But when the time came it would be Blake who she turned to for support. At least he hoped so. He'd make sure that he was there to give it.

* * * * *

Ally and Shep were sitting at the kitchen table laughing and chatting like old friends when the three men arrived. Ally was wearing a pair of jeans and a white t-shirt and she looked so cute sitting there in her bare feet with her long hair in a ponytail and no make-up. Shep wore only a pair of jeans with the top button open.

The jealousy slammed into Blake and he almost stumbled. It would never have bothered him before what Shep would do with a woman while he was gone. But this time was different.

Ally was different. Blake didn't like the idea of Shep having sex with Ally when he wasn't there. The only thing that kept him from losing it was Ally's bright smile and the way she was focused only on him.

"You're back. If you want to hit the shower, I'll bring you a cup of coffee." Ally smiled at him and he wondered if she realized what she had just disclosed to the other men in the room about their relationship. It wasn't like they hadn't guessed as much, but she had just confirmed everything.

"I'm afraid that the shower will have to wait 'til after we all talk. But the coffee sounds good." Blake dropped a kiss on her head, showing his possession in that simple gesture. He wanted them all to know that she was his and that meant if they hurt her or made her upset then they would have to deal with him as well. Ally was no longer on her own and it was time she knew it.

Ally stood quickly and went to the coffee pot. She took three more cups down and poured them full and set them in front of the men at the table. She grabbed the pot and refilled both her and Shep's cups, then turned back to the counter and busied herself making a fresh pot. She could feel their eyes on her and knew what was coming. This was why she had traveled to Legacy in the first place. It was time to put her skills to use and see if she could reconnect with the man who killed her family.

"He killed again." It wasn't a question that she asked as she turned back to the men watching her. She had known when Blake left that morning that The Messenger was striking again. Shep reached out and squeezed her hand and she caught sight of the tightening of Blake's jaw. Was he jealous? Did he think that she and Shep had spent the rest of the morning in bed making love? She wasn't sure how she felt about all of this right now and it would all have to wait anyway.

"A young woman about your age," Gil said softly and Ally closed her eyes.

"There is almost always a woman involved." She spoke softly then opened her eyes. "I've only known of one fire he set that was two men. They were both gay."

"So he has a thing against women?" Ben asked.

"He has a thing against sin," Ally corrected softly. "And he sees women as the original bearers of all sins."

"Wow, so this guy believes that all sins start with the woman?" Ben looked surprised by this.

"He calls himself The Messenger. He feels that he has been sent to earth to carry out God's plan of redemption. So The Messenger cleanses the sin from people with fire." Ally looked really sad for a minute and Shep reached out to squeeze her hand again. She had told him earlier about her mother's death while they were talking.

"Why fire?" Blake asked sharply and they all glanced at him. His glare was directed firmly at the linked fingers of Shep and Ally. Ally tried to pull her hand free but Shep just grinned at her and tugged until she was leaning against his chair.

"The Messenger believes more in the Old Testament God. You know, fire and damnation. The vengeful God?" At their nods she continued. "He sees it as a way for them to atone for their sins by facing the fires of hell. If they walk out, then they were pure and God protected them. If they burn, then they have now earned their way into heaven through his intervention."

"That is sick," Gil stated matter-of-factly. "What else do you know about him?"

"I know that he quotes scripture all the time, including at the scene. He blesses the victim before he sets the fire." Ally closed her eyes trying to remember the things she had picked up on so many weeks earlier. "I know that he usually follows his victims home from somewhere before he kills them. He gets into their homes while they're out and sets the scene up."

"How does he do that?" Blake wanted to know. He had to know how much she knew about the way the room was.

"He places old rags and newspapers, magazines, whatever is available in the victim's home under the bed. He places a special pillowcase under their cases to help them sleep better." She looked up at them all. "He laces it with chloroform."

"Holy shit," Ben muttered. "No one knows about that."

Blake and Gil shared a look. That was another thing that they had managed to keep out of the press. No one knew about the pillowcases laced with chloroform. "What else do you know?" Blake demanded.

"He is an ordained minister from the internet. He's very proud of that fact as he sees it as having God's official seal of approval." Ally was trying to remember anything else that she could.

"Unfortunately, that won't narrow it down any. Anyone can get ordained over the internet nowadays," Shep shrugged his shoulders.

"He leaves a sign that he has been there on the front of the house somewhere. On a porch if it is available, or sometimes the doorstep." She locked her eyes with Blake's. "It is a long match like the ones people use to start a fire in their fireplace. He leaves it so that you will know that he has been there."

"Why does he leave it?" Ben wanted to know.

"Because you have to know that he has been there and saved another soul. How else will the world know of his good deeds?" Ally had that sad look again. "He killed my mom and her lover Tory." She looked defiant, waiting for the same response she always met when she spoke of her mother. But none of them seemed surprised by it. Or even concerned.

"No questions? No comments about my being the daughter of a lesbian?" Ally demanded.

"Hate to break it to you, toots, but your mom wasn't always a lesbian," Ben told her. "She and your dad met and fell in love. Then they met Tory and she became the third in their relationship. When your dad died, Roni and Tory never wanted another man so they just stayed with one another."

"How do you know all of that?" Ally wanted to know.

"I heard my mom and dad talking about it one day," Ben admitted. "It was bad enough that your mother had hooked up with a man and not married him, then accepted another woman into the relationship. But it was a carnal sin to remain with the woman after your dad died." He looked at Ally sadly. "At least before they could tell people that she was controlled by the man in her life and had no say in what he did. But with your dad gone and Roni staying in the relationship it made it seem that your mother wanted to be with Tory."

"She did," Ally stated with pride. Her mother had been happy with Tory, very happy. And Ally had been surrounded with love and acceptance by the two women who raised her.

"But they couldn't accept that, Ally. You know how Preston and Virginia St. John are." Ben practically sneered the names of his parents, showing his own dislike of them. "He sent a man to talk to your mom once. Shortly after that is when she changed your last name to Samms." He looked up at Ally and smiled. "Sam was your dad's name."

"I know," Ally said softly. Her mother had told her all about her dad and what a wonderful soul he was. He was searching for his little brother who was in the service somewhere. It seemed that her uncle was under the impression that her father was dead. Ally didn't know the entire story, having only listened to the things that her mother and Tory shared with her. After the fire, she no longer had any pictures of him either. She had lost everything in that fire. And everyone.

"I need something from the scene of the fire," Ally said firmly, getting them back on the subject at hand. "I need to reconnect with The Messenger so that we can find him and stop him."

"What do you mean?" Gil asked.

"I need to touch something that he held, something that he left his emotional imprint on. I've already connected with him once before so I'm sure that I can again. If I'm lucky then I can get inside his head and find out where he is, see what he sees. But I need something that he has touched first. I need that connection." Ally looked at Blake, somehow knowing that he would be the one to get her what she needed. And that he would stay with her while she did what she had to do.

Blake got up and left the room only to return instantly with what looked like a Ziploc bag. "You mean something like this?" he asked and held it up so that everyone could see the match inside.

"Shit," Ben muttered, while Gil gave an outright, "Fuck!"

"Are you sure?" Ally asked, knowing how much he risked by bringing her such an important piece of evidence.

"I can't let you keep it, Ally, but I can let you use it for what you need to do." Blake held the bag out to her but refused to release it when she reached for it. "Are you sure about this, honey? No one is going to think any less of you if you don't want to do this."

"I will," Ally smiled sadly. "I will." She took a deep breath and tried to center her thoughts. She held the bag against her chest and closed her eyes. "I'm not sure what, if anything, will happen when I hold this in my hand. Maybe nothing. Maybe I'll only see bits and pieces." She opened her eyes and looked straight at Blake again. "I may connect with the victim instead. I never know. The important thing is to remember not to touch me while I'm seeing. No matter what I say, don't touch me. You'll sever the link and I won't get all that I can." She let her gaze roam to include everyone. "Do you all understand?"

She waited until they all nodded their agreement before locking eyes with Blake again. "No matter what I do or say, Blake."

"I promise." Blake pulled her into his arms and held her tightly for a brief moment. They both seemed to need it.

Ally grabbed a chair and pulled it away from where they all surrounded the table. She placed it in the corner and sat gingerly in it. She took several deep cleansing breaths and closed her eyes trying to center herself on the task ahead of her. This was it. The moment she had been waiting for. This was her chance to stop the man who had killed her family. With trembling hands she opened the bag and slowly reached inside.

The scent of smoke filled her nose and the room took on a hazy shadow. It took her a moment to realize that it wasn't another fire but something else entirely.

"He's at a bar. Sitting at a table along the back wall keeping watch over the flock." His words, not hers, but that was how it was when she was linked. She could see what he saw, hear what he heard, feel his thoughts and emotions as if they were her own. It was scary at times how deep the link could and did go.

"He's waiting for someone. He knows that she will be there tonight. He's watched her before. But she's not here. So he's sitting and waiting." Ally took a deep breath and closed her eyes, centering her thoughts completely with his. She had to learn all that she could. And who knew when she would get another chance. When her voice emerged again she knew that it would be deeper, harsher, more in line with his than hers.

"For the wages of sin is death." She boomed and vaguely she sensed the confusion of the men in the room. "Only through the fire can a sinner gain entry into the hallowed halls of heaven. It is my duty, Lord, and I don't take it lightly. I know that you have set this task for me and I live to serve you. Your fire and damnation live through me. I am but a humble torch of Your power and might."

His thoughts were chaotic as he sat there waiting. It was a jumble of scripture and reverence for his version of God. She could feel his contempt for the other people in the bar. He didn't like that they drank and flirted. There was a couple in the corner almost having sex and he was appalled and disgusted. His gaze moved around the room again but she still wasn't there. It had to be her tonight. The Lord had already made his selection and The Messenger would follow. They were both startled when a waitress stopped by the table.

"Hey there, sug." She stuck her hip out and rested the tray below her well-formed breasts. "Can I freshen that drink up for you? Or you want to try something else?" The suggestion was blatant and made Ally wish for a mirror so that she could see the reflection of The Messenger. She could feel his contempt for the woman and her sexual offer.

"I'm fine, thank you." The Messenger spoke to the waitress and, in a silent kitchen miles away, Ally repeated it to an audience of four.

"Just let me know if you change your mind." The waitress leaned close and whispered in his ear. "I get off at midnight and if you'd like, so could you." With a saucy smile she walked away, her hips swaying and drawing the gaze of many eyes.

"The devil is tempting me with the sins of the flesh. But I am strong in Your love, my Lord. I will not waver from my task and give in to the jezebel sent to torment me. I am simply The Messenger." She felt the tension course through his body. His gaze locked onto the back of a woman who had just entered the bar. She was speaking to the waitress and laughing.

Ally tried to break out of The Messenger's mind enough to describe her. She was almost positive that this woman was his next intended victim. It would be up to her to try to stop him. "She has long dark hair. Petite frame. I... There is something about her that is familiar. I can't place her but I know that I've seen her before." Ally wanted to see the woman's face more than she could say, but it was only the woman's back presented to The Messenger and Ally as well. What was it about her that tugged at Ally's memory?

The waitress came back with a takeout order but all that was going through Ally's mind was The Messenger's voice repeating over and over, "she is leaving." The Messenger was getting up and making his way across the room to follow her. Ally was hoping that they had lost her, but The Messenger seemed to know exactly where he was going. He was whistling a song, "Onward Christian Soldiers", as he walked down the sidewalk and headed to a small compact car parked along the curb.

"He knows where he is going. He's been there before." Ally suddenly realized what The Messenger had in play. "He visited her home earlier today and set the scene for her salvation." Ally tried to pull at his memory of the woman's home. She needed an address, a street name, anything to point them in the right direction. "He was very displeased with her. Her home was filled with Oriental art and different depictions of the Buddha. It angers him that she might believe in something other than his own one true God. Her punishment must be carried out right away. He placed the magazines and newspapers from her recycling bin under her bed, as well as some of her cleaning cloths that were under the sink. He must be sure that the flames burn hot enough to cleanse her completely of her sin.

"I can't see an address or any street names. He thinks of her house as the candy house. I don't know what that means." Ally could feel the taste of excitement in The Messenger's mouth, feel the anticipation in his veins. Although the waitress in the bar had turned him off, the thought of fire had his cock at full mast beneath his jeans. It was a sickening bit of information that Ally could have done without. The Messenger pulled his car to the side of the road and his gaze locked on a house that sat by itself at the end of a cul-de-sac.

"The house is a pink-and-white gingerbread-style home. It sits on the curve of a cul-de-sac by itself. There's a car parked in the driveway and lights on. This is where she lives and this is where he was earlier. He is sitting in the car and watching the house." Ally shook her head from side to side as she tried to focus on the streets around him. She still couldn't make out the number on the house. "He is waiting for the lights to go out. He'll give her five minutes once the lights are out before he'll enter the home and grant her the salvation of eternal life. He is pulling on thin latex gloves." Ally struggled with in The Messenger's mind urging him to turn and look at the street sign. She tried to make him wonder where they were by placing questions in his mind but nothing worked. Although she was linked with him, he was unaware of her.

"The lights are out." Ally's voice was deadly calm when she dropped those words into the room. Everyone knew what that meant. "He's set his timer on his watch. He'll give her five minutes before he enters through the back and begins the Lord's work."

The kitchen was quiet as the minutes ticked by and Ally sat, focused on the events taking place inside her head. The Messenger opened his door and stepped out into the night. He glanced down at his watch and smiled at less than a minute to go. Whistling again, he began to make his way to the house and around the side, giving Ally a chance to take in more details.

"The number of the house is 1975. It is on the house in big gold letters just beside the front door. There is a walkway that leads to the back of the house. A little gate that opens through the white picket fencing. The yard is filled with flowers and there is a pond of some kind in the corner. It is surrounded by lush plants. There's a grill on the patio but it looks as if it has never been used. He's doing something to the door, I can't... He's opening it. He picked the lock. He's entering the house and pulling it closed behind him, relocking it. He is in a little living room filled with the Oriental things."

Ally tried to look around and take in as much as she could as quickly as she could. She knew that a woman's life depended on it. "The couch and easy chair are an orangey color, soft. Leather, I think. There is a throw on the back of the couch. Black with a dragon design on it. There's a picture on the shelf over the fireplace. A woman and a man. The man is big. He looms over the woman. There's another photo. It's a blonde woman." Ally tried to focus on that picture. There was something about it that was clicking in her mind. Not only had she seen the woman before, but the place where the picture was taken. Who was it? Where was it? Suddenly it hit her. "It's a picture of Moira. Taken at her gym. The woman in the house. I've seen her before. At the dinner earlier. She was there. She left with Catherine."

Things spiraled out of control then and Ally was left drained and shaking. The Messenger passed a mirror hanging in the hall and stopped to straighten it. It was the first good look that Ally had of him. Simultaneously the room around her exploded into action and she heard the name Michelle spoken. Before she could focus intently on The Messenger's thoughts again someone touched her.

"No," Ally screamed as she felt the jolt through her body when she slammed back into her own consciousness. "I told you not to touch me," she murmured before pitching forward into a secure set of arms and passing out.

Blake scooped her up and glared at Ben. "She said not to touch her. Didn't you fucking listen to her?"

"I was worried. She didn't look good." Ben hadn't even realized that he had touched her 'til Ally screamed and Blake shoved him out of the way.

"Roman's on his way over to Michelle's. Jack's right behind him." Shep interrupted them. "I'd suggest someone stay here with Ally and the rest of us head over as quickly as we can."

"I'm staying," Blake stated. It was the first time that anyone had ever come before the job and he knew that from this point on Ally would always come first. He loved her. "You guys go on. We'll meet you there when we can."

"I'll call the station on the way," Gil said pulling his phone out as the three men hit the door running.

Blake nodded and watched them go. It was the first time that he didn't feel a need to be in heat of the moment. His entire life had been one adrenaline rush after another. He glanced at the woman he still held in his arms and headed down the hallway to the bedroom. From now on she was all the excitement that he needed. He had a feeling that she would be more than enough.

Chapter Ten
෨

Roman could see the smoke and flames when he pulled into the housing addition where Jack's sister Michelle lived. Someone would have already called the fire department, but he still had to try to get in and reach Michelle. She was family and you never walked away from family. He'd learned that lesson once already in his life.

He was out of the truck and running when the first sirens filled the air. Three powerful kicks to her front door and he had a way in. The flames were everywhere and the heat was intense. Smoke filled his nose and mouth, and Roman lifted his arm to cover both with his sleeve. It couldn't have been more than three minutes since Shep's call. Yet the fire was already raging out of control.

Roman forced his way through the house, but the closer he came to the room he knew Michelle was in the hotter the fire and the thicker the smoke. He dropped to his hands and knees trying to crawl. He never saw the figure obscured by the smoke, who stepped out behind him. Couldn't hear over the crackle and roar of the fire. But he felt the slam of something into the back of his head and turned even as he fell. Slipping into unconsciousness, the last thing on his mind was a woman. Not the one he was trying to save. But the one who had saved him. If he made it out of this alive, he'd keep her any way that she demanded. Suddenly he knew that being with her was all that mattered.

"Rin," he whispered. But the only one who heard was The Messenger.

* * * * *

God had brought him another soul to save. The man was big, though, and solidly built. The Messenger decided to leave him in the hall, knowing that the smoke would get to him long before the flames did. He went out the back door and made his way through the yard to the side gate, the match still in his hand. He had to leave it on the porch so that they would know that the woman and man had been saved by The Messenger. It was his sign to God that these were the souls that he had sent.

He made his way to the porch. The sirens were closer and he could make out the glow of lights. He placed the match carefully on the edge in plain sight and turned to walk away. He was met by a fist to the jaw that knocked him flat on the ground. He was flipped and his hands were tied behind him. Harsh hands jerked him to his feet and headed him away from the beautiful flames toward the sidewalk.

Fire trucks screamed into the area followed by police cars and an ambulance. He had never seen the aftermath of what God's work demanded. He was only The Messenger and it was not his place to see. The man holding him was met by another in uniform as organized chaos convened around them as the fire fighters engaged in yet another battle with the house behind him.

"This the one?" A rich baritone filled the air as the muscular black man with the deep green eyes spoke to the man holding him.

"Yeah, Teddy. This is the scumbag who's been setting the fires all over." The man stepped around him as the one called Teddy grabbed him and The Messenger recognized him from one of the pictures on display in the house behind him. The man's eyes scanned the growing crowd around them. "You see Roman anywhere? I saw his truck when I got here. He went in to get Michelle."

"And the flames of salvation shall grant them passage into the halls of heaven and the Lord will welcome them with open arms." He told them grandly, willing to share his wisdom.

The men ignored him.

"I haven't seen him, Jack. Where would he have taken her?" The name on the uniform was Simons, so The Messenger took him to be Officer Teddy Simons. A fine-looking man perhaps sent by God to take care of him.

"His truck is still here or I'd say that he took her straight to the hospital." The other man said, the one called Jack.

"He is being cleansed by the fire," The Messenger proudly told them. He was sending the Lord two more souls today. "Soon he and the woman shall walk in the halls of heaven and bask in the presence of the Lord."

"What?" The one called Jack grabbed him and shook him violently. "Are you telling me that they're both still in there? Is that what you're telling me, you sick, twisted fuck?"

"Vengeance is mine, sayeth the Lord." Didn't they get that it wasn't him? Didn't they understand that he was just the Lord's Messenger?

The man thrust him back toward Officer Simons and started running back to where the firemen still battled. "There are people in there!" The man yelled. "There are still two people in there."

"And the flames shall set them free. The cleansing fires of salvation shall wash away their sins and they will be anointed in the Holy Spirit. God's message is delivered." He had saved two more souls. He was a faithful Messenger.

* * * * *

The room was lit by the dim glow of a lamp when Ally opened her eyes. She was resting on the bed in Blake's room and he was lying close beside her, one hand stoking softly over her hair.

"You're awake." He spoke softly making her wonder just how long she'd been out. It varied with every encounter. Sometimes she never passed out at all.

"How long have I been out?"

"Maybe five minutes. Not long at all." He moved so that he was looking down at her and she was overcome by the emotion shining so vividly in his eyes. "The others left to head to Michelle's house. Hopefully they'll make it in time." He took a shaky breath and traced his fingers down her cheek. "I almost killed Ben when he touched you and you screamed. I didn't know if he had hurt you or not."

"I'm sure that he didn't mean to." Ally almost laughed at the way she felt compelled to defend a cousin who had walked out of her life without looking back. Or had he? She was beginning to understand Ben's reasons. And he was happy now. Wasn't that all that mattered in the long run? "You stayed with me?" She couldn't believe that the man who had rushed out the door in the wee hours of the morning was still with her now.

"Yes," was all that Blake answered, but he continued to run his hands over her body.

"I'm fine now, Blake. You can go on if you want. I'll just rest a few more minutes and then I'll join you." She wouldn't keep him from where he wanted to be. God help her but she loved him.

"You're not going anywhere." Her startled gaze locked with his and she felt the pool of liquid between her thighs at the look in his eyes. "I'm not going anywhere. They can handle it just fine without us. We'd only be in the way."

"But your job…" Ally started to say, but her words were cut off by the touch of his lips, the slip and slide of his tongue against hers. The kiss was hungry, consuming, but filled with something more. Something she prayed was love but was afraid to believe. They were both gasping for air when he pulled away.

"They can handle it. My job is to be right here with you." He skimmed his tongue across her jaw and nibbled his way down her neck. "For now I want nothing more than you and me, making love. I want to feel your skin against mine. I want to taste you everywhere until neither of us can hold back." His eyes connected with hers and there was no more denying the love that reflected there. "I want to love you. For now and every day for the rest of our lives." He cradled her face in his hands and brushed at her tears with his tongue. "I want you to stay with me, to be with me, to love me. I don't want to be without you." She watched him take a ragged breath before continuing. "If you want Shep to be with us, then I'll accept that. I'll take you anyway that I can have you. I…"

She stopped him with a finger to his lips wanting to put his mind at ease. "Shep and I didn't have sex when you left, Blake. He took me down to the basement and let me work out. He's a good friend and I'm pretty sure that he knows how I feel about you."

"He's the best friend I've ever had and I'm—" He stopped and looked intently at her as the rest of what she said sank in. "How you feel about me?"

"I love you, Blake. I love you more than I ever thought possible. I know that we haven't known each other long and that my gift can be hard to handle, but I hope that you'll give us a chance." She was so afraid to believe his earlier words.

Blake laughed and bent to nip her bottom lip with his teeth. "Did you not hear me, woman? I love you. I want to spend the rest of my life with you. Your gift doesn't change that at all. I've never been so jealous in my life as when I thought you and Shep were back in this bed without me."

"Well, maybe we could invite him back sometimes. I'd hate to come between your friendship." She smiled brightly and was rewarded with his rich laughter.

"We'll see what we can do," he agreed before turning serious once more. "I'd like to marry you, Ally. I never thought that I would again after what my first wife did. But with you I want it all."

"What did she do to you?" Ally wanted to know what had put the sadness in his gaze.

Blake closed his eyes and Ally could feel his turmoil as he struggled for the words to tell her. "My first wife was young when we met. We both were. I was in the military back then and thought it would be great to have someone waiting at home for me when I got back. I was Navy and was gone for months at a time. She couldn't handle it and she slept around." He looked her in the eyes and his pain became hers. "She got pregnant and aborted the baby. It was mine. She didn't want it in the way, curbing her fun while I was gone."

"Oh, Blake." Ally wrapped him in her arms and held him close. She couldn't imagine doing anything like that, but who knew what the other woman was thinking at the time? Honestly, Ally didn't care about the other woman. Her only thought was for Blake and what he had lost. "I'm so sorry. I can't imagine losing a child."

"I wouldn't wish it on anyone." She was startled at the fire in his eyes and it must have shown on her face.

"Any woman who really loved you could never make such a decision, Blake. You have to believe that." Ally wanted him to know that she wouldn't betray the man she loved in such a way.

"It's water under the bridge now," he murmured as he pulled her to him. "All I want to do is spend the rest of my life loving you."

"Then do it," she whispered seductively. "Make love to me, Blake. Make love to me."

Slowly, they began to undress each other, stopping and exploring with each new inch of skin exposed. Fingers caressed, tongues stroked and teeth nipped as they explored each other. It was like the first time with everything wondrous and exciting. He found the ticklish spots behind her knees and spent long moments teasing the piercing in her navel. She discovered how much he enjoyed having his nipples sucked and nipped. Arousal built and grew with each stroke and rub until they were both panting with need. He moved away and knelt between her thighs, running his tongue along her dewy slit.

"I want to taste you too," Ally moaned. Wanting him to turn so that she could take him in her mouth. He sucked at her pussy lips and nipped them gently with his teeth before complying and lying beside her on the bed. With a roll he was up over her with her knees hooked behind his arms, his engorged cock bobbing just above her mouth. She was just about to taste him when he attacked her pussy, using his tongue to spear deep and fuck her.

She screamed and arched closer to his eager mouth. She reached up and gripped his pulsing cock with her fingers and guided it down to her mouth and he lowered his hips giving her easier access. She ran her tongue over the bulbous head before sucking the drops of semen already slipping from him. He was like ambrosia on her tongue and she greedily sucked more of his length into her mouth. She heard his groans and joined him when he thrust two fingers inside her channel and began to torment her clit with his tongue and teeth.

Ally reached her hands up and clasped his buttocks, tugging him even closer to her mouth before taking as much of his cock as she could into her mouth. She could feel the large head against the back of her throat and swallowed several times, breathing through her nose to help combat the gag reflex. Slowly she slid him out, only to take him just as deep again. He rewarded her with another taste of his cum, which she eagerly swallowed. Before she could take him deep again, Blake was gone.

"Hands and knees," he grunted and his hands were shaking as he helped her turn over into the position he wanted. "I love the look of your ass when you're on all fours. I like to feel it against me when I fuck that sweet little pussy of yours."

Ally bent further down in the front so that her forearms rested on the mattress, lifting her ass higher for that first stroke. She loved this position as well. Loved how deep Blake could fuck her. She watched as he left the bed and grabbed a condom from the table. It was sheer torture to watch him roll it on, wanting it to be her hands caressing his flesh. She trembled with anticipation as she felt him move onto the bed behind her. She couldn't stop the groan when he rubbed along her folds seeking entrance.

The first thrust was everything that she wanted. Hard, fast and as deep as he could go. Quickly it was followed by another and then another until the rhythm was set and they were both rocking their hips together. She could feel her nipples rubbing against the afghan and she flattened her arms along the bed so that she could reach the headboard and brace against it. Blake knew just what he was doing. Every hard stroke rubbed the bundle of nerves inside her that stimulated her pleasure. Every stroke threw her closer to nirvana and left her keening and moaning out loud.

"So good, Blake," Ally tried to form the words to tell him. "So good."

"Only gonna get better, honey," Blake grunted in reply, his thighs slamming against her ass again. "Every time like the first time." It was a promise that she knew he would do everything to keep.

"Yes," she cried out when he leaned back and added two fingers to her ass, pumping them in time with his cock. He used them to rub against the thin flesh that separated fingers from plunging cock. She could feel the tightening of her belly, the clench of her cunt around his cock and she knew that orgasm was only seconds away. "I love you, Blake," she cried out as the first wave hit her. "I love you."

She heard his harsh moan as he continued thrusting, pounding impossibly harder and faster until she felt the harsh blast of his hot seed exploding inside her. He held deep for a moment before pulling back and slamming in again. With each burst from his cock it was the same. He'd thrust inside, filling her with his length as more semen pulsed into the tip of the condom. Then he'd slide out only to slam home again for the next burst of seed. It was hot and thick and she could feel it through the thin layer of the rubber. Blake gave one more thrust and wrapped his arm around her waist, turning them so that they lay on their sides with him still inside her.

"I love you too, Ally." He brushed her hair out of her face and snuggled his mouth in, placing kisses along her jaw and neck. When she turned her head, he caught her lips in a breathless kiss that lasted forever, yet not nearly long enough. "You never answered me. Will you marry me, Ally? Will you stay with me forever?"

"Yes, I'll marry you." Ally snuggled closer back into him and smiled.

"You make me feel like a randy teenager all over again." His words were followed by a gentle thrust and Ally was amazed that he was already hard again.

"What stamina you have," she murmured.

"Only with you," he thrust in and out again before pulling out and replacing the filled condom with a new one. It was mere seconds but it felt too long to be without him inside her.

"Ummm..." Ally moaned and lifted her leg back and over his hip, deepening the angle of penetration. "Maybe we won't need Shep after all."

Blake stopped for a minute and then slammed deep, making Ally cry out. "You wench. You'll pay for that comment." His chuckle filled the room as he continued with the slow, easy rhythm of their lovemaking. "I'll love you until you can't stand up and then I'll invite Shep back and we'll share you for the rest of the night."

"No, please, anything but that," Ally moaned but there was no disguising the blatant grin on her face and Blake chuckled again.

"I can see that life will always be interesting with you."

Ally glanced back and the grin was gone. "Does that bother you, Blake? Can you deal with all that will come with having me as a wife?"

He placed a soft kiss on her check before answering. "I wouldn't want you any other way, Ally. I love you and no matter what the future brings, we'll deal with it together."

"I don't know what I did to deserve you, Blake, but I'm so glad that I found you. I love you." Ally caught his lowering mouth with hers and slid her tongue inside to duel with his. It was a slow exploration filled with love and acceptance.

"I'm the lucky one," Blake sighed when they finally broke the kiss. "I'll never forget that."

Ally lay in his embrace after they had both come again. The second time had been all that the first time wasn't, soft and slow and saturated with a level of emotion that left her more drained than ever before. Her last thought before she feel asleep was for Jack and Moira. There was one last thing that she had seen before she was brought out by Ben's touch. Two people were in the burning house. But only one would leave alive.

* * * * *

Catherine was pulled from sleep by the incessant ringing of her bedside phone. She groped blindly for it as she tried to focus on the blurry numbers on her alarm clock.

"Hello," she answered.

"Rin, it's Jack."

She could hear something in his voice and suddenly she was wide awake and fear was clawing at her. "What is it Jack? Who is it?"

"There's been a fire at Michelle's house," Jack's voice was ragged through the phone.

"Michelle? Is she all right?" Catherine and Michelle had recently become friends as they were the only two older women at the family get-togethers.

"We weren't in time to save her." The pain was evident in Jack's voice, but only to someone who had come to know him as she had. Because of Roman, they had gotten to know each other well.

"Where are you, Jack? I'll be there as soon as I can." She was already pushing the covers off and heading to the closet for clothes when his next words came through what felt like a tunnel.

"I'm on my way to get you, Rin. We need to get to the hospital."

"Who else was in the fire, Jack? Who else is hurt?" So many names were going through her mind. Gil and Ben were both working on this case, as well as Blake. Moira could have been at Michelle's house, or Katie. But her heart stopped at his next words and she thought that she might die.

"It's Roman, Rin. He went in to save her and the smoke was so thick..." Jack's voice trailed off and Catherine blinked and landed hard on the carpeted floor of her bedroom. "He inhaled a lot of smoke, Rin. He's at the hospital. They're not sure yet if he'll make it."

Her keening cries filled the air as her heart beat faster. It hit her like a tornado out of nowhere. She loved him and wanted him in her life no matter what her children thought. And yet she had been the one pushing him to accept the crumbs of her life that she was willing to share. She remembered every time that he had hidden in the bedroom when someone had shown up unexpectedly. She remembered all the times they were around one another but couldn't be together because it was what she demanded. Now she might lose another man that she loved, only this time she didn't have all the years of memories and laughter to help her through.

She dropped the phone and ran to the closet to pull out a pair of jeans that Roman had talked her into buying, and slipped into them. She tugged a t-shirt on that he had given her. It was gray and bore the words *Semper Fi*. Always faithful. She was only just now learning what his gift was supposed to convey. She grabbed one of his sweatshirts from the back of her closet where she had placed it out of the way and slipped it over her head, needing the comfort it gave her.

She grabbed a pair of slip-on shoes from her closet floor and slid her feet in before making her way to the front door. She would meet Jack downstairs. She needed to be with Roman. She had to tell him that she loved him, that she needed him. She wanted to tell him that she was sorry. Most importantly, she wanted to tell him that she chose him. Every day for the rest of her life she would pray that he was there with her. The first face she greeted every morning and the last vision she took to bed. If only God would grant her the chance, she would show Roman that she was no longer afraid.

Chapter Eleven

ஒ

The ride to the hospital seemed to take forever. Catherine could hear Jack's voice, but his words were a jumble that she couldn't decipher right now. Her only thoughts were of Roman and all that she had to make up to him, all that she had to tell him. Never again would they act like they were anything other than two people who were very much in love. God had given her a second chance at happiness and she had hidden it in shame. Now she just might lose it again.

The truck stopped moving and Catherine realized that they were in the parking lot of the ER. Before she could reach for the door handle, Jack grabbed her arm and demanded her attention.

"Damn it, Rin. Pay attention to me." His face showed how tired and worn he was and for the first time Catherine remembered that Jack had told her Michelle hadn't made it. Michelle, the sister who he had just discovered and started to get to know. Now he might lose his best friend as well.

"I'm sorry, Jack. I'm so sorry about Michelle."

The pain came and went in his eyes, but Catherine saw it. "They said she never felt a thing. Smoke killed her in her sleep." She watched as he rubbed his hands over his face and tried to shake off whatever he was feeling. "What I've been trying to get through to you for the last few minutes is that the waiting room is full in there, Rin. Ben and Katie are here, as well as Moira and Gil. By now Griff, Chetan and Shep will be here as well. You need to pull yourself together, Rin."

"No, Jack, I don't." Catherine knew exactly what she had to do. "I need to get in there and be with the man I love." She reached for the door and shoved it open. For the first time in a long time she wasn't concerned about what her children would think or feel. She had devoted most of her life to them. Now it was time to devote herself to seeking her own happiness.

She ran across the lot with Jack on her heels and shoved through the double doors nodding at the cop who sat on duty at the entrance. The first thing that she saw was her family overflowing the chairs in the waiting room. She had no intention of going to them and every intention of finding Roman when Griff came over to her.

"Mom? What are you doing here?" Griff reached for her arm and led her over to where everyone else was sitting or pacing. "Jack, you didn't have to drag her out of bed for this. There are enough people here for Roman."

Catherine caught Katie's and then Moira's gazes and it hit her that they knew exactly why she was here. There was compassion there and understanding.

Catherine tugged at Griff's arm and took a deep breath. "I want you to sit down for a minute, Griff. I'd like to talk to all of you."

"Can it wait, Mom? This isn't exactly the time for a family talk." Griff stood to the side, noticing absently the way that Moira and Katie moved into the arms of their husbands and Chetan and Shep moved next to Jack. "What's going on?"

"You're right, honey. This isn't the time for this discussion. I should have told you all a long time ago. But I was afraid and I let that fear control me." She turned to Katie and felt a jolt at the nod her daughter gave her. At least Katie seemed accepting of what Catherine was about to say. She turned back to Griff, sensing that her youngest son would take this the hardest. "I've been dating someone for a while now and…"

"What!" Griff exploded and she could tell that he wasn't thinking about where they were any more. "You're a married woman. You can't be dating."

"Your father has been gone for two years now, Griff." She could see the little boy in the eyes of the man standing before her.

"So you just don't love him anymore? You just shove him in a grave and go on with your life?" She knew it was the same little boy talking, but her hand was out and flying before she could stop it. The crack of her palm across Griff's cheek left the room in silence.

"How dare you speak to me that way? How dare you say something like that to me?" She was shaking with pent up emotions that she had kept inside for too long. Maybe she had been wrong to try so hard to be the rock her children needed when their father passed away. Maybe she should have allowed herself to be the woman instead.

"Do you have any idea what it is like to love someone so much that your entire life becomes rooted in that person? I loved your father with all I was for thirty-four years and I don't regret one moment of it. I died with him that day and it took all I had to stand strong and be there for you. You wanted to convince yourself that you were the one comforting and watching over me. I knew that and I let you believe it even as I soothed your wounds. I've given my life to your father and then to my children and I have loved every moment of it."

"Obviously," Griff sneered and although she knew it was pain and confusion speaking, it hurt deeply.

"I deserve better than that from you, Griff. I raised you better than that." Catherine closed her eyes and did nothing to stop the tears that flowed down her cheeks. "As much as I wanted to die with your father, I didn't. I had to accept that and go on whether I wanted to or not." Her eyes opened and there was no denying the pain inside her. "I had to. I met and married the love of my life and was blessed with thirty-four wonderful years and four beautiful children. I could never ask for anything more than that. And I didn't."

Catherine shook her head trying to find the words to express what she wanted — no, needed — to share. She glanced toward her older son Gil and was pleased to see Moira wrapped in his arms and understanding on both of their faces. Maybe it was the fact that he had recently found the love of his life. She looked back at Griff, so much like his father Mick that he took her breath away. "I didn't ask for anything. But God saw fit to give me a wonderful gift anyway. I never expected to fall in love again, not at the age of fifty-seven. Not when I'd already been given so much in my life. But I did. And instead of being grateful I hid it in fear."

Griff looked at her and the print of her hand still stained his cheek red. "Who is it?" was the only thing he asked her.

"Roman and I have been seeing each other for months. I asked him to be discreet and not let anyone know about it." She glanced behind her when she felt Jack step up. "Except for Jack, who is Roman's best friend, we've kept it private. I've walked away from him when all I really wanted was to go straight into his arms. I've made him hide in shame when I should have kept him proudly at my side. Now, I may lose the man that I love—again."

"You love him?" Again it was Griff who spoke while everyone else remained silent around them. "You can put Dad in the past and love another man?"

"Oh, Griff. I'll always love your father. Always. But even he wouldn't expect me to give up on a second chance for happiness. I'm still alive and it's time I started appreciating that and living." She wanted nothing more than to wrap her baby boy in her arms and hold him close. But the boy was gone and in his place was a man who was struggling to deal with a woman she'd kept hidden from him.

A nurse stepped out and called out for the family of Caesar Davis. Catherine went to step forward when Griff grabbed her arm and stopped her. "This is what you want? You choose him?"

"I choose life and everything that it still holds for me." With that she pulled her arm away and followed the nurse to where Roman was, with Jack right behind her.

"You okay?" Katie stepped away from Ben and went to Griff.

"Are you okay with this?" he demanded, looking from her to Gil and back again.

"She's found a chance at happiness again, Griff. How can we deny her that?" Katie asked softly.

"I don't know how to deal with this. I don't know if I can accept this or not. She's Mom." His eyes pleaded with Katie to understand. "She's Mom."

"She's also a woman, Griff. You have to let her be that as well." Katie hurt for her brother, but she believed that her mother deserved every ounce of happiness that came her way.

Griff shook his head and turned and walked away without looking back at any of them. Katie started to follow, but Gil's voiced stopped her.

"Let him go. He needs some time alone right now. He'll be okay eventually." Gil pulled his wife closer to his chest and held her tightly. "He just needs to be alone right now to think and deal."

"You think he'll ever accept mom with another man?" Katie asked and Gil heaved a weary sigh.

"Maybe. You never know what the future will bring." Gil looked down at the woman in his arms and felt the truth of those words in his very soul. He might not have been so understanding either before he found Moira and learned how love changed everything. Doug would feel a need to let Roman know what would happen if he hurt their mother and Gil and Damon would be right there with him. Hell, even Katie would. But love had opened all of their eyes lately and they couldn't want any less for their mother. Griff would find that out for himself someday. Maybe someday soon.

* * * * *

Catherine felt her heart stop when she stepped around the curtain encasing the bed where Roman rested in the emergency room. He had an oxygen mask on and an IV attached to his left arm, as well as other hospital paraphernalia that recorded different things. Her strong warrior lay as still as death and the beep and hiss of machines surrounded them.

She went to the bed and took his right hand in hers, squeezing it and bringing it to her lips. The smell of smoke was so strong that it almost overpowered her but Catherine refused to let go. She stroked her fingers through his hair and almost sobbed when she felt the singed ends. The doctor had been happy to tell them that Roman would pull through. He had inhaled a lot of smoke and his throat would be raw and sore for a few days. He might have some headaches, but all in all he had been lucky. They had reached him before the flames did any damage to him. Just the thought made Catherine shudder in fright.

"Rin…" Roman was trying to pull the mask away from his face. His grey eyes were open and the most beautiful sight that she had seen in a long time.

She eased his hand away from the mask, making sure it was back on securely. "I'm right here, Roman." She brushed his face with her fingers, needing to feel him, to touch him. "I'm not going anywhere."

"So sorry…" he murmured under the mask, his eyes opening and closing as he struggled to speak. She could hear the rasp in his voice and k his throat must be hurting. "No choose…okay…"

"Shhh…" Catherine leaned close and kissed his jaw letting her tears bathe his tender skin. "I'm the one who's sorry. But that's all over now, Roman. I promise you that it's all over."

He looked up at her with pain in his eyes and it hit her how he might take her words. "No. No, Roman. I mean that the hiding is over. I told everyone that we've been dating. I told them that I loved you and was ready to grab life with you and hang on." She leaned close again and kissed his cheek.

"No more hiding, Roman. So you better be ready to show the world that you're mine from this moment on."

She felt his smile before she eased back to see it. "Was always ready," he murmured and pulled his hand from hers to reach up and trace the tear tracks on her cheeks. "Love you, Rin." Harsh coughs racked his body and left him panting for air. The nurse came in and said that they were ready to move Roman into a room now. Catherine knew he didn't want to stay, but she also knew that it was what was best for him. When he was in his room and settling in for the night, she would be there with him. She'd never walk away from him again.

Jack found them together when he entered the room later. He had sweet talked the nurse into letting him in after visiting hours. He wanted to see Roman again and make sure that he was okay. He had slipped away earlier to identify Michelle down in the morgue. He had seen too much death in his life and he was sick and tired of it.

"Hey," the hoarse croak came from the bed and had Jack glancing over to see Rin curled up asleep with Roman. They looked so natural together with an aura of happiness radiating around them for everyone to see. He wanted that for himself.

"Hey, yourself."

"I'm sorry, Jack. I'm so sorry." Roman stated softly.

"You have nothing to be sorry for. You did everything that you could and you almost died as well." Jack blew out a harsh breath and sat gingerly in the chair by the bed. He was feeling too antsy to sit, but needed to be close so that he could whisper and not disturb Rin.

"You're leaving?" It was uncanny the way his best friend could read him like a book. It was a skill that they shared when it came to one another.

"Yeah. I need to make sure of what I think before I say anything. I don't want to say anything to her until I know."

"So you really think that Ally is your brother's daughter?" Roman asked.

"She has the Madigan eyes. The shape of her face. There is so much there that makes me believe. But I have to make sure that I'm seeing fact and not just what I want to see."

And that meant that Jack was going away for a while. He'd come to say goodbye to Roman and let him know that he'd be gone for a bit.

"How long you planning on being gone?" Roman questioned Jack.

"As long it takes to find out what I need to know." Jack stated.

"And if she is your niece?"

"Then I'm going to come back and tell her. I hope that she'll be happy but either way I'll be her family. We all will. And I'll do everything in my power to make up for not being there when he died." Jack's expression was fierce with his determination to make amends for that.

"Will you tell her about her dad? About his gift and why the two of you weren't in contact at the time?"

"I don't know. I'll have to see what is what first. I'll keep in touch. Call me if you need anything." He stood up from the chair and walked the few inches closer to the hospital bed. "I'll leave Chetan in charge 'til you're up and ready to come back in."

"I'll be back soon," Roman vowed.

"Take your time," Jack nodded toward where Rin was curled against him. "Enjoy the newness of not having to hide. Enjoy being with the woman you love."

"It'll be you some day," Roman said and Jack couldn't hide the need for just that, not from someone who knew him so well. He had loved once and lost out on so much when he had discovered that Moira's mother was dead. Only Moira's will had kept her alive for him to find when he returned to the states from too many years spent trying to die. And he would have hunted for her years earlier had he even known she existed, but Moira's grandmother had done her best to keep Moira hidden. So he had taken every impossible mission that he could, even the ones that no one expected him to come back from. He had wanted to die, to join the woman he loved, but someone had been watching over him. He liked to think that it was her, keeping him alive for their daughter. He remembered it like it was yesterday, could still see the face of the girl he first lost his heart to. He didn't think that he would ever find someone to love like that again.

"Yeah," he agreed, but he felt sure Roman heard the doubt loud and clear. "Someday maybe it will be me."

* * * * *

Shep slipped into Blake's house through the front door and sat in the darkness of the living room, absorbing the silence. He had waited a few minutes before following Griff to make sure that he was okay. The two men had talked a lot on nights that started with a full bottle of Wild Turkey and ended in a drunken haze. Gil had nodded at him as he left and he realized that the older brother wasn't as clueless as he thought.

Maybe they all knew just how close Griff had been to his father and the things the man had shared with his youngest son. Shep had heard it all. About how Mick Daniels had pressed Griff to keep an eye on his mother and make sure that she was safe and no one took advantage of her. The man had spoken of love and fidelity and expressed how it was forever when you were with the right woman. But then Mick had never planned to die and leave Catherine. What man ever did?

What Griff had to realize was that his father was gone and his mom was a grown woman who didn't need his protection. But Griff had made a promise to his father and Shep knew that honor and trust meant a lot to Griff. It would be hard for him to accept his mom's new love, even though he liked Roman, which Shep knew that Griff did. A promise was a promise, especially when it was made to a dead father. Shep shook his head and let the day's weariness settle in his frame. Griff would have to deal with it in his own way. All Shep could do was be there as a friend.

A noise caught his attention and he looked up to see Ally heading toward him wearing one of Blake's t-shirts. Her long black hair hung in waves around her and she had the look of a well-fucked woman. She also had the look of a woman in love. Shep felt a slight twinge of regret but let it go. Blake deserved a woman who would love him and Shep would have to accept that there would be no more threesomes for them.

Ally sat on the couch next to him and placed her hand on his thigh. There was compassion in her eyes and all he longed for was passion. He tried to shake the feeling off but her hand began gently rubbing his thigh and his cock answered with a definite "hell yeah".

"Are you okay?" she asked him and he realized that she had known what he would find when they got to Michelle's house. For the first time he really thought about what it must be like to see things that you didn't want to. To have no choice.

"I'm fine. Roman's in the hospital." He leaned his head back and tried to get his cock under control. It wasn't happening.

"Is Catherine with him?" The voice was soft and sweet and the hand was still torturing him. Where the fuck was Blake? It hit him what she said and he closed his eyes for a moment. It appeared that Ally did see everything. Even he hadn't known that Catherine and Roman were seeing each other until tonight's ER confession.

"Yep, she's with him. Probably stay the night as well." His eyes snapped open when he felt her hand move up his thigh. What the hell was she doing?

"Griff didn't take it well." It was a statement, not a question. The woman was batting a thousand but he was done with the questions. He had to get out of there before he did something that he would regret.

"Look, Ally, I appreciate your concern but I should probably be heading out." He went to get up and Ally leaned over and straddled him, placing her bare pussy over the hard ridge under his jeans.

"We heard you come in, Shep. I know that you are feeling lonely. So much has happened. So much has changed." Her eyes were a deep dark green and Shep could feel the heat of her cunt where she rubbed against him. "But not everything has to."

His gaze locked with hers. "What are you saying?"

"Blake and I are getting married."

"Congratulations," was what made it past his lips when all he wanted to do was demand what the fuck she was doing on his cock, then.

"I know the type of relationship that you and Blake often share, Shep. There's no reason for it to stop." Her eyes were clear and bright.

Shep caught his breath. "What are you saying, Ally?"

"She's trying to tell you to bring your sorry ass into the bedroom," Blake appeared in the doorway. He was naked and had one hand wrapped around his dick stroking it from root to tip. Shep almost laughed when he saw Ally's gaze focus on it and heard the small moan as she licked her lips.

"I thought that you were going to let me do this?" she asked, never taking her gaze off Blake's erection. She ground her pussy down against Shep and this time it was his moan that escaped.

"You were taking too long, woman. Just tell the man that you want to fuck him and get your ass back into the bedroom." Blake's gaze was centered on her pussy and where it rubbed blatantly against Shep.

Shep stood with Ally and she wrapped her legs around him, her arms around his neck, while he headed them toward where Blake stood.

"Sure you're okay with this?" he asked Blake. His cock was screaming just to accept what was offered and fuck her. But his head was telling him to make sure that his friend was really okay before anything happened.

"Ally and I talked about it earlier," Blake nodded and turned to lead the way to the bedroom. "We both agree that we'd like our relationship with you to continue if you want it to."

Hell yeah he wanted it to. "You sure?" he looked down at the woman filling his arms, needing to hear that she was okay with it from her own lips although her body was already sending its own response if the dampness on his jeans was any indication.

"Yes, Shep. I'm sure. I mean, Blake's not getting any younger and I'm still in my twenties." Ally's giggle was cut short by the sound of Blake's hand slapping her bare ass. She moaned and ground harder against Shep.

"Wench," Blake grunted and settled himself crosswise on the bed on his back. "Get down and bring that sweet pussy over here to me."

Ally eased away from Shep and turned to head to the bed and Blake. When Shep just stood there watching she turned back. "Do you need some help with those clothes, Shep, or are you just planning to watch this time?" She grabbed the hem of the shirt still on her body and slowly lifted it over her head and let it drop to the floor. Her breasts were high and firm, her nipples already hard points begging for his lips and tongue. How the hell had he gotten so lucky? His buddy may have found the love of his life, but he was still willing to share her with Shep. And she wanted it as well. He was a lucky man indeed.

His hands began making quick work of his clothes and Ally laughed at his impatience to be naked. She turned, giving him a great shot of her tight ass before getting on the bed and taking Blake's cock in her mouth. He watched Blake wrap his hands in her hair and help guide her up and down his length.

Finally Shep was naked, his dick screaming to get inside the hot clasp of her pussy. She had her ass up high in the air and he could see the cream glistening on her thighs and slit.

He looked at Blake asked the question with his eyes. Blake nodded and tossed him a condom, which he caught easily and tore open. He had to chuckle when he saw that it was ribbed. Ally would like that. Shep stepped up and stood behind where she was kneeling on the edge of the bed. He palmed her ass in his hands and with one smooth stroke placed his dick where it was screaming to go. She felt like heaven wrapped around his cock and he groaned in pleasure at the clasp of her wet heat. Her moan joined his and he pulled all the way out enjoying the sight of her juices glistening on the thin sheath covering his shaft before he plunged it back home inside her.

"Such a tight, sweet pussy Ally," Shep grunted as he rode in and out of her. "I could fuck this forever."

"Ummm..." she offered around the thick cock filling her mouth. Her checks were taut from the fierce suction she was applying to Blake's erection and from the look of pure pleasure on Blake's face, he was enjoying every hard pull.

Shep covered his fingers in her juice and used them to manipulate her anus, making it slick and wet before he worked one thick finger inside. She was tight and Shep shuddered with the desire to take her there. Blake had been the one to work his cock inside her ass the last time. Shep wanted to be the one to fill it this time. He worked a second finger in with the first and began scissoring them to prepare her.

"You want to take us both like this again Ally? A cock buried in each of these hot little holes, fucking you, giving you pleasure?" Shep slipped a third finger in and thrust hard spearing her on his hand.

"Ohhh..." Ally moaned and he could see her face look up at Blake. Some silent communication past between the couple and Blake pulled his cock out of her mouth. "Get up here and sit on my cock," he said to Ally, grabbing a condom from the pile on the table before turning to Shep. "Lube's in the top drawer in the table." Shep knew where the lube was, where it always was. But Blake's words told him exactly where his cock would be going. He was going to get his chance to fuck that sweet little ass already making its way up to Blake's cock. Fuck. The way she felt around his fingers he wasn't going to last long.

He grabbed the tub and squirted a generous amount on his fingers, preparing to work it into her tight pink pucker. She was lifting her ass high enough to place Blake's cock at her entrance and Shep had a great view as she slid slowly down the length of his friend's erection. He heard Blake's groan, followed by Ally's, and felt a glimmer of jealousy when she leaned forward and the two shared a passionate kiss.

Shep shook the feeling off and joined them on the bed. He put his legs outside Blake's and crept up behind Ally. With one hand on her lower back he held her down against Blake's chest while he used the other one to work his lubed fingers in and out of her anus. He grabbed the tub of lube back up to squirt some just inside the haven he was eager to fill. He snapped the cap back in place and dropped the tube on the bed. He used his hands to spread her back cheeks, then moved one to center the head of his cock where he wanted it. He pressed into her demanding entrance where she had only taken one other cock before.

Shep felt the give of that first ring of muscles and then the head of his cock was inside where he wanted it. She was like a vice around him, the tight channel made even tighter by the cock already buried in her pussy. He did his best to take it slow and easy when all he really wanted to do was ram home with one hard thrust. Finally, what felt like a lifetime later he was deep in her ass, his balls resting against the lower globes of her ass mere inches from Blake's balls.

Fuck, it was incredible. "Not going to last," he grunted out and Blake threw him a look.

"I've just been waiting for you, buddy," was all he got before Blake pulled out and slammed in again.

Ally cried out and shifted between them. On the second stroke, Shep joined in so that one pushed in while the other pulled out. Back and forth they went, the rhythm gaining momentum with every stroke until they were both slamming deep into her body at the same time. Ally arched between them and bent forward, latching her teeth into Blake's shoulder. Both men could feel her orgasm as it ripped through her body. She tightened around them both and with a few more strokes both men were joining her.

Shep threw his head back and gave a harsh cry as the hot jets of cum spewed from his cock. She tightened even further around his shaft and he was milked of every drop of seed. Blake's grunts and groans joined in and he could actually feel the other man's release through the thin membrane that separated them. Ally collapsed against Blake's chest and Shep couldn't help but over hear the whispered I love yous that the couple exchanged.

They might welcome him into their bed, but he would never be a part of what the two of them shared. He felt like a third wheel, like an outsider. He had loved Moira but she had ended up more like a little sister. He had feelings for Cass but the spark hadn't been there for the two of them either. Katie he could have had something with but the baby of the Daniels family had eyes only for Ben, even before they were together. He glance down at the woman whose body still cradled his cock. Ally he could have had something more with as well. But fate had placed her with Blake first.

She reached a hand back and urged him to lean forward, covering her with his weight. Blake shifted until they could all lie on the bed Ally firmly held in place between the two men. Yeah, they wanted him with them. He'd be welcome in their bed. But Shep wanted something more. He wanted someone to look at him the way Ally was looking at Blake. He wanted a woman of his own. For the first time he longed to strip bare and show a woman the real man he kept inside.

With a sigh, he pulled free of Ally's body and rolled off the bed to his feet. He had no idea what the hell was wrong with him.

"You okay?" Blake's voice cut into his thoughts.

"Just going to jump into the shower," he tossed a careless grin over his shoulder as he headed across the hall to the bathroom closing the door behind him.

"He's lonely," Ally leaned closer into Blake's warmth and stroked her hand up and down his chest.

Blake sighed. "I know. I felt the same way before I found you."

Ally could feel Blake's worry for his friend and smiled up at him offering him what she could. "He won't be lonely for long." She supplied that bit of information with a smug smile.

"You know something, woman?" her lover demanded with a tap of his palm on her ass. God she loved this man.

"I know that someone is coming. Someone who will turn his life upside down and inside out." She snuggled closer to the man she was going to marry. She wouldn't tell him everything. She could see the woman and the danger that followed behind her. She was meant for Shep, but it would be up to him to make sure that the woman lived to see a future. No matter what she said it wouldn't change what was meant to be. Some things were best learned on your own.

Also by Lacey Thorn

Bare Beginnings

Bare Love 1: His Bare Obsession

Bare Love 2: Bare Confessions

Ellora's Cavemen: Jewels of the Nile III (*anthology*)

Island Guardians 1: Earth Moves

Island Guardians 2: Fanning Her Flames

Island Guardians 3: Washed Away

Island Guardians 4: Breathing Her Air

Merciful Angel

One Good Man

Seducing Sampson

About the Author

෨

Lacey Thorn spends her days in small-town Indiana, the proud mother of three. When she is not busy with one of them she can be found typing away on her computer keyboard or burying her nose in a good book. Like every woman, she knows just how chaotic life can be and how appealing that great escape can look. So toss aside the stress and tension of the never ending "to do" list. For now sit back, relax, and enjoy the ride with Lacey as she helps you to unlace and unleash the woman inside.

Lacey welcomes comments from readers. You can find her website and email address on her author bio page at www.ellorascave.com.

Tell Us What You Think

We appreciate hearing reader opinions about our books. You can email us at Comments@EllorasCave.com.

Why an electronic book?

We live in the Information Age—an exciting time in the history of human civilization, in which technology rules supreme and continues to progress in leaps and bounds every minute of every day. For a multitude of reasons, more and more avid literary fans are opting to purchase e-books instead of paper books. The question from those not yet initiated into the world of electronic reading is simply: *Why?*

1. *Price.* An electronic title at Ellora's Cave Publishing and Cerridwen Press runs anywhere from 40% to 75% less than the cover price of the exact same title in paperback format. Why? Basic mathematics and cost. It is less expensive to publish an e-book (no paper and printing, no warehousing and shipping) than it is to publish a paperback, so the savings are passed along to the consumer.

2. *Space.* Running out of room in your house for your books? That is one worry you will never have with electronic books. For a low one-time cost, you can purchase a handheld device specifically designed for e-reading. Many e-readers have large, convenient screens for viewing. Better yet, hundreds of titles can be stored within your new library—on a single microchip. There are a variety of e-readers from different manufacturers. You can also read e-books on your PC or laptop computer. (Please note that Ellora's Cave does not endorse any specific brands.

You can check our websites at www.ellorascave.com or www.cerridwenpress.com for information we make available to new consumers.)

3. *Mobility.* Because your new e-library consists of only a microchip within a small, easily transportable e-reader, your entire cache of books can be taken with you wherever you go.

4. *Personal Viewing Preferences.* Are the words you are currently reading too small? Too large? Too... ANNOYING? Paperback books cannot be modified according to personal preferences, but e-books can.

5. *Instant Gratification.* Is it the middle of the night and all the bookstores near you are closed? Are you tired of waiting days, sometimes weeks, for bookstores to ship the novels you bought? Ellora's Cave Publishing sells instantaneous downloads twenty-four hours a day, seven days a week, every day of the year. Our webstore is never closed. Our e-book delivery system is 100% automated, meaning your order is filled as soon as you pay for it.

Those are a few of the top reasons why electronic books are replacing paperbacks for many avid readers.

As always, Ellora's Cave and Cerridwen Press welcome your questions and comments. We invite you to email us at Comments@ellorascave.com or write to us directly at Ellora's Cave Publishing Inc., 1056 Home Avenue, Akron, OH 44310-3502.

MAKE EACH DAY MORE *EXCITING* WITH OUR

ELLORA'S
CAVEMEN
CALENDAR

☥ WWW.ELLORASCAVE.COM ☥

erridwen, the Celtic Goddess of wisdom, was the muse who brought inspiration to storytellers and those in the creative arts. Cerridwen Press encompasses the best and most innovative stories in all genres of today's fiction. Visit our site and discover the newest titles by talented authors who still get inspired - much like the ancient storytellers did, once upon a time.

Cerridwen Press

www.cerridwenpress.com

Discover for yourself why readers can't get enough
of the multiple award-winning publisher

Ellora's Cave.

Whether you prefer e-books or paperbacks,

be sure to visit EC on the web at
www.ellorascave.com

for an erotic reading experience that will leave you
breathless.